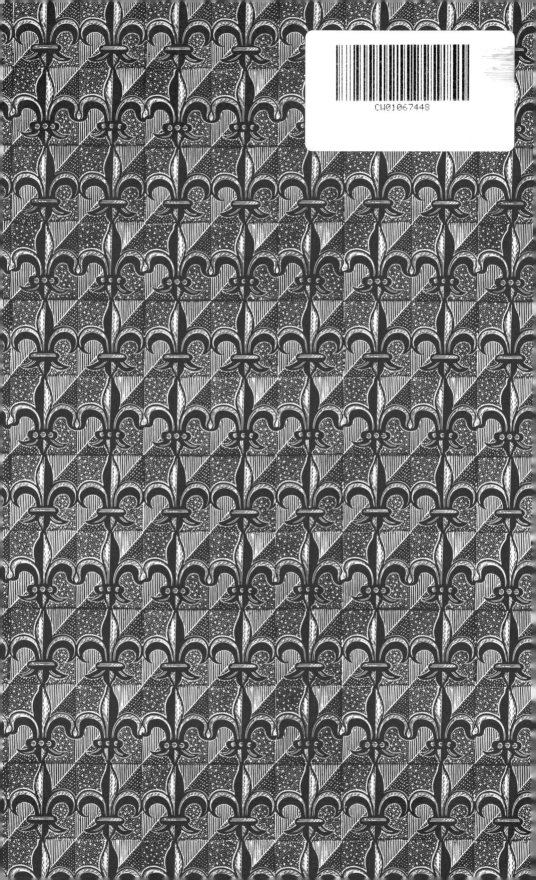

NO RETREAT

NO RETREAT

John Bowen

Sincair-Stevenson

First published in Great Britain in 1994
by Sinclair-Stevenson
an imprint of Reed Consumer Books Ltd
Michelin House, 81 Fulham Road, London SW3 6RB
and Auckland, Melbourne, Singapore and Toronto

A CIP catalogue record for this book
is available at the British Library

ISBN 1 85619 398 5

Typeset by Deltatype Ltd, Ellesmere Port, South Wirral
Printed and bound in Great Britain by
Mackays of Chatham PLC, Chatham, Kent

Dedicated to the memory
of the people of Lidice,
10th June, 1942

My grateful thanks to Frank Kermode and Charles Wood, both of whom read this novel in manuscript and made valuable corrections and suggestions: Charles also kept me supplied with a copious flow of military information while I was writing it. Thanks also to Colin Rogers for being in at the beginning, to Dr Marisa Viegas for vegetative states, to Dafydd Wyn Phillips and Phil Rickman for Welsh, to Professor Ladislav Vanek for the difficulties faced by any resistance movement in protecting from discovery a couple of uppity amateur assassins sent in from outside, to Mark Tyrrell for radio communications, to Arnold Rubinstein for Dutchess County and to Jon Hardy for boats. Books I have found particularly helpful have been *The Killing of Obergruppenführer Reinhard Heydrich* by Callum MacDonald (Macmillan: 1989) and *The Last Ditch* by David Lampe (Cassell: 1968).

'No retreat, no retreat
They must conquer or die who've no retreat.'

John Gay, *Polly*

Preparation

The Prime Minister, the Chief of the Imperial General Staff and the Head of Military Intelligence stood on a hill among maple and black walnut, looking down on the valley below. All three men were overdressed for the sunny October weather. The Prime Minister had been told that in upstate New York the leaves begin to change colour in August, and had anticipated mists and mud. He wore expensive brogues with thick socks and a trench-coat over his tweed jacket, button-down shirt and twill trousering. At home with his family the Prime Minister dressed American-style, but he judged it prudent on public occasions to look like an Englishman and put up with the discomfort in the cause of public relations. The two soldiers were in uniform, top quality barathea, and their peaked caps were adorned with red silk and gold braid. The badges of the top brass are of real gold, not brass at all, and never highly polished – which would wear away the metal – but worn dull; yet they caught and reflected the sunlight like a heliograph, so that those whom the three men had come to watch were well aware of the presence of spectators on the hill.

The Prime Minister wiped the eye-pieces of his binoculars with a handkerchief which had already been used to sop sweat from his forehead. 'Bloody things keep misting up.'

'Don't bother with them. Take the general view.'

The general view was bare. Across the valley, an unfenced country road ran downhill in wide curves before turning to take a parallel course with the river at the bottom. There was no road, nothing man-made, on the side where the three watchers stood, only

1

a rocky slope down to the river. To reach this place, they had been driven first through populated and prosperous country, a country of second homes, vineyards and apple orchards; then by roads progressively less well-maintained through land which seemed to have no particular use, with the houses poorer, often unoccupied and more widely spaced; finally through deep woods in the heart of which the road had ended, and they had been conducted uphill along a track, at the side of which groves of discarded refrigerators sprouted, with a 1938 Chevrolet, a rusty plough, barrels which had once held toxic chemicals, plastic sacks, empty carboys and the usual litter of cans and broken glass which form the detritus of an advanced civilisation.

Then, at the brow of the hill, the trees were sparser and the track ended, and there was only the empty valley in front of them, with its rough road and narrow brawling river, and on both sides open land of tussocky grass, tree-stumps, scrub and a plenitude of rocks, some of them outcrops from the slopes of the valley, others which seemed to have been scattered there deliberately like the pieces of some large-scale modern sculpture. 'They grow a lot of rocks in Dutchess County,' their conductor said, touched his cap and retired out of earshot.

The Prime Mininster said, 'I assume they'll start fairly soon.'

'They're starting now.'

At the top of the road opposite, a very old army truck had appeared. Its mottled green and brown camouflage paint had faded and its shape looked somehow clumsy and old-fashioned. Everything about it said to the three watchers, 'I am not a battle-worthy vehicle, and cannot be trusted to run for long without intensive maintenance.' The truck began to descend the hill. There was a uniformed man in the driving-seat, but he did not appear to be driving. Instead the door of the cab was open, and another man, dressed in a frogman's suit of black rubber, stood in the door frame and seemed to be controlling the steering. This man was wearing a turban-shaped crash-helmet with side-flaps, as worn by parachutists, and his elbows and knees were padded.

The truck took the first bend. The Prime Minister raised the binoculars to his eyes again, and the eye-pieces at once misted over. 'God dammit, Victor,' he said. 'I don't want the general picture. I want the detail.'

2

'There should be a demisting cloth in the case. They're standard issue.'

The truck had negotiated the first bend and gathered speed for the second. The turbaned man was in no position to control either the foot-brake or clutch, and his colleague in the driving-seat seemed to be incapable of doing so; the truck took the second bend faster than was prudent and the third dangerously. After the fourth and last bend, the road straightened to follow the river, and the turbaned man, his task presumably completed, threw himself off the side of the truck and into the side of the road, where he rolled over twice and lay still, his arms covering his face.

A man in British Army battledress appeared from behind a rock and stood in the road, facing the truck which did not – could not – slow for him. It could not because, as the Prime Minister now discovered, the uniformed person behind the steering-wheel was not a person at all, but an arrangement of stuffed hessian in a peaked cap. The man in battledress, who was armed with an Ingram Model Eleven sub-machine-gun, fired two bursts into the cab of the truck, and stepped nimbly aside. Meanwhile another man in battledress, holding a pineapple grenade, emerged from the river bank, drew the pin from his grenade, and rolled the grenade neatly under the truck, which immediately exploded. There was a short pause, during which pieces of the truck dispersed themselves and what was left caught fire. Then the two men in battledress bowed to right and left as if taking a curtain-call, and from behind rocks, scrub and folds in the ground all over the hillside other men in battledress appeared and applauded.

'I suppose they'll expect us to pay for that truck,' the Prime Minister said. 'Do you have dossiers on those two? I'll take a look at both of them in the aircraft on our way back.'

The British government-in-exile was pleasantly situated in a leafy suburb of Washington: it occupied two floors of an old frame house, above a discreet shop selling Sexual Aids and Candies. The British had been canny. By the late forties, when it was already clear that the liberation of Western Europe would not be achieved quickly, they had sold the embassy and the various consulates, and invested the proceeds both for growth and income. Consequently the British government-in-exile enjoyed well-maintained air-conditioning, an ample secretariat and the latest electronic office-equipment while the Dutch had to make do with two part-time secretaries and an electric fan.

Two floors were more than adequate. A government-in-exile is not as large as a government; it has, for instance, very little use for a Home Secretary. Back in the summer of 1942, with the fighting over in North Africa and an invasion of the British Isles by sea and air imminent, most of the Cabinet had escaped to what was then the USA, while the Royal Family flew south to New Zealand, believing it to be more like home. Only Churchill had remained to face the invaders and his own subsequent trial and execution as a war criminal. Since the Nazis were accustomed to hanging those whom they considered to be public enemies not by hempen rope, but by wire, and Churchill, even after the privations of the blockade, was a man of full figure, his head came off and was pickled and exhibited at the Tower of London until the gentler nineteen-sixties, when it was quietly removed and buried at Woodstock.

Meanwhile his colleagues, under Clement Attlee, had set up in Washington. They were determined to carry on the struggle; they would never cease their efforts until Britain was free again. The French, Dutch, Belgian, Danish, Czech, Polish and Norwegian governments-in-exile, which had read the signs and left London a little earlier, made similar noises. But they were in a neutral country, however friendly. There was very little action they could take in the struggling line, and still less after the British capitulation in November.

The British government-in-exile had not recognised the capitulation; no Free Briton ever would recognise it. Nor was it a government without a people, even if the people did not amount to very many, and the laws they were required in daily life to obey were those of a host-country. There were British citizens already abroad in 1942 to be represented and more who escaped over the succeeding years. There were remnants of the Air Force and Navy which made their way to American ports and airfields. There were Free Britons still in Britain, who regarded their present lack of freedom as temporary, and who, by whatever means they could and at great personal risk, sent intelligence reports to Washington, all of which were read diligently, reduced to précis and filed on cards.

Such was the business of government, but it did not add up to a full-time job. Most ministers laid aside their portfolios and found other employment, in business, in journalism and on the lecture circuit; some were already old, and soon died. A few – Attlee, Eden, Cripps and Anderson, with Lord Halifax, the Ambassador in Washington, Sir Alan Brooke, CIGS, and Lord Louis Mountbatten, Chief of Combined Operations – formed themselves into an Inner Cabinet and continued to function, but even they had to look about for directorships and consultancies which were remunerative without being onerous and would allow them to maintain a standard of living suitable to their station.

Time passed. The unstoppable Germans mopped up the Russian half of Poland in 1943, went on to liberate the Baltic States and Finland in 1944, then, pausing only to announce that they had no further territorial ambitions, moved into the Ukraine, Moldova and Byelorussia; and, after a pause for digestion, on eastwards to take in Georgia and Armenia, proceeding piecemeal as they had done before 1939, a mouthful at a time, until the Soviet Union had shrunk to Greater Russia and points east, its army discredited, its economy in disarray. Thereafter Hitler halted the movement east; he had no intention of going the way of Napoleon. Instead he returned his attention to what remained of Europe, and by the time of his death from cancer of the prostate gland in 1953, only United Ireland (as a sop to the Americans) and Switzerland (as a sop to the bankers) enjoyed a government outside the control of the Third Reich.

Time passed. Sir John Anderson died in 1958, Lord Halifax the year after. In 1957, Sir Anthony Eden began to sicken; he was having trouble with his bile duct. Since by then the Foreign Secretaryship involved little more than showing the flag at various social functions, Sir Anthony struggled on because – resembling Ronald Colman as he so strongly did – the Washington wives found him attractive. For five years longer Sir Anthony's bile duct endured the State Department's hospitality. Then he gave up and was succeeded by Harold Macmillan, who was in his mid-sixties but reckoned, in a good light, to look even more like Ronald Colman.

Time passed. Hitler's successor was Heydrich, who systematically got rid of anyone whom he considered a threat, so that by 1960 when he was incapacitated by the first of a series of strokes, there was no one person to take over from him, and a Council of State governed in his name. By the time he died in 1966 this system had become established. There was no need any longer for government by terror; it was not cost-effective, and people were sick of it. The old European states became federated provinces, with a central currency but considerable local autonomy. The intelligence reports from occupied Britain to the Free British government in Washington, which had already dwindled to the merest trickle, dried up altogether.

Time passed. Sir Alan Brooke died in 1963, and Lord Mountbatten combined both offices, but the young Lord Willoughby de Broke was brought in to assist him as Head of Intelligence. None of the other governments-in-exile included members of the aristocracy; the British considered it a diplomatic bonus that they could always produce a peer to grace a dinner-table. Willoughby de Broke was the peer in reserve – a lord-in-waiting, one might say. He became the only lord in 1967 when Mountbatten, emotionally exhausted by a messy divorce, was killed in a pile-up on the San Antonio Freeway. The provision of peers would eventually become a problem, with the pool of hereditary peers growing smaller and no new peers being created by a monarchy resident in Auckland, but for the time being there were other problems more pressing.

The question of succession to the Cabinet offices was one of them. When Clement Attlee died, he was succeeded as Prime Minister by his son, Martin. This was an *ad hoc* decision by the Cabinet and a troubling one. The government-in-exile was a democracy; freedom was an essential part of the British ethos and distinguished the Free Britons from those enslaved by Germany. But in practice there were no party differences among the Free British politicians, and very few of the Free Britons in America actually wanted to participate in their own government; the job had become increasingly esoteric and ceremonial.

By the mid seventies membership of the British government-in-exile had become, practically speaking, hereditary. The full Cabinet, which met twice a year, included an Attlee, a Morrison, a Bevin, a Cripps, a Macmillan, a Mountbatten, an Eden, a Wood, a Grigg, a Lyttleton and an Anderson. They confirmed the appointment and ratified the actions of the Inner Cabinet of three ministers and two military advisers. The appointment of the military advisers constituted the third and most pressing problem of government. The pool of those Free Britons who had any actual experience of warfare was even smaller than the pool of hereditary peers, and grew smaller at a much quicker rate.

Time passed. The Americans were not pleased at the consolidation of the German Empire in Europe, but they had to accept it, just as they had to accept the rapid growth of the Japanese Empire in the East. Meanwhile they considered it wise that their own nation should grow – not by conquest, of course, but by invitation. The USA became the USNA, a federation of states with territory stretching from Ellesmere Island to Panama. King Charles III reigned over Australia and New Zealand as Governor-General for the Empire of Japan.

Time passed. By the mid seventies, the world was effectively dominated by three enormous confederations, each safely insulated from the others. It was a world at peace. How could the three empires have made war? With the whole width of what was left of the Soviet Union between Japan and Germany and the width of the Atlantic between the Germans and the USNA, they would have been like three boxers squaring up to fight, each in a different ring. They had sophisticated computer-operated weaponry; they had satellites in orbit; they each had – and no other country had: they saw to that – nuclear capability. And they had no experience whatever in using any of these weapons. Time passed. In 1991 the three empires were at war: Japan and the USNA against the German Empire.

'Traditionally those who won the last war always begin by losing the next. This is because they rely on the tactics, and very often the weapons, which brought them victory before, whereas the previous losers have to find something different and usually better. Just the same with us in 39–42. Thought we knew it all, so we were knocked off our balance by the Blitzkrieg. Absolute bloody shambles in Crete. Chased all over North Africa by Rommel. Historically the British have always recovered from that sort of thing, but this time we didn't.'

The lecturer paused to study his audience, twenty young men dressed in British battledress of 1939, meticulously recreated by a firm of theatrical costumiers in Dayton, Ohio. 'Blitzkrieg . . . Crete . . . Rommel . . . Doesn't mean a thing to you lot, does it?' he said. 'Never mind. You'll learn.'

Up to now their instructors had been American: West Point was just down the Hudson Valley. This one was British – British-British not American-British: he had fought in the British Army and had only recently retired as Professor of Military History at Yale. 'None of you has ever been in battle,' he said. 'Nor your fathers. You've never even seen it in the movies, because there haven't been any war movies for years, and anyway it never was like the movies – much more messy. People don't die cleanly in battle; that's one of the first things you discover. What's it like, do you think, battle, eh? Hah!' His laugh was only half a laugh, the other half a bark. 'My dears, the noise! And the people! Old jokes are best. However, let's get on.'

He had called them his dears. Could this man be a faggot? Some of the young men shifted uneasily in their seats. Trouble had been taken to ensure that none of the first intake of volunteers was homosexual, and the twenty had the normal prejudices of young American males. Throughout their schooldays, often during college, they had been mocked by contemporaries to whom it was an article of faith and folklore that all Brits, even those born in the USNA who had never seen their homeland, were secret queens until proved otherwise, and they had felt obliged to prove it otherwise. Now here was this professor, their countryman, brisk and dapper, with his thin silver hair combed across his pink and polished scalp, with his silver bi-focals and his closely clipped silver moustache, wearing the kind of pinstriped suit which their own grandfathers wore to funerals but with a silk handkerchief spilling from the top pocket, and by the way he spoke and used his hands . . . But no, they had already been told about the professor. He had been a tank commander, awarded the Military Cross for bravery in battle. It was probably just the way his generation communicated. He was not, could not be, a fag.

The twenty Free British volunteer commandos looked at the professor, and wondered. He looked at them and wondered. Why had they volunteered? His task was not merely to instruct them but to make a confidential report on the suitability of each to undertake what would be required of him. They were all said to be of above average intelligence, had all passed various psychological tests and received university education, but so had sixty per cent of the adult population of the USNA. University education was a device to keep young Americans off the labour market; only the four who had been to Graduate School were, in the professor's terms, educated at all. To do this job they needed to be officer material. That was his responsibility. Their American instructors could teach them weaponry. He had to evaluate their officer qualities.

Of course one must be careful in writing any report, however confidential. One of these lads was an Attlee.

How was he to connect with them? A history professor! Most Americans were utterly uninterested in history. Theirs was an immigrant culture; they looked hopefully into the future, and preferred to forget about the past. His own speciality, Military History, he had found to be even more deeply lacking in interest, at least to the students at Yale: there had been semesters recently when he'd had no pupils at all, and his retirement had been delayed because of the difficulty in finding a replacement. Why should anyone care? The United States had not been directly involved in any kind of war since 1918. Until now.

'Would someone like to tell me how and when this war started? Mr Parry-Jones?'

'Never stopped, sir. Nobody signed a peace treaty. Britain has been at war with Germany since 1939.'

'Ideologically correct, Mr Parry-Jones, but of little practical use in understanding our present situation. Mr Attlee?'

'August last year, sir, Iraq invaded Kuwait. The independence of Kuwait was guaranteed by Persia and Saudi Arabia. They were bound to resist the invasion, and did. However, the Iraqi armed forces, the largest in the Middle East, had been equipped and trained by the Germans. Finding themselves in trouble, fighting on two fronts, the Iraqis appealed for assistance which Germany supplied, both in arms and military advisers.'

'And our own involvement?'

'The USNA and Saudi Arabia had signed a Treaty of Mutual Assistance in 1977, and there was a Concordat between Japan and Persia negotiated during a state visit by the Mikado to the Shah in 1980. Both the USNA and Japan were therefore obligated to provide military assistance, which was also restricted initially to the provisions of arms and advisers. At first it was hoped that the conflict might be confined to Iraq and her neighbours. However, in February of this year, troops of the German Empire entered northern Iraq by way of Turkey, and a state of war exists.'

'Very good, Mr Attlee, an extremely clear summary.' What a constipated young man he was: it must run in the family. 'That's the diplomacy of it. But diplomacy is usually a cover for economics. What are the economics?'

Silence. They stared at him, blank as planks. Then Parry-Jones said, 'Well, it's oil, isn't it?'

'Yes, it's oil. Oil and arms, but chiefly oil. The USNA and the Japanese and German empires are all very large territorial units, and could be self-sufficient, if they needed to be, in most essential resources. But not in oil. All three do have sources of oil, but not enough, and certainly not produced cheaply enough; all three are net importers of oil. Cheap oil – easily produced oil – comes from the Middle East, and over the years the oil companies of the Great Powers have built up connections there, the three American companies with Saudi Arabia and the Gulf States, Shell and Reich Petroleum with Iraq and Palestine. The Japanese Hanimotu Company came late into the game and made connections with Persia. And what did these great industrial empires use to pay for their oil?'

There was no answer. He had not expected one. 'Arms, gentlemen. State-of-the-art weaponry, constantly improved and updated so as to maintain a very profitable market, provided to Arab states each of which was governed by an absolute ruler with no nonsense about democratic accountability. It was a situation bound to lead to trouble. Easy enough to see that now, but arms were what the Arabs wanted, and they called the tune.'

He was lecturing. It came easily to him. But as a lecturer he would learn little about their own capabilities. Better to promote a dialogue. 'What is the greatest danger that any of you can envisage in the conduct of this war?' he said.

They were bright enough to know that 'Losing' could not be the right answer, but most of them lacked imaginative reach and they resented being asked questions which might more properly be put to the General Staff. Why couldn't he just talk to them? They had brought notebooks and pencils. Questions were for the end of the day, when they might reasonably be examined on what he had said to see whether they had got it right. A dark-haired young man in the back row said, 'Escalation, sir?'

'Good. Why?'

'Economics again. Uncontrolled escalation could cause the widespread destruction of oil-wells, leading to a world shortage of oil. Could mean economic collapse – inflation first, then everything running down. Not much point in total victory if everyone goes bankrupt.'

He had such a wretched memory for names these days. He had taken pains to learn the names of these young men, to read the records, get some kind of preliminary feeling about each of them, but the names just went; it was the same with the names of flowers. However, there was a list in front of him. 'So the Great Powers can't afford to go all out? They have to fight a limited war?'

'Yes, sir. Just as well in my opinion. I mean, we've got all sorts of modern weapons, but we've no experience of using them in battle.'

Ah, yes! Sinclair! Dark hair, brown complexion – but they were all tanned. A little older than his fellows, a little more lived-in. The Heathcliff look. 'These weapons have all been thoroughly tested, Mr Sinclair.'

'Not on anything that fights back, sir.'

Sinclair. A common name, but one ought always to check out the First Families. There had been an Archibald Sinclair, who had made a devasting speech in the Commons after the débâcle in

11

Norway, which had helped to hound Chamberlain out of office. He had joined the Coalition Cabinet and had presumably escaped with them. A Liberal. Scottish. All Liberals were Celts, but not all Celts were Liberals.

'And what is the great disadvantage of a limited war, Mr Sinclair?'

'Could go on for ever, sir.'

'And how does one break out of that?'

Sinclair . . . Yes. Mid-twenties. Had been married – some woman who played the cello. There'd been a scandal – drug overdose – she was dead. Might have been his reason for volunteering. That kind of reason was never good enough, because the pain wore off, and one began to have second thoughts. Also he was clearly more intelligent than the others, which might be dangerous. They needed intelligence and initiative to do the job, but too much of either might lead one to question whether it were a job worth doing. The professor made a mental note to check Sinclair's academic records.

Sinclair said, 'I think that's why we're here, sir.'

Much too intelligent. The professor said, 'Someone else, explain.' Nobody could. The professor said, 'Mr Sinclair, you appear to be some way ahead of your friends.' That should hold him for a while. In the United States it never did to be too far ahead of one's friends.

'Sorry, sir.'

He wasn't sorry, of course, but had to appear to be. The professor put the knife in. 'My fault. I may be going too fast.' Sinclair's lips narrowed, his brown cheeks darkened, and he looked down at his knees. The young man next to him, a bumpy fellow with butter-coloured hair, moved a little away. 'Let us consider why we are here together,' the professor said. 'So far your instruction has been mainly operational.' Most of them wrote 'operational' in their notebooks, but not Sinclair. 'You have been taught to use automatic weapons and plastic explosives . . . high frequency radio and the use of codes . . . unarmed combat . . . the preparation of ambushes and booby-traps . . . simple first aid and so on. This is training to operate on your own and in small groups. Guerilla warfare – commando operations. It makes sense, doesn't it? Since the Free British government has no aircraft, tanks or heavy artillery and no money to buy them, any forces which we ourselves raise to assist the USNA have to be irregulars.'

Some of them wrote 'irregulars'; a few wrote 'no money': most wrote nothing but looked puzzled and angry, first because the professor seemed to be putting down the Free British government, secondly because most had supposed that their training so far was only a preparation for the big stuff, when they would command tanks, pilot helicopters and walk tall amongst civilians. All they knew was that the Free British government had offered to raise a force of volunteers to serve with the US forces in the present war against the German Empire. That war was located in the Middle East in support of Arab allies who would do most of the actual legwork. There was no conscription; the war was being fought by professional soldiers, the enlisted men mostly black, the officers mostly white. Since the Free British volunteers were white, they had expected to reach officer status fairly quickly.

The professor said, 'From now on your training widens. It also becomes informational.' None of them wrote down 'informational': they were all watching. 'Some information you've had already, mainly about the organisation and weapons of the German Army, which is, as I think you know, a conscript army, like that of Japan. You will no doubt have been told, or worked out for yourselves, that some of the troops on the German side in Iraq will actually be British conscripts, and if you were fighting there, you'd be expected to kill them.'

It was clear that nobody had told them, and they had not worked it out for themselves.

'Do any of you have a problem about that?'

It was clear that they did not know, had not given it any thought, whether they had a problem about that.

'However . . . back to information. Many of your new instructors will be civilians – diplomats and business persons. They will inform you about the day-to-day details of life in Europe generally, but particularly of life in Britain. Not in the Middle East, gentlemen. In Britain.'

The direction of Sinclair's gaze was no longer down at his knees. His chin was up, his full lips slightly smiling. 'Yes, Mr Sinclair,' the professor said. 'You've taken us in this first session a little faster than I'd intended to go, but what's done is done.' He looked around at what was still unfortunately for the most part only an audience and wondered how quickly he could transform it into a seminar. 'My own assignment with you, gentlemen,' he said, 'is not informational but evaluational. I have to assess the quality of your thought and your capacity for judgement. So let's begin. Before our next meeting, I wish you to have considered the following subject for discussion – write it down, please. "How long and to what effect can a resistance movement in an occupied country function without supply and support from outside?" You'll find books in the library to help you. Good day to you.'

He walked quickly from the platform, making the involuntary movement he always made after a lecture of pulling his gown down and around him – except, of course, that he no longer wore a gown. They had asked him to wear his uniform, but really that would have been too vulgar, so he had told them that it no longer fitted, which was untrue. Sinclair, it had to be admitted, was something of a dish. However, the professor was long past that sort of thing.

As they left the lecture room together, Parry-Jones said to Sinclair, 'What was all that about?'

'You didn't think we were being trained for desert warfare?'

'We're not supposed to know what we're being trained for. When they want us to know, they'll tell us. Therefore we don't ask.'

'I didn't ask. I do know.'

Parry-Jones and Sinclair were the two who had attacked the truck, Parry-Jones with the grenade, Sinclair with the Ingram. They were the cream of the first intake of trainees, renaissance men, physically and intellectually pre-eminent: Parry-Jones had completed a course in Classical Welsh at the University of Idaho. Theirs were the two dossiers to which the Prime Minister and the Head of Military Intelligence were giving particular attention.

Soon all the volunteers knew. They were to be the vanguard. The Free British Special Service Unit was to free Britain. It seemed rather a tall order for twenty people.

The way to end a limited war is to cause trouble somewhere else. The provinces of the German Empire were not like the federated states of the USNA, which had voluntarily joined the Union, but had been created by force and the threat of force, by the conquest of proud and independent nations with a long tradition of freedom. For fifty years, these proud nations had groaned beneath the jackboot of the German oppressor. It could not hold. They were ripe for trouble. All the European governments-in-exile agreed on that, so it had to be true. Resistance movements still existed, dormant for almost fifty years but ready to burst into flame as soon as the sparks were fanned. The volunteers would fan those sparks. Small groups would be infiltrated into Britain to make contact with the Resistance, create unrest, provide intelligence, organise acts of sabotage, and generally prepare the ground for an invasion which would lead to liberation.

Almost fifty years. It was a long period of dormancy – two generations. The volunteers had no memories of Britain, nor had their parents. Only the grandparents remembered, and the Britain they remembered had greatly changed. The English in America still sang 'There'll Always Be An England' on Empire Day, and the Welsh sang, 'Land of My Fathers' on Saint David's Day, and the Scots sang 'Auld Lang Syne' and sometimes 'Scotland the Brave' on almost any occasion, but what was this England there would always be? It existed in old photographs, the plays of Shakespeare, the novels of Dickens and the songs of Vera Lynn, in black-and-white movies still sometimes shown on Public Service Television, in letters and diaries and scratchy recordings of Churchill's speeches. None of this was a practical preparation for what the volunteers would find when they landed.

Nor had there been any contingency plan for the operation, nothing kept on file and updated year after year. Nobody had expected war in the Middle East; the participants had blundered into it. Then the British had jumped in and made the offer of a special force, and the Americans had accepted it with many graceful expressions of gratitude and regard. It was a considerable coup for the British, and a proof that the Special Relationship between themselves and the Americans was as strong as ever, even in adversity.

In fact the Americans had no intention of invading the European mainland, but calculated that the best way of inducing the Germans to pull out of the Middle East and make peace on generally acceptable terms might be by encouraging disaffection at home. The Iraqis would withdraw from Kuwait if the Germans told them to do so, and then everything would be back as it was before, with a hard lesson learned by all concerned. The American government did not say as much to the British; the Special Relationship did not involve telling the truth, but was a purely British piece of self-delusion. And the British did not, in their turn, inform the Americans that they intended such a deed as would astonish the earth, partly because it is not certain that the British knew, when they made the offer, exactly what they did intend.

It was all so haphazard, but after fifty years of peace it was bound to be. Nobody said so, nobody questioned it, but even the training that the volunteers had so far received from their West Point instructors was based on British Army commando training manuals of the 1939–42 war. The volunteers would have been better taught by Mafia hit-men, and since the Honourable Society is notoriously patriotic that might have been arranged, but West Point would have considered it unprofessional.

Now, although the rough-and-tumble continued, they spent more time in the classroom, as the professor had said they would. Their new instructors were civilians, staff from the US consulates of London, Bristol and Liverpool, travel agents and trusted business persons whose work had required them to live in Britain for a while.

The volunteers were given maps, town plans and scenic guides to areas of natural beauty. They were taught to measure distance, weight and volume on the metric scale, provided with coins and currency notes – ten pennies to the shilling, ten shillings to the mark – and told not to think like tourists, never to calculate how much is this worth in dollars, but instead how much bread will it buy, how much petrol, how many potatoes and metro tickets. They were told that they must carry an identity card (with which each would be supplied) at all times and be prepared to show it to any official as a matter of routine; they would also be given credit cards, but not, for obvious reasons, American Express. They were told how to use public transport, open a bank account, what to drink in a pub or beer-cellar, what clothes to wear on formal and informal occasions – they would each be kitted out with clothing and luggage of British manufacture. They were taught the differences between British and American behaviour, and that they must learn to take their new ways of behaviour for granted, not to think of them as different at all. All this they were taught by Americans, who had seen nothing of British social and family life except from the outside.

They were not taught German, because most British did not speak German; it was the 'second language' taught at school, but only lawyers, senior management and the higher ranks of the Civil Service actually spoke it. Instead they were taught the British accent, what was still called 'BBC English', and to recognise and understand the most common variants – Cockney, West Country, Northern, Brummy, Welsh and Scottish.

This business of the accent was a killer. The volunteers themselves spoke in various American accents from the West Coast, the Middle West, the East Coast and the South, but they had lived in a mobile middle-class society, in which accents were mutable and un-important, and did not instantly signal class, status and education as, they were told, one's accent did in Britain. Consequently the ears of the volunteers were not attuned to differences in accent: very few of them could tell when they were doing it wrong. Those who had no ear at all, and could not even tell that there *was* a difference between their own accents and the British, failed the course. It would not have been safe to send them out.

In all, nine of the first twenty failed, five because they could not master the accent, three for lack of physical dexterity, and one because he fell out of a tree and sustained brain damage. There was then a problem of what should be done with them, since they knew too much to be returned to the community. The problem was solved by assigning the three who lacked dexterity to clerical duties in Fort Lauderdale and promoting the five who could not manage the accent to the rank of sergeant and allowing them to assist in the training of the next batch. Meanwhile they continued to listen to tapes and attend conversation classes in the hope that they would improve. If they did not, the Free British Special Service Unit was in danger of ending up with more instructors than trainees.

Meanwhile the war in the Middle East was hardly progressing. The word used by journalists to describe the conflict was 'probing'. With a curious harking back to the early days of the 1939–42 war, there were probing 'leaflet attacks'. Bomber aircraft flew high above the armies of all sides, dropping leaflets. The leaflets dropped by the Iraqis asked the Muslim subjects of the Shah of Persia and the King of Saudi Arabi why they had chosen infidels to be their comrades-in-arms against the Faithful, and the leaflets dropped by the Allies asked the same question of the Iraqi troops. No aircraft was damaged by enemy action in the course of any of these raids.

Both sides announced that they would not be the first to strike at defenceless civilians. Instead US and Japanese aircraft made probing attacks on essentially tactical targets – railway lines, bridges, power stations and airfields – and German aircraft retaliated. The Allies also bombed Kuwait City and reduced it almost to the condition of an open plain. This did cause a great many civilian casualties, but Kuwait City had already been fought over, so one might assume that the civilian population was used to it, and clearly the Allies had to bomb at least one city if only to prove that they were not intimidated by threats and that the thing could be done. In these bombing raids, unlike the leaflet raids, many aircraft were destroyed, since the targets were heavily defended. Those who had designed and tested the missiles used by all three Great Powers were amply justified by their performance. The airborne missiles destroyed with great precision the targets at which they were aimed, and the ground-based missiles destroyed the aircraft.

There were also probing manoeuvres by tanks. The village of Al Fat Hafrah on the Saudi border was taken by German and Iraqi tanks, retaken by Saudi and US tanks, taken again and taken back again in four textbook actions spread over as many weeks; a village of much the same size on the Iraqi border with Persia was the scene of similar action. These probing tank attacks seemed to suffer the same disadvantage as the probing aircraft attacks; you could knock out an opposing tank, but usually lost one of your own tanks in doing so. Tanks were individually less expensive to produce than aircraft, but their loss was more damaging in one respect: the crew of a destroyed aircraft could bale out and become prisoners, but the crew of a destroyed tank were almost invariably incinerated, and the incineration of tank crews was highly unpopular at home, at least in the USNA.

Even more worrying to the belligerents was the presence of the media. The journalists were as unused to war as the soldiers, and seemed to regard it as some sort of international sporting event at which they were entitled to special seating. There were nearly a thousand of them, the strength of a battalion, and they came from all over the world. Accommodating them and providing them with food and drink on the scale to which they were accustomed could be managed, and so could preventing them from being caught up in the action and accidentally slaughtered, since there was so little action; but the actual business of news management was much more difficult.

What could a military spokesman say at a press conference when nothing had happened but a couple of foot patrols and a little defensive digging in? The media will only take so much analysis, then they demand action. The war was like a football match at which, after an initial exhibition of skill and tactics, the teams have started to play for time, and the spectators are becoming bored. The danger was that the reporters would begin to press for something to report, and the armies be pushed by a manipulated public opinion into an escalation of the war, which would end in the most horrifying carnage.

The first training course ended at Christmas. It was decided that the eleven who had qualified might be trusted to spend Christmas at home. They were to encourage their families and friends to believe that this was an embarkation leave before they were flown to join the army in the Middle East, and warned against saying anything at all to anybody about the real nature and object of their training.

Peter Alloway, twenty-two, assigned for further training as a radio operator, returned to his family home in Laramie, Wyoming, where his father, once an attorney, was now a respected judge, and his grandfather, Gavin Alloway, still worked part-time in the university hospital as a consultant in thorassic surgery. The Alloways were

19

Home Counties people, sound professional middle class; they had been doctors, lawyers, accountants, teachers as long as anyone could remember, and would not change their nature in changing their country of residence. There still were Alloways in Berkshire, cousins and second-cousins, and the Alloways of Laramie had until the outbreak of war, kept in touch, with letters three or four times a year, occasional phone-calls and parcels of knitwear and rich plum cake at Christmas.

Peter Alloway obeyed his orders. He told his family and his girl nothing, and they were careful not to ask. But his English cousins did come into the conversation, as it was natural they should do at Christmas, and this put it into his mind, when nobody else was by, to borrow the family photograph album and look over the collection of letters kept by his grandmother, and to make a note of the village between Newbury and Wantage where his grandfather's brother still lived, with the rest of his family not far away. He wrote down the addresses and the telephone numbers on a piece of paper which he placed in his wallet. He believed that in doing so he was using his initiative as he had been taught to do. The Berkshire Alloways might come in useful.

Arwen Parry-Jones and his sister Bronwen took the solo voices at the carol service of the local Pentecostal Church in which his father and mother were both ministers. Arwen loved his parents but did not share their faith; it was still a cause of private shame to him that, at the age of thirteen, when it had begun to cause comment among the congregation that the Spirit had not yet visited him, he had felt obliged to fake a public manifestation of being touched by Divine Grace which he had followed by speaking in tongues. Away from home, among friends, he was agnostic, intelligent and urbane. At home it was easier to pretend to believe. His parents would not be able to understand the agnosticism and would be distressed by it, since they would believe him damned eternally. While they were up among the Chosen, he would be burning below.

Arwen's enthusiasm and his attachment was to his parents' nation and language (which they themselves did not speak), not to their religion. For as long as he could remember, it was his Welshness which defined him and marked him out of the ordinary. During his

20

last year at the University of Idaho, he had begun to make his own translation of *The Mabinogion* into modern American. The only previous translation available was well out of date; it had been made in 1838 by Lady Charlotte Guest and reissued in 1903 by Jonas Lewis of Ruabon in a three-volume edition with a commentary by Dr Gwenogvryn Evans, and was not demotic. Arwen's project was primarily a labour of love, but might also score him brownie points in the academic world. He had already been promised publication by the University Press and would not be asked to contribute towards the cost.

The professor said to Ian Sinclair, 'Do you have anywhere to go over Christmas?' He knew already from the documentation that Sinclair had nowhere in particular to go. Since his wife's death he had been at odds both with his own parents and hers.

'Friends? I might stay with my sister for a while. Her husband's an asshole and the children take after him, but I'm fond of her, I suppose.'

'Would you like to stay with me for a couple of days? I have a small but tolerably comfortable house in Canaan, which is in Connecticut, some way outside Newhaven.'

'I think I should tell you, sir, that I'm not queer. Not even sometimes. Not ever. Sir.'

'Whereas I am, as you correctly surmise. However, at my age the lustful appetite has considerably diminished. That's not why I ask you to come. Nevertheless if you find yourself unable to believe me, let us forget the invitation, Mr Sinclair.'

'No, sir. I'd very much like to come.'

The professor wondered whether he should ask Sinclair to stop calling him 'sir'. Most of his pupils at Yale had proceeded to 'Iestyn' or even 'Yesty' almost from the moment of first meeting. But he decided that 'sir' had its uses in removing their relationship even further from the sexual. When Sinclair wished to use the professor's Christian name, no doubt he would make his wish known.

It was Christmas. They performed the rituals appropriate to Christmas in their world.

On Christmas Eve they went out for a light dinner at an Italian restaurant in Newhaven. They ate Californian asparagus with butter and Parmesan cheese and *scallopine al marsala*. The marsala was Californian also, the cheese from Wisconsin, and the bottle of sauvignon they drank with the meal came from Northern Ohio.

On Christmas morning they exchanged presents. Since the volunteers would not be allowed to take with them any object made in the USNA, the professor produced an object from his past, a silk tie made by Charvet of Paris in 1938. It was the most elegant piece of apparel he had ever owned, and he had stolen it as a teenager from a disliked uncle staying with his parents. He had kept the tie always with him, had taken it into battle, into captivity and into escape; it had been a talisman. It seemed to him appropriate that it should return to England with Sinclair, whose need for a talisman was now greater than his own.

Sinclair accepted the tie gratefully. In return he gave the professor a sensotape of Couperin's *Trois Leçons de Ténèbres*, and although the professor already had a recording of this work, he did not say so, and managed during the morning to hide it. To the professor – perhaps wanting to deceive himself – Sinclair's choice of a piece of music which he himself already knew and loved was an indication of a deep and instinctive mutual understanding.

They attended Matins together at the Episcopal Church because it was seemly to do so, and went on afterwards to a Faculty party; the professor was still invited to such functions since he still lived amongst those who had once been his colleagues. 'You will have a choice of drinks,' he said. 'Either overstrong Martinis or a non-alchoholic fruit punch, both equally unpleasant in their different ways. Two years ago I tried pouring one into the other, but my action was not well regarded. To eat, there will be corn chips with a guacamole dip. Can you bear it, do you think?'

'Good practice.' It had been agreed that Sinclair would speak only in his acquired English accent while with the professor, who still spoke Standard English. If he could carry it off in the company of half the Faculty and their wives, all unbuttoned by overstrong Martinis, that would be something; it would be like the Embassy Ball in the film of Shaw's *Pygmalion*. But how to explain him? Who should he be?

'You shall be my nephew. This is Yale. None of them is capable of analytic thought. They will think it natural for my nephew to have an English accent.'

In the event, nobody noticed. But Sinclair noticed. He could hear the difference between themselves and him. And the professor noticed and congratulated his pupil. They walked back in an alcoholic haze, and the professor had a little zizz after lunch.

That evening the professor roasted a rib of beef rare for their Christmas Dinner, and brought out a bottle of imported claret of 1981, which was a good year. Afterwards they sat together by the fire.

The professor said, 'I wanted to talk to you.'

'Once I knew you weren't going to make a pass at me, I thought that might be it.'

'I shall talk round about, I expect. Wander a bit. I'm not very clear what I should say, or if I should say anything.'

Silence. The professor said, 'I'm in good health, Ian. I'm still an active man; my mind is active. I volunteered, you know – volunteered to be a Free British volunteer; I thought it more appropriate for someone like myself to go. I told our people in Washington that none of you has the experience that would allow you to operate successfully, and we can't give it to you here, whereas my generation has some knowledge of war and we remember Britain because we were born and grew up there. And we're eminently dispensable. It was an empty gesture. I suppose I knew they would not take me.

'There are two sorts of English queen among my contemporaries in this country, Ian. Some are men like myself, semi-closeted. There are a few outright areas of deceit in our lives, but much which is never spoken. We avoid scandal, and die a lonely death. And there are the men like Auden the poet, outright and upfront and obvious, making a virtue of it and enjoying the perks. I knew him slightly. I asked him here once: I was asked to ask him. He read his poems to the Literary Society for a very large fee. That lot died off in their sixties mostly of hepatitis, various diseases relating to drink and drugs and sex, some them murdered by rough trade. My lot just grow skinnier and we last depressingly long.

'When Eighth Corps surrendered in Libya, we were taken to a prison camp outside Tripoli. The sanitation was not good there, and

many died. The Nazis at that time had no great objection to killing
defeated soldiers – mainly the officers, mainly in Poland – but
preferred to do so intentionally; they would not tolerate death by
inefficiency and waste. So we were moved to Italy, and there I
escaped. I spoke Italian with reasonable fluency. I walked a great deal
in various directions. I was fed and sheltered – as you hope to be. I
made . . . friends. Good friends.' His lips tightened. 'I don't know
what happened to them. Finally I managed to get to Spain, which
wasn't then a part of the German Empire. Nor was Italy, though they
were allies and the Italians in the inferior position. I worked my
passage from Bilbao to Boston on a cargo vessel. Olive oil and salt
fish. The barrels of oil leaked and the fish stank.'

'Sir?'

'The point is, Ian, that nobody's told you . . . None of your
instructors, myself included, has come out with it clearly and
forcefully because to say it is to admit what our government can't
afford to have admitted, but life under the Germans is not like that
now. Killing off the priests and officers, lining them up blindfold in
front of a mass grave, machine-gunning them, then shovelling earth
over the dead and dying – once it's done, it doesn't have to be done
again. Consequently the concentration camps and the prison camps
have long since been closed down. People have stopped noticing that
there aren't any Jews and gypsies in Europe any more. Someone of
your age wouldn't know what a gypsy was.'

'What are you trying to tell me, sir?'

'I think you know. You're bright enough to know.'

'There isn't going to be a resistance movement? We'll have no
support on the ground?'

'Correct. Britain is not an enslaved nation desperate to throw off
the German yoke. The Britons in Britain, for as long as most of them
can remember, have enjoyed full employment and a relatively high
standard of living. They accept direction of labour and much that we
might find irksome; they don't actually want to be free. They believe
that – practically speaking – they *are* free, or at least as free as any
reasonable person might wish to be.'

Sinclair said, 'Thank you for telling me. I'll have to think about it.'

*

24

After Sinclair had gone, the professor cleaned his house, as he usually did before the arrival of Mrs Cecchetti, his weekly cleaning lady, but more thoroughly and four days early. Then he made himself a sandwich from the left-over beef and ate it slowly with a glass of claret. The snow was thin on the ground and not particularly slippery, so that he was able to go for his usual constitutional, meeting and greeting the other walkers whom it was usual for him to meet and greet. There were a number of places and prospects, not particularly old or odd or even memorable, places of merely personal significance, which this afternoon he chose to visit, so that the constitutional was longer than usual, and the street-lamps were already lit by the time he returned to his tolerably comfortable home.

He ran a bath, and undressed, hanging his trousers and jacket on wooden hangers in the closet and throwing everything else into the laundry basket. The bath should be hot, he knew, as hot as he could bear it. Should it also be perfumed? Had the Romans added herbs – rosemary, lavender and camomile perhaps? He could not remember. Rue might be more suitable. He poured half a bottle of cologne as a gesture into the steaming bath, then lowered himself into it and added more hot water. The convention required a cut-throat razor, preferably one which had belonged to his father, something from the past to link him with his ancestors, but of course he had brought no such object with him to America. Instead he had provided himself with a kitchen knife which he had sharpened with a steel shortly after Sinclair's departure.

Perfume or no, his father's razor or no, all that was window-dressing. The only important element of a Roman self-slaughter was that both veins should be opened, that his life-blood should drain away, turning the bath-water into amniotic fluid, so that he ended as he had begun, drifting into death either by loss of blood or by drowning. He picked up the knife from the side of the bath and tried the blade against the ball of his thumb.

'Lord, *but it stung like a nettle!*' That was Mr Polly, he remembered, on the night of the Great Fishbourne Fire, when Polly sat on the stairs which led from his draper's shop to the living-quarters above – stairs over which paraffin had already spilled from the lamp he had intended to drop – tried to cut his throat, and was

25

surprised because he had not expected it to hurt. Well, the professor did expect slitting his wrists to hurt, but not all that much. He had endured worse.

The History of Mr Polly had been a set book for School Certificate. He had answered context questions, analysed (even then the Military Historian) the strategy and tactics of Polly's three battles against Uncle Jim, with particular reference to the use of the eel as a tactical weapon, and had been awarded an 'A'. He had been awarded many marks of academic excellence since and the Military Cross for gallantry in the face of the enemy. He looked down at his body, stretched out in the scented water. It was better than many at his age, with really not much of a pot-belly, only a little subcutaneous fat plumping out the breasts, the knees only a little scrawny, the veins in the legs certainly not varicose though one could as certainly see where they were. His skin was withered now and dry, there were liver-spots on the backs of his hands and on his thighs, his penis was a withered twig with an oak-apple at the end, his scrotum a discarded dorothy-bag and – oh shit! what did it all matter?

But it did matter. This apology for a body to be discovered days hence in the bath, cold and sticky with blood, by the unfortunate Mrs Cecchetti . . . it would not do. The whole enterprise would not do. The blood ebbing gently into water scented with herbs in the old Roman way, that would not do either, and never had done. The professor had seen men die when their veins had been opened, violently opened by shrapnel in battle, and the blood had not ebbed, but gushed out like liquid from a pump. He had no objection to that, but there was no dignity in it, and no honour in inflicting the consequences of it on an unprepared middle-aged Italian lady who liked to consider herself more friend than cleaner. The Roman way might have been all very well for the Romans, who were often bounced into suicide, but was ultimately inappropriate to the conditions of twentieth-century America where the practical choice for someone whose life had become meaningless lay between an overdose of barbiturates and a retirement home in Florida.

The professor soaped his body and washed it in the hot perfumed water, then removed himself from the bath and dried himself vigorously with a towel the size of a small sheet. He dressed in clean underwear, warm woollen socks, comfortable corduroy trousers, a plaid shirt and a pair of soft leather moccasins. He combed his damp silver hair neatly across his pink scalp so that it would dry in place, and he trimmed unsightly tufts from his nostrils and ears. Then he went to the living-room which was also his study, and lighted the fire already laid in the grate.

He returned to his bedroom, and took from a locked drawer in the bedside table seven pill-bottles, none of them full but each containing sleeping pills. Like many men and women of his age, the professor had put together a hoard of such pills, the relics of past prescriptions, against a time when they might be needed. He went to the kitchen and boiled a kettle. He tipped the pills into a cereal-bowl, filled a jug with boiling water, fetched a bottle of whiskey from the dresser, and took whiskey, water and pills back to the fire, now burning briskly, and placed them on a table beside his chair. 'If it be now, 'tis not to come,' he said. 'If it be not to come, it will be now. If it be not now, yet it will come. The readiness is all.'

He set the tape of the Couperin so that it would rewind and begin to play again when it was over, settled himself in his chair, put on headphones, taped the sensapads to the insides of his wrists and switched on the music. Yes, this was it; this was the way, without fuss or inconvenience to anyone, not even himself. He poured whiskey into his glass, added hot water and sipped, rolling it around in his mouth, savouring and relishing the taste. Then a couple of pills, then a little more whiskey, then pills. The only danger, he knew, was that he might be sick, vomit up the cocktail of alcohol and barbiturates and have the whole job to do again. Therefore he must take it slowly, space out the pills, not trying to cram them all down at once, must continue to savour the whiskey, not rush into the second glass and the third, but work his way gradually through the bottle, remembering that he had all night and the music would continue to play.

Couperin. *Trois Leçons de Ténèbres*. An appropriate choice. He had never been able to persuade Lucio to enjoy any music written earlier than 1850, which was one reason why it would never have worked with Lucio, not in the long term, probably never with anybody. The professor closed his eyes, and the image of Sinclair formed behind the lids. There had been no way of saving him; all one could do was to warn. The image of Sinclair became full-length and arranged itself upon a chaise-longue. Methodically, bit by bit, the professor began to undress the image of Ian Sinclair, who moved himself about obligingly so as to allow the professor to do so. 'There is no doubt,' the professor said aloud, 'that, objectively speaking, the man Auden was the most complete and utter stinker.'

Those were the professor's last words, not particularly memorable, perhaps not even true, and with no one to record them. When Mrs Cecchetti found him four days later, she thought at first that he had fallen asleep with the music machine playing.

Landfall

They had been twenty, and then they were eleven. They had been eleven, and then they were five. Two groups, one of three volunteers, the other of two, had been chosen to infiltrate the homeland. The other six volunteers remained at base in support and under further training; they would be sent out as the next two groups in a couple of months when the experience of the first two had been evaluated. Base was at High Peaks, formerly an artists' colony in South Dakota, a charitable foundation which had run out of funds and had been sold cheap by its trustees to the Free Brits.

They had been five and now they were two. The other three volunteers had not yet left the submarine: they would be carried further and make their own landfall elsewhere. Neither group was to know anything of the whereabouts of the other. They had been forbidden to make contact after landing.

Much thought had been given by Operations Section of the Free British in Washington to the selection of landing-places. The approach would be from the Atlantic. Therefore the landings would have to be made on the west coast. But the coast of south-west England would be too highly populated for a secret landing, that of Scotland too far from those centres of population in which one might expect the Resistance to be capable of effective operation. North Wales would be less populated and probably less policed than the South West, yet easier to get away from than the Highlands and Islands and nearer to London. A further consideration was that Parry-Jones, one of the volunteers in the first group, was said to speak the local language.

29

Wales, then. The planners had provided themselves with a selection of tourist guides and the Automobile Association's *Motoring Atlas*, published in 1979. *The Visitors' Guide to North Wales & Snowdonia* by C. Macdonald informed them that the beaches between Harlech and Barmouth are among the finest in Wales, shallow and sandy and backed by dunes. Sandy beaches would be easier for a landing than shingle; the approach would be free of rocks, which elsewhere on the coast of Wales abound, an important consideration when the landings would have to be in darkness.

That the beaches were backed by dunes was also an advantage. They could not be overlooked from the coast road or any dwellings close to it; the presence of an observer on the beach itself was unlikely since the holdiday season would be over and that part of Wales experiences heavy rainfall in February. Then there were the mountains, in this area never far from the coast. If a hiding-place were needed to begin with, some mountain hut or slate-cutters' cabin would provide it. The decision was that the first group of two men, Sinclair and Parry-Jones, should be landed between Tal-y-bont and Llandenddwyn.

Sinclair and Parry-Jones were the Attack Group: their mission was special. The second group of Attlee, Cape and Alloway had a more mundane job: Organisation and Information – information to begin with, organisation once they were in place; they would know what and whom to organise when they'd had a bit of time to look around.

The two groups must be landed far enough apart for them to work separately and in ignorance of each others' whereabouts, but near enough for the whole operation to be completed in one night. North of Harlech the Lleyn Peninsula stretches westwards, on its south side the holiday resorts of Criccieth and Pwllheli, again with sandy beaches but much built up, and in any case too close to the first landing-place. Its north side would still be within easy reach of the submarine, and although there were no sandy beaches, and the charts indicated stretches of cliff and rocks, what else could one expect from Wales, which was not Atlantic City after all?

There was a place called Aberdesach, no more than a dot on the atlas, where the railway no longer ran, the coast road came down to the sea, and there seemed to be a break in the cliffs: one might almost call it a little bay. The Head of Military Intelligence said, 'What do you think? If the place has a name, there'll be houses. People. Not many . . . a place this size, but even so . . .'

'It's a beach, sir. They don't have to land close to the houses.'

'And they'll be the second group to land. 0300 hours, sir. Nobody awake. And it looks like uninhabited country inland.'

'Swings and roundabouts, sir. If there are houses, there could be a vehicle unattended and easy to steal. They'd be out of there and into the hills in no time.'

'Swings and roundabouts, eh?' This was the language of planning, comforting for a military man to speak and to hear spoken. 'Right! Swings and roundabouts. Aberdesach it is.'

The Head of Military Intelligence knew, they all knew, that a three-man O & I Group, burdened with expensive and irreplaceable radio equipment, needed a safe and secret landing-place more than the first two-man Attack Group, but his emotional commitment was to the Attack Group, which had been entrusted with the more daring and important mission. He regarded the setting up of radio communication and the intelligence-gathering function of young Attlee's lot as considerably less exciting.

2359 hours on 8th February 1992. A new moon was obscured by clouds and steady rain. The submarine had come to the surface five miles offshore so that the coast could be surveyed for an absence of lights. Three elements were required for success – a calm sea (which there was), darkness (which there would be until 0630 hours, though there was still the second party to be landed on the other side of the peninsula at 0300) and a stretch of beach in a relatively unpopulated area (which they hoped they had found, but only the actual landing would confirm). Parry-Jones and Sinclair entered the rubber dinghy which had been prepared for them, and began the final stage of their journey.

It was a journey into the unknown. They knew what they had to do, but not how to do it; had been briefed in general terms, but all the particularities had been left to them; their battle plan consisted of an objective with no method. What if the landing were discovered or even opposed? The dinghy would already be returning to the submarine, which would not hang about to find out what had happened to the volunteers. If they were in imminent danger of capture they would have to resort to the cyanide capsule which each carried in a gold locket on a thin chain of gold links worn around the neck. This would be a great waste, and would warn the Germans that a covert operation was under way, thus making the task of the O & I Group more difficult. As for the Attack Group, Operations Section supposed that it would have to be started all over again from scratch.

Parry-Jones and Sinclair were not required to paddle the dinghy. There were two crew-members to do that. It had an outboard motor, which had been used at the beginning of their journey, but as they drew closer to the shore, the engine was switched off so that their approach might be silent. The rain was drenching and the dinghy itself shipped water, as dinghies do. The two sailors paddled energetically, partly to keep themselves warm and partly because they wished the whole business over and themselves safely back on board, yet they shivered in their oilskins. Parry-Jones and Sinclair sat, one at the bow and one in the stern, sleek and snug in wet-suits. They had not been provided with authentic English suiting from Saks Fifth Avenue, with tweed jackets and comfortable corduroys, only to have them ruined at the outset by rain and seawater. Their clothing, weapons, papers and rations for two days, together with the travelling bags of toughened waterproof cloth from Burberry in which they would be carried, were in zippered back-packs which were themselves waterproof in case either volunteer should fall over while wading the last few yards to the beach.

Sinclair, at the bow, was wearing light-enhancing goggles to improve his night-vision: like the submarine they were under test. He had worn similar goggles during exercises at the training centre, but never in driving rain and never at sea. Raindrops exploded against them in bubbles of enhanced light; it was like having one's face inside a jacuzzi. Beyond the exploding drops was a bead curtain of rain, hiding from him whatever in the way of submerged rocks, bobbing mines and entanglements of barbed wire might lie between the dinghy and the beach. But there would be no submerged rocks – they had been assured of that – and no reason for man-made barriers either since nobody in Britain knew they were coming. Sinclair had been given the responsibility of a look-out without the means to look out effectively but with the assurance that there was nothing to look out for. The words *'Finita la commedia'* floated into his mind, but this comedy was still at its beginning, and when the end came it was not likely to be comic, at least for the leading players.

What had the professor expected him to do? He could not back out; he had volunteered for danger; they all had. They had not known what kind of danger until the training course was well in progress, but nobody had backed out. Even then they had not been allowed to know the full extent of the danger, that they would find no resistance movement, no friendly underground to shelter them, because those who had sent them did not know that, or would not allow themselves to know it. Did the CIA know, Sinclair wondered, did the Americans know that the Free British volunteers were being sent like wasps to buzz and sting where they could but in the end – which would come soon enough – to be swatted with rolled-up newspapers or drowned in jam-jars? And do no more real harm than wasps?

Sinclair knew. He could have worked it out for himself without the professor, but he had gone on anyway because there did not seem to be any honourable way out and he had wanted to make a gesture, some sort of gesture which would give meaning to a life which had seemed meaningless after Ellie's death.

Death. *Half in love with easeful death*. Too much death. The professor had committed suicide. Did Sinclair carry some kind of taint which brought despair to those who loved him?

That had been, now he brought it back to mind, a very odd afternoon above the Sex Shop. The general older than God, all kitted out in chestnut brown with polished leather straps and bits of red silk (but you could see the bulge of the colostomy bag) and the Prime Minister like an advertisement for Country Casuals.

Did the Americans know what the orders of the Attack Group were? Sinclair did not think so.

Interesting! Not for the first time, Sinclair found his own thought processes interesting. 'Some sort of gesture which would give meaning to a life which had seemed meaningless after Ellie's death.'

Three months ago his state of mind would not have allowed the possibility of doubt. He would have thought 'had become meaning-less' not 'seemed meaningless': there was a hell of a difference. Had time done this or was there a point to his gesture after all?

The rain stopped suddenly and there was a break in the clouds which allowed a sliver of moon to give what help it could to the light-enhancing goggles. Sinclair plucked at the side of his wet-suit as if at a pocket, searching for a handkerchief with which to wipe them, but wet-suits had no pockets. He shook his head. He could see the froth of breaking waves and light reflected from the sand of the beach. 'We're nearly there,' he said. The two sailors discovered a reserve of energy and the dinghy shot forward. Now that the rain had ceased, the sound of the waves could be clearly heard. The dinghy rocked among the surf. Then there was a bump as its bottom hit the shallow beach, and the two paddles became anchors to hold it steady while the passengers disembarked.

They stood there in the shallow water, feeling the slight tug of the receding waves, two tall two-legged creatures with black rubber skin and white faces, their back-packs like humps for the storage of blubber to take them through the winter. It should have been a moment of high drama, but the sailors knew nothing about the nature of their mission and were in a hurry to return. One of them said, 'Good luck, you guys!', the other said, 'See you!' and then they were turning into the waves and on their way back to the submarine. They did not need Sinclair and his light-enhancing goggles to guide them. They had a radio beacon for that.

Parry-Jones and Sinclair walked together out of the water and onto sand. They walked clumsily, their frog-feet flapping. The sand became shingle, beyond which Sinclair could see the shapes of the dunes. Parry-Jones said, 'Hold it here a moment,' and collapsed slowly from the knees onto the shingle like an apprentice actor rehearsing a stage fall. He had not tripped; the action was intentional. Once down, he placed his head amongst the pebbles, kissed those within easy reach of his mouth, and spoke a couple of lines of verse in a foreign language.

'What are you doing?'

'I'm saluting the soil of my homeland.'

34

'Couldn't it wait?'

Parry-Jones scrambled to his feet, which was not easy in flippers. 'Has to be done on landing. I would have warned you, but I anticipated a negative reaction. It's a protective ritual. The Welsh warrior – a king's son usually; we can't rise to that, but we're both warriors, at least, and my father's a minister of religion – anyway the Welsh warrior returns from exile to claim his inheritance against the usurper. First thing he does, he salutes the soil of his homeland and asks it to protect him. I included you in the invocation, you'll be glad to know, even though you're not Welsh.'

Sinclair said, 'Very generous; I appreciate it.'

'Common sense really. If you get into trouble, it's bound to affect me.'

'Do you really believe that stuff?'

'All my life since I can begin to remember,' said Arwen Parry-Jones, 'I've taken part in rituals in which I did not believe in order to please other people. At least now I'm doing it to please myself. We'd better find somewhere to shelter for tonight, then get out of these wet-suits at first light, dispose of them and turn ourselves into solid citizens.'

They both knew, because they had discussed it, what was next to be done. While they were in wet-suits they were at their most vulnerable. If the weather had been kind, they could have changed into civilian clothes in the shelter of the dunes, buried the wet-suits and back-packs in the sand or burned them, and been out on the road with their travelling bags by early morning, a couple of unremarkable young men on holiday or looking for work. But the weather was not kind. Therefore some barn or byre must be found, a shed on an allotment, a beach hut, even a church, any building likely to be unoccupied at night in which they could shelter until daybreak.

They knew what to do; they would do it. They went forward together towards the dunes, Parry-Jones a little behind, and walked smack into a fence of wire mesh which had been erected to cut the dunes off from the beach.

First there had been nothing, nothing at all, and then the voices. The nothing could have lasted for any length of time – five minutes, five hours, five days, five weeks, five months, five years – how could one know?

Five. Why had he fixed on five? There was a clue in that somewhere.

At first the voices had been strange to him, and what they had been saying was strange. Instructions had been given, usually by males, and received usually by females: there was a hierarchy, male-dominated. Occasionally he had been directly addressed, and required to open his eyes or move his fingers if he could hear what was said, but there had been a lack of logic in this. He could hear, and understand much of what he heard, but was unable to make any physical motion in response: the voices should have known that. Certain physical tests and actions were also performed on his body. He could deduce as much by the nature of the instructions given by the voices to those who served them, but felt nothing of what was done.

After some while – again he could not know how long, having no way of measuring – familiar voices had joined the unfamiliar, the voices of his father and mother, of his sister Kate and of Bernadette. These voices . . . unhappy . . . halting . . . had told him stories he already knew, stories of his childhood and of the more recent past. They told him that they were sitting by him, holding his hand, and that he was to press their fingers to show that he remembered. In this they showed the same deficiency in logic as the hierarchs: he could remember, but could not press or even feel their fingers. Bernadette told him that she loved him and that she would always love him and always be near him, but he could hear the uncertainty in her voice, and would not have bet money on it.

The voices from his home told him of their pride that he had volunteered to serve his country, but nothing about his time at the training centre, since all that was Top Secret; they knew nothing about any of that. There was only one voice from the training centre, and that was the voice of his buddy Geoff.

Geoff told him that they had been in the woods on the other side of the valley, preparing an ambush for elements of A Group, representing the advance party of a column of motorised infantry, and that he – David – David Piper – he was David Julian Piper: he knew that, did not need to be told that, knew it perfectly well; he had always been David Piper – he had been concealed in the upper branches of a tree commanding the track by which A Group's vehicle was expected to approach, that his field of fire had been obstructed by foliage, and that in attempting to clear it he had fallen out of the tree and onto his head, suffering concussion and some injury to his back. Of what the voices from home told him he remembered everything, of what Geoff told him, nothing. Geoff's voice had been oddly formal and constricted, not at all like Geoff.

Five. That was it. There were five of them, three and two, very hazy at the edge of his consciousness, hardly there at all. There had been five together and now there were two, with the other three not far away. Five dots in two clusters, five points of anxiety within the dark, five fearful, five at risk. His mind was a nebula into which five alien stars had somehow intruded, and he was picking up their signals. That was why five had been the first number to come into his mind: it had been there already. Five minutes, five hours, five lives to which his one life was somehow attached. David Julian Piper, secure within the shelter of his coma, not brain-dead (his parents had been assured of that), by no means brain-dead and therefore capable of revival though with many functions considerably impaired, knew almost nothing about the five except that the signals would grow stronger and he would know more.

The fence continued for several miles, and they had to feel their way along it. During this time the rain began again.

At last they came to a gap, clearly intended for access since the fence continued beyond it. This gap was the width of a path, a winding path among the dunes, but still fenced on both sides so that one could not break away from it. The steeper parts of the path were stepped and elsewhere it became a boardwalk. In season, and perhaps even out of season, it must be in frequent use by the public. It was a path to get away from.

The path ended at a metalled road. To one side was an asphalted car park with a wooden table and benches for picnics. There was also a toilet, which was locked. Presumably someone would arrive to open that toilet. They were still nowhere near to finding a safe place to lay up, and did not know how much time they had wasted in feeling their way along the fence. They must go on.

Once again rain was blurring the light-enhancing goggles, and walking in frog-feet was not easy, yet if they took the flippers off they would have to go barefoot, and there was broken glass about. Such difficulties had not been anticipated by their instructors at the training centre.

They found a wooden gate giving access to the dunes from the car park. Here at least there were no fenced areas, though there was evidence of public resort in the empty cans and plastic beakers which were scrunched beneath their flippers, and Parry-Jones walked into a single coil of barbed wire, left lying in the sand, and cut his leg. The dunes were like sandy mountains which had shrunk to no more than ten times the height of a man, with valleys meandering between, along which the summer visitors had impacted the sand.

They found a concrete pill-box, and this also seemed to have shrunk since it was built. Although there were horizontal slits for a couple of machine-guns in the wall facing the sea, the door on the landward side was only big enough for a child to enter. Nevertheless they crawled inside for shelter, discovered that the floor was covered with broken glass, shit and slime, and crawled out quicker than they had crawled in.

They applied reason to their predicament. If a wet-suit is able to keep one dry against the sea, it will keep one dry against the rain. They spent the rest of the night lying on the slope of a dune, sheltered from the wind, and slept as well as they could until the dawn.

While they slept the wind dropped, the rain stopped. Dawn came to a clear sky. Getting out of the wet-suits and into their civilian clothes in the open and on wet sand was not easy, but in rain it could not have been managed at all; they became convinced of their good fortune and consequently cheerful. These clothes were old friends. They had been worn at a costume parade in the gymnasium of the training centre and thereafter for a fortnight before embarkation to give them that lived-in appearance. Parry-Jones and Sinclair looked at each other as if in a mirror, and grew in confidence: they were so impeccably British. Both were wearing expensive brogues by Lobb of St James, socks and underwear by Wolsey, soft comfortable trousers of best quality corduroy by Aquascutum, button-down shirts by Turnbull and Asser, V-necked sweaters of Shetland wool by Pringle of Scotland and jackets of hand-woven Harris tweed by Daks. Sinclair wore the Charvet tie given to him by the professor, Parry-Jones the tie of Jesus College, Oxford. It did not occur to either that they were considerably overdressed for the Welsh seaside in February.

The rest of their gear was packed away in the travelling bags. Outerwear would be a problem. Raincoats or rainproof overcoats would have taken up too much room in the back-packs. However, Burberry also manufactured collapsible foldaway umbrellas, and these took up very little room. The volunteers did not know, as Operations Section had not known, that they were only made for export.

There remained the wet-suits and back-packs. If they were discovered, the Free Brits' secret invasion would no longer be secret: the commando training manual used at the centre had emphasised that agents dropped by night into enemy territory must always bury their parachutes immediately after they hit the ground. It would not be easy to bury the wet-suits because the volunteers had nothing but their hands to use for digging, but wet-suits were smaller than parachutes; the thing could be done. They would have to be buried deep, because the nature of sand is that it shifts, and this was an area, as one could tell by the numerous turds lying about, where people exercised their dogs, which are also digging animals, their curiosity easily aroused. Deep digging by hand in wet sand would almost certainly ruin the volunteers' expensive British outfits. Perhaps they should have done the digging while still naked, but what if they had been discovered? The digging might just be explained away, but not the nudity. 'We'll have to burn them,' Sinclair said.

Burning would not be easy either. There were plenty of discarded newspapers littering the area, but they were soggy with the rain. The volunteers looked about for driftwood, for flotsam driven onto the dunes by high tides and the wind, and they could see through the fence of wire mesh that there was plenty on the beach, but they could not get at it unless they went back by way of the path; it was too risky. But there was brushwood, some of it bramble, lying about on the tops of the dunes, apparently placed there intentionally to stop the sand blowing away. It was wet, but would dry quickly enough if a fire could be started beneath it.

Only non-smokers had been chosen for the Special Service Unit, partly for reasons of fitness, partly because any form of addiction was thought to indicate a weakness of character, but the volunteers had been provided with Dunhill cigarette-lighters as part of the general cover and in case they were needed for just such a purpose as this, to start a fire. Sinclair and Parry-Jones made a collection of plastic beakers and cartons of waxed cardboard, piled them together, placed on top the crumpled inside pages of tabloid newspapers (which were less damp than the outside pages) and brushwood on top of that. Soon they had a fire. Burning brushwood dried out more brushwood. The fire blazed up. The first pair of flippers was placed on top of it, began to melt and then the rubber took fire. A back-pack followed, and a column of black smoke rose from the bonfire. 'I suppose that's bound to be seen,' Parry-Jones said.

'Nobody's going to make anything of it. Anyway who's looking at this time of the morning?'

Someone was looking. There was a small boy in jeans and a blue anorak standing among marram grass and sandwort at the top of one of the dunes, and watching them.

The volunteers had been taught that if any unfortunate person were to happen upon them while they were engaged in some activity which would reveal who they really were, that person was to be killed immediately, silently and without scruple, using one of the approved methods. Neither Sinclair nor Parry-Jones for a moment considered putting this part of their training into operation in the case of the small boy. Sinclair said, 'We'll go up to him. He mustn't see what we're burning.'

Parry-Jones said, 'If he's local he may be Welsh. I'll talk to him. You get the rest of the stuff on the fire.'

So Arwen Parry-Jones climbed up to the small boy while Sinclair piled the rest of the brushwood on the fire and the second back-pack and the wet-suits on top of it. The stench of burning rubber was now strong and the smoke looked as if a raiding party of Apache had set fire to a wagon-train.

Arwen said to the small boy, 'Dydd da iti, ac o ba wlad yr wyt ti'n hanfod?' which was the question put by Pwyll, Prince of Dyfed, to the King of the Dead, and may be demotically translated as 'Hi, stranger! Where are you from?'

The small boy stared at Arwen, and his eyes flicked sideways as if checking on his escape-route. Arwen repeated the question.

Sinclair had climbed up to join them. He said, 'He doesn't understand you. He thinks you're a foreigner. It's probably your accent. Let me try in English.' To the small boy he said, 'Do you live near here?'

The small boy nodded.

'What's your name?'

'Tommy.'

Arwen said, 'He's not from the Principality, then. Probably a holiday-maker.'

'In February? What's your other name, Tommy?'

'Griffiths.'

Arwen said, 'There's nothing wrong with my accent. There's no one in the Department at Idaho speaks with a purer accent.' He said to the boy, 'Listen to me, Tommy Griffiths. My name is Arwen. My sister is Bronwen, my father Owain.' It had not been possible to fit the volunteers out with the identities of Britons who had died or absconded. Although supporting details had been invented, the forged identity cards, driving licences and credit cards with which they had been provided were all in their own names, because they were used to answering to those names; only Attlee was spelling his with an 'eigh'. The credit cards had been issued to add verisimilitude, not for use. They must never be used, since accounts in those names did not exist.

Arwen said to the boy, 'Parry-Jones is my family. We are Welsh – a Welsh family. Our bloodline is pure, and goes back hundreds of years. Are you a Welshman, Thomas? Are you from around here? Cymro? From Merioneth?'

The question was simple enough, but seemed to puzzle the small boy. However, after he had given it consideration, he nodded.

'But you don't speak Welsh? Your family don't speak Welsh?'

Again it was clearly a worrying question to which the small boy was not prepared to offer a reply.

41

'Do you also have a sister as I do, Thomas?'

A shake of the head.

'A brother?'

Shake of the head.

'Friends at least? Do you have friends of your own age? Welsh boys?' At last a nod. 'And what are their names?'

'Peter . . . Joe . . . Karl.'

Arwen said, 'Oh, Christ! English names. German names. What's happening here?'

Sinclair said, 'There's been a lot of intermarriage, I suppose.'

Arwen looked as if he were about to burst into tears. Sinclair said, 'If we're looking for a Welsh-speaker we're more likely to find one among the old-timers. Tommy, is your grandfather alive?' Nod of the head. 'Both of them?' Another nod. Sinclair did some calculations. 'Boy's about ten. Father probably in his early thirties, both grandparents in their fifties – hardly born when the war ended.' He spoke again to the boy. 'What about your great-grandfathers? Do you have a great-grandad alive?'

'He's old.'

'Yes, he would be.' Sinclair said to Parry-Jones, 'There's your Welsh-speaker. If anyone.' And then again to the boy, 'Will you tell us where he lives? Can you take us to him?'

'He's in a Home. My mum and dad visit Wednesdays. I don't go.'

Dead end. The old man might well be gaga and anyway had no privacy. Arwen said, 'What are you doing out here, Tommy, so early in the morning?'

The small boy produced a key from the pocket of his anorak. 'Come to open the toilet.' He looked down at the bonfire, and sniffed. 'What's that you're burning?'

'Oh! . . . Nothing important. Don't worry about it.'

'It's rubber, isn't it? Shouldn't do that. Pollutes the atmosphere.'

The boy seemed already to have established himself in a commanding moral position. Sinclair felt the situation slipping out of his control. It was natural that American schoolchildren should be taught not to pollute the atmosphere by burning noxious substances, but oddly disconcerting to find the same lessons in the mouth of one educated within the evil German Empire.

'Sorry. You're right.' The boy would talk to his parents. Some explanation was required. He looked down at the fire. The burning rubber was no longer identifiable. 'Sleeping-bags. We're on holiday, you see. Thought we might try sleeping rough, but it's not really practical in this weather. They're old. Not worth keeping. Decided to get rid of them.' He had a sudden vision of Arwen and himself through the boy's eyes, walking up the road to Harlech in their tweed jackets and expensive cords, sheltered from the drenching rain by collapsible umbrellas of waterproof silk. 'How did you get here? Bicycle? We'll walk with you back to the main road. I imagine there'll be a bus along soon enough.'

They had made a terrible start. They must get off the road as soon as they could and find somewhere to hide until they could work out how the land lay.

The Prime Minister was in conference with the CIGS and the Head of Military Intelligence. They sat at one end of a long table in the Operations Room, which had until recently been the Cabinet Room, but the military had taken it over. It seemed to the Prime Minister that both men had grown in the last few weeks, not physically but in presence – something about the set of their shoulders, about the way they were sitting, each master of his own space. He himself, as was customary and proper, occupied the head of the table, but had begun to wonder if it had not somehow become the foot.

'We've heard from the O & I Group – your nephew's group. All quite safe, you'll be glad to know. Got ashore without incident, stole a van, and now they're up in the hills somewhere outside Blaenau Ffestiniog. Bloody cold, I expect.'

'Lieutenant Attlee is my second-cousin, not my nephew; I think you know that, Victor. It's the Manitoba branch of the family. We don't see much of them.'

The CIGS was teasing, of course. There had been some argument over whether young Attlee should be among the first five. He had not graduated *summa cum laude* from the training centre. He had been a conscientious and meticulous student but lacked flair; the professor's confidential report had been tactful but tepid. Yet he had been promoted to lieutenant when the others were all sergeants, and put in charge of a group.

The Prime Minister had opposed the appointment, but had been outvoted. It was not a matter of merit but of expedience. Once the flame of freedom had been rekindled and the brush fires of resistance were crackling from Lands End to John o'Groats, when the waves of English-speaking reinforcements from the New World were breaking against the beachheads and Britain was on her way to becoming Great again, then the fact that an Attlee had been among the first five would be a bonus in terms of PR, and whether he died gallantly in action or lived to lead the victory parade would not really matter. 'No question of favouritism; it's the name,' the Head of Military Intelligence had insisted. 'Not the man himself but the name we need. And you can see it for yourself in Iestyn's report, Prime Minister – "should make a competent officer": one can't say fairer than that.'

Too much had been arranged over his head. It was time to take charge. The Prime Minister cleared his throat. It did nothing for his charisma. 'I'd like to be clear about this,' he said. 'Organisation and Intelligence! What intelligence are we expecting to get?'

'General picture to start with. Then the targets – arms depots and factories. We'll be sending in new units on a continuous basis, some of them Attack Groups assigned to sabotage. But for the time being, what's most important is to be receiving intelligence bulletins at all, not what they contain. In order to keep this thing rolling, first we have to prove it can roll, do you see?'

'No.'

'We had a bit of a chat with Casey yesterday.'

Had they, indeed? Casey was the head of the CIA. He had not until then given much of his attention to the Free British Special Service Unit; he had seemed to regard the whole operation as an exercise in amateur theatricals. His attitude had been galling to the British Cabinet, and particularly so to its military advisers. No wonder there was an atmosphere, almost a miasma, of smugness in the Operations Room. 'Without me?' the Prime Minister said.

'Oppo to oppo, off the record.'

'I thought you were having some difficulty in talking "oppo to oppo" with any of Casey's people. With any of his more senior people.'

'Not any more.'

The CIGS said, 'Let me try to focus your thinking, Prime Minister. What overriding aim have we in sending these units to Britain?'

Shut your eyes, and you wouldn't know who was speaking, Victor or Hilary. They were two mouths of the same monster. The Prime Minister said, 'You know our War Aims as well as I do.'

'There are Aims and aims, Prime Minister – big "A" and little "a": big "A" comes later. Our immediate aim, without which we can achieve nothing, is to establish credibility with the State Department and the Pentagon.'

'We have credibility.'

'When were you and Doris last asked to a State Department dinner? I don't mean one of the minor league affairs with a stand-up buffet and a couple of folk singers. I mean a real, white-tie diplomatic dinner as guests of the President and the First Lady.'

'Independence Day.'

'That's right. You never spoke to the President; you were greeted by Annenberg. And you and Doris went in to dinner at the bottom table behind the Venezualan *chargé d'affaires*. I remember you mentioned it in Cabinet. You were very bitter.'

'It's water under the bridge.'

'We aim to change all that. Casey wants in. His people are thin on the ground in Europe. We have credibility now, Prime Minister. We have something the Yanks want. They'll treat us as equal partners, and they're ready to share.'

'Ready for us to share our intelligence with them or ready to share theirs with us?'

'Ours is better. It'll be better still as we get more groups in position.'

'Has it ever occurred to you . . .' He found it difficult to continue. What he wished to say had first occurred to him at the briefing meeting with Sinclair and Parry-Jones, had occurred several times since, but he had not been able to bring himself to mention it; there would almost certainly be a simple reply which would expose him to ridicule. 'Has it occurred to you . . .' he said. They were waiting, polite as owls. 'Have you considered that we've never actually discussed how we get these people back?'

'We don't have to get them back. They remain in position until the invasion begins.'

He had expected a simple answer, and now had it. It was simple but not really an answer: that was the military way. 'You didn't tell Casey about the Attack Group?'

'Good God, no!'

They would not, could not have done so. For that at least they would have needed his permission. Casey must know, of course, that two groups had been landed. Odd that he hadn't asked about the purpose of the smaller group. 'When are we going to tell the full Cabinet?' A blank. He looked each of his military advisers full in the face, challenging them, willing them to be unable to meet his gaze. They returned it, clear-eyed and innocent as nuns, infinitely tolerant of their civilian master. 'Any of them?'

The Head of Military Intelligence said, 'You know what they are, Prime Minister. They enjoy attention and don't often get it. You can't trust them to keep their mouths shut, that's the long and the short of it.'

The CIGS said, 'In time of war, Prime Minister, who knows least knows best.'

In time of war, the Prime Minister thought, the military get above themselves. He had been talked into the Attack Group. It had seemed a good idea at the time, but already there was no way of stopping it. But all he said was, 'Have you considered an element of contradiction in all this? If the Attack Group succeeds in its mission, that could foul up everything the other groups have been sent to do. Foul up getting into bed with Casey – foul up the equal status – Special Relationship – everything. There'll be such a retaliation. Such a hunt. They'll roll up the Resistance, roll up our own units, and we'll have no intelligence anyway.'

'We'd start again.'

'They'd be expecting us to start again. Waiting for us on the beaches.'

'I don't think you quite understand the military way of doing things, Prime Minister.' They could say *that* again. 'Most strategic planning contains some element of contradiction; it's inbuilt. We have two plans, Plan A and Plan B, each, if successful, bringing us a considerable advantage. A layman like yourself might think it a disadvantage that if A works, it could prevent B from working. Not a bit of it. The military mind knows perfectly well that either A or B is going to get cocked up anyway. In practice the two objectives have to be treated as totally independent. They'll never collide.'

The Prime Minister supposed that Lloyd George must have had trouble of this sort from the military. Churchill perhaps not, since Churchill had been even loopier than most of his own generals. Yet Lloyd George had ended on top. He made a mental note to get a good biography of Lloyd George from the library, and find out how the thing was done.

It was true that the Free British volunteers had been able to land unopposed because they were not expected, yet the Germans were prudent people. They did not anticipate invasion, but had prepared against it. They were confident that the Japanese could not attack through Russia, but the Atlantic provinces of the Empire might be open to nuisance-raids from the Americans, and this was particularly the case with the province of Britain because the language was the same.

The imperial government was represented within each province by a Reichsprotektor. At first the Reichsprotektor had been the real administrative authority within the province, but after years of peace and stability he had become more like a constitutional monarch. He still had the authority to govern by decree, to appoint ministers, to propose and to veto legislation within the provincial parliament, but no longer needed to do so. Now, as the war brought a shift in the balance of power within the Council of State in Berlin, the generals had decided that security must be tightened.

Everything had been done constitutionally within the framework of provincial self-government. The gracious and easy-going civilian Reichsprotektors of the Atlantic provinces were replaced by younger, harder men, with the youngest and hardest assigned to Britain. This was Dietrich Druckermann, a career soldier, a General of the SS.

Druckermann had his own ideas. His secretariat presented to the British Parliament a bill which empowered the police to round up and imprison for their own safety 'disloyal elements'. Parliament reluctantly voted it into law. By 'disloyal' the new Reichsprotektor seemed to mean members of certain dotty nationalist organisations – the Children of Rebecca in Wales, the Men of the Glens in Scotland and Albion Awake, a social and sporting society, which had the bulk of its membership in the Home Counties. These groups could hardly be considered disloyal in any real way. The Welsh and Scottish groups were only agitating for Home Rule within the Empire and it was hard to make out exactly what Albion Awake stood for except that King Arthur and the Round Table came into it somewhere.

The war had not up to that time involved much hardship in Britain. Petrol was rationed, and some consumer durables had gone into short supply as the factories producing them were converted to the production of weaponry, but there was no general call-up beyond the normal conscription for military service at eighteen, and no shortage of food. This business of arresting people for holding peculiar opinions was new. Nothing like it had happened since 1950. The British did not understand what was going on, and did not like what they did not understand.

'Don't say "and stuff". Never say "and stuff". Don't ever say "and stuff" or "blah-blah-blah" or "you guys". Not ever. Even to me.'

'I don't ever say "blah-blah-blah". I'm not a fucking New York queen.' There was dried blood down the side of Parry-Jones' face from a gash at the top of his forehead and matted blood in his hair at the back from a gash in his crown. 'I just want to know when we can get out of here.'

'When we know enough. When your accent stops relapsing. When we begin to stand some small chance of melting into the fucking landscape.'

'Don't overdo it, Ian. You're not in charge.'

'I'm in charge to this extent, Arwen,' Ian Sinclair said. 'I'm better at it.'

Rain. A narrow metalled road, only just wide enough for two cars to pass dangerously, climbed in steep zig-zags to a car park set halfway up a hill of granite and slate. To one side of the car park was a one-storey wooden chalet, its windows crowded with locally produced ceramic mugs and pots of Welsh honey. Behind and above it there was a great hole in the hill, the mouth of the mine. Slate spoil had spilled down the side of the hill: the road had been made through it.

A chunky, middle-aged woman in yellow oilskins – cape, trousers, fisherman's hat – was pushing her bicycle up the road through the rain, followed at a little distance by a man in a soggy brown anorak and a blue waterproof pixie hood, also pushing a bicycle. This man clearly wished to walk beside, not behind the woman, but every time he made a little run to catch up, he had to stop, breathing heavily, to wipe his spectacles with a handkerchief taken from somewhere beneath the anorak, and consequently fell further behind.

The woman reached the car park and leaned her bicycle against the wall of the chalet. To one side of the door, set among granite chippings and between a pair of urns which in summer held geraniums, there was a wooden notice:

HISTORIC SLATE-MINE
OPEN TO THE PUBLIC
APRIL TO OCTOBER
ADULTS M2.50
CHILDREN & OAPS M1.50

and pinned to the notice a card which read:

IN CASE OF EMERGENCY PHONE
LLANBEDR ACUPUNCTURE CLINIC
034 226817

The man had arrived at the top of the road, and came running across the car park, splashing through puddles. 'Any sign of a disturbance? Break-in? Vandalism?'

The woman shook her head and left him. Another wooden sign, smaller and in the shape of an arrow, read simply ENTRANCE and pointed to a much smaller hole in the cliff: no road or path led to the great mouth higher up, from which the spoil spilled. This smaller entrance hole was closed from floor to roof by an iron gate. The woman tried the gate. It was locked – as it should have been at this season. She returned to the chalet, and went round to the back.

There was another door, marked STAFF, at the back of the chalet; beside it was a heavy dustbin of galvanised iron. The woman began to tilt the bin, and the man ran to assist. There was no key under the bin. 'Taken it with them.'

The woman went back to the notice by the main door, put her hand deep into one of the urns, groped amongst wet potting compost, and found a Yale key on a wire ring. With it she let herself into the chalet, the man still following, then opened a drawer in the enquiry desk, and took from it a much larger iron key labelled SPARE. By the desk there was a display case of slate ashtrays, boxes and small pieces of abstract sculpture, and above it was a rack of white plastic safety helmets. She removed her yellow oilskin hat and put on a helmet. The man took one also and jammed it over his pixie hood. The woman picked up a flashlight from the desk.

'Aren't you going to put on the electric?'

'Safer not.'

The iron key opened the iron gate. They entered a dark tunnel sloping downwards under the rock and could see light ahead of them. Halfway along, the level of the roof changed, and the man hit his head against it, but was protected by the helmet. 'Always do that,' he said.

They came out of the tunnel into the light. To their left was a slope of scree, rising to the mouth of the mine, which was like a huge window in the cliff, lighting the chamber in which they stood. Beyond it two other chambers could be seen. 'Won't be in there.' The woman lifted her head, puckered her mouth and whistled four times sharply on a single note. From a niche in the wall an owl rose, circled the chamber once, then flew out into the daylight. The woman turned right to where shallow steps leading to a lower level had been cut in the rock, with a ramp beside them and the marks where a winch had been used to raise the tubs of slate.

The man said, 'Should I stay here?'

'Do whatever you think best.'

The man hesitated. 'Better come with you, then. Protect you in case things turn ugly.'

He was shorter than she and slighter. His thin wrists stuck out from the sleeves of the anorak, his moustache was sparse, exhausted by the effort of trying to grow, and his spectacles were still misty with rain. The woman said, 'Thank you, Hastings,' and began to descend the stair.

With the electricity not turned on, it was gloomy at the foot of the stair, and dank, and one could hear the steady drip of water falling into a basin in the rock. There were tunnels leading to other chambers both to left and right, those on the left still faintly lit from the upper level, those on the right pitch black.

The man said, 'They might have gone away. Packed up and left.'

'Save us a lot of trouble.'

'Or they might have gone out somewhere together.' He glanced over his shoulder up the stairs. 'They might be back any moment and find us.'

'Hope so. I'm not hanging around.'

'How can they live down here?'

'With some difficulty, I should say.'

'I wish you'd let me turn on the electric.'

'They might think it was the police. You don't want to get shot. Anyway, if they're still here they must have heard us by now. Sound carries underground.'

'I'm not leaving these stairs.'

'No need. They know where we are.' She flashed the beam of the torch to right and left, and called, 'Hey, you two! If you're in there, come out and meet us. If not, I'm going, and I shan't bother to come back.'

A voice came out of the darkness of the tunnel to their right. 'Who are you?' It sounded close, yet they had heard no one approach.

'Friends.'

'You may have to prove that.' Hastings gave a small, involuntary moan. Sinclair moved out of the darkness of the tunnel into the dim light with Parry-Jones at his shoulder. Both men were wearing heavy sweaters and jeans, and were in their stockinged feet. Sinclair stood silent at the mouth of the tunnel, flexing his hands. Parry-Jones moved unobtrusively, his back to the wall, towards the foot of the stairs to cut off the visitors' retreat.

51

Hastings' head jerked, his adam's apple twitched, his eyes rolled, his body shook with fear. The woman said to Sinclair, 'You didn't have to take your boots off. You'll catch your death; those socks are soaked already.' Hastings closed his eyes, and his lips moved in silent prayer. The woman said, 'You just try not to be stupid, you two. Make the effort. If I'd meant you harm, I'd have sent the police, not come myself. And I'd have left Hastings at the top. I'm beginning to think I should have done that anyway. Which is the one that speaks Welsh?'

'He does.'

'Does he speak only Welsh? I don't speak it myself. Nobody does round here. No one under seventy. He'd be starved for conversation.'

'How did you find out about us?'

'Tommy Griffiths told me. I'm his teacher. He didn't know what else to do. Didn't want to tell his parents. Didn't know how they'd take it. Came to me in confidence. I encourage that with all the children.'

'Doesn't explain how you knew where to find us.'

'Where else could you be? Look, mister. Listen. Learn.' She had fallen easily into her teaching mode. 'Day before yesterday, you stood there in the bus-shelter down on the main road, dressed up to the nines with your little umbrella, and you took the bus to Harlech – fifty mark note for a two shilling bus-fare, and you think you won't be noticed! You bought food and necessaries at the Castle Self-Service. Then you bought shirts and thick socks at Davies' Drapery; you should have gone to the Bethesda Charity Shop and got them second hand. Wyn Davies served you; she said you were very well-spoken. Wondered where you'd come from, though, maybe another planet.'

'Did she say that – another planet?'

'No, I'm teasing. You're English, as far as Wyn's concerned, an English eccentric. Finally you went to the Marine Stores, and bought two pairs of jeans, two fisherman's heavy-knit sweaters, boots – two pairs of different sizes – two tin mugs and a billy-can, candles and a paraffin stove with a can of fuel – paid cash for them and said you'd taken them with you, though Hwyel offered to deliver. You had more than you could carry for the return journey on the bus; it caused a lot of interest.'

'I remember.'

'Should have taken your friend to help you.'

'There were reasons against.'

'And of course you got off the bus where you'd got on, at the road below, though you weren't staying in the village, and there's no caravans nearer than Tal-y-bont. So where else could you be keeping yourself this wet and windy weather?'

'Careless.'

'Correct. And continued as you began. Yesterday same bus, different direction; you went to Barmouth. You had some change for the fare by then. You bought two sleeping-bags at Llanaber Camping. Seemed strange to me, that, when you'd told Tommy it was sleeping-bags you were burning on the beach.'

Arwen said, 'We've got to get out of here.'

Sinclair said to the woman, 'You're sure Tommy told no one else? Not even his friends?'

'Only me. It was a secret between us. And I told Hastings.'

'You put yourselves at risk, then, by coming to look for us.'

'I don't think so. I'm reasonably certain, mister, that you need help, and you need it quickly, and there's nobody to give it but Hastings and me. X marks the spot of your hiding-place here as soon as anyone besides me bothers to work it out. Your friend's right; you've got to get out and find somewhere else, but you can't do that on your own because you leave a trail, you two, like a one-legged moose with an incontinence problem. I think you can turn the electric on now, Hastings. Shed a little more light on the proceedings. It won't alarm these gentlemen now. And bring a couple of safety helmets back with you.'

Hastings was off up the stair like a jack hare, and they could hear his helmet bumping against the roof of the tunnel above. The woman looked at Arwen and said, 'There's more than Hastings been hitting his head, I see. You should have broken into Reception and borrowed a helmet.'

'We didn't want to draw attention to ourselves.'

Sinclair said, 'Why do you want to help us?'

'I don't want to. And Hastings certainly doesn't want to. I'm not a religious woman, but I said my prayers last night. "Let this cup pass from me, Father," I said, but God didn't answer; he keeps his own counsel mostly, I find, and mostly I don't bother him.' The light went on, sixty-watt bulbs, not many of them, set behind plate glass in niches in the walls of the tunnels. 'What I wanted was to come here and find you already gone. I'll sit down for a while if you've no objection. You've a right to know my circumstances if you're going to have to trust me.'

She sat on the stairs, well protected from cold and damp by the yellow oilskins. From above a distant bumping announced Hastings' return, and soon he appeared on the stairs behind her. The woman said, 'The reason Tommy Griffiths came to me . . . it's not just because I'm his teacher. My brother's been arrested; he's in a detention centre. The children know that; everyone's aware of it; there's not much the people around here aren't aware of, as you've already gathered. They don't know what to make of it. My brother was a respected man, you see, worked for the County Architect's Department; he's younger than me, but gone further.'

Hastings said, 'Extremely respected professionally and recognised outside the Principality for contributions to the Concept of Rural Community Housing within the Public Sector. A fine man.'

'But he's in prison?'

'They don't call it a prison, though it's the Prison Service running it, and the rooms are locked at night. The people kept in there – men and women too – they can write and receive letters, wear their own clothes; there's recreational facilities – sports, concerts and amateur dramatics; they had the carol-singers in at Christmas. And I'm allowed to visit once a week, only it's in Norfolk, there's no cross-country train service, and I don't have the petrol coupons to go by car. Technically, Hugh isn't a criminal. He's being held in custody for his own safety, though he wasn't in any danger, not from anyone around here. Except this danger.'

'It's a concentration camp?'

'They don't call it a camp either. Too many worrying associations with that word, not that many people alive today can remember Belsen. It's a detention centre in which potentially disloyal elements

54

are confined for their own safety until the end of the Present Emergency: I have the words by heart. My old professor from Aberystwyth is there too. He was a cranky old sod, to put it bluntly, but he cared for his students. He hasn't anybody else to write to, so he writes to me, mostly in poetry. He says Hugh is a comfort to him in adversity. All the Welsh are in the Norfolk centre; it's only Welsh. There must be Scots and English potentially disloyal elements as well, but I don't know where they're kept.'

Hastings said, 'It's ridiculous. There's no disloyalty. It was a hobby with her brother.'

'Dangerous hobby?'

'He couldn't know that. Nobody could know it.'

'What was it?'

'Welsh language. Like your friend. That's what caught my interest. Hugh always needed something to occupy his mind. So he started to learn Welsh. As a hobby. Only . . . simply to get hold of the books . . . historical materials . . . mutual discussions on disputed textual questions . . . he had to join a club of like-minded people.'

'And the other people in the detention centre? Are they like-minded people?'

'Mostly.'

Sinclair's voice was sharp. 'How many locally?'

'Better you shouldn't know how many. Not many.'

'All arrested?'

'All who were at home or at their place of work when the police came.'

'And the others? Hiding?'

'I wouldn't be able to say.'

Arwen said, 'Learning Welsh is more than a hobby.'

'Is it? Not these days. After the war they stopped teaching Welsh in schools – wasn't allowed; you had to learn German. It was a military government in those days; I suppose they didn't want people jabbering away in a language the soldiers couldn't understand. It wasn't a crime to speak Welsh, you understand, not in private; they didn't send the old ones to prison even then. They just stopped the teaching, called in the books and pulped them, Hugh says. Banned the Eisteddfods, both local and national. Stopped the programmes on the radio. Not many people cared. There was too much to do, just getting back to normal. Then all that passed. Apart from a few pilots on attachment at the airfield, the only Germans we see these days are tourists, and not many of them; they go south mostly, for the sun. But there's generations of children grown up, never hearing a word of Welsh in their lives. There's no advancement in it, the way there's advancement in German, nothing but curiosity-value for university-educated people like my brother.'

Arwen said, 'There's not a day passes they don't hear and speak their own language. The place-names are Welsh, every town and village, every brook and hill.'

'Everything's got to be called something. Our villages are called what they've always been called.' She said to Hastings, 'There's a touch of Hugh about him, wouldn't you say? That could have been Hugh.'

'There is a touch. I recognise a touch.'

Sinclair said, 'The duration of the Present Emergency could mean any length of time. It could mean until the end of the war, and who knows when that will be?'

'My thinking exactly.'

'Once you start locking people up for their opinions . . .'

Hastings said, 'Hugh doesn't hold opinions. Not in that sense, not political. He has no aspiration to overthrow the government. He works for the County Council.'

'Once you start locking people up for trivial reasons . . . learning Welsh . . . wearing national costume . . . joining oddball societies . . . then you can't really afford to let them go again, because they'll have a grievance and may want to do something about it. And their families and friends the same. And those who weren't home when the police called, the same.'

The woman rose to her feet. 'Now we're quits in the trusting stakes,' she said. 'Hastings and I don't know much about you, and you'll notice we've asked no questions about why you're here, but we knew enough before we arrived to put you in danger. And you don't know much about us, but you know enough about my brother and my job here to make it easy for them to trace us if they caught you and you talked. You weren't intending to stay around here anyway, I shouldn't imagine.'

'Only until we'd got ourselves organised.'

'You've got plans? A destination? Don't tell me where.'

'Nearer to London.'

'We'll do what we can for you, if only to get rid of you. You're a danger to everyone in the area if you stay. Have you got food for a couple of days?'

'Yes.'

'Don't go out. Don't be seen. I'll send you a message by Hastings – nobody else – or come myself if I need to communicate. Make yourselves a look-out post at the top of the scree in the upper chamber so you can't be taken by surprise, and get out that way and lose yourselves somehow if anyone else tries to get in. Give them the helmets, Hastings.' He did so, and she began to stump upstairs, turning like a French classical actress making a false exit to say, 'Just as well for you I'm a teacher. I've spent my professional life protecting children from the consequences of their own incompetence.'

Underground

Sir Gervase Acland, forty-five, seventeenth baronet, Liberal Member of Parliament for Richmond and Twickenham, sat on a bench in Tower Gardens, protected against the sharp March wind by a heavy overcoat and cashmere scarf, and wondered whether he had been too clever by half.

He had deliberately put himself at risk in order to avoid a greater risk, had drawn attention to himself in order to divert attention from himself. By accepting the smaller risk he had learned a little about the greater.

Yes, he had probably been too clever, unnecessarily clever. Even his secret thoughts were expressed in the language of cleverness. Safer to be stupid, much safer not to think at all, but Gervase Acland's own stupidity lay, and had always lain, in being clever; that was his nature, and he could not change it.

Gervase was on the humanitarian Quaker wing of his party; he was what was called a Chocolate Bar Liberal. Since the end of the war the Liberals had become the main party of opposition again, and the Choccie Bars were the opposition within the opposition. *Plus ça change, plus c'est la même chose.* Acland's grandfather, Richard, the fifteenth baronet, had been a Liberal MP in 1935 – Liberal inclining to Socialist. The Germans had shot him in April 1943 as part of a tidying-up operation; his had been among the last batch of executions.

Plus ça change . . . Gervase was in no danger of execution; all that had quite gone out. But he might be in some danger of a detention centre if his little plan had been too subtle.

59

He had put down a Parliamentary question to the Home Secretary; any MP was entitled to do that. It was a question relating to persons detained under the Emergency Powers Act of 1991. He had considered asking how many people were currently in detention, but that would have been too easy to block; the answer might aid and comfort an enemy only too eager to know how many potentially disloyal elements there were among the British people. So he had chosen instead to base his questions on *habeas corpus* and to ask when the detainees might expect to be released or criminal charges be laid against them; his line would be that he had been approached by distraught wives and parents within his constituency and it was his duty to inform them if he could. He had expected this question to be blocked also, but privately and unofficially. What he had not expected was that the blocks should be imposed by the token Chocolate Bar in his own Whips' Office.

'Inadvisable to ask?'

'Right.'

'Who's giving the advice?'

'I am.'

'Look, these are my constituents. I've got to face them. They come crying to me – "Peter was never a traitor . . . James isn't political . . . Joanie only wanted to lend a helping hand." What am I to tell them? I've got to tell them something.' He had wondered whether the room might be bugged. His gaze had flicked over the portraits of Gladstone, Asquith and Lloyd George, the brass paperweight on the leather-topped desk, the heavy black old-fashioned telephone. It would be convenient if the room were bugged.

'We've all got the same problem, Gervase. It's just not a good idea at the moment to rock the boat.'

'Because of the war? You can't be serious. It's thousands of miles away. It doesn't affect us.'

'Because of . . . Look, Gervase, indulge me. Let me remind you of what you must already know. Ever since Parlimentary democracy was restored, the Tories have hung on to office because they've had a working relationship with the Reichsprotektor's Secretariat. Yet we're the natural majority party, because the Liberals are the party of business in this country, right? And always have been.'

'Wrong. We're the party of reform. Fair dealing. Fair shares. Looking after the underdog.'

'All of which depend on a healthy economy. Otherwise there's no dealing at all, fair or unfair, nothing to share out, and the underdogs just go under. I'm talking contracts here, Gervase. Productivity. Jobs. I'm talking wealth. That's Liberal language: the chaps in the Secretariat are beginning to realise that. And there's a General Election due, provided the war doesn't get in the way.'

Could this be Tony the Choccie Bar Terrier? Tony who had pushed through the Abortion Act as a Private Member's Bill? Tony who had harried the Home Office on the abolition of capital punishment and on prisoners' rights, which the tabloids had called Sex in the Cells? Well, they had taken him into the Whips' Office as a token humanitarian and already he had become more flagellant than they.

Not tactful to say any of this, however. Don't push it, Acland. He had done the business he came to do. It was time to be convinced.

Tony said, 'Of course these detentions are a miserable business for everyone, but they won't last because the war won't last. Von Neustadt says it's only a matter of time before the Americans realise they've made a mistake in getting involved in a purely Arab affair. And when the Yanks pull out, the Japs will pull out.'

'Who's von Neustadt?'

'Chap I know in the Secretariat.'

'If I could give my constituents any idea just how long . . .'

'Still as long as a piece of string, I'm afraid. But not a long piece of string, Gervase; that's the point to get across. After all, in the bad old days, as von Neustadt reminded me, these people used to be treated quite harshly – forced labour . . . summary execution . . . torture even. There's nothing remotely like that these days. Quite a high standard of comfort actually: they asked my advice on that. I gave them a few tips – just the little things that make the difference. Library facilities. Special diets for diabetics. Friendly football matches with the prison officers.'

'Okay, you've convinced me. I'll withdraw the question and talk to the families as best I can. You really believe that at the next election . . .'

'I really do. We're on our way.'

And he had withdrawn the question, as he had always intended to do. It had served its purpose. It had shown him to be a concerned constituency MP, doing his best in his muddled humanitarian way to help even those of his constituents who had been taken into protective custody as potentially disloyal. Such further contact as he might have – might be expected to have, would have to have – with the families of those potentially disloyal elements would be to explain matters to them, to reassure them and to support them; the authorities could make no more of it than that. He now had a cover of sorts; he was on the side of the explainers, and, emollient and accommodating, might expect political preferment to some junior office after the next election.

More than that, the interview had given him a lively sense of the true extent of the greater danger. *'Von Neustadt reminded me that these people used to be treated quite harshly.'* They were already prepared to threaten. How much further would they go?

What was the future? What could one do? The moral imperative to do something was clear – clear to an Acland anyway. There were people in Britain, not only his constituents, who needed protection. Some were already locked up in the centres, for whom not much could directly be done, but more importantly there were those on the run, in hiding, trying to keep themselves out of the centres. Was it possible to help such people, to do only that, without in some way fighting back?

'Okay. You put your money where your mouth is, mister. Speak some Welsh.'

The old man's nose was pitted like a strawberry and very much of that colour. He had not shaved and his striped flannel shirt was without a collar. Behind the thick spectacles, his eyes were faded blue and milky with incipient cataracts and the whites were bloodshot. He had two tufts of dirty white hair on either side of a bald pate splotched with liver-spots. The landlady had procured him under instruction. Apart from Hastings and the schoolteacher, who were now part of the past and much regretted, the landlady was the only one of their protectors whose face they had been permitted to

see, and now there was also this old man's face and they did not care
for it. There was malice in this face. It was most unlike that of the
landlady, which indicted at all times an almost rebarbative readiness
to please. The landlady was a woman of the utmost gentility, as was
shown by the furnishings of the room in which she had accommo-
dated Sinclair and Parry-Jones. Dainty pillows of fine net, six inches
square and trimmed with pink roses and velvet bows, had been
scattered on the coverlets of the beds, on both armchairs and on
every vacant surface not already occupied by a china ornament or
glass animal.

Arwen lifted his chin, smoothing the skin beneath it so that his
throat should be relaxed and the words emerge sweetly. He said, 'Ac
mi glywaf grafangau Cymru'n dirdynnu fy mron. Duw a'm gwaredo,
ni allaf ddianc rhag hon.'

'Very bad Welsh.'

'Bad!'

'Flowery. Old-fashioned. And the accent all to cock.'

Arwen decided that it would do no good to bristle. What he had
spoken was from a poem by his own professor at Idaho, the purity of
whose diction was much admired among the Welsh-speakers of the
USNA; he had been awarded the Bardic Crown at the Kansas City
Eisteddfod of 1986. The sentiment and elegance of its expression
were wasted on such a man as this. Arwen had been a fool to choose
it, but he and Sinclair had lost a lot of self-esteem over the past few
days, and he had been trying to regain a little.

They had been taken from the slate-mine blindfolded in a closed
van, and had been driven many miles on winding roads uphill and
down. They had guessed that this was being done to confuse them,
so that they could not tell in which direction they were being taken,
and what with the darkness, and the changes in temperature, and the
twisting and turning, they had been confused but not frightened,
knowing that the arrangement had been made by the schoolteacher
and Hastings, whom they trusted, and that it was common sense that
they should not see their conductors. They had not allowed anyone
to touch the travelling-bags containing their weapons, however.

When the blindfolds had been removed they had found themselves in this double room with bathroom ensuite in what was clearly

a small hotel or guest-house, sited on the edge of a cliff by the sea. The windows on the landward sides were shuttered. Their view was only of the open sea and sky, obscured for most of the time by rain dashed against the glass by the persistent gales, which also rattled the shutters of the landward windows so that neither of them had been able to sleep for long or well. This place would not be occupied out of season, yet if anyone were to notice their occupancy they could be explained as unexpected lodgers taken in to turn a penny.

Two meals a day were brought to them by the landlady, and the door otherwise kept locked. These meals had been cooked long ago to be ready for summer visitors who never came, then frozen and now reheated in a microwave oven. They also had an electric kettle in the room and a small wicker basket in the shape of a shell containing tea-bags and sachets of instant coffee, sugar and a powdered milk-substitute, and a portable television which Sinclair insisted they watch continually, partly to pick up the BBC accent, partly to keep them abreast of what was going on in Britain, so that they would be able to converse in pubs and on buses once they were again at liberty. And he had paid the landlady to supply them with all the newspapers, not just *The Times*, the *Daily Telegraph* and the *Manchester Guardian*, which had been required reading during their training at the centre, but with the more popular papers, the *Daily Express, Daily Mail, Daily Herald*, and *News Chronicle* and the tabloids, the *Daily Mirror* and *Daily Sketch*.

Yes, they had lost face, much face. Their identity cards had been taken away for inspection by their unseen protectors, examined and returned to them. It appeared that this documentation would not do, was of no use at all. The landlady had attempted to turn the scorn of her colleagues to something like apology, but the scorn had shown through. 'What it is, you see, the situation if you was to express it bluntly, what you'd have to say, the plain fact is they're out of date. To still have one of these you'd have to be at least fifty and not moved from your place of permanent domicile since the age of twenty-one, and even then there'd be questions.'

'You mean they're no good?'

'I wouldn't go that far. There's work gone into them, care been taken. They're very well done for what they are, though of course they haven't the ageing so even as antiques, I'm afraid they wouldn't pass muster. But as documentation, no; they'd be bound to arouse suspicion. And then there's the matter of your work certificates.'

'What are they?'

'That's the point. You shouldn't have to ask; you should have one each. Since the Present Emergency we've all got them, everyone except the children; we've all got to carry a certificate to show we're engaged in essential employment. Even Senior Citizens and the Disabled have special documentation. Housewives have them; it says "Housewife" or in some cases "Single Parent". I have one myself, being in the catering trade: even the pot boy has one. And you haven't.'

'We've got jobs. I'm an insurance salesman for the Provincial Mutual. My friend's in electronics. We're on holiday at the moment, if anyone asks.'

'In February, yes: it's not the season. And no vacation certificates. Even if you were sick . . . convalescent, there's sick notes to be duly signed by a qualified medico.'

'Oh! How vexing!' Normally Sinclair would have said, 'Oh, shit!', but the volunteers had been taught that British males do not use scatological language in front of their womenfolk. During their time together, the professor had said, 'How vexing!' and Sinclair, delighted, had picked it up as a typically English usage.

The landlady had not responded to it, but glanced down again at her notepad, dainty as the little pillows in its frilled cover. 'Then there's the next thing. You say you work for the Provincial Mutual. I'm to ask you the name of the Area Manager in Merioneth. And where your local offices are, all down the coast. If you don't have that information at your fingertips, who's going to believe you?'

It was humiliating, utterly so, and with the added worry that, if their own documentation was so inadequate, that of the other group must be as bad. Had they already been discovered? Was the hunt up, the whole operation already blown? 'There's another small matter I shan't embarrass you with,' the landlady had said, 'which is the fact that all your paper money has been printed in Wuppertal, whereas British marks are printed in Port Talbot. It's legal currency, or I should have refused to accept it, but it does show carelessness, to say the least.' And now they had called in this elderly Welsh person to check that Arwen could actually speak the language of his forefathers.

The landlady said to the old man, 'What does it mean, Brynfor, what he said there in the old language? I have to make a report on every aspect.'

'Means? What's it matter what it means? Load of self-conscious rubbish, that's all. Means, "Christ, I'm bloody homesick," more or less.'

Arwen said, 'It's from a poem. A more exact translation might be, "And I can feel Wales clawing at my heart. God help me, I cannot escape from her." '

The landlady poured oil on troubled waters. 'Now there's a commendable sentiment!'

The old man said, 'Peth byw yw iaith. Mae'n tyfu fel mae dyn yn tyfu.' He spat into his handkerchief. 'Ac yn marw fel mae dyn yn marw.'*

'Are you testing me? Do you want a translation?'

'No. Just think about it.' The old man turned away to the landlady. 'He'll pass. We'll go down now.' And they left the room together, the landlady smiling and nodding, as she was wont to do, as if in apology, but locking the door behind her.

Downstairs in the hall Trefor was waiting, a massive man, big in Haulage, and with him Mr Goronwy Watkyns of Abersoch.

'Well?'

'Brynfor says he'll pass.'

'Then he's true Welsh? He speaks the language?'

The old man said, 'After a fashion. Yankee fashion.'

Mr Goronwy Watkyns said to the landlady, 'When you informed them that their documentation was invalid, how did they receive that information?'

'With amazement. As I told Trefor. Swore they'd no idea. Documents supplied by impeccable sources. Wouldn't name them. Under orders not to talk.'

'And in the luggage?'

---

* A language is a living thing. It grows as a man grows. And dies as a man dies.

'Won't say.'

'Radio communication?'

Trefor said, 'Mrs Phillips doesn't think so. We're not experts, of course.'

'And their intention in coming here? The object of their mission? That's it, Trefor; that's the nub of it.'

'They're our countrymen, come to help us.' The old man spat again, this time at an already ailing Swiss Cheese plant. 'Free Britons, come to make us free: they're not prepared to say how. As a consequence, we end up helping them.'

'That's often the way with unsolicited offers of assistance in my opinion.' Mr Goronwy Watkyns chewed his upper lip. 'And one of them claims to be Welsh with a bloodline pure all the way back for hundreds of years. Owain bloody Glyndwr in person, come back from the dead to put the cat among the pigeons!'

The landlady said, 'True Welsh or not, they can't stay here much longer. I've never been in trouble with the police: I've got my licence to think of. One way or another, you've got to get shot of them. Something painless and herbal in the early morning tea would be my choice. Save a lot of trouble in the long run.'

Trefor said, 'If we were into saving trouble, we wouldn't have become involved in the first place.' He sighed. His enormous stomach shook the hall table and the landlady grabbed at a glass elephant to save it from being swept away. 'Children! Bloody kids playing at soldiers! No idea what they're getting into. Dangerous to themselves and us.'

'You agree with Mrs Phillips, then? Poison in the tea and a couple of weighted sacks off the cliff at midnight? There's much to be said for it.'

'No way we could justify it. Not to Megan. Not to Hastings. Not to our own consciences. But I agree we can't keep them here, and anyway they don't want to be kept. I could take them out tomorrow and leave them at a Comfort Station on the autobahn. It'd be on their way to wherever they want to go but what's the use of that? They'd be picked up the same day, and the trail leads back through Megan to us.' The landlady put her hand to her mouth, squeezing it into a fist, and the glass elephant broke and cut her fingers. 'There's bugger all we can do but play Pass the Parcel. The problem is to find another player ready and able to receive it.'

'Oh God, Protector of fools and the innocent, forget not these little ones under Thy hand,' said the old man, and Mr Goronwy Watkyns said, 'Amen!'

Upstairs Ian Sinclair said to Arwen Parry-Jones, 'What *was* the translation of that bit of Welsh the old man threw at you?' and Arwen replied, 'I don't know. I couldn't understand the accent.'

To a thoughtful and prudent man there will always be more reasons for inaction than for action.

Let me rephrase that in a way which Lieutenant Attlee himself would have preferred. In any covert operation, inaction will be the norm, and action only undertaken for a compelling reason. Since it is the nature of compelling reasons that a response to one will usually give rise to another even more compelling and so on to some unforeseeable and usually disastrous climax, one must consider long and carefully before committing oneself to any response. If one considers for long enough, there is always the possibility that the compelling reason will go away.

The O & I Group had begun with a compelling reason, which was to get away from the landing-place as quickly as possible, but that had been planned for. They had stolen one vehicle, then another, then another, abandoning each to make a trail which – if anyone were interested in following such a trail – would seem to lead east towards the English border. They had enjoyed one piece of luck. One of the vehicles stolen had been a doctor's car, and he had carelessly left his petrol coupons in the glove compartment. They had abandoned the car almost immediately, but kept the coupons. None of their instructors at the training centre had warned them about petrol rationing. The incident reinforced Lieutenant Attlee's natural caution. There might be other important aspects of life in wartime Britain about which they had not been warned.

They were cold and wet. Their expensive brogues squelched as they walked and their damp tweed jackets stank in the squash of Morris Minor or van – they were careful never to steal any expensive vehicle which might be fitted with an alarm. They had slept rough and badly in or beside one vehicle after another for four nights. But Attlee would not be hurried.

They had stolen bicycles also, one each, and kept them, transferring them from one vehicle to another and devoting half an hour a day to mastering their use, since bicycles were not common in the USNA except among newsboys and middle-aged health freaks, and neither Cape nor Alloway had ridden one before. At four o'clock on the afternoon of the fifth day, with the dusk already thickening, the last of their stolen vehicles was driven along a track both muddy and rocky to where it ended below a shepherd's cottage.

They had found the cottage the day before. Both doors had been locked and the light summer curtains at the windows closed. There were no signs of occupancy. The dustbin outside the back door was empty, there was no toilet paper in the outside privy and no water ran from the stand-pipe beside it when the tap was turned on. They had been trained to open locks considerably more complicated than that of the front door; it gave them no trouble. They had inspected the cottage upstairs and down – two bedrooms above, kitchen and a little parlour below. They had found a stopcock under the kitchen sink and an electricity mains with a fuse-box under the stairs. The place was habitable and they would be able to operate their radio.

Now they unloaded their gear and two of the bicycles, which Attlee and Alloway would carry to the cottage while the dusk held: it would not be safe to use lights. Bernard Cape would get rid of the van. He would take it beyond Llangollen towards Oswestry and leave it in a ditch some time during the night, and make his way back to the cottage next day, using the third and most powerful of the stolen bikes, a Carrera Kratoa, only thirty-two pounds in weight with a gel saddle and toe-clips.

The O & I Group had fallen on its feet. They settled into their new home. By the cheapness and battered condition of the furniture, it had probably ceased to be a shepherd's cottage and become a holiday let. No matter: they would be undisturbed for at least a couple of months provided they did nothing to attract attention. There were two electric hobs set on top of a mini-oven, there were basic cooking utensils and crockery; they could cook and eat. There were blankets and beds; they could sleep. There were chairs and a sort of sofa. They improvised shutters from cupboard doors and heavier curtains from spare blankets; they could light a room at night, and the light not be seen. They acquired more suitable clothing.

They must be like mice on the hillside, lying low to avoid the attentions of predators. Twice a week, whatever the weather, one of them would cycle to town for provisions and the newspapers, a different town each time (Ffestiniog, Blaenau Ffestiniog, Betws-y-coed or Bala) and a different volunteer, so that with three volunteers and four towns, none of them need be seen twice in the same place. If questioned in shops, they were to say they were youth-hostelling. Of all the trainees, Attlee had read most greedily among the holiday brochures and travel guides. He knew that there were hostels open all year round all over Britian in which young people on a walking or cycling holiday could stay the night cheaply, and he knew where the hostels were. North Wales was rich in them.

Of course the group did not do nothing. It had a mission, which was to provide intelligence. Its Intelligence Reports were compiled from the newspapers, brought back in quantity twice a week. Isolated in a shepherd's cottage (or holiday let) halfway up a Welsh mountain, it was unlikely that the O & I Group would chance upon any hard military intelligence at first hand. Even Bala and Blaenau Ffestiniog seemed to be singularly free of the movements of armoured columns or testing of secret weapons, and troop trains did not use the light, narrow-gauge steam railway which only functioned these days for summer visitors. The volunteers looked dutifully about as they cycled along the winding roads or walked the hillsides, but there was no industry that they could observe, either high-tech or low-tech, nothing to do with the war at all: even the quarries had been turned into museums. For news of the war, for economic analyses, for political developments in Berlin and London, the quality newspapers and such of the egghead weeklies as could be found locally were the only sources.

Lieutenant Attlee's mind was well suited to précis and compilation. He sat down twice a week with scissors and sellotape, and at first his reports were much admired in the Operations Room of the British government-in-exile. 'Pure gold!' the Head of Military Intelligence said, and had the reports copied, labelled TOP SECRET and sent by motor-cycle messenger to his contacts at the CIA. But as report followed report, all much the same, unspecific and containing nothing which could not be picked up anyway by CIA operatives in neutral countries who had access to the same censored sources, the CIA's response became more and more tepid, and British Intelligence began to ask itself what the fuck young Attlee thought he was playing at, and there began to be a feeling that it was time the O & I Group got off their arses and into the field. Before this feeling could be turned into a positive order, the group's Intelligence Reports were interrupted anyway.

The reason was – unfortunately – compelling, nor did it allow time for any prolonged consideration. Bernard Cape arrived back from town in a stolen Mercedes with his bike in the boot. 'We've got to get away from here. Quickly.'

'Why?'

'These identity cards are crap.'

David Attlee clicked his tongue. First the petrol coupons and now this. One could never be too careful, must never take anything for granted. The Mercedes was obviously a mistake: Cape had allowed haste to lead him into incautious behaviour. But all he said was, 'Do the British say "crap"? Is it idiomatic?'

Peter Alloway had already begun to pack up his equipment. 'I think they do actually. My grandfather does.'

'Tell me what happened.'

'The woman in front of me at the check-out was caught shoplifting. She'd have been okay, I suppose, if she'd said sorry and offered to pay, but she tried to bluster her way out, then got hysterical and made a run for it. No way I wasn't a witness, no way I could get out of making a statement. I said, "You can see she's upset," and offered to pay for her, but maybe that wasn't so clever; maybe they thought I was an accomplice.'

'Maybe. It hardly ever does to put oneself forward. I think I may have said that before.'

'I think you may have, David,' Cape said. 'Anyway they called a cop off the street – a young one luckily, not very experienced. But the first thing the police do – this much our instructors have got right, David – is to ask to see your identity card. I expected it so I wasn't bothered until I saw his face as he looked at the card, and knew I was in trouble.'

Each of the volunteers had a mantra, which he was to use if he felt the approach of panic. It had no meaning in itself, but would put one's mind into the calming mode. Lieutenant Attlee closed his eyes, and thought the words, 'Ah! The ineffable orderliness of being!' Then he said, 'Did you kill the policeman before you stole the car? Is it in fact a police car?'

'I spoke to him in German, and he let me go.'

Ah! The ineffable orderliness of being! The relief! – but one must not show it. Cape was the linguist of the group, fluent in French and German at graduate school level. 'What did you say to him?'

'He didn't understand German, so I said I must talk to him privately, and we went into the manager's office. I told him that I was German Army Counter-Intelligence working undercover, and checking on the efficiency of the local police forces in this area. I congratulated him on recognising an obvious fake, and told him that none of his colleagues from Harlech to Carnarvon had done as well. I said I wished to talk to his Section Officer – only a sergeant here, apparently – but I mustn't be seen entering a police station because that would blow my cover. So I made an appointment to meet his sergeant in plain clothes at a fish-and-chip restaurant this evening. He called it a chippie, but I guess it's some sort of cheap diner.'

'Not "guess", Bernard: they never say "guess". "Suppose". . . "Imagine" . . . either of those. Didn't he ask to see your security classification or whatever?'

'Told him I never carry it with me. In my game you're on your own: you can't trust a piece of paper to get you out of trouble. Said I'd bring documentation with me to the meeting with his sergeant tonight. I'd like to think we've got that long, but the moment he makes his report they'll be looking for us. They don't know where to look yet, but you can take it they'll be looking. So should we be on our way? We'd better start with the Mercedes and change it as soon as we can.'

'I agree.' Ah, the ineffable disorderliness of being! Moving in a hurry was bound to lead to loss of control. If one could not maintain control, how was one expected to lead, how even to function?

72

The sergeant sat in the chippie for two hours that evening, but nobody from German Army Counter-Intelligence turned up. Although he was wearing plain clothes as instructed, everyone in the chippie knew perfectly well who he was, and his presence caused some perturbation, particularly to the staff, so that he was twice offered, and once accepted, free portions of plaice and chips.

Next morning he was faced with the problem of whether or not to report the incident.

Who could the young man with dicey documentation have been? Some wanted person, criminal or political, on the run? If so, the incident had better be forgotten. A report would only lead to trouble and accusations of inefficiency. It would be a black mark on Constable Pomeroy's record, which was fair enough, but also, the people at Sub-Division being the bastard lot they were, against himself.

But the identity card had been out of date. A criminal might be expected to have a forged card; a Politically Unreliable trying to keep out of a detention centre would probably produce his own and hope it was not on anyone's list. Either way the card would be current. But this, according to Pomeroy, had been a card of a sort he had never seen before, yet the photograph had been of the holder and the stamp of the issuing office fairly recent. Two hours waiting at the chippie! Could it have been a practical joke?

The young man had spoken to Pomeroy in fluent German. Pomeroy had not been able to understand him, but had recognised the language. No petty criminal, no PU would be fluent in German. So what if the young man had been what he had said he was, an undercover agent, testing the security of the local police? Setting up a phoney assignation would have been part of the test. Pomeroy had jumped the first hurdle – he had spotted some obviously false documentation – and fallen at the second: he should have insisted on bringing the man into the police station in spite of all protests made in whatever language.

But that would mean that the whole shoplifting episode had been a set-up. How could that be? Gwynneth Parry was a local woman, known to be light-fingered: she had been in trouble before, hence the hysterics. Only a local man could have known that: no German snoop would know it. It was a puzzle what to do. Either way he was bound to be wrong.

After considerable cogitation the sergeant decided to report the incident in writing, with the embellishment that he had reprimanded Constable Pomeroy for departing from standard police procedure in this case, but had decided to keep the appointment anyway in order to regularise the situation before it got out of hand.

At Sub-Division they had a good laugh at the hoax which had caused that pompous little prick, Sergeant Rees, to hang about the chippie half the night, exposing his best blue suit to hot fat and vinegar, but decided that they had better forward his report to Division anyway, partly to cover themselves and partly to share the joke. At Division, tongues were clicked and the report forwarded, with much other routine paperwork, to County.

At County the report was passed sideways from Uniformed Branch to CID. County CID spoke downwards to Divisional CID who spoke to Sub-Division who sent a Detective Constable to talk to Constable Pomeroy. There had been no consequences to the incident, no other young men posing as German Counter-Intelligence agents or even the same young man doing it again. A Mercedes saloon, the property of a local estate agent, had been stolen from the multi-storey car park on the same day, but had been discovered abandoned in a lay-by on the B4407 the next: there was no obvious connection.

County decided that they had better refer the incident to Special Branch in London. It was uncomfortable to have to consider the possibility that the German military were secretly checking on the security of the local police forces, but if that were really so, why had there been no other similar cases? It was not clear what 'German Army Counter-Intelligence' might mean. The Army did not usually refer to itself as 'German', since Germans were a minority among the soldiers: only the SS was entirely German. If the SS really were behaving in such a way, then Special Branch would probably know, and if they did not know, they ought to know.

Special Branch had no direct contact with the SS or even with the military generally. The report would have to be discussed with their masters at the Home Office, who would decide whether to speak to their opposite numbers at the Reichsprotektor's Secretariat.

All this took time.

'I've had a word,' said the Permanent Under-Secretary to the Commander of Special Branch. 'And got a dusty answer. Politically Unreliables are the responsibility of Special Branch. Nothing to do with the military unless assistance is specifically requested by the civilian authorities.'

'That was my own understanding. But one never knows.'

'Well, I've asked. They are. So you do know. Except . . . now that I have asked . . . brought it to their attention . . . you know what they're like at the Secretariat. The problem with our asking is that it's bound to have set them thinking. I mean, who the bloody hell was this fellow with an identity card twenty years out of date? He couldn't really have been a PU?'

'I imagine we'd better find out.'

'And how many PUs actually are there, running around on the loose? If you ask me, it was a great mistake locking them up.'

'Nobody did ask you, Henry. Or me either. It's just a feature of the Present Emergency that we have to learn to live with.'

Megan Wynn-Morris travelled by cross-country bus and train to visit her brother at the detention centre. To their surprise, all the visitors were searched on arrival before being admitted.

Megan was not allowed to see her brother. His visiting privileges had been withdrawn because, along with an (unspecified) number of other prisoners, he had been guilty of unruly conduct towards members of staff. She would be informed by letter when she might come again. This was the first time in Megan's experience that the word 'prisoners' had been used to describe the detainees at the centre.

The little B and B where Megan usually stayed overnight was modest but run by friendly people. They were less friendly on this occasion. Detectives from London had been round the village asking questions about all those who visited the Welsh prisoners regularly. Instead of watching television by the fire with the family, Megan spent the evening in her bedroom alone and the night awake and restless.

'Remember. Always sit on a hard chair, never on an upholstered armchair, and certainly never on a sofa; you're bound to catch headlice. Hard to believe in 1992, but you're up against folklore, you see. Bugs are thought to be lucky. Even the clean houses in the slum areas have bugs.'

Sinclair was riding a lady's bicycle with a basket on the front. It bothered him that he was unused to the braking system. On the cycle he had ridden as a child, the brake was worked by pedalling backwards. Over here there was a doohickey on the handlebar which one had to press. This road would have been dangerous to any cyclist, and was especially so to one who had to use his feet as a brake because there was no time to take thought and remember the doohickey, but Dorothy was singularly unruffled. 'None of the ordinary misfortunes of city streets ever happen to a District Nurse,' she said. 'The police don't bother us, muggers don't mug us, articulated lorries mount the pavement to avoid us; we have our own professional misfortunes, and that's enough. While you're with me, you're an honorary District Nurse.'

They had been taken from the Quick Service Counter of a Volkspeise Transport Café off the A417 by a man with a DKW who had driven them through increasingly built-up countryside to a Recreational Forest Area (it was in fact Burnham Beeches) where he had left them in the Picnic Facilities with a packet of ham sandwiches and a screw-top bottle of Tizer. A light snow was falling, but the trees gave good shelter and the Tizer was warm from the car-heater, and soon enough a van had arrived, one of those drive yourself vehicles which can be hired by the day. The driver had worn a scarf over the lower part of his face and dark glasses, and they had been put into the back, and the door not opened until they were at the end of their journey, inside a bare shed or garage, again windowless, which had been fitted out with a couple of camp-beds and a commode. The van-driver had not spoken on meeting them and did not do so on leaving. He simply left them and locked the door.

It had been like this since the slate-mine. They had been chosen for an important and dangerous mission, briefed by the Prime

Minister of the British government-in-exile himself and his Chief of
the Imperial General Staff. They were the cream of the cream of the
Free British Special Service Unit, pre-eminent in the commando
qualities, self-reliant, self-sufficient, intrepid, decisive, trained to
kill and to control events. And they had made nothing happen, killed
nobody, controlled no events, had relied not on themselves but
others, and owed their freedom to the people they had come to free.
They were hot potatoes, passed from hand to hand by people anxious
to get rid of them; if they were dropped, they could only go cold. 'It's
the rock and the hard place, Ian,' Arwen Parry-Jones said. 'Either we
lose patience and do something silly, or else we get used to other
people taking care of us, and we turn into bloody cabbages.' The
shed was dark, the door locked, their only warmth to lie under coarse
blankets on a narrow bed: the situation lent itself to vegetable
imagery.

Then Dorothy had come. She had wheeled her bicycle into the
shed, and from the basket on the front she had taken bottled water,
cold chicken and chocolate cake and a sixty-watt bulb for the empty
light-socket.

She had told them her name: that was new. And her profession:
she was a District Nurse. Sinclair had said, 'Aren't you telling us
more than we need to know?'

'No. If you survive interrogation, I'll probably be looking after
you, and you'll need to know much more about me and my family
and my work. Now get that food inside you, and I'll be back at six to
take one of you to the boss.'

'One of us?'

'Either. Doesn't matter which. Whichever's in charge, I suppose,
the one with authority.'

Arwen said, 'We don't give each other orders. We work together.'

Sinclair said, 'Why can't we both go?'

'Use your noddle. Even if I could get the extra bike, there'd be
questions asked. One of you is a trainee, helping out; two are
conspicuous. I'll be on my rounds. Leg-ulcers to dress: they all
smoke like chimneys and then complain when their circulation
packs up. Two terminal cancers for morphine injections. A
tracheotomy tube to be changed. Three confused old women living

alone – I've no baths to do this evening, but there's an enema: I'll need help for that. She's a great kicker, that one, used to play for Tottenham Hotspur.' Arwen gulped, but a volunteer who had been trained to crush a man's windpipe with one blow from the side of his hand should not flinch at an enema. 'We'll finish the evening round and that'll take us conveniently close to where I'm to deliver you, and I'll bring you back here afterwards.'

'I don't like it.'

'You've got no choice. I'm to bring one; that's the order. You say you're soldiers; you should be used to orders. If you don't like it, you can stay where you are. Anyway it's in your own interest. One of you has to stay to look after your gear. You couldn't take those bags with you on a nursing round in Battersea, even if you could get them on the bikes. And from what I've heard, you won't be parted from them.'

It was true. Their weapons were in the bags. 'Why can't the boss come here?'

'Because he doesn't choose to. You need him; he doesn't need you. I'll tell you frankly because you've probably gathered as much by now anyway, nobody needs you. You're a responsibility, not a deliverance. Will you decide between yourselves which of you goes with me, and let me know when I get back? And one more thing – no weapons! I'm to make a body-search before we set out. Since I'm a State Registered Nurse, and well used to bodily bits and pieces, that shouldn't embarrass you.'

And she had left them. The chicken had been cooked with rosemary; the cake was a sachertorte. Neither had eaten such food since leaving the US. Arwen said, 'What do you think she meant? – "if we survive the interrogation"?'

'We've got to convince them we're genuine. That shouldn't be difficult, since we are. I find that reassuring. They're worried we might be German Counter-Resistance trying to penetrate their organisation. That means there's an organisation to penetrate. I've been worried that there might not be.'

'We know there's an organisation. How else could we have got as far as we have?'

'Oh, sure! But hasn't it occurred to you that it's all been rather thrown together – improvised on the hoof? This is the first time we've made contact with people who seem to know what they're doing.'

Arwen said, 'Don't say "Oh, sure!" Never say "Oh, sure!" Stick to "Absolutely spot on!" or "Ready when you are, squire." '

'Shut your fucking gob and finish your chicken.'

Arwen said, 'Isn't it convenient that the word "fucking" is idiomatic in both languages?'

The evening round ended at the bottom of a row of terraced houses where a block of flats had been built to fill what had once been a bomb-site. It was called Peabody Building. Dorothy said, 'I've a call to make on the second floor, but I'll take you first to where you're going.'

Where they were going was the top floor. There was no lift; they left their cycles at a friendly flat on ground level and walked up concrete stairs open on one side to the weather. At the top of each set of stairs was an open landing with a communal toilet and a cold-water tap near it. The flats were built round an enclosed courtyard into which the tenants indiscriminately dropped their garbage. 'These are post-war,' Dorothy said. 'One room to a tenant. Mostly they live alone, but you sometimes get one family sharing a room. No sense of community. The old streets are better, but so many were bombed and nobody bothered to rebuild the way it was.'

Some of the flats on the top floor seemed to be in poor repair and were unoccupied. Dorothy took Sinclair to one of these, knocking three times on the door before opening it with a key. Damp ran down the walls and there was rubble and plaster on the floor, but a cheap office desk had been brought into the room and a hard chair set behind it. There were two men in the room, both wearing Mickey Mouse masks. One sat behind the desk; the other stood at the window. Dorothy said to Sinclair, 'I'll leave you here and come back for you.'

So the interrogation began, and was at first simple enough. These people clearly were the Resistance; their conduct so far had indicated as much. They were the people whom the Free Britons had come to assist and to organise. There was no reason why they should not be told that the two volunteers were members of a special force which had been recruited by the British government in Washington and that there would soon be more of them – though it seemed wiser not to mention the O & I Group which had already landed, and since they themselves did not mention it, the presumption must be that they did not know of it. There was no reason not to tell them where the two volunteers lived in the USNA and about their family backgrounds and their education. The old man at the hotel had already confirmed that Parry-Jones spoke Welsh. Sinclair's own family was impeccably British – which was to say Scots. His great-grandfather was the very Sir Archibald who had been leader of the Liberal Party and a member of the war-time Cabinet, and Sinclair was said to resemble him. This detail appeared to interest Mickey Mouse One greatly.

'So far satisfactory. We believe you.' Mickey Mouse One opened a drawer in the desk and put his hand inside to take something from it.

Sinclair's fingers tingled. A warning sounded in his brain. Messages of danger came to him from his childhood. He knew this sequence well. In comic strip or TV series, the crooked businessman or politician, the Syndicate Boss, the alien space-invader in human guise, the not-so-benevolent millionaire, each would reach into the top drawer of his desk. First the false sense of security – 'We believe you.' Then the pay-off. The drawer would contain a gun. Zap! Powee! The poor fool standing in front of the desk, blackmailing subordinate or small-time competitor, would be blown away. But Sinclair was the hero, his every sense alert, his muscles like tensed steel. He was not expendable; if *he* were blown away, the series could not continue. What amateurs they were after all, these people! They needed organising, needed Sinclair and Parry-Jones, even Attlee and little Peter Alloway, to put them in order. He rose slightly on the balls of his feet, ready to pounce. He had been trained for this. Mickey Mouse One had no chance against him.

Mickey Mouse Two said nervously, 'Please don't get agitated. He only wants to make notes.' Mickey Mouse One took from the drawer a reporter's notebook with a cheap ballpoint pen stuck through the coiled wire of the binding. 'That concludes Part One of the interrogation. We'll proceed. What have you been sent to do?'

'Help you.'

'That's not good enough. Nobody asked for help. All you've done so far is to add yourselves to the number of people we've been trying to keep out of the clutches of Special Branch. What's your mission?'

'My orders are not to discuss it.'

A long pause. 'Very well. We'll go at it another way. What do you want from us?' Sinclair did not reply. 'You've been sent for a purpose. You can't accomplish it without our help. You can't even keep out of prison without our help. You can't function in any way. What help do you want specifically?'

'Good documentation. Identity cards that will pass as genuine.'

'That's already in hand.'

'Something from a qualified doctor to say we're sick – convalescent from some industrial accident. I don't imagine that insurance salesmen suffer much in the way of industrial accidents, so I'd better change my profession.'

'Won't Vacation Certificates do? Three weeks?'

'Not long enough.'

The two mice turned their heads to look at one another. Then Mickey Mouse One said, 'You have a fixed time, then, after which your people will pick you up? Another rendezvous on a Welsh beach? We already know that you're not in contact with them, because you're reported to have no radio equipment. So how long is your mission planned to take?'

'I told you. We don't discuss it.'

'Open-ended, your mission? No time-limit? It takes as long as it takes?' No comment. 'Even convalescence doesn't last for ever. Tuberculosis might be more convincing than an industrial accident. That way you won't have to learn another trade.'

'Up to you.'

'And what else do you need?'

'Somewhere to live where we can come and go and our presence won't be questioned.'

'Any preference where?'

'Could be in London. Or just outside. Somewhere near Windsor perhaps.'

'Why Windsor?' No reply. 'Seat of government – not the provincial government, of course: that's in Westminster. But the

Secretariat works out of Windsor Castle. Not a good place, I'd have thought. More security around Windsor than any other location you could pick. Interesting!' No comment. 'And what else?'

'Use of a car and petrol coupons.'

'Difficult to get hold of and easy to trace. You'd be better with bicycles; they're less conspicuous. And public transport for long distances. You're not used to driving in this country and any accident involves the police.'

'We might need a car in exceptional circumstances. Bicycles wouldn't be much good if we had to get away fast.'

'A getaway car?'

'Yes.'

'Get away from what?' No reply. 'Open-ended mission. Takes as long as it takes. Centres on Windsor. And you're asking for a getaway car.' The two mouse faces turned towards Sinclair, intent, and the fingers of one mouse drummed on the desk. 'Oh sweet Jesus!' Mickey Mouse One said. 'Oh, heaven and all angels! I don't know why you're asking for a getaway car; you won't have anywhere to go. You're on a bloody suicide mission, aren't you?'

Muscles twitching at the side of the face betraying turmoil within the calm of a trained volunteer. The Prime Minister, the CIGS, they had neither of them used the word 'suicide' during that afternoon above the Sex Shop, but they had said nothing about getting back to the USNA either and Sinclair and Parry-Jones had not thought to ask. Fools, idiots! They could not say that they had been deceived; they had deceived themselves by simply assuming that arrangements would be made. How could they be brought back when, from the moment they landed, they would be out of contact with Washington and had been instructed to keep away from the O & I Group? The evidence had been there for them to make the obvious deduction, but they had not made it because it had never occurred to them that they, Ian Sinclair and Arwen Parry-Jones, might not be the heroes of the series after all, that they might be expendable bit parts in the pre-credits sequence. The PM and the CIGS had also made an assumption, but with more justification. They had assumed that the Attack Group had fully realised that theirs was a suicide mission, and had patriotically accepted the fact.

It was too much to be taken in at this moment. He would have to talk about it seriously with Arwen. It was they who had shown themselves to be the amateurs; the mice saw more clearly. What was the use of a getaway car without a getaway destination? So far he and Arwen had thought only of how to achieve their mission. Now they must begin to consider the aftermath.

'How many times do I have to tell you? My orders are not to discuss it.'

The mouse said, 'I'm afraid you're going to have to discuss it, Sergeant, but not yet. We have to discuss it amongst ourselves first. You'll find Dorothy waiting outside. She'll take you home. We'll talk again soon.' The situation seemed to have moved outside Sinclair's control. Before he had even reached the door, Mickey Mouse One aka Sir Gervase Acland MP, turned to Mickey Mouse Two and said, 'They've been sent to murder the Reichsprotektor.'

'There's activity there,' the neurologist said. 'No doubt of it. Look at the chart. He ticks over for hours at a fairly low level, and then suddenly – bezoom!' The neurologist knew that legally it was always safer to keep patients alive, however low the quality of that life might be, and it was certainly more lucrative for himself and the hospital as long as the parents were prepared to pay.

Retreat

The two mice removed their masks. Acland said, 'I discover that I'm very frightened.'

'It's the risk to Dorothy that worries me.'

'If that's all that worries you, Stephen, you've more courage than brains.'

'No, of course it's not all. I'm as scared as you are, shit-scared to such an extent my mind blocks it out.'

Acland said, 'One drifts into things. Such things. Never intended.'

'I think I may have to sit down. There isn't a chair.'

'Sit on the desk.'

'Are we going to help them?'

'Since they clearly are what they say they are, we have to. Without proper papers and with no real idea of how to behave, they'll get picked up otherwise. Then Special Branch will know, first that there's an organisation helping people on the run, and second – worse – that the Americans are trying to infiltrate secret agents into Britain. Everything will get much tighter and much more unpleasant. Not helping them is riskier than helping. Dorothy said herself that she'll make a relationship of trust with them. That way if they . . . get into trouble, get caught, they'll feel a responsibility to her: they won't betray her or us through her. That's the hope anyway. She's offered to take them into her own home. She's very bright, Dorothy. More guts than you or I, and bright with it. She says they have cyanide capsules, so if they were caught they should be able to kill themselves without being made to talk. And even if they couldn't manage that, well . . . interrogation in the old style . . . Gestapo stuff . . . that kind of thing . . . It's quite gone out.'

'It could come back, and quickly, if they manage to murder Druckermann.'

'I was watching Sinclair's face when I told him he was on a suicide mission. It came as a shock to him. He simply hadn't realised that the kindly old gentlemen in Washington didn't intend the two of them to survive. No medals except posthumously. When that's begun to sink in, we may see a change of attitude.'

'Meanwhile it's not safe to let them out into the street.'

'They'll learn. Dorothy will teach them. I think they're bright. They have to be bright, or they wouldn't have passed the course.'

'We don't have to protect them. You ignore the alternative. Everyone else has been able to pass them on. We can't; they've ended up with us. There's nowhere else for them to go, but they're too dangerous to keep.'

'I find I've rather got into the habit of protecting people. Haven't you?'

'Not good enough. We should get rid of them. If Dorothy's going to make a relationship of trust by taking them into her home, it should be possible to manage something.'

'You're just saying that, Stephen – making noises because we're both scared: you don't mean it. If you or I or any of our friends were in the habit even of letting people perish, let alone of having them killed, we shouldn't be doing what we're doing.'

'Maybe not.'

The two men sat in silence for a while. Then Acland said again, 'One drifts into things,' and Stephen Grenfell said, 'No way back, though,' and then, 'Perhaps they'll think better of it. The Druckermann business.'

'We have to give them that chance.'

'And then do what with them?'

'What are we going to do anyway? I've been thinking about this a lot, brooding about it. We've been telling ourselves that the war will be over, and the detention centres be emptied, and we'll all return to normal, with no questions asked, as citizens of an independent self-governing democracy within a federation of equals. But it's all self-deception. The reality is that there's nothing normal to go back to. This whole business has shown that our freedom can vanish overnight if there's a change of policy in Berlin.'

'Killing the Reichsprotektor isn't going to alter that.'

'No, it would make it worse. That's why any help we give those two has to be slow and drawn-out. We can't actually refuse to help, because being under orders they'll try it anyway and fail, and the consequences will be just as bad as if they'd succeeded. We've got to give them time to make friends here, get comfortable and think better of it. And then we've got to think what use they can be in our own work. Because they can be of use, if we butter them up a bit and tell them how much we value their organisational skills.'

'You've stopped being frightened.'

'For a while. Time and thought, they cast out fear, at least for a while. Look, Stephen, think about the PUs – as I have. Not just about how to help them, but about their nature and possibilities. They're not really politically unreliable, we both know that; they're a bunch of cranks and enthusiasts, and it was a great mistake to lock them up. But we can profit from that mistake, because – if we choose to be – *we're* the Free Britons – you and I, Dorothy and Jack, little Carrie Baines and all the Yeovil *condottiere*, not that poncey lot of has-beens in Washington. What's been done to the PUs is going to turn them . . . and those who know them . . . certainly those who love them . . . into people who really are politically unreliable, people with a grievance, people who've suffered injustice and couldn't get it set right, people who've discovered what it means not to be free. And when there are enough of them, and they're organised, we can begin to put a bit of pressure on Berlin.'

'Have you talked to the others about this?'

'I'm trying it out on you.'

Stephen Grenfell stood up and stretched. 'PUs are a strictly British problem. The Reichsprotektor, with the consent of the democratically elected British Parliament, has decreed that politically unreliable persons, to be nominated by the British Security Services, shall be kept under detention in order to protect them from attack by their indignant fellow-citizens who might otherwise be tempted to take the law into their own hands. I speak for the Ministry of Information, which I represent.'

'Bollocks!'

'Of course. That's my job – the fabrication and dissemination of high-quality bollocks. Only . . . I'll tell you an interesting thing.'

'Tell me an interesting thing.'

'It's about the Albion Awake detainees. Their average age is greater than of the Welsh and Scots groups. Bound to be: there's a long tradition of sloppy nationalism among the Celts – Welsh language . . . haggis . . . lava bread – so even some of the younger ones catch it. But Albion Awake is full of Battle of Britain pilots and Desert Rats – Finest Hour stuff – and naturally they're all getting on a bit. No wonder the wives and families have been so cross. Carting old gents in their early seventies off to detention centres: it's not on. So it's had to be carefully handled. A lot of them have gone to the centre at Pitlochry, which used to be an Old People's Home – very useful actually, basically a granite barracks with security facilities and tranquillising drugs for those who've gone senile, but colour-washed exterior walls and fitted out with a sun lounge and cable TV. Easy to keep the PUs under restraint and supervision, but it looks humane – and is, Gervase, is – more nurses than security guards, though of course even the nurses have been trained in techniques of restraint.'

'Don't enjoy it, Stephen.'

'What nobody realised was that the old gents would regard themselves as prisoners-of-war, just like in the old days: they'd remember – where was it? – Colditz and those places, form themselves into escape groups and start tunnelling. Takes a bit longer when you're seventy, short of breath and stiff with rheumatics, but it can be done. There's been a mass break-out. Most of them were recaptured very quickly, particularly those who went straight home to the Little Woman, but a few are still free. It's been a tricky problem for us at the Ministry, deciding how to deal with it. Just kept it quiet at first, but too many people know. Since our official line is that there's no censorship, we have to say something. Took time, lot of inter-departmental to-and-fro but we've decided to play it down, make a joke of it, something for the "Isn't the World a Funny

Place?" inside pages of the papers and the "And finally" bit of the BBC News. We're breaking the story tomorrow.'

'You're right; it is an interesting thing. But how does it affect us?'

'News management can deal with one break-out. Two would be serious, so it can't be allowed to happen again. Not anywhere, not from any of the centres. The detainees have to be managed and contained. There's a new man at the Secretariat . . . Von Neustadt – clever little monkey.'

'I've heard of him. He seems to be ubiquitous.'

'Energetic certainly: he gets around. I think he has designs on a Reichsprotektorate, not necessarily here. Make his mark in Britain, then take over Luxemburg and work up. He's devised two new approaches. One is Re-education and Training, but that's still experimental – hypnotism, group therapy, drugs – it's bound to be slow and nobody's sure it will work. The other has more serious implications: I don't know how it affects us, but I'm sure it will. The Home Office is moving prisoners out of Dartmoor and getting the place ready for some new arrivals.'

Mickey Mouse One had said they would talk again soon, but in fact they did not talk again. The mice communicated with the two volunteers through Dorothy who had become their aunt, as her husband had become their Uncle Jack and her daughter their cousin, Sally. They were country boys from a farm in North Devon. This would account for their both having caught TB, easily done when they were sharing a bed, and anyway TB is common in country areas. One gets it from the cows, who are infected by badgers; so much is common knowledge, or at least widely believed.

Parry-Jones said, 'But we can't be brothers. We don't look at all alike.'

'Nonsense. All Yanks look alike,' Dorothy said.

'We're not Yanks.'

'No, you're not. Quite right to remind me. You're my sister's sons from Kingscott.'

Kingscott was a hamlet, not far from St Giles in the Wood, which was not far from Great Torrington. In the matter of false identity, Dorothy said, it was much safer to pick a small place of origin. They could not hope to learn the street-by-street geography, the local politics and personalities of a town the size of Leicester or Kettering from maps and guide books, and the more people lived in such a town, the greater the chance of their meeting one and being found out.

But very few people lived in Kingscott and fewer ever left it. Dorothy had been brought up on a farm there. She could describe every building from the manor to the village shop, run by Mr and Mrs Newcome. She told them about old Mr Folland, who had tried but failed to cut his throat when young for unrequited love, and whose voice had been funny ever since, and about the watercress beds in the little stream behind the cottage next door which had once belonged to someone from the Indian Police but was now a guest-house, and about Farmer Hookway who had paid Reuben from the garage to fix the controls of his Morris Minor so that it could not be driven at over fifty kilometres an hour. She told them where one used to be able to find mushrooms and where wild daffodils, though the indiscriminate use of herbicides had long since killed off both. She showed them photographs.

There was time for all this while they waited indoors for their supporting documents and for their clothes to arrive from the country, horrible old corduroys, flat caps and thick flannel shirts suitable to farm-workers, and shiny blue suits for best. She instructed them to smear their hair with Brylcreem, which was white gook from a bottle, and to comb it back from their foreheads. No gel, no spray, no form of fixative had ever been allowed to touch Sinclair's hair, which was frequently washed, smelled delicately of itself and fell poetically over his brow. He refused. Dorothy rode over his refusal as if he were one of her old ladies refusing an enema. He gave way. They were able to leave the house and to familiarise themselves first with the neighbourhood, then with the city. Since they *were* strangers, there was no reason why they should not behave as strangers.

'They've taught you silly games at that training centre of yours in my opinion,' Dorothy said. 'They've taught you caution: there's nothing more suspicious. What you've got to realise is that everyone you meet expects you to be what you say you are, unless you give them cause to believe otherwise. Nobody's looking for secret agents. There may be a war going on, but it's a long way away, and it doesn't touch most people's lives here; we don't think of ourselves as an occupied country, even if we are. So off you go and enjoy yourselves.'

It was like stepping back in time; the social and moral values were so old-fashioned. Their instructors at the centre had given them some warning of this, but the reality took a bit of getting used to.

Women did work but only in certain capacities – nurses and teachers, secretaries and shop-assistants, in catering and in domestic service: the other jobs and professions were for men. Prostitution was legal but divorce made difficult. Contraception was for women to manage, usually by saying 'No' or by contriving some form of *coitus interruptus*; only the wealthy could afford the contraceptive pill developed in the USNA. If an unmarried woman had the misfortune to become pregnant, the father of the child would be expected to marry her unless he were rich enough to pay someone else to do so; if he were married already, he would deny paternity. Consequently abortion was common and generally carried out in secret at home, after which District Nurses like Dorothy might have some tidying up to do.

There was very little opportunity for privacy. Young men and women did not usually leave home except to marry, and if they did were expected to live in hostels or boarding-houses. Landladies were not complaisant; neighbours observed every action. There were no drive-in movies, but what the volunteers would have called heavy petting, and Dorothy's family called courting, took place in the back rows of conventional cinemas, some of which were provided with double 'sofa-seats'.

Dancing was a decorous activity, far removed from anything the volunteers had ever experienced, even at High School: there were foxtrots and veletas and a dance called the Military Two-Step in the objective reality of which Parry-Jones could not make himself believe. The theatre and cinema offered romance as a substitute for passion, and the television and radio services of the BBC still had it as their remit to inform, educate and entertain in that order, were licensed, as they had always been, by government, and were required to be tasteful, balanced and responsible in their treatment of social and political questions so as to avoid the necessity for censorship.

They had been advised to take things easy, get used to British life first and to their new identities, forget about their mission for a while. They could not, would not and did not forget about it, being under orders, but the business was too important to be rushed. Meanwhile there could be no harm in looking. They went to Windsor by train on a Cheap Day Return, changing at Reading.

The day was fine, with spring already on its way: there were crocuses in the flower-boxes set around the lamp-posts in the main shopping street. They loitered outside the castle with its swastika flag set in the red, white and blue of the province of Britain and its guards in their SS uniforms of black and burnished silver. The guards made fine figures, obviously were meant to do so. They held their chins high, their hair was yellow, chestnut or ash-blonde; none of them was under six feet tall and they had chests like football players. Sinclair and Parry-Jones suspected that this was all for show. The real defences of the castle would not be on public display outside the gates; they would be elsewhere. They bought a street-map at a newsagent's shop, and took the train back to London.

It was odd that they saw no blacks as they went about the city. They were used to the presence of blacks, and, although they themselves had no black friends, nor did their friends have black friends, they had developed the friendly manner common among young liberals of their income-group which indicated equality without familiarity. The same manner also did for Hispanics and for the under-class. Dorothy said that there were blacks amongst her patients, and Chinese and Indians too, descendants of the old immigrant families. There was no discrimination against them; they had the same rights and privileges as anyone else. They were not numerous, but that was to be expected, since immigration of any sort was strictly controlled and of the inferior races totally forbidden.

Sinclair and Parry-Jones wondered whether Dorothy expected a reaction to her use of the word 'inferior'. Was she testing them? But no, they were past all that. They had been accepted; between Dorothy's family and themselves there was now trust and liking. It was possible that even someone like Dorothy did not realise the unacceptability of what she had just said, that she had been brought up in those beliefs and did not question them. It was all part of what the Free Britons had returned to their homeland to correct.

The O & I Group had slept in barns, they had slept in sheds, they had slept in an empty boat-house by the river. Though they themselves had been trained to fitness, the radio equipment was delicate and required a lodging out of the wind and rain. They moved from one town to another, leaving the suitcase containing the radio in a left-luggage locker at the railway station, then cycling out of town again to find a place to sleep; if they had tried to sleep in the warmth of a railway waiting room, close to where they had left the radio, they would run the risk of being questioned by railway staff or the Transport Police.

They could not use the radio because they had no source of power; the joy of the MTI super-portable was that it could be operated from an ordinary power socket, the disadvantage that, if no power socket were available, it needed a 650-watt generator or a car battery with a transformer. They had used it once just before leaving the cottage to let Washington know what had happened – since it was important that no more groups should be despatched with out-of-date identity documents – and then discontinued transmission. They had money, and could have paid for rooms in any hotel or boarding-house, but would have had to produce identity cards: even the Youth Hostels they claimed to be touring would have to keep records. Also the money, as Attlee frequently reminded them, would not last for ever, and without adequate documentation they could not find jobs. Though they were trained to fitness, they did all develop heavy head colds.

They did not see how they could go on like this. They did not see that it would ever change.

They discussed ways in which they could obtain genuine identity cards. They visualised themselves sitting in a bar together, drinking and talking companionably, but watching the door to the gentleman's washroom. They would know when it was empty, know when a man on his own of roughly their own age went to use it and would be alone inside. They would follow him in, silence him, knock him out, steal his money and identity documents, and leave. By the time he recovered consciousness or was found, they would be gone.

They discussed whether it would be better to kill the man, so that he could not describe them. While two of them went back and remained outside the door to prevent interruption, the third would drag his body into a cubicle, lock the door from the inside and climb back over it so as to delay discovery. Invariably they decided that it would not do. It would not do for one card, and certainly not for three. The hunt would be up for a group of three men, perhaps even three men on bicycles, the details of the stolen identity cards would be on every police computer, and anyway the photographs would not match.

They discussed getting rid of the bicycles and going back to a series of stolen cars for transport; they could sleep in a car, the radio equipment would be kept in the boot; they could buy a transformer and transmit from the battery. But stolen cars were risky, bicycles hardly noticed. Once on a country road, little frequented, they had cycled round a corner and found themselves at a police check-point. The police had only been checking cars, and had waved them on.

Though they had weapons, there was no use for them. They had been taught many ways to murder, but always there had been the presumption that those murdered would be the enemy. The people amongst whom they moved, the people of the railway stations, the cheap eating-houses, the bars and the self-service shops were not the enemy. They never saw the enemy.

They stood on a hill below woods and looked down across rough pasture to the abbey. The track they had been following ended here, where clear water emerged from a crack in the rocks and ran on downhill along a rocky channel which seemed to be partly man-made. At the bottom of the hill, where the slope became gentle, was a large kitchen garden. There the water was caught by a sluice-gate, part of it to be pushed out as needed into irrigation channels, and the rest confined within a culvert, disappearing beneath the east wall of the abbey and reappearing from beneath the south, completely tamed, to run on down the valley and join some larger river. Cape said, 'We could ask for sanctuary.'

Lieutenant Attlee well knew that patience is an essential quality of leadership. He said, 'Is that a serious suggestion, Bernard, or ironic?'

'Oh, ironic of course. When am I otherwise?'

Cape was the cross one had to bear. Attlee had no objection to irony in its proper place, but that place was not in a commando unit on active service when the unit's morale was already low. Cape was an intellectual, or probably considered himself to be, but like many intellectuals he did not always think before he spoke. Attlee always thought before speaking. He was the commissioned officer, had been appointed leader by superior authority and bore the responsibilities of his office like a badge to prove it. One of those responsibilities was to maintain morale.

Cape said, 'We need a rest. We need medication. Peter's cough is getting worse.'

It was Cape's opinion that linctus bought from a supermarket was unlikely to cure bronchitis. Well, he was entitled to his opinion, but there was no need to reiterate it when, as he must know perfectly well, it had already been taken on board and was under active consideration.

There was a monk on a mountain bike coming up the track towards them, making heavy weather of the gradient in spite of the plenitude of gears, but apparently determined not to get off and push, which would have been quicker. The three volunteers turned to watch him. Cape wondered whether applause would encourage or embarrass him. Attlee's fingers twitched: it was possible that they had been observed from below and this person despatched to investigate.

The monk's bicycle swerved and wobbled; if he did not dismount, he would fall off or go over the side of the track. His hand moved to some switch or toggle. There was a whine and a popping noise, the wheels straightened and the monk completed his journey with the assistance of what appeared to be a small hairdryer. He smiled and nodded at the volunteers, switched off the engine, leaned his mountain bike against the rock, took from somewhere beneath his habit a rubber hot-water bottle, unscrewed the top, filled the bottle from the spring and screwed it up again, then cupped his hands to take a drink himself.

Cape said, 'Excuse me, father. Are you under a vow of silence or is one allowed to talk to you?'

The monk said, 'Oh, my dear chap, I talk all the time; I'm notorious for it.' He nodded down towards the abbey. 'We're Benedictines, not Cistercians. Basically the same Rule, I always like to say, but far less harshly applied. That's a nasty cough your friend has.'

Cape looked across at Attlee, and Attlee stared back at Cape, daring him down, imposing leadership. Cape thought, *That's it, of course; he's frightened. We're all frightened. David's fear takes the form of trying to turn survival into a routine. He'd rather go on as we are, drifting to disaster, than take a chance on some way of breaking out.* Meanwhile Peter Alloway, his head dizzy and aching, pain tearing at his lungs whenever he coughed, his spirits already lowered by his illness and now brought even lower by the knowledge that he had become a cause of hostility and danger to his comrades, felt his eyes filling with unmanly tears so he covered his face and coughed into an elder bush.

Cape turned back to the monk, who stood politely waiting for further conversation, panting a little and sweating from the exertion of cycling so far uphill and clearly disinclined to begin the return journey at once. He seemed to be in his late sixties, perhaps even older, bald with heavy spectacles on a pointed nose. His white habit had food stains down the front and was as ample as a maternity gown, yet his pot belly showed beneath; if he were pregnant, his time was close. He held out the rubber bottle and said, 'Water sample. We test it here at the spring, test it again when it leaves the premises. Discover what pollutants we put into it. Take them out if there's too many.'

Cape thought of the lakes of Northern Ohio in which, these days, nothing lived. 'You seem to be very responsible people. Or is that a legal requirement?' Attlee closed his eyes. A primary rule had been broken. Never ask questions about any details of life in Britain. They were supposed to know.

The monk said, 'Gives me something to do. Idleness is the enemy of the soul. We all work, but somebody of my age is reckoned to be past the heavy stuff – gardening and so on, getting the coal in – so I have to find jobs for myself.'

'I don't know much about what you do in the monasteries, apart from worshipping God an' all. (*Don't say "an' all". Never say "an' all".*) Do you still feed the poor at your gates, like in the Middle Ages? Minister to the sick?'

The monk looked sideways at Alloway, then back at Cape. 'Not really. One of our community is a herbalist, but if we need a doctor, we go to the local practice like anyone else. As for feeding the poor, since any religious community these days has to make its own living, we've found it more profitable to feed the rich. Tea rooms. Conducted tours. Week-end retreats for executives and professional people who need to recharge their spiritual batteries. We used to feed tramps at the Buttery door but the District Council asked us to stop. It was an attraction to tramps. They came from all over the country.'

'What about sanctuary?'

A long silence. The monk tucked away the rubber hot-water bottle, took off his spectacles and polished them with a fold of his tunic. Attlee cleared his throat. Leadership had passed, at least until it could be reasserted. There would be a crisis and he would have to pick up the pieces and somehow fit them together so that the group could go on as before. The monk said, 'You're Americans?'

'British. Free British.'

'Free . . . yes. I was at the Vatican for ten years. So much displaced royalty hanging about! How it all comes back.'

'Sanctuary, father. We're asking: we're – what's it called? – supplicants: we're in need. Or has that gone out as well, along with ministering to the sick and feeding the poor?'

'Wouldn't do. You'd be clinging to the altar. We'd have to work round you.' He glanced at his wristwatch. From below they could hear the clock of the abbey church begin to chime the hour. 'Anyway there's a reason why our community is one of the last places in the country you should go for sanctuary.'

'What reason?'

'Watch the road.'

On the other side of the valley a blue police van was turning off the main road and onto the side road leading to the abbey. It drew up in the public car park, which was otherwise empty. This was odd in view of what the monk had told them about the tea rooms and the guided tours, but perhaps the season had not yet started. A uniformed policeman in the front passenger seat jumped out and opened the rear door of the van. From the interior there came two men wearing dark blue overalls, cowboy boots and motor-cyclists' helmets and armed with machine-guns. They turned to face into the van, weapons at the ready.

'Who are they?'

'Security guards. Outsiders. We don't get many in Gloucester-shire. They do bank deliveries mainly.'

Two civilians emerged from the interior of the van, each carrying a suitcase. One of the civilians was wearing a white hat, the other was bare-headed.

The monk reached into the recesses of his habit again and this time brought out a pair of binoculars which he handed to Cape. They were of excellent magnification. The white hat was a cap, a flat cap, worn with a plaid jacket, knickerbockers and blue suede shoes; the wearer, a man of early middle age, looked as if he had been plucked off a golf course. His companion was younger, dark-haired, in a polo-necked sweater and jeans with heavy boots. Both were nervous of the security guards and unsure where to go. One of the guards indicated a small door to one side of the main gate. They went together towards it, the guard rang the bell, the door was opened by another man in dark blue overalls, but without the gun or helmet, and all four were admitted. The police van waited.

The monk said, 'Our facilities have been requisitioned.' Alloway began to cough again. Cape said, 'Your manner so far doesn't suggest that you're going to hand us over.'

'Have you killed anyone?'

'No.'

'Illegal acts generally?'

'We've stolen cars and abandoned them. Stolen bicycles. These.'

'Venial. Hardly counts.'

'And of course our presence here is illegal.'

'Why do you need sanctuary?'

'It seems our idenity papers are no good. And my friend is ill, as you've already noticed.'

'What's your purpose here?'

'To locate elements of resistance to the German occupation and assist them.'

'Locate?' The monk grunted. 'Good word. You haven't located any elements so far, I take it, or you wouldn't be asking for shelter. Locate! You'd have to turn a few stones, look into a few dark corners. Generally speaking, the British are perfectly happy to be part of what is now beginning to be called Greater Europe instead of the German Empire. You won't find a Maquis.'

What the fuck was a Maquis? Better not to ask, but to proceed on the Attleean priniciple of pretending to know. 'And those people down there?'

'There you have it. You could call *them* elements of resistance, I suppose. I'm not sure what they'd call themselves. However, the police who brought them are British, their guards are British, the psychiatrists who treat them will be British. No Germans involved, except that one must assume that a German gave the order.'

Attlee said, 'Who are the people and why have they been brought here?'

'I told you our facilities have been requisitioned. The people are PUs – Politically Unreliables – members of . . . I'm not quite sure . . . nationalist groups mainly, I think. Harmless, eccentric people: I find the whole thing very difficult to take seriously, yet it clearly is serious. They're brought here for reprogramming. With those two, we now have twenty-four, which is as many places as we are usually able to offer to spiritually exhausted businessmen in need of a retreat. However, they don't worship with us, aren't allowed to share in the life of the community at all; they're hardly permitted a community life of their own. They're isolated, even from each other, quite early on. They clean their own rooms. We do nothing for them but provide food, which must be served in silence. Their Rule is stricter than ours, but that's the way of psychiatry.'

For Lieutenant Attlee the situation was beginning to become clearer and therefore perhaps more manageable. They had located elements of the Resistance, but these elements were powerless and could not be organised for guerilla operations by the O & I Group because they were already being reorganised by the occupying authorities. However, if one were able to make contact with them before their reorganisation was complete, they might lead one to other elements who were not so powerless. 'How does this reprogramming work?' he said.

'I'm not sure. It's new – an experiment, we gather; it's only just begun. Obviously we're not part of it ourselves. A mixture of auto-suggestive techniques and drugs, I suppose; you know the sort of thing – an intensification of what already goes on in psychiatric practice anyway. A couch in a darkened room. Tranquillisers injected. Group confessions. Audio sensotapes. Videos. Electric shocks whenever they're shown something to be avoided.'

'Injections, you said?'

'We know there are injections. Their waste-bins are emptied into ours.'

Cape said, 'But the injections could be . . . could just as easily be lethal. Nobody outside would know.'

'We've discussed that within the community: we've got that far. There's no evidence of it up to now; they could not avoid our finding out. However . . . when one considers the circumstances . . . These are people already held in a detention centre who have volunteered as candidates for reprogramming, have been assessed and been judged suitable. What one can't know is whether all of them really have volunteered. We're told so; their fellow-detainees are told so. If the reprogramming is successful, they're released: they don't go back to the centre. If they were killed here by lethal injection, they wouldn't go back either. It would be possible to make the whole intake believe that they were being reprogrammed and released, whereas actually . . . It would be possible. It isn't happening, but it would be possible.'

'But the people operating the programme, you said, are all British.'

'Yes. And the programme itself still experimental. No need for nightmares. Yet.' Down below, the two security guards came out of the abbey and climbed back into the police van, which was driven out of the car park. 'I'm not a young man. I can remember the late nineteen-thirties and I do. I was an oblate here. We knew, even we boys knew, what was happening to the monastic orders in Germany. After the war was over, we kept our heads down and hoped it wouldn't happen here, and by and large it didn't. But in Germany in nineteen thirty-seven . . . monks and nuns imprisoned . . . shot . . . trumped-up accusations . . . show trials. There were Franciscans working with the disabled, charged with homosexuality because they held the penises of sclerotic patients to help them to piss. Convicted, they were sent to camps and processed in the way usual for homosexuals – hard labour first and the gas chamber when they were of no further use. Never happened here. Doesn't happen anywhere now. But some of us remember. I'll have the binoculars back, please.' He took the binoculars from Cape and prepared to mount his mountain bike. 'You'd better come with me. I'll take you to the abbot. That cough certainly needs attention.'

The monk's name was Father Theodemar; he had been named after an eighth-century abbot of Monte Cassino. 'Fashions change,' he said. 'Most of my lot were given rather obscure names when we came into the Order – little-known popes and reforming abbots mainly – then in the sixties there was a rash of Julians and Gregorys, Nicholases, Dominics and Fabians; now they're all John, Peter and Philip.'

There were thirty-eight of them. By the Rule of St Benedict, all had to be consulted, though the abbot need not be bound by their opinions. In any case, since the only way of concealing the O & I Group was that they should be disguised as monks and take part in the work of the abbey, the other monks were bound to know. But the abbot did not expect objections. None of the monks was happy about the Humane Re-education Programme.

There would be conditions. While they were at the abbey they must not function as an O & I Group; they must function as monks. They would work in the garden and the kitchen, attend the Offices and Readings six times a day (though they need not take part), eat vegetarian food from wooden bowls and drink plain water in the Refectory at meal-times, abstaining from refreshment at all other times, rise at four in the morning and go to bed at nine-thirty in the evening. They assured the abbot that they would find none of this difficult to accept; the regimen seemed very like that of the training centre. Their weapons and the radio would be kept by the abbot until they wished to leave. Lieutenant Attlee disliked this condition and it worried him greatly, but one must give something to get something. What they would get, besides safety and temporary shelter, were identity cards.

The method would be daring but simple. The identity data of all PUs were held on police computers – not only on the Special Branch and MI5 computers, but on the computers of every regional police force. As those who have tried to have their names removed from a junk mailing list well know, computers resist amendment. It would be easier to issue re-educated PUs with new identity cards than to amend the old, and it would have a symbolic significance also, as von Neustadt himself pointed out, because the process of re-education would have transformed them into new people: they would be born-again reliables. In making use of the abbey's retreat facilities, the authorities had not been able to take over more than there was. There was only one Administration Office and the abbey itself had to be administered as well as the programme. The psychiatrist-in-charge and the officer commanding the security guards shared that office with the abbot. The blank identity cards were kept in the office safe.

Penicillin is not usually thought of as a herb, but the herbalist seemed to have access to it. Peter Alloway was put to bed and treated with streptomycin, aspirin, heartsease and inhalations of comfrey. The clothing of all three volunteers was taken from them, washed and ironed, repaired where necessary and put away in a press until it should be needed. Their hair was cut short and shaved at the crown of the head to make a tonsure, they were given breviaries to carry at all times and kitted out with gowns and hoods of cotton and polyester.

How did the three volunteers react to the monastic life?

To Attlee it was a job, to be performed meticulously. He was out in the vegetable garden every day, hoeing between the rows of onions, shallots, garlic and broad beans which were already showing, earthing up potatoes, digging well-rotted manure into what would be the seed-beds of beetroot and broccoli, carrots and kale, peas and spinach, turnips, radish, lettuce and swede, harvesting cauliflowers and winter spinach for the kitchen. He sat decorously in the refectory at meal-times, eating everything in his bowl and listening to readings of the Rule, one chapter a day. He opened his mouth during the choral offices, but did not sing.

Cape was deeply uneasy. He had got them into this, and he had been right to do so; it was the way out of a dead end. But the pervading atmosphere, the unquestioning obedience to rule, upset him. Cape was a questioner. By questioning, by the testing of hypotheses, by the words 'Show me' and 'Prove it', the human race advanced. It seemed unnatural to Cape that any human being should try to destroy the self, whether in the service of a God of highly speculative reality or for any other reason. That was what humans were: selves. In their individuality was their humanity: that was what distinguished them from termites.

As for Peter Alloway, given only light duties as a convalescent, he spent hours in the abbey church, which had been rebuilt in 1928 from local stone on the foundations of the original building (torn down, a bit at a time, during the sixteenth century by predatory local landowners). Sometimes he sat watching the changing light through stained glass; sometimes he knelt, head bowed, waiting for a voice.

Infantry were not the answer. Infantry were an embarrassment in modern warfare. The function of infantry was to define a front. The soldiers would construct deep and secure emplacements for artillery and a system of shallow, less secure trenches and dug-outs for themselves. In front of these they would lay mines, dig ditches and construct various barriers against tanks. The infantry of both sides would do this, just as the infantry had done at the beginning of World War Two, but with less and less conviction, and they would remain within their defensive positions, facing each other across dead ground, always vulnerable to air attack but attempting with every day that passed to make themselves a little more secure. They would fall victim to various debilitating diseases from foot-rot to typhoid, and be supplied with food, water, ammunition and petrol over great distances at enormous expense, until the real fighting started, when most of them would be blown away.

Infantry in this war were not the concern of the governments of the three Empires; they did not send their own foot-soldiers to the Gulf. It was the Iraqi infantry who drew the lines on the sand, facing Persians on one side, Saudis and Omanis on the other. The Great Powers provided the armour, the aircraft and the ships. And these were not the answer either because, as has been said, it would be madness to commit them in any real way unless one could be sure of winning.

Stalemate. The Germans, having the shortest line of communication and that by land, sent five more armoured divisions into Iraq, and made sure that this was known. The Japanese brought another squadron of fighters, equipped with heat-seeking missiles, into Persia. The Americans sent another aircraft carrier. The American and Japanese Commanders held a press conference to express their delight at hearing of the German reinforcements since so many extra tanks would provide a larger target.

Stalemate. After weeks of inaction, perhaps by simple error, perhaps as a ploy to see what would happen, one night a battery of Persian heavy artillery began to fire. The gunfire was taken up all down the line, like firecrackers setting each other off, and all down the Iraqi line there was a similar counter-action, and since the commotion in the night sky was so great and could be seen and heard over such a distance, and particularly by the infra-red cameras of the aircraft despatched to see what was going on, the guns of the Saudi emplacements also began a barrage, and the Iraqis replied, and so it went, Armageddon in April, only ceasing with the dawn.

Many, many infantry were killed that night. A whole battalion of the Saudi Tenth Regiment, some of them on camels, misunderstood or misheard a muddled order and attacked across the dead ground, to be slaughtered by mines and machine-guns. Their corpses could not be cleared away. Maggots grew fat on them and then (it was believed) having acquired the taste for human flesh, crawled from the dead to the living, so that gangrene killed more infantry on both sides than the battalion could ever have hoped to do by its attack.

Stalemate. In Berlin the balance of power within the Council of State continued to shift. It had become a War Council in which the generals predominated, and the generals were beginning to grow impatient. In Washington the British initiative had been written off.

The Pentagon made friendly noises, but went no further, and the CIA no longer shared information. The British continued to train volunteers, but there was no transport available now to take them to the Welsh coast and no more expensive state-of-the-art equipment except for ready money. The project continued to be interesting to the Pentagon and of great potential value, but the British were not able, as it seemed, to deliver. The CIA had begun to flirt with the French, but the French were coy.

Stalemate. In the Operations Room of the British government-in-exile, they bit their upper lips and told each other that there would be bluebirds over the white cliffs of Dover soon enough. They had only to hang on, and news would arrive from London which would change their status utterly. Then the whole world would see that the Brits had a long arm; they could pull a string and set the puppets dancing. All they had to do was wait.

The only contact between the community of the abbey and the community of the re-educated was, as has been said, that the monks cooked for the Re-eds and served their meals. Those who were undergoing Intensive Conscience Examination Therapy were served individually in their rooms: the word 'cell' was not used except by the monks about their own accommodation. It was odd how much overlap there was between the two regimes, religious and re-educational. The monks were also required by Rule to assemble at regular times to recite predetermined texts to the sound of music; they were also required to examine their consciences in solitude. They did so every night before settling to sleep, but without the assistance of drugs.

There were guards supervising the service and clearing away of meals, but not enough to block out all conversation, particularly with the solitaries. If the O & I Group wished to question the re-educatees before the re-education process had been completed, it must be done then. Attlee offered his own services as monk and waiter. But the abbot had given an undertaking that the meals would be served in silence; the fiction was that conversation with monks might disrupt the therapeutic process. He refused the offer.

It was frustrating for Lieutenant Attlee that, now that he was almost within touching distance of dissident elements, he was forbidden to speak to them. It was his first test of obedience as a pseudo-monk. 'I can't trust you, David, because you couldn't trust yourself,' the abbot said. Attlee's lips tightened and he nodded. Though he might promise to obey, he would be tempted in the greater cause, and he would fall. 'And Bernard would rationalise it by telling himself that since he's only pretending to be a monk, he only has to give a pretended obedience.'

'What about Peter?' Peter Alloway had already proved himself to be a weaker vessel. He was a technician, a radio person and nothing more; Attlee had little faith in his ability to rise to any sort of challenge. But even a weaker vessel may be better than none.

'Peter's a simpler character. Blessed be he.'

'Oh, yes,' said David Attlee. 'Indeed, yes. Blessed be Peter. Will you allow him to do it?'

'He might pick something useful up simply by observation, I suppose. No harm in that. And he'll keep the silence. Peter can be trusted.'

Peter could be trusted. He had already heard a still small voice speaking to him in the chapel. He had known it to be his own voice – no miracle there – but had known also that it was telling him what he really wanted. He had asked first his closest friend among the monks, Father Philip, then – on encouragement – the abbot whether he might be accepted as a novice if he were to return after the Present Emergency. He would have applied immediately, but had sworn an oath of obedience to the Free British government which would take some time to fulfil, and did not think it right to start a new life by breaking one promise to make another.

It seemed to the abbot that, although it was too early to be sure, and one must allow for back-to-the-womb behaviour brought on by stress, there might be a vocation there. 'Yes,' he said, 'Peter can serve the meals. He's still on light duties anyway. I'll get Father Anselm to show him the ropes.'

Bernard Cape's friend in the abbey was Father Theodemar who, although assiduous in the performance of his monastic duties, seemed to be more interested in the outside world than the other monks. They strolled together in the cloisters, and the good father discoursed at large.

'Some of us read the newspapers,' he said. 'After all, monks do live in the world. Not "of" but "in": we can't avoid it. There was a news story the other day which might have interested you, a humorous story humorously told. A group of old age pensioners in a detention centre in Scotland – every one of them over seventy – dug themselves a tunnel and broke out. Came up in the shrubbery. "Is this France?" But, reading between the lines, some seem to have got away.'

'You haven't kept that newspaper, I suppose?'

'It all goes to be recycled. There's always an enormous increase in the consumption of paper during a war, and of course the pulp no longer comes from Canada. You know, I can't help feeling that you and David are mistaken in wanting to talk to the poor devils upstairs. If they really volunteered for the programme, they're not dissidents, just people who already very much regret having joined – probably for social reasons – whatever dotty organisation or club they did join, who long to return to their normal lives, and will happily denounce anyone who suggests otherwise. Only a psychiatrist could make such a performance of re-educating people who, practically speaking, are re-educated already.'

Peter Alloway served meals from a trolley and took away the dishes afterwards. Most of the patients did not try to talk to him, perhaps did not want to talk, perhaps could not talk. They lay on their beds or sat in an armchair by the window, staring out. There were no pictures on the walls of the rooms, no family photographs on dressing table or bedside locker, few books and those always the same books – *The Enemy Within*, *A Positive Approach to Mental Health* and *Eysenck's Guide to Normal Behaviour* – which were provided for private study. Some of those who had been longest in the programme twitched and mumbled, some left their food untasted and these, when it was reported as it had to be, were force-fed by the psychiatric staff.

One of the patients, an anxious, elderly person, always gave the same greeting, 'Hullo, young man! Are you all right? Are you sure you're all right?' Peter Alloway, his back to any supervising guard, would smile to indicate that he was all right and very much so. Then the elderly person would say, 'I'm going to be all right too, aren't I?

I'll be all right.' And Peter would nod. He had been forbidden to speak, but not forbidden to nod.

The man in knickerbockers, whose arrival they had witnessed from the hill, talked non-stop and seemed to understand that he must not expect a reply. It was possible that he was not talking primarily to Peter, for he sometimes directed his remarks upwards to a corner of the room or to the overhead light, enunciating particularly clearly those he considered particularly important.

'I'm not an Albionite, not in my views, and never have been,' he said. 'I only joined in order to further my business career. I'm in corporate videos: you can't get anywhere in the corporate video business unless you put yourself about to make the social contacts. It was purely a business decision.'

He spoke louder and to the light-fitting. 'Which I now see was ill-advised and which I deeply regret, but we're in rather a trough these days owing to the Present Emergency. I don't know what I'll find when I get back to the office. It's a one-man operation really, just me and the wife and some expensive equipment for which we've not yet paid. What we should really do – and I see that now – is put our entire operation at the disposal of the armed services as information technology. Please don't go: I haven't finished. We had a very interesting lesson yesterday; I found it extremely useful. They showed us a lot of badges and logos, not just the Albion Awake and the Welsh and Scottish, but all sorts, foreign movements, Basques and such, and of course the Japanese and Americans with their nasty national emblems. All the people who were wearing the badges – mean-featured, untrustworthy lot – they were frowning, but in between we had pictures of our own brave boys, not just the Army and the Air Force and the jolly Jack Tars, but the police and traffic wardens, council officials, bus conductors, and every one of them had this great, beaming, friendly smile. And when they showed us the bad people, we all had a little electric shock that came out of something they'd strapped to our chests with our full consent and approval. But the good people came with inspirational music and healthy scents like pine and rosemary. It certainly reinforced my belief.'

*

'I tell you frankly, squire,' the junior psychiatrist said to Bernard Cape, 'I don't know what we're doing. Most of the time it's a doddle, our job; we do it by the book.' The junior psychiatrist was a gregarious fellow and had been glad to find, among this community of loony, gloomy monks, one like-minded body to whom he could talk.

'Flashers,' he said, 'sexual deviants of any sort . . . people who've been warned to give up smoking . . . most compulsions . . . All they need is a bit of simple aversion therapy . . . bit of stick and carrot with the emphasis on stick. Phobias . . . cats, birds, spiders, all the usual stuff – get them used to it gradually – Accustomisation Therapy. The rest is mostly drugs. Anxiety – benzodiazepines. Depression – tetracyclics. Manic Depression – lithium. Schizophrenia – phenothiazine and ECT. But with this lot there's nothing clear cut. We've got to make it up as we go along, try a bit of everything. We're going to have to release somebody soon or they'll stop funding the programme. Problem is that all the ones who've been here a while have begun to go catatonic and we daren't let them out.'

'You can't stay here for ever. You're going to a cottage in the Chilterns for a month. The woman who owns it lets it out to summer visitors, so the village is used to strangers. Anyway the cottage is outside the village. Isolated. You won't be overlooked.'

'Near Windsor?'

'Near enough. About ninety minutes by cycle. Anywhere nearer is all built up.'

'A car would be quicker.'

'Ian, let's not go into this again. How would you get the petrol coupons?'

'If you can get us identity cards, petrol coupons shouldn't be a problem.'

'Well, they are. And we'd have a better use for them. It won't hurt you to cycle; you're supposed to be in top condition. You really vex me sometimes. You're not stupid, but you're behaving stupidly about the car. You know you have to be inconspicuous, but you're all the same, you Yanks –'

109

'We're not Yanks.'

'British Yanks. It's a masculine status symbol, that's all. Well, you don't need it.'

'Does the woman know about us?'

'Why should she? I told you, she's just a woman who lets out her cottage. Advertises in *The Times*. It's her living, I suppose.'

'Do we pay the rent?'

'It's been paid in advance.'

Sinclair knew, and Dorothy must know he knew, that they would not take the chance of any old advertisement in *The Times*. The woman must be one of them, have connections anyway, but it would be safer if he and Arwen believed her to be just the landlady.

'Will Carrie be coming with us?'

Little Carrie Baines had left Yeovil and come to London. She had grown restless since her father, grandfather and brother had been taken away in a police van, and wanted to be of use, so she had been put to use as courier, guide, emissary, finder of safe houses, and temporary friend; one of her uses had been to act as cover and company for Sinclair and Parry-Jones. She was a demure girl, almost virginal, the respectably reared daughter of a male-dominated family, but from the moment she saw Arwen, and her hand touched his too briefly in greeting, somewhere inside her the words, 'I'll have him' had formed themselves into a sentence, and within a week she had.

It was upsetting for Sinclair. Upsetting professionally because he did not know whether to welcome her as an ally or discourage her as an emotional entanglement, and upsetting personally because, although a soldier on active service may accept that masturbation is the only sexual outlet practically available, he knows well enough that it is not as good as the real thing, and to have one's buddy enjoying the real thing in the next bedroom does nothing for one's concentration on the task in hand. Luckily Carrie was often otherwise employed.

'I expect she'll visit.'

'How soon can we leave? It's time to get on with the job. We've been long enough learning to be British British, and according to you we're no good at it anyway.'

But he was not really miffed with her. One couldn't be miffed with Dorothy. 'Miffed': that was a good word, a totally British word. He must try to work it into his vocabularly on a regular basis.

April turned to May and it was time for the O & I Group to leave the abbey. They collected their clothing, which no longer looked at all new or smart, their rucksacks, their weapons, the radio and their bicycles, which the monks had been using communally, and departed by daylight as they had arrived. Their new identity documents allowed them to work anywhere and at any job commensurate with their abilities, provided that the work was of national utility and obtained within fourteen days of leaving the Re-education Centre. Attlee, Cape and Alloway had no need now to fear interrogation; the new cards showed that they had been purified, purged of error by qualified psychiatrists employed by the State, were loyal to the bone and squeaky clean. On a more practical level, they could pass as British; they had picked up so much in accent, behaviour and attitude from the monks. The tonsures would grow out.

The sun shone, the air was balmy, the hawthorn in blossom. They ate a packed lunch in an open field and discussed the future. They knew now that dissident elements were not going to be easy to find and that the British generally did not groan under the oppressors' yoke. Yet people had been arrested and a few had escaped; there must be discontent. That there were detention centres was common knowledge; their location was not. Would it be feasible to find one, settle near it, maybe even find employment within it, make contact with the detainees and organise a break-out? Dissident elements would be disseminated like the spores of a puffball all over Britain, and could be organised into the cells of a resistance movement which would permeate every stratum of British society.

Alternatively they might settle close to a factory making – oh, some essential electronic equipment, something expensive and difficult to replace – and blow it up or set it on fire or both. This would have the advantage of doing immediate damage and would be likely to provoke reprisals which would, with any luck, lead to more discontent. Again, they would have to find out the location of such a factory. Would Washington know? Would the CIA know? It was the kind of knowledge the CIA certainly ought to have on file, and would, Attlee assumed, gladly pass on to their Free British colleagues with a team already on the ground. Clearly the group's first action must be to reopen communications with the Operations Room in Washington.

Except that there was still the problem of a power-source.

First things first. They would cycle to Gloucester, leave the radio and the rucksacks at the railway station, then scout about un-encumbered for a top-floor furnished apartment which they could rent by the week.

They left the bicycles leaning against the railings outside the station for anyone to take: it was easy come, easy go with those bicycles. The three rucksacks required a 'jumbo locker' each; there were only three available; but the radio, constructed to look like an attaché case, would, as it always had so far, fit into an ordinary left-luggage locker. Alloway took the case over to the bank of lockers on the other side of the concourse, inserted a five-shilling coin, opened the locker, put in the case, locked it away and stowed the key in the top pocket of his jacket. Attlee and Cape were buying local papers at the railway bookstall as a start to their search for accommodation. He would join them there. A voice said, 'Hullo, then! What are you doing in civvies? Running away?' It was the knickerbocker man.

He still wore the white hat, plaid jacket and blue shoes in which they had seen him arrive at the abbey, and carried the same small suitcase. Alloway supposed that there would have been no room in it for another suit: it would contain only spare underwear and toiletries. What was the man doing here? Were there guards with him? No. None were to be seen, or policemen either. It was a moment for quick thinking and decisive action. Alloway said, 'Sorry?'

The man held out a hand to be shaken. 'Kevin Pargeter. You used to bring me grub. Three meals a day, very much appreciated.'

Pretend not to know him? Too late: the moment had passed. 'I'm afraid I wasn't allowed to talk to you.'

'I know. I did the talking. You let me. I was grateful, still am. You

112

having a day out or what? Didn't know they allowed that sort of thing. In for life without the option, eh? Burn your clothes and put you in a frock.'

Alloway realised that this man, however friendly and grateful he might appear, was very dangerous. He may have been a dissident element once, but was not now. If he had been released from the Re-education Centre – the first to go – it must be because he had been programmed to run to the nearest police station the moment he suspected even the smallest disloyalty in any of his fellow-citizens; a Free Briton would be even more upsetting. Excuses would not convince him; his antennae would sniff out prevarication. Only a big lie would do. 'I was a novice. Discovered I didn't have a vocation. They let me go.'

'Good grief! I'm very sorry. Making stupid jokes! What a fool! Insensitive!'

'I'm keeping you from your train.'

'Don't worry. I've just arrived. Van dumped me outside. Make my own way. Haven't even looked at a timetable yet. Look, we must have a drink.'

Somehow this Pargeter must be moved away out of the concourse. Attlee and Cape would have bought their local newspapers by now, would be wondering what was holding him up, might even be looking across at them, might decide to come over. It was unlikely that Pargeter, shut up in his room, had seen them as monks, but not impossible. If he had, he could hardly be expected to believe in three lost vocations. All lies of whatever size lead to other lies. If Attlee or Cape or both were to come looking for him, how could they be introduced as friends or even acquaintances when, as a lapsed monk, he had no friends in the outside world and certainly not in Gloucester? And even if the story were that they were friends from a former time who had come to take him back to where he lived . . . where did he live? 'It's all too difficult,' he said.

'You what?'

'I'm sorry if I'm not making sense. I feel rather vulnerable. The world's so strange to me.' He had to get to them and warn them to keep away. The man had said something about a drink. 'Yes, I would like a drink. Nothing alcoholic.'

'Oh, no, no. Right. Start as you mean to go on. You don't mind if I do?'

'Not at all.'

Settled at a table in the station buffet, Alloway said, 'Would you excuse me a moment? A call of nature.' He left the buffet quickly and looked about for the Gents in case the man was watching. Then when he was sure he was out of sight, he veered to the bookstall at a run.

Attlee and Cape were waiting. 'Where the hell have you been?'

'There's a man recognised me from the abbey. One of the reprogrammed people; he's been released. He mustn't see you. I've got to get rid of him.'

'You have got rid of him, haven't you, or you wouldn't be here?'

'He's waiting for me in the buffet, thinks I'm in the john. (*Don't say "john".*) Loo. If I don't go back he'll be suspicious.'

Give Lieutenant Attlee a soluble problem, and all his qualities of leadership were shown at their best. 'Locker key,' he said. 'For the radio.' Alloway gave it to him. 'You'd better leave your rucksack where it is and retrieve it later because there's too much in it to compromise you.' There was an automatic machine-gun in it; there were explosives in it. 'You've got money?' Alloway had money. 'Don't rush. Let it take as long as it takes.' He glanced at the station clock. 'One of us will be back here at the bookstall at six. If you're not here we'll wait fifteen minutes and then go. Same at noon tomorrow. Same again at six. Same procedure every day until we see you. Understood?' Alloway nodded. 'Okay, Bernard, let's go.' He turned on his heel and left the concourse with a military stride. Cape shrugged, then followed him.

Peter Alloway watched them go. What did David mean, 'Let it take as long as it takes'? He began to have a sick feeling in his stomach. Unless he could make the story of the lost vocation stick, there was only one way of ensuring that the knickerbocker man did not tell anyone else about the pretend monk at the Re-education Centre.

'Where are you bound?'

He had expected the question and had prepared an answer. 'London.' That should be anonymous enough.

'Great! We can travel together. Someone to talk to. I'm not one of those unsociable buggers who buries his head in a paper, pardon my French. I take an interest, always have. Ask people about themselves. First rule of salesmanship, and I tell you straight, in my business salesmanship is what it's all about; you've got to sell the service and that means selling yourself.'

Alloway was finding it difficult to understand what the man was saying. What *was* his business? He had talked about it in his room at meal-times. Something to do with video. 'You're going to London as well?'

'Paddington. Tube from there to Victoria, then off again to the south coast.' Had Alloway made a mistake in choosing London? It was clearly a complicated place to get around in. He tried to remember what a tube was: one of his instructors must have mentioned it. 'Eastbourne, do you know it? We're just outside. National Trust land, as a matter of fact, near Beachy Head. Beautiful spot. Card!' The man opened his wallet and produced a card, all in one movement like a conjurer. 'Take it. Drop in some day if you're down our way.'

The talk went on like a river, but one could not allow it merely to bear one along, because there were alligators in the river, pike, piranha fish suddenly surfacing and demanding a response. The man insisted on buying Alloway a ticket. 'Expect you're skint, aren't you, bound to be? Not exactly rolling in the stuff myself these days, as you may have gathered, but one good turn deserves another.' As the London train arrived, and they were about to board it, he stopped suddenly, one foot in the air, and said, 'No luggage?'

'Just what I stand up in.'

A mistake. He had been seen putting a suitcase into a left-luggage locker. But the knickerbocker man made nothing of it. Was he playing some sort of game? What game? Why? *Let it take as long as it takes.* Easier for Attlee to say than for Alloway to do.

Now they were in an open carriage with seats on both sides and a centre aisle. What had to be done could not be done here. The knickerbocker man was still talking. They were on the sunny side of the carriage. 'It's hot in here. Why don't you take your jacket off?' Sweat ran down Alloway's cheeks and the side of his neck: his shirt was sticking to him. 'Put it on the seat and nobody'll sit next to you.' Nobody would sit next to them anyway if there were other seats free: a woman opposite them had already moved across the aisle.

Alloway took off his jacket and put it on the seat beside him, and the knickerbocker man, though he did not seem to be sweating to anything like the same extent, did the same. 'The wife won't be expecting me, you know,' he said. 'Give her a surprise. If you phone first it's only an anti-climax when you get there. I'll take a taxi from the station, go round the back. Bound to be in the garden in this weather. Creep up behind her. Hands over her eyes. "Guess who." She'll have a heart-attack and I'll collect on the insurance. What about you?'

Alligator question again, and as usual Alloway unprepared. 'Sorry?'

'Nobody expecting you?'

'No, I'm afraid not.'

'No family?'

'A married sister. Our parents passed away when I was a little boy.'

'What part of London do you live in?'

Blank. What parts of London were there? He could remember nothing of what he had been taught at the training centre. A word came out of the blankness. 'Walthamstow.' He prayed that the knickerbocker man would have no acquaintance with it.

'That's south of the river, isn't it?'

Either 'Yes' or 'No' would have a fifty per cent chance of being wrong; 'I can't remember' would be wronger. Alloway put his hand to his eyes. 'I'm sorry. Just talking about it makes me feel dizzy again.'

The knickerbocker man looked at the sign at the end of the carriage. 'Toilet's free. Why not go and splash your face with water? You'll feel better.'

He would. Just getting away from the chat for a while would make him feel better. He rose quickly to his feet and headed for the 'Toilet' sign, remembering when he reached it that he had left his jacket on the seat, but to return for it now would be insulting. There were two toilets tucked away in an enclosed space where the two carriages were joined, with doors on both sides by which the passengers boarded and left the train. It was, Alloway realised, the only space where there was any privacy, where – provided the train was in motion – any act could be performed without being witnessed. He sluiced water on his face and looked at himself in the mirror, flexed his fingers and watched the fingers flexing, looked back again in the mirror and stared at the reflection of his fingers and his face.

Meanwhile Kevin Pargeter, who was indeed playing a game, because he believed that Alloway might be someone from the Security Services who had been disguised as a monk for purposes of entrapment and was now monitoring his homecoming, swiftly and inconspicuously removed Alloway's wallet from the jacket he had left on the seat, and examined its contents. What he found surprised him. There was an identity card just like his own, stating that Alloway had been re-educated at the centre and was now certified as a reliable citizen, there was much more money than one might expect a monk to possess and there was a piece of paper with a list of names, all of people named Alloway and living in Berkshire. He returned the identity card and the money to the wallet and the wallet to the jacket, and put the piece of paper in the back pocket of his knickerbockers, to be considered more carefully at some later time.

As Alloway returned to his seat there was an announcement on the train's communication system that the passenger buffet was about to open for the service of beverages and snacks. 'Don't sit down. Let's get a bit to eat before the rush. Passes the time and stretches the legs. My treat.' The knickerbocker man took his wallet from his jacket, but left the jacket lying across the seat. 'Leave these. They keep the place.'

The buffet car was in the front of the train, the bumpiest section, to ensure maximum spillage. They queued and Pargeter paid for two plates of cold wurst with potato salad and two cardboard cups of coffee with cardboard handles; then they began the long journey back to their own carriage. The voice on the system cleared its throat to attract attention, and announced that the train would arrive at Swindon in approximately five minutes, fifteen minutes behind schedule, and that the management and staff of the Great Western Railway Company apologised for the delay which was due to track maintenance.

They were in the little space by the toilets between carriages. One toilet was occupied, the other vacant. There was space for Alloway to draw level. He said, 'Er . . .' and the kickerbocker man stopped and turned halfway towards him. Alloway lurched forwards and sideways. The plate of potato salad went into the face of the knickerbocker man like a custard pie, and he fell back against the door of the vacant toilet, his own food spilling down his front. 'Sorry! Terribly sorry!' Alloway dropped the cardboard cup and turned the handle of the door with one hand while pushing the knickerbocker man into the toilet with the other. Behind him he could hear the other toilet being flushed; his private place would not be private for much longer. He closed the door behind him. The mouth of the knickerbocker man was open: it might only be surprise or he might be about to speak or shout. The side of Alloway's right hand, rigid, smashed against the knickerbocker man's windpipe, then the left hand similarly to the bridge of the nose, then the neck taken in both hands as he fell and twisted sharply to displace the vertebrae and break the spinal cord. Done. Textbook stuff. *Let it take as long as it takes.* He did not think he would be proud of himself.

Alloway took the wallet, the brand new identity card, all that he could find which would identify the knickerbocker man, and put them in his own trouser pocket. He did not think to look in the back pocket of the knickerbockers. Something else was needed to divert attention. He must think quickly; they would be at the station soon. He removed one of Pargeter's shoes and used it to smash the mirror over the washbasin. He pulled out a sliver of glass and stabbed the dead man in the neck. With the sliver of glass dipped in blood he wrote the word 'PERVERT' on the mirror. That should provide a false track for the police.

The train had begun to slow down as it approached the station. Alloway left the toilet, shutting the door behind him, and went quickly back to his seat. Passengers were requested not to use the toilet while the train was standing at a station, and he hoped that nobody would. He collected his own jacket, Pargeter's jacket and the suitcase and white golfing cap from the rack. 'We get off here,' he said to the woman across the aisle, and left the train at Swindon.

118

Honeymoon

It seemed to him that the voices no longer spoke to him as often as they had done earlier. One could not be sure of this, because one could not be sure of anything in the nothing-world in which he lived, but he knew the difference between the past and the present, had a fairly accurate recollection of the events of his life before the training centre, and, even within this nothing-world where the passage of time could not be measured, knew that there was an extensive period of then before the immediate now. During that period of then many familiar voices had spoken to him, but now his buddy Geoff did not speak, nor did Bernadette, nor did his father, nor Kate. Only his mother spoke, with long gaps between, and even when she was close to him and seemed to speak directly to him, there were spaces between the sentences, and much of what she said was like a letter written to a stranger.

The nurses spoke (he knew now that they were nurses) and their voices were of frequent occurrence, far more frequent than his mother, but the nurses spoke mainly to each other, and if to him then as to an inanimate contrary thing, difficult to handle and of inferior workmanship.

In fact the patient, David Piper, was not particularly difficult to handle. He was a healthy object, although vegetative, his brain stem undamaged, and although nobody, not even his mother, any longer believed that he would regain consciousness, there was no reason why he should not continue to live for many months, even years, perhaps decades, given the level of nursing care he presently enjoyed. His breathing had never been interrupted; he had never had to be put on a respirator, so there had never been any question of turning it off. His heart pumped, his blood circulated, his kidneys functioned, so did his liver, pancreas and other organs. He was fed a liquid formula of concentrated proteins, minerals and vitamins through a very narrow nasal gastric tube, and although this tube did sometimes become clogged, that was the nature of the equipment, not a fault in him. He urinated through a catheter running up his penis into the bladder, and (since his diet contained no solids) shat infrequently, a thin diarrhoea into nappies which were regularly changed. Every two hours his body had to be turned so as to avoid bed-sores, but this was not difficult, since the feeding-tube was taped to the side of his nose, the catheter to the side of his leg, and he was not overweight. Whenever he was turned he farted, and the nurses complained about that.

The patient, Piper, continued to be something of a mystery to the neurologist. There was no justification for the continued use of expensive neurological equipment to monitor a brain which merely persisted in a vegetative state, but all the same it was hard to resist taking a look from time to time, since the patterns of activity were so very odd. The PET scan showed a pattern which was totally new to the neurologist, neither normal nor the pattern of any known mental illness, while the electroencephalograph indicated the steady pulsing of delta and theta waves one might expect to find but with sudden bursts of inexplicable alpha activity which did not appear to affect the patient corporeally in any way.

The signals were stronger now, more confused and more confusing, no longer clusters of two and three, but two clusters of two and a singleton, and within one of the groups of two there was disharmony. Mostly what he received was still generalised emotion – anxiety often, anger, fear, a kind of relaxation of tension for a while and even happiness; without knowing what it was, he picked up some of the joyful urgency of Arwen's first coupling with Carrie Baines, and the nurses found an emission of semen in his urine-bottle and wondered at it.

Sometimes there were flashes of vision and of sounds which were definite and particular – a mouth opening wide, an interior voice crying, 'Why? Why?', the fingers of two hands seen clenching and unclenching in a flyblown mirror. He did not know what the flashes meant, but the emotions which went with them were not pleasant. They were not like the complaining voices of the nurses or his mother's uncomfortable bulletins of family news. All those came from outside and were now beginning to be fainter and difficult to hear. The signals were from inside. They did not have to force a way through the thickening exterior air, but were received direct.

Attlee and Cape found an attic flat in Gloucester, one large room with bed and sofa-bed, a kitchen alcove and shared toilet and bathroom on the floor below. The bath-water was heated by a gas appliance totally new to them called a 'geyser', which had to be fed with money, and erupted into noisy flames whenever the hot tap was turned on: a notice on the wall of the bathroom warned bathers of the danger of asphyxiation, though nothing was said about what one must do to avoid it. There was a gas-fire in the living-area, with a coin-meter which ate shillings at an amazing rate, and another meter on the wall outside the door which also had to be fed with coins to provide electricity for light and power: the TV set had its own coin-meter. Clearly those Brits who occupied furnished accommodation during the winter months needed to keep themselves well provided with shillings and must often be cold during extended bank-holidays.

One window faced west. The view was all sky, no trees or buildings between the volunteers and the Atlantic East Satellite. They could resume communication with Washington, and did. To operate the radio was extremely simple. All they had to do was to open the suitcase. The lid acted as an aerial and they spoke directly into a telephone hand-set. Six digits put them into the Marisat system, three more scrambled the voices, seven for the number required and Bob's-your-uncle, a telephone rang in the Operations Room of the British government-in-exile. Alloway had not kept the six o'clock appointment, but that was not yet a worry: no doubt he would turn up. His title of 'radio operator' was a misnomer. Both Cape and Attlee could operate the radio, but Alloway was the mechanic; if it failed, only he could repair it.

The resumed contact caused both relief and perturbation in the

Operations Room. Why was the O & I Group asking them for targets? The volunteers should already have been informed of appropriate targets by their contacts in the Resistance.

'It seems that there isn't a Resistance as such. Just a few nutters who have already been locked up.'

'Then who's been hiding them this last month?'

'They'd rather not say.'

'What' is not a word which can easily be uttered slowly, but the CIGS managed it. The expression in his eyes lowered the temperature in the room by two degrees centigrade. He was like a Baked Alaska in reverse, blue ice without and hot meringue within. 'Make it an order.'

'I'm disinclined to make it an order, sir. I have the feeling that they might be tempted to disobey.'

'Why?'

'Paying a debt, I think.'

In fact Cape had put his hand over the mouthpiece of the telephone and said to Attlee, 'If you tell them, I shall walk out of that door and not come back. I'll get a job through the war, and make my own way home when it's over.' In Cape's view, any information, however classified under whatever system of security, sooner or later became disseminated. They had an obligation to protect the monks, as they themselves had been protected, and Cape intended to honour it. Also it would save them from having to report the matter of Alloway's temporary absence.

'Very well. We won't push it.' The Operations Section knew that they could not ask the CIA for targets because they could not admit that there was no resistance movement as such in Britain. The CIA had its own sources, such as they were, and must have known about the loonies being locked up, but had neglected to inform the Brits. It was probable that the CIA people were already laughing at them. They would laugh on the other side of their faces when news came from the Attack Group.

What had happened to the Attack Group? Should the O & I Group be ordered to find out? But how would they do so? So many precautions had been taken to keep the two groups separate.

There was that business of the inadequate documentation. Could the Attack Group already have been caught and killed or even turned? Could the O & I Group have been turned? Had this unsatisfactory report of theirs, made after a long break in communication, asking for orders and refusing information about their recent whereabouts, been set up by German Intelligence? No. Unlikely. It is less easy to turn an agent when communication is by voice. Messages in morse are easy to fake, but the human voice gives itself away. Young Attlee was not an actor: he was the apotheosis of straight behaviour. Nevertheless they would do well to have the tapes analysed by a trustworthy shrink.

Pending confirmation by the shrink, it was probably safe to assume that the O & I Group had not been turned. As for Sinclair and Parry-Jones, if they had been captured their capture would have been used for purposes of propaganda, since there was no point in trying to turn them when they were not in contact with Washington. Same if they had been killed; their bodies would have been put on show as sacrificial victims of the so-called 'Free British government', the crazed power-hungry puppets who were being manipulated by the Pentagon for its own evil purposes. Therefore Operations Section could safely assume that the Attack Group had not been turned either, that they had solved the documentation problem and were at large and on the loose. So what the bloody hell was holding them up?

After discussion it was decided that the O & I Group should be ordered to proceed to London, search for the Attack Group through Resistance channels (what channels? Never mind: find some: do it), and assist them to achieve the object of their mission (which was? Don't ask – classified on a need-to-know basis). The O & I Group's role in this operation would be only to assist and support. It would have no command function: the Attack Group had its own orders and was authorised to act independently (translation: for political reasons Attlee held the higher rank, but Sinclair and Parry-Jones were better soldiers). The Intelligence Officer who was required to transmit this order began to feel that there were advantages to communication in morse after all. The human voice talks back.

Sinclair and Parry-Jones loaded the bicycles and their suitcases into the back of an old van, squashed into the front with Jack and were driven out of London. There were more suitcases now. Even the baskets on the handlebars of their bicycles contained an overflow of underwear and aftershave.

They left the main road between Henley and Marlow and drove uphill along lanes so narrow that two vehicles meeting could not pass each other and passing places had been constructed at intervals of fifty metres. Uphill and down and precious little on the flat: this was not cycling country. Jack seemed to know the road well. They drove through beech trees and came to a village in a valley with a windmill on the hill above it. They drove on beyond the village and left the road for a metalled track which took them a short way into woods and then ended in a circle of gravel with a battered sign reading CARS HERE. They wheeled the cycles and carried the suitcases along a muddy winding path further into the woods until they reached a clearing in which stood a small cottage of flintstone and slate with a patch of garden at front and back and an outdoor privy.

Arwen said, 'Who builds a cottage in the middle of the woods except a witch?' and Jack explained that it had been a gamekeeper's cottage in the days when the land had belonged to some big estate, but the estate had not survived the death of one son in Norway, the other in North Africa. The land had been sold in parcels during the fifties and the big house had become a Convalescent Home, which it still was, although it now specialised in what were called 'addictive disorders', which broadly speaking meant drugs, booze and food – patients had been seen at the village fête, their jaws sewn together with silver wire, weeping over the home-made cakes at the Women's Institute stall.

Jack left. They explored their new home. The exploration did not take long. One large room and a kitchen downstairs, two bedrooms up. The floor downstairs was of quarry tiles over stone, upstairs of polished wood; there was a tin bath in the kitchen. But the cottage was provided with mains water, electricity, a telephone, comfortable armchairs and a sofa, well-sprung beds and a well-stocked larder with a fridge and freezer. There were books, a television set and a tape-deck with a catholic selection of tapes from Mantovani to Monteverdi. The tin bath and outdoor privy seemed peccant to the volunteers, a self-consciously eccentric gesture towards the rustic life, but they supposed they could live with it.

An hour and a half by bicycle to Windsor. They would be away for whole days often. They found a loose floorboard on the landing, but decided to leave it as a decoy. Instead they prised up a board in Sinclair's bedroom, hid the two Ingram machine guns, the grenades and the plastic explosive in the gap beneath, replaced the board securely and covered it with a rug. They would only have to lift it again once.

Carrie Baines was to meet them in Windsor next day. Unbeknownst to them, she was under orders to delay their project. Like many a heroine of romantic fiction Carrie was torn between love and duty. She packed an overnight bag and sandwiches for three, put her bicycle on the train and met Arwen on the steps of the public library.

'Ian's at the post office, putting some money into his savings book.' The volunteers had been issued before they left the US with five thousand marks each in fifty-mark notes, consecutively numbered and, as they had discovered, printed in Germany; it was dangerous stuff to flash around. As part of their new identities, Dorothy had provided both her nephews with post office savings books, issued in Torrington, each with a balance of 500 marks which they had repaid her. The rest of their money was to be laundered little by little into these accounts at discreet intervals at different post offices and never more than 200 marks at a time.

Ian Sinclair stood in the queue at the post office and brooded. From Dorothy's house they had visited Windsor three times to reconnoitre; this was their fourth visit and they were no further forward. They very much wished to question the mice, had asked for a meeting and had been politely put off. They still knew nothing about the administrative and domiciliary arrangements of the Reichsprotektor and his staff in Britain. Dorothy did not know, or said she did not. Such matters, she told them, were not the concern of a District Nurse; she had enough to do keeping up with the whims and fantods of the Ministry of Health and the various charitable societies for which she worked. And Carrie knew no more than everyone knew which was that the Secretariat was based in Windsor

Castle, and that ordinary people had no contact with it because everything was done through the British Parliament. Carrie supposed that the tradespeople of Windsor itself must know where and how the Germans lived. Arwen and Ian would have to ask about. Discreetly.

They were under orders to keep their mission secret, but the mice had guessed it at once. Now Dorothy and Jack knew, and Carrie, and the whole circle of those who worked with the mice would probably know, yet about the activities and purpose of the mice Sinclair and Parry-Jones knew only what they were permitted to know, that the mice helped and sheltered people on the run. The volunteers had been sent to organise the mice and to command their assistance, but the mice were organising them and gave them only what assistance they wished to give, which was to wrap them in cotton wool and try to keep them out of sight. Even Carrie – what was she but comforts for the troops? They were being treated like children, and he would stand for it no longer. He had reached the head of the queue and stepped forward to pay four new fifty-mark notes into his savings account.

'What you been up to, dear? Robbing a bank?'

'Just about.'

'Long way from home, aren't you?'

'I've had TB. I'm convalescing.'

'Oh!' The counter clerk moved back a little in her high chair, stamped Sinclair's book rapidly and passed it back to him. That was the reason for the TB, of course. It frightened people, so they wouldn't get too close.

They sat on a bench by the river to eat their sandwiches. Sinclair said, 'I've come to a decision. I'm sick of all this pissing about. Bloody gamekeeper's cottages! Bicycles! Picnics in the park!' He bit angrily into a sandwich and a mixture of chopped apple and herring with sour cream squirted into his lap. Carrie closed her eyes. Ham would have been safer, cheese and chutney more usual, but a sudden access of love for Arwen had tempted her into fantasy. Sinclair said, 'We're not gentlemen amateurs: we're professionals. We've got a job to do and we should get on with it. We'll move our gear here to Windsor, rent a room and apply for a job in the Castle.'

Alarm. Was he serious or was this just petulance? Dorothy would have known, and dealt with it in her comfortable no-nonsense way, but Carrie was a little afraid of Sinclair who was too intellectual, too sharp for her, unlike Arwen who knew a lot, particularly about Wales, but was not sharp at all, at least not to Carrie. She said, 'You can't. You'd have to be vetted. Your identities won't stand up. They'd ask questions in Devonshire.'

'Okay. We'll watch outside the Castle. All day – days on end if we have to. We'll see what tradesmen's vans go in and out regularly and get a job with one of them.'

'You can't do that either. You've got TB.'

'We'll make a miraculous recovery.'

'They'd send you back to your local Employment Office in Devon. You're agricultural workers; it's a reserved occupation.'

'Shit!' Carrie breathed again. She was temperamentally unsuited to manipulation and her relief showed. Sinclair thought, *One more push will do it.* He said, 'You'd better go back to London tonight and tell those bloody mice that unless we get some positive information, we'll do something spectacularly silly which will almost certainly lead to our being caught.'

'I thought I was going back to the cottage with you tonight.'

Arwen said, '*I* thought she was.'

Carrie said, 'I'll phone Dorothy from the cottage. Then you can listen to my end of the conversation.'

The front door of the cottage was open, and there was a middle-aged police constable in the kitchen with a teenage girl, drinking tea. Carrie said, 'Great! Biccies! I'm starving.'

'Mr Ian Sinclair and Mr Arwen Sinclair?' Dorothy had not been happy at allowing Arwen to keep his own first name in his new identity as her nephew, but had decided that it was safer, since he was accustomed to answering to it, and Sinclair to using it.

'Arrwen. We pronounce the "r".'

'Our . . . win. Very good. I'll try to remember that.' The constable took a notebook from his top pocket and wrote in it. 'Our . . . win.' The volunteers had not brought biscuits with them to the cottage and there had been none in the kitchen cupboard. Had the

127

police brought their own? 'I just called in,' the constable said. 'Mrs Brooking always gives me a note of visitors, as she's required to do by law, and I've come round to inspect your particulars.'

'Bobby, you're putting it on,' the teenage girl said. 'He puts it on horribly, particularly in spring.'

'You button your lip, my girl,' the policeman said cheerfully, 'or I'll put *you* on. Identity cards?' Sinclair and Parry-Jones handed them to him. 'Vacation certificates?'

'Sickness. Convalescence. We've both had tuberculosis.' That produced the usual reaction. The policeman put the documents down on the table quickly. 'You needn't worry. We're not infectious any more. We've stopped spitting blood.'

'I'll just make a note of the numbers and you can have them back.' He sat at the table and copied the numbers without touching the documents. Carrie took out her own identity card and work certificate and gave them to him. 'And I'm not sick at all. I work for a travel firm in London, but I may be spending the night here from time to time.' The constable glanced at them and returned them to her. 'Staying long?' he said to Sinclair.

'Indefinitely.'

'In . . . def . . . in . . . itely. Agricultural workers, eh? Farming? You've an educated way of speaking for a farm labourer, sir, if you don't mind me saying so.'

'We're gentlemen farmers.'

'That would explain it. We've got a lot of those around here.' He drained his mug of tea and stood up. 'Well! Duty, duty must be done. No need to take up any more of your time: I'll be on my way. Enjoy your stay. You'll find we've very pure air in the Chilterns – the lungs of London, I always say. I won't shake hands.' He stopped at the kitchen door. 'Our . . . win. Devonshire name, is it?'

'Celtic.'

'Like Uncle Tom Cobbley, I expect. Bill Brewer . . . Jan Stewer. We used to sing that at school when I was a lad.' And he was gone. They heard a motor-cycle start up at the back of the house. He had left the teenage girl behind. Should they run after him and try to pop her on the pillion? Carrie added more hot water to the teapot.

'Don't worry about him taking notes,' the girl said. 'They don't go anywhere.'

'What happens to them?'

'He enters them in a ledger. Fills one, starts another: he's got dozens. I've been polishing the floorboards upstairs so I had to move the rug. You'd better dirty down that place where you've taken a board up unless you want people to notice.'

Arwen said, 'What did you mean about him putting it on?'

'There's not many men in the village so he gets pressganged by the Drama Group. He always has to play the policeman. It's very muddling for him.'

'But he really is a policeman?'

'Oh, yes: *the* policeman – the village policeman, our one and only. We don't get much crime around here, so the job's a bit of a sinecure, but of course it doesn't lead to promotion. My grandad wants to see you when you can manage it. Tomorrow morning will do.'

Peter Alloway never seriously considered keeping the rendezvous with Attlee and Cape at the bookstall. His rejection was instinctive. Those two were trouble, the mission was trouble; because of it he had done something so terrible that his mind was trying to block it out, yet it must not be blocked out but seen clearly for what it was, and its effects calculated so that they might be avoided.

He needed to be alone, to take stock, to get his mind together. London might be a good place to get lost for a while. He already had a ticket to London bought for him by Pargeter. It had been clipped once, but would be valid from Swindon. Silly to buy another. Like the other volunteers Alloway had been issued with five thousand marks, and had spent very little of that money, but, as he had heard Attlee say so often, it would not last for ever.

He bought a return ticket from Swindon back to Gloucester, where he retrieved his rucksack from the left luggage locker. He was now a little overburdened with luggage. He dropped Pargeter's white cap into a litter bin. His knowledge of British geography was still weak, but he knew that London was to the south east, and he could remember the names of the towns to the west through which the three of them had cycled on their journey from Wales. He found a local train for Ross-on-Wye standing at a further platform, boarded it, left the plaid jacket on the rack of an empty compartment, got off again and watched the train pull out with the plaid jacket still in place. The suitcase, with his rucksack, was manageable. He did not wish to leave it or to send it anywhere until he had been able to inspect the contents.

He arrived at Paddington that evening and found a cheap hotel near the station in Sussex Gardens. This was the first test of his new identity card. It passed. The woman at the reception desk looked at it cursorily, noted the number, and gave it back to him. 'How long you staying?'

'Just the night.' It would be safer to move about. He remembered that there was a condition: he had to find work within fourteen days. There would be time to think about that tomorrow.

'Room Thirty-five. Bath and toilet at the end of the corridor next to the fire escape. Here's your key.' The room was small. There was just space for a single bed, straight chair, a desk-cum-dressing-table under the window, a washbasin and a wardrobe. He ran some water in the washbasin to wash his face and hands. There was a faint smell of urine. Male occupants of the room, he assumed, did not bother to walk along the corridor when they wished to piss during the night.

He sat on the bed and examined the contents of the suitcase. Two pairs of pyjamas, one dirty, one recently washed probably by Pargeter himself. Underwear, socks and handkerchiefs, mostly dirty, the rest similarly washed. A woollen pullover with no maker's mark, probably hand-knitted. Four shirts, all dirty, all clearly mass-market garments with the label Deutsche Hemdenschimmer. A wedding photograph in a leather case: Pargeter had taken it with him into protective detention but had not been allowed to display it, at least during his period at the abbey.

Peter Alloway looked closely at the photograph. Would it speak to him? Pargeter had been married in his late twenties or early thirties, already a little overweight, a man of substance. His wife looked younger and rather less confident. It had been a white wedding. The men wore grey top-hats; the women's hats were heavy with imitation flowers. Pargeter stood next to his new wife on the steps of the

130

church, surrounded by friends and relations, daring the photographer not to get everybody in.

There was nothing in the suitcase which could identify Pargeter. No laundry marks. In the detention centre he had done his own washing; previously his wife must have done it. Could Alloway reasonably assume that there would be nothing on the body to identify him either? Dental work? – but there is no way of linking a corpse with a dentist unless one already has a fair idea who that corpse might have been in life. Pargeter would not be missed. The psychiatrists were finished with him, but since the Re-eds were not allowed any outside communication during the process of their re-education, his wife would know nothing of his crafty progress towards discharge. Most husbands would have run to a telephone the moment they were outside the abbey gates, but not Pargeter. *If you phone first it's an anti-climax.* He had not told his wife he was on his way home, so he would not be reported as missing.

He had fallen between the chinks. The police would be presented with the body of an unknown pervert who had been murdered by some hysterical young man encountered on the train to whom his advances were unwelcome. The white hat and plaid jacket had been successfully dispersed. Only the knickerbockers, should they have been made to measure or ordered from some specialist manufacturer, might lead the police to Kevin Pargeter. Alloway would have to take a chance on those knickerbockers.

He went out to look for a cheap meal and found one both cheap and nasty in a snack bar on the Edgware Road. He took a scenic route back to his hotel, and in Titchborne Row came upon a notice in a shop-window informing the public that the Women's Voluntary Service would receive cast-off clothing for people in need on weekdays from 10 a.m. to 5 p.m. This was better than litter-bins. He would return in the morning. It would be a charitable act, as well as prudent, to disperse Pargeter's underwear and warm woollen pullover among the needy.

The pink and blue neon lights of the hotel sign shone unremittingly through the unlined curtains of Room Thirty-five. Alloway lay awake in the single bed, listening to the noises of the street outside. All round the vicinity of Paddington station, spilling

by way of Praed Street into Sussex Gardens, women were offering
what was presumably a voluntary service, though not to the needy.
He heard car doors slamming and engines revving, the clicking of
stiletto heels along the pavement, voices raised in argument, men
laughing and a woman shouting, 'Bastards! You bastards!' Well, he
had not expected to sleep. He must make plans: there was so much to
plan. Could he return to the abbey? Would they accept him? No, he
was in mortal sin, and dared not confess, even to Father Philip. He
needed a friend and knew, or thought he knew, of another person
who would also need a friend.

The hotel's breakfast egg was still wet from the poaching, the
sausage grey outside and pink within, the toast both old and cold, the
coffee grainy with milk that had little bits floating on the top; there
was jelly marmalade in a tiny plastic container which resisted
opening. Peter Alloway remembered the snack bar on the previous
evening and the buffet car of the train. Did all Brits at a cerain level of
income live like this? When they married, was it mainly so as to get
away from the likes of Sussex Gardens and the Edgware Road? He
paid his bill without complaint and returned to Titchborne Row
where a middle-aged lady in a mist of Chanel accepted the contents
of the suitcase without comment.

The rucksack contained his own clothing, which he would need.
There was still the problem of what to do with the gun, ammunition
and plastic explosive. Too many complications in that one; it would
have to wait. Next he must lose the empty suitcase. *Tube to Victoria*:
he knew what the tube was now; it was the subway. At Victoria
station he examined the timetables of the Southern Railway with
care. Many trains south seemed to go by way of Clapham Junction;
the routes diverged after that. He bought a ticket, left the train at
Clapham Junction and allowed it to carry the empty suitcase on to –
where? – was it Hythe? – Southampton? Someone somewhere
would find it useful. He waited on the platform for the next train to
Eastbourne.

I'll take a taxi from the station. He took a taxi from the station,
showing the taxi-driver the card Pargeter had given him. 'Do you
know this house? I think it's just outside the town.' *National Trust
land, as a matter of fact*. 'It's on National Trust land, not far

132

from . . .' He could not remember the landmark the house was not far from. 'Beachy Head,' the taxi-driver said. 'I know where it is.'

They turned off the main road and followed a metalled track for about a mile. It ended at a group of four detached houses. He stopped the taxi at the first house, and paid the fare with a large tip to cover the inconvenience of having come so far out of town. 'I'll find it from here.' *Bound to be in the garden in this weather.* She was at the end of a lawn behind the house, on her knees with her back to him. *Creep up behind her. Hands over her eyes.* '*Guess who.*' Peter Alloway coughed to draw attention to himself, and she turned to face him, wondering at this tall young man on her lawn with his crumpled tweed jacket and enormous rucksack.

Alloway said, 'I'm sorry to disturb you. I'm Peter Alloway. I've come to give you news of Kevin.'

It was not so much the knickerbockers – which were undistinguished as knickerbockers go – but the list of names in the back pocket that interested the police. Pargeter's body had not been found during the journey to Paddington because it had slipped forward as Alloway left the toilet and the heels had ended up against the door, leading passengers wishing to use the toilet to believe that it was occupied in spite of its 'Vacant' sign, and they had used the one opposite or gone angrily elsewhere. The train had arrived in Paddington one hour and a half later and been turned round for the journey back to Cheltenham. Again, passengers wishing to use that toilet had been disinclined to push, and by the time the train arrived at Cheltenham rigor mortis had begun to set in. By next morning the late Kevin Pargeter was like a metal bar pressed tight against that door; no passenger, however great the need, could have forced it open. He was eventually discovered two days later, when beginning to soften, by a cleaner, and taken out of service for forensic examination. The police found the remnants of potato salad still spattered in Pargeter's face particularly puzzling.

In death faces change and are further changed by the processes of photography and reprography. Nevertheless the police followed procedures. Pargeter's beard had continued to grow after death; they shaved him. A cosmetician plumped up the inside of his cheeks with cotton wool and applied make-up to the outside: it was intelligent guesswork and took no account of what the police could not know, which was that he had been kept indoors for several months, so they overdid the suntan. Then they photographed his face, omitting the wound in his neck, the sight of which might have diverted the attention of anyone asked to make an identification, and showed copies of the photograph to railway staff along the line.

They were not asking for any great feat of memory. By the state of rigor, the rectal temperature, the amount of bacterial growth in the potato salad and so many other indicators they knew the day he was killed and that it must have happened in the late morning or early afternoon somewhere between Cheltenham and Ealing Broadway. The question was simple enough, 'Do you remember seeing this man, who would probably have been wearing knickerbockers, either boarding the Cheltenham Flyer at your station last Thursday or as a passenger on the train itself?'

But they did not know about the white cap and the plaid jacket. The casual observer notices the white cap not the face beneath the cap, the plaid jacket not the knickerbockers below the jacket. A porter at Gloucester thought he remembered a man in knicker-bockers boarding a train on that day, but not this man; he could be positive; it was a much younger man. The ticket-inspector on the Cheltenham Flyer remarked that one could not tell, unless one made a point of looking, whether a seated passenger with a table in front of him was wearing knickerbockers or not, but there might be something about the nose, while the buffet-car attendant thought there might be something about the chin. A ticket-collector at Reading had a vague memory of a man wearing a full beard of naval cut and a short coat of soft leather above knickerbockers who had left the station on Thursday morning after the arrival of the 9.50 from Basingstoke. A full naval beard was added to Pargeter's likeness and the ticket-collector's identification became positive. It was certainly the same man, who must have shaved off his beard, returned to Reading station during the ticket-collector's lunch-break and boarded the Cheltenham Flyer to Paddington. The murderer would have purloined the black leather coat. Unfortunately no other member of the station staff at Reading remembered such a man.

There was another puzzling aspect to this murder. Forensic believed that the wound in the throat had been made after death. It was hard to be sure, but injuries to the trachea, the pre-frontal area of the brain and to the vertebrae had been quite sufficient to kill the man, and the removal of his shoe to break the mirror must have been done afterwards. This was not to say that the dead man was not a pervert – the glass would have been broken to obtain blood to leave the message – but where would some casual pick-up have learned how to kill a man unarmed and with such economy of effort? The police had to face the fact that there might be a military aspect to this murder, which was bound to lead to trouble.

Meanwhile there was the list of names, all of people named Alloway living in Lidlicote, a village up on the Berkshire Downs. Some of these Alloways had better take a look, not just at the photograph but at the man himself laid out on a sliding shelf in the mortuary.

Scotland Yard was in charge of the case. It had to be so, since no one knew in what county the man had been killed and the Transport Police were not accustomed to dealing with murder. Two officers from the yard took the A4 to Newbury, then north on the A34, leaving it to climb to the Ridgeway, where cars were parked in a row, and picnics spread, and in the distance the serious walkers in baggy shorts were strung out like pilgrims. No picnic for the police; they would stop at a pub if there was time. They drove through West Ilsley, turning this way and that along minor roads until they reached the village. 'Good horse country, this!' said the Chief Inspector, who fancied a flutter. 'Watch them on the Gallops from the road near Lambourn. It's not Newmarket, mind. Too gentrified. They lack the killer instinct.'

So it proved. The village was picturesque, all the old houses of the old village lovingly preserved, the modernisation hidden away, thatch (where there was thatch) brought from the reed-beds of East Anglia and renewed every seven years, slate (where there was slate) rescued at great expense from abandoned Baptist chapels or imported from Wales. In these houses lived comfortable people with comfortable families, some retired with comfortable pensions, others still employed in comfortable and lucrative employment, mostly at a rather uncomfortable distance.

On the outskirts of the village were council houses where the remnants of the old village families now lived. Some of the men were agricultural workers; the women worked in the pub or cleaned house for the newcomers. Some were old, some on Assistance Benefit, some scratched a living from odd jobs of all sorts as and when they could find them. Their houses were small, built of cheap yellow brick with doors and windows of standard sizes painted in approved colours, a tiny garden at the front, a shed and strip of vegetables at the back, every aspect of occupancy controlled by bye-law, but nevertheless, as the comfortable people often told their visitors and each other, 'in keeping': they did not detract.

There were four Alloway families in the village: they were among the oldest of the new villagers. Walter Alloway (seventy-seven) had retired from legal practice, his wife had died, and he lived in a small self-sufficient apartment in the house of his daughter Cecily (forty-eight) who had married a doctor, James Dart, and produced two teenage girls, Sarah and Rachel. Julian Alloway (fifty) Walter's son, once the junior partner of Alloway & Alloway, solicitors in Oxford, had succeeded his father, and had since taken his own son Justin (twenty-five) into partnership. Justin, so far married only a year, had not yet produced a son to become the next junior partner, but he was working on it. Stephen Alloway (sixty-four) Walter's brother, who occupied the old rectory with his wife Janet and unmarried daughter Grace (thirty-one) was an accountant with an office in Newbury. His married son Piers (thirty-four) lived in London and worked for the Ministry of Agriculture and Fisheries. This was as close as the Alloways, or any other of the new villagers, had ever got to agriculture.

The Alloways looked carefully, as they were asked to do, at the photograph brought to Lidlicote by the police. They had no idea, none of them had the slightest idea, who this person murdered on a train might be. They did not know and could not guess how he might have come into possession of the list of their names and addresses. They had nothing to hide, were not and could never be potential subjects of blackmail, there was no possible reason why their names should be on any list more sinister than a Christmas card list. Reluctantly Walter, Stephen and James Dart accompanied the two police officers to the mortuary in Bristol where the corpse was still being held. One by one they were taken to the refrigerated tray: each, one by one, shook his head. They had never seen the man before. He had never been either a client of Walter or Stephen or a patient of James.

Yes, it was odd, it was extremely odd that the man should be in possession of such a list. No, they could not explain the writing of the word 'pervert' on the mirror. It was clearly nothing to do with them; there had never been any suggestion of that kind of thing in their family, nor (Stephen felt bound to point out) could any link with homosexual perversion explain the inclusion on the list of the names of the wives and his daughter Grace. The list appeared to be what it almost certainly was, a Christmas list, but the Alloways could not understand why a complete stranger should wish to send them seasonal cards or presents.

Could it be intended as some form of introduction? Perhaps, but the Alloways were not expecting, had not been warned of some friend of a friend about to visit them, and one would expect letters of introduction, not a list of names. Could it be a list some criminal might carry, a list of people possessing valuable property, easily portable, pictures, say, or jewellery, antiques, gold and silver objects? No. The Alloways were comfortable, not seriously rich. Many of the families of Lidlicote owned objects choicer than theirs.

They were driven home, indignant and innocent, the two professional men fretting at a day wasted and appointments cancelled. Conferring afterwards the two police officers agreed that the whole case continued to be a puzzle. Local police sources confirmed that the Alloways were model citizens, a force for good within the community: Janet Alloway had been for many years a Justice of the Peace. It was highly unlikely that any member of the family, let alone all of them, should have criminal connections. So why did the dead man keep the list in the back pocket of his knickerbockers and why should it have been the only piece of paper of any sort found in his possession?

The girl's grandfather had asked to be called 'Cakehole'. His name was Harry Simnel. 'Simnel . . . Cake. Get it?' The lads in the Auxunit had always called him 'Cakehole'.

It seemed to Sinclair and to Parry-Jones that England was full of the most extraordinary characters. Cakehole! It was clear that their use of the old man's nickname would be a symbol of mutual trust, an equivalent to the mingling of blood. They would have to bring themselves to do it.

The girl earned pocket-money from Mrs Brooking for keeping an eye on the cottage and coming in to clean, usually between visitors. June was the month of preparation for exams – something called School Certificate. Failure doomed a sixteen-year-old to menial exployment in later life: success offered the possibility of further education culminating in another exam, Higher School Certificate, which could take one on to college and professional status – or at least to marriage within the professional class. The girl, Juliet, doggedly revising algebra, had missed cleaning up before the volunteers' arrival, and had sneaked in to get it done while they were out. She had noticed the place where the board had been lifted and had told her grandfather, with whom she lived. He had come with her to the cottage, looked beneath the board, replaced it and warned her to say nothing to anyone of what they had found until he had been able to talk to the two young men.

He said, 'Don't tell me no lies and I'll believe you.' He was predisposed to believe them. One by one the lads of the Auxunit had died off, leaving only him. For fifty years he had believed that his skills and his training would not be wasted. Some day the call would come. Now it had.

In 1939 he had been of an age and fit to fight, but had been discouraged from joining up. He was a blacksmith: it was a reserved occupation. Even in those days a smith had less to do with horses than with machines. Cakehole alone, his skill, his empathy with metal and oil, piston and sump, battery and cable, kept the elderly farm machinery of the Hambleden Valley in operation; he could not be spared to go as a soldier.

He had joined the LDV, later the Home Guard, but that was nothing – playing silly games. Then, in the summer of 1940, Colonel Gubbins, back from the débâcle in Norway, had been instructed to create an underground army, Britain's last line of defence, to come into action when the Germans invaded. Simnel's name had been put forward by his Commanding Officer, only too readily since he found the man's inadequately concealed scorn difficult to bear. Special Branch officers came to the village, asking questions. They were vetting Simnel but had not been told for what, so their questions were general and the villagers thought he had been in trouble, and spoke up for him. The reports being so good, he had gone for interview to the War Office in London, signed the Official Secrets Act and – once the harvest was in and before the autumn ploughing began – was sent for training in Coleshill, where he was taught the use of explosives, sabotage, booby-traps and unarmed combat, promoted sergeant and returned to his own house, his old job, the secret leader of an underground patrol. There had been six patrols in the Chilterns, each of six men led by a sergeant, and although they had a lieutenant as Group Leader, that was mainly an administrative responsibility. The patrols worked independently: no commissioned officer came between Sergeant Simnel and his lads.

'We operated a cell system, you see.'

Sinclair and Parry-Jones did see. It was their own system, their own training.

'I knew it,' Cakehole said. What had disposed him to trust them from the beginning was finding a Fairbairn Field Service Fighting Knife just like his own under the board with the rest of their armoury.

The lads of the Auxunit had patrolled, they had exercised, they had brought themselves to a peak of efficiency and fitness, the whole operation kept secret, even from their wives (some of whom believed in consequence that they were spending nights away from home adulterously). They knew that the war was going badly; they were ready to be used. Then the Royal Family had been moved secretly out of the country, the Government had done a bunk to America, such units of the Royal Navy and Royal Air Force as could manage it had been ordered to make for neutral ports and airfields, and the army had capitulated unconditionally. The Germans arrived, not as invaders to be fought openly on the beaches by the Home Guard, then covertly by the Auxunits after those incompetent sods had got themselves slaughtered, but as a victorious occupying force, and there had been nothing for Colonel Gubbins' last-ditch line of defence to do but to destroy every piece of paper which might indentify them, burn their battledress, bury their weapons and pretend that they had never left civvie street.

Under the Occupation the lads of Sergeant Simnel's patrol had avoided each other as far as they could, perhaps for reasons of safety, perhaps because they all felt a little dirty, felt that somehow they should have defied the orders and fought on. He had turned them into a machine, since machines were what he knew best, and now they were just spare parts lying about and rusting. Over the years one by one they had died off, the Group Leader too, the spunk gone out of them. Cakehole had not rusted; he had kept himself oiled and ready for action. He had not even burned his battledress. It was with his weaponry, his explosives, booby-traps and incendiaries, all stored in the secret Operational Base built by himself and the lads beneath the outdoor privy of the cottage. The Fairbairn dagger he kept with him at home.

There was a proper water closet in the privy, connected to the septic tank, not a mere thunder-box. Beside it was a cabinet of stripped pine varnished with polyurethane, on top of which there were back numbers of *Picture Post*, Trollope's *Barchester Towers* in the Everyman edition and a toilet roll. 'We move this.' They moved the cabinet. 'Stand back a bit.' The old man pressed against the floorboards, and smoothly, instantly, without a squeak or groan, one side of a trap-door moved downwards, the other upwards, and they could see the room below.

'Counterweight. Beautiful workmanship. Locks from the inside. Jump down.' They did so. There was headroom even for a tall man. Cakehole followed them, landing neatly on his toes. Above them the trap-door returned to its former secondary function of being part of the floor of the privy. Cakehole struck a match and lit a paraffin lamp hanging from the ceiling. It lit at once. It was clear that every object and article of furniture within the Operational Base was maintained to be ready for immediate use. Sinclair wondered how the old man managed it when Mrs Brooking had a long let. Answer: she would not accept long lets.

Cakehole reached up at full stretch to the trap-door and pushed the bolt across. 'Unbolt to leave. Tug on the rope.' A rope with a wooden handle was attached to the opposite side of the door. 'Stand on that box and pull yourself up. We don't waste space on a ladder. And there's an emergency exit comes out in the woods, but that's for emergencies.'

'Doesn't it get damp in here?'

'Insulated walls, ventilation and drainage. Sleeps six.' There were six wooden bunk-beds in two tiers, each bunk with a sleeping-bag, and a wooden table with a bench and three wooden chairs. 'Radio.' There was an old-fashioned portable radio with an *art nouveau* facia which would have fetched money at a Collectors' Fair. 'Heat.' There was a paraffin heater with an enamel saucepan on top of it. 'Water tank with purification tablets. Bottled water in the cupboard. Tinned food – bully beef, beans, stew. Soup powder, milk powder, Marmite, cocoa, instant coffee, tea, sugar. Toilet in there. We joined up with the overflow from the one above so it all goes down to the septic tank. Rum.' There was a bottle in the cupboard, which he produced with a flourish. 'Want some?'

The liquid inside looked like treacle. 'It's rather early for us.'

'Right! Keep a clear head. Didn't expect you'd say Yes. Medicinal purposes really.' The bottle was half empty. 'Keeps the cold out.'

'It's a great place. You've done a great job.'

'You might need it. Built to be used. I'll show you the emergency exit, then we'll pull down the trap-door and leave the toilet at five-minute intervals in case anyone's watching.'

Anyone watching might have thought it odd to see three men leaving the privy separately at five-minute intervals when they had all gone in together, but the volunteers did not say so. They were disposed to cherish Cakehole. He was the only element of the Resistance they had so far encountered who seemed to approve of their mission and was eager to assist. 'Should have been done long ago,' he said. 'Put the cat among the pigeons and see what flies out. True colours would be my guess.'

They sat together at the kitchen table, where the large-scale Ordnance Survey Map was spread out among bread and cheese and pickles and bottled beer. They knew now that the Reichsprotektor lived with his family in a large and well-guarded mid-nineteenth-century manor house between Burchett's Green and White Waltham. Preceded by a motor-cycle escort, he was driven every day by his driver/bodyguard, a captain of the SS, to and from his office in Windsor Castle. They had gawped at the house through the lodge gates, a family party of two young men, an old man, a young woman and a girl, out on their bicycles with a picnic for a day in the country. They had asked if the house was open to the public, and been turned away by the soldiers at the gate. Then they had cycled off all together on the road back to Maidenhead, stopping where it grew steeper to help the old man wheel his cycle up the hill.

To Cakehole the assassination was not a problem of morality or politics, but only of logistics. 'It can't be a booby-trap operation,' he said, 'because we'll only have the one chance so we have to be certain, and booby-traps are *un*certain: that's the nature of the beast. And it can't be a wire-hawser-across the-road operation, first because it takes time to get the hawser into place and other motorists use that road and we might end up taking the roof off a Morris Minor and second because there'd be no time to get rid of it afterwards. No, what we want is something simple and flexible which can be easily aborted, makes nobody suspicious, and we clear up as we go along. We'd better begin by stealing an old open lorry and a few traffic cones. Do it in the Midlands or the North. We don't want to draw attention to ourselves before we have to.'

At the abbey, to the vexation of the psychiatric staff and the dismay of the monks, the Re-eds were deteriorating. Some refused food, were forcibly fed, yet wasted away. Some became confused, replying in vague and fanciful ways to the simplest factual questions. The senior psychiatrist diagnosed depression with, in the more severe cases, some indication of a regression towards catatonia, and dosed them with tetracyclics, increasing the dosage as their condition grew worse.

The consequent side-effects were interestingly diverse, ranging from schizophrenia in those already confused to liver damage and massively increased blood sugar with renal failure in the rest. Early in June the first Re-ed died, to be followed by other deaths of which two were suicides. The next-of-kin were informed: so was the Home

Office. Post-mortems were conducted. Everything was done in a proper manner. Nevertheless the abbot became increasingly concerned and so did the monks.

Luckily the British class and educational systems provided their own channels for the expression of concern upwards. Father Theodemar's contemporaries during his schooldays at Ampleforth had become widely disseminated in various positions of influence and eminence. After consulting the abbot he wrote privately to a friend in the Home Office.

'It never was a suicide mission. There'll be too much to do afterwards.' Arwen found that these days he shared his thoughts more readily with Carrie than with Sinclair; she was in every way a more receptive listener. 'Hit and run. We'll have the initiative. Pop up all over the place like the Scarlet Pimpernel.'

They were in the parish church, looking at the wall-paintings. The Church consisted of an early Norman tower with bits added in later centuries; the chancel was in two sections, like two Monopoly houses ochre-washed and pushed up against the tower. The murals, now faded and patchy, had been painted in the thirteenth century, plastered over in the seventeenth, uncovered and over-enthusiastically restored in the nineteen-thirties, with the touching-up removed in the nineteen-seventies. There was an iron stove (unlit on weekdays) with a scuttle of anthracite beside it and pews of dark wood, highly polished, crowded together, which would seat sixty at a crush. The pulpit was of oak, stained and magnificently carved; a notice beside it read, PLEASE DO NOT USE THE PULPIT AS IT IS INSECURE.

Arwen was fascinated by the church, and visited it often. It was so unlike his own father's church. This had an auditorium seating sixteen hundred, used for interdenominational services on Good Friday – only Catholics were excluded – and was part of a complex, all dedicated to the Almighty, in which there were conference and lecture rooms, a self-service restaurant, a cinema, play-rooms for the kiddies, and sheltered apartments for senior citizens at the eventide of their lives. He said, 'Shall we get married?'

'Who'd give us away?'

'Ah, there's the danger!' And they both began to giggle, soon helplessly, holding on to each other in case Carrie fell over, extracting every drop of juice from that indifferent pun. 'Any cause or just impediment?' It was no good, they could not stop, and a village woman who had looked in to refresh the flowers went away again, banging the heavy door of oak and iron behind her.

No sexual relationship had ever been like this before. Arwen had suffered the usual ·disadvantages of a religious upbringing, never knowing when or how or where to make his pass, jeans humiliatingly creamed after any close encounter. He still remembered with horror an inability to get to first base during a gang-bang in the back of a schoolmate's father's sedan – he had engaged the girl in *conversation*, would you believe? Then at university he had set himself to learn to do the thing properly, with theoretical advice from experienced sophomores and practical instruction by the wife of a professor of ergonomics. But it had not been like this, nothing like this, no real sharing, no joy.

For Sinclair life was not so joyful. He had bad dreams.

He dreamed of Ellie, once his wife, now two years dead. Two years, four months, some days – 13th February 1990: she had been dead before the ambulance arrived: they had phoned her parents first and then him. It was not an overdose, not in the usual sense. You can't overdose on hucks: that was what everybody said, so it had to be true: the worst that could happen is that you'd go through the wrong door. Hucks – huxleys, after Aldous Huxley whose books had popularised the drug among creative and open-minded people. Ellie's mind had been opened. She had died of fear.

She had said, 'You're so cold, you're so fucking cold. Why can't you lose your temper?' But he could not. He never lost his temper. Irritability, sarcasm, ironic detachment, even contempt, but never rage openly expressed. He could not. Ellie had been buried; Sinclair had insisted on that; she was afraid of fire. Her parents had paid for the funeral; there had been a supplement because of the hardness of the ground. He had stood apart from them all, and felt nothing but the cold.

In the church there had been a group of her friends on gilt chairs between the altar and the communion rail, a chamber group of strings and woodwinds and a soprano; they had placed her cello by an empty chair and an extra viola had taken the cello line. Pieces by Haydn and Corelli and then the Andante of the Schubert C Major Quintet as they left the church. Local people who had known her as a child had spoken; some had been asked to speak and some had been moved to pay a tribute. Sinclair had not been asked, nor had he been moved.

Did they hold him responsible? He had never taken hucks or any mind-opening drug, would never do so. The doors of perception, as far as Sinclair was concerned, would be opened by logic and empiricism or they could stay shut.

She had moved in groups, was happiest in groups, first among the country people who were her kin and her neighbours, then among the community of musicians. Both groups had their own ways, their own language, and he was not accustomed to those ways and did not speak those languages; they excluded him without – they would say –intending it. His own friends – hardly a group – people he had known at college – people he had met since – people one could talk to, exchange ideas with, they made allowances for Ellie. Perhaps it was sometimes a little obvious that they made allowances.

When they became lovers, he and Ellie had been a group of two, and thought that would take them on through marriage and a family, but it never does. She said, 'I didn't want to fall in love with you. You looked like Heathcliff in the movie. I was afraid of you.' What she meant was that she thought she had found another father, younger and better looking than her own. There was a natural authority in Sinclair, a sort of habit of command. He knew it and distrusted it, tried sometimes to repress it, but could not. She had found it at first reassuring, later overbearing.

And he? He had wanted to be in love – that was the first thing – and to have his love returned; he had wanted the state more than the person. Then, because his own mind was critical and analytic not creative, and he was dissatisfied with that and felt it to be a lack, he had wanted to 'have' – literally to have and to hold – a creative artist of his own, who would be his, known to be his, guarded and guided by Ian Sinclair. And, as he now recognised because his dreams were

145

telling him so, he had wanted his wife to be his daughter. So reasoned Sinclair, the self-analytical, lying alone during the long wakeful nights.

She had died of fear. Why? She had loving parents, a loving brother, loving friends. She had no habit of fear, no history of insecurity; she was, and had always been, in all relationships secure – except of course that *he* . . . that he, Ian, her husband, could not give her the warmth, could not easily express . . . did not actually feel, if he was honest, did not seem to be able to feel . . . Oh shit!

She had taken those fucking hucks, had first of all lain on the rug, her head on a cushion, listening to the music, seeing the patterns the music made, the coloured threads intertwining, entering the music, pulling it to her, pouring it over her, bathing in the colours and fabrics and the liquid warmth of it, and then . . . All this he knew. She had talked about it as it happened; her friends had enjoyed her initiation with her. Gerry had told him. And then . . . First the wanting to throw herself downstairs, out of the window – quite normal, almost usual; anyone might do that and it was the business of one's friends to stop one doing so, hold, hug, cuddle, talk one through. And then crouching, her back against a corner, foetal, trying to push herself inwards, compress herself into a nothing, an empty space. And all the time the weeping, the dreadful babble of sounds that were nearly words, and then the screaming, and then the silence and then . . . And then she was dead. It had taken them by surprise. They could not believe it. It had never happened before. They had telephoned for an ambulance to revive her, but she was already dead.

If he had been there, he supposed, he could have stopped it. If he had been there, it would never have started. It had started because he had not been there, increasingly had not been there, because he had reminded her that she had her own friends, her own career, and that they could not spend their whole married life in each others' pockets.

Bad dreams. He walked with a child, his daughter; they were together; he was in charge. At first they walked through familiar places, the streets of her home town or his, the campus, the woods, along the river bank, through snowscape or green fields. At first he knew the dreams for what they were, *his*: he could control them: he could make them happy.

146

Not so. Everything changed before he noticed and could prevent it. The streets became dark alleys slippery with vomit where only rats and winos lived, the campus a quagmire strewn with rubbish, barbed wire and the sharp edges of rusty metal; brambles, briar, rotting fungus and trailing ivy grew over the paths of the woods; there was blood and shit beneath the snow. And she . . . he could never save her. Sometimes, when they came for her, he was made to watch what they did to her, unable to move, offering to take her place (which was never allowed), taking revenge in various bloody ways afterwards, always too late. Sometimes she would leave him for some innocent reason and only for a while, but would not return, and he could not find her, knew that without him she would wander deeper into danger, increasingly afraid and calling his name, and he would search . . . search, going further and further away from the place where she would expect him to be waiting, becoming lost himself, unable to find either her or his own way back, always searching . . . imagining . . .

Usually the girl, his daughter, was Ellie; this was invariably so at the beginning of the dream. But sometimes, just as the surroundings changed without his noticing, so the girl herself changed, and she became Juliet Simnel, grand-daughter to Cakehole, still a school-girl, intelligent and industrious, preparing to sit for her School Certificate examination at the end of July.

He gave her news of Kevin; she gave him coffee and fruit-cake. He told her that re-education was a long haul, and Kevin missed her badly, but was keeping his spirits up by positive thinking, and getting good grades in his course work, better than most of the other detainees; with luck he would get his clearance within a year. 'Clearance' was a good word, very British, somehow vaguer than 'parole' or 'release': Alloway was proud of 'clearance'.

Mrs Pargeter – Susie – had not known that Kevin had volunteered for re-education; she had been told nothing at all about his progress since the police took him away or even where he had been taken. Re-education was clearly a step in the right direction; you could trust Kevin to find his feet and put them on the nearest ladder. Alloway described the re-education process imaginatively, using a little of what he had observed at the abbey, supplemented by memories of his own student days at the University of Wyoming and the tougher parts of the regimen of the training centre. At least Susie could take comfort from the knowledge that Kevin was fit, in tip-top condition, due to regular exercise and a healthy diet with no tobacco and alcohol.

How was she managing the business with Kevin away? Kevin had often wondered and worried about that.

Not very well. The bottom had dropped out of corporate videos when the Present Emergency began. ('Right!' Peter said, 'Right! I remember. He told me.') And anyway Eastbourne probably wasn't the best place for making corporate contacts, but they'd had to work from home and her father had bought them this house. What they mostly did was what Kevin called 'video packages' – weddings and funerals and functions, far more effectively shot, lit and edited with far better sound quality than any amateur could hope to achieve. A professional actor (from the Pier Pavilion) would narrate a professionally written script (by Kevin) and the finished article would be attractively packaged in a red box of simulated leather with gilt lettering.

That was their bread and butter. The jam was a new initiative, thought up by Kevin, by which privately owned boarding schools and nursing homes in the area would commission promotional videos – *The School Year at Bareham Hall* or *Changing Seasons at the Sunny Pines Sanatorium* – and these would be put together over a longish period to demonstrate to potential customers the quality of life and the service offered at these establishments.

She took him to the office, which was a wooden building at the end of the garden, hidden by trees. The previous owner of the house had fitted it out as a sauna, but the Pargeters had reconverted it. Now, along with the usual office furnishings, the desks, filing cabinets, typewriter and telephone, photocopier and fax, revolving chairs and functional sofa, there were racks of cassettes, reels of videotape and something which looked like a greatly enhanced video-recorder with two screens which Susie called 'the off-line' and which was used for the preliminary editing. Final editing, she said, had to be done at an editing suite in London, hired by the day and very expensive, and so had the sound-dub. These were the pricey elements of the business. For the rest, Kevin operated the camera and had taught her to use the off-line; he hadn't the patience himself. They had some lights of their own, hired any extra as needed, and employed a man part-time to rig them, a nice old man in his late seventies, still very nimble up a ladder; he had been a rigger at Ealing Studios when young, and had worked on the early George Formby films and with Gracie Fields in *Sing As We Go*.

Susie was at home in the office. She bustled about, switching items of equipment on and off, showed him bits of weddings and a retirement presentation, then grew impatient and turned it off with the carriage clock still on the table. 'Would you like to see a Quality of Life? Have you got time?'

'All the time in the world.'

They settled down together on the functional sofa to watch seriously. It was Kevin's conviction that these Quality of Life videos would make them rich. It was an idea which had found its time, he said; once it took off there was no stopping it; the possibilities were endless. Each Quality of Life video was a unique selling proposition, hard sell and soft sell seamlessly combined.

They watched one and then another. The first, which was intended for parents with children to put away, showed a spacious traditional building, chockful of history with modern extensions, laboratories with bunsen burners, Oxbridge graduates in gowns and mortar boards teaching Latin for university entrance. All the traditional trimmings were there – Eton collars and compulsory chapel, cheerful adolescents gulping teaspoons of Bemax administered by Matron in a starched white uniform, the OTC, Sports Day, Speech Day, the swimming pool, brisk games of rugby football and hockey in crisp winter weather and cricket played in spotless white shirts and cream flannel trousers.

The second video – for children with parents to put away – reassuringly lingered on the individual bed-sitting rooms with lavish provision of space for those special things, beloved of dear old people, which the residents would be encouraged to bring with them, the photographs of grandchildren in silver frames, the walnut writing-desk, the ivory elephants, the watercolours of Le Touquet.

149

Then tea in the Sun Lounge with dainty napkins, triangular sandwiches, three-tiered cake-stands with prettily coloured sugar icing on the fancy cakes. Onwards and outwards to the grounds, both sunny and sheltered in summer and winter, with flower-beds and statuary of reconstituted marble and a riot of bulbs in springtime. 'They're not really as big as that,' Susie said. 'We made them look bigger. You cheat it by choosing the angle.' Everywhere there were old folk in friendly conversation, dancing to the gramophone, playing Housey-Housey, walking in organised parties by the sea, lining up with a giggle to be inoculated against influenza. That was what the old really wanted, the video suggested; that was what absolved one of guilt. Old folk preferred to be with each other.

'How many have you done?'

'That's the problem. Just these two and bits of five. Then they took him away.'

'You're finishing them yourself?'

She shook her head. He looked at her. Feeding him fruit-cake, showing him the office, talking about Kevin, she had forgotten that she was unhappy; now it came back. He had better not pursue this, or she would begin to cry. He pursued it. 'Why not? It's obvious you could manage. You know the business inside out.'

'No confidence.'

'Comes with practice.'

'It's not as easy as that. You're right in a way. If it was just confidence in myself, that does come with doing it. But it's the punters. Customers. People I'd have to sell the ideas to, people I'd have to satisfy. They're the ones with no confidence, Peter. Even the videos which are partly done . . . they think they have to wait until Kevin comes back. You men don't realise. It's very hard for a woman to run a business. We've no authority; we're not brought up to it. I need a man.'

He had not planned this, not consciously. He had known that he would find a need to match his own need, and had followed his instinct. She must be lonely. The cottage was already isolated, and local people would be wary of a woman whose husband had been taken away by the police. He said, 'I need a job.'

It was as if a light came on inside her. 'Oh God! Would you? Just until Kevin comes back.'

'I've no experience.'

'It's easy. I'll teach you.'

'I'm supposed to get a job of national utility.'

'No problem. Daddy knows everybody in the Town Hall.'

So he stayed to supper, and slept in the spare room.

As for the documentation, it was as easy as she had said. Her father was a party member. The Nazi Party was no longer politically active, even in Germany, but in Britain it had succeeded to the position and influence once exercised by the Freemasons. National utility was not an issue to Daddy's friends at the Town Hall. There was a going concern to be rescued, commissioned work to finish or the fees (already spent) might have to be returned. Kevin could bloody well take care of himself, wherever he was, but nobody wished to see Billy Wheeler's daughter in Queer Street.

It seemed natural to them both that he should move in with her. There was so much he had to learn and a backlog of work to be completed. 'Anyway,' Susie said, 'I need someone to cook for. Living on your own, you can't be bothered; it's all poached eggs and cheese on toast. And too many chocolates, to tell you the truth.'

He was introduced to clients as an associate – not Susie's associate, but 'This is my husband's associate, Mr Alloway.' Everyone accepted him, even old Henry, the rigger from Ealing, very tolerant and free with his advice. And Peter found that he enjoyed the work and learned quickly.

She was sixteen years older than he, neither beautiful nor plain, but attractive, likeable, pleasant to be with, a home-maker; she made a home for him, and he settled into it naturally. She was not sexually voracious, not at all the sort of woman who makes passes at the janitor; she had been satisfied within her marriage and sexually shy outside it. As for Peter, he had the randiness of his age, but was not a sexual adventurer. They were alike in that way; both looked for emotional security. Yet both knew well enough what was bound to happen, and, because they knew, could wait for it to happen.

During the third week, after a day spent with a riding academy on Pevensey Levels, an evening with fish pie and television, they climbed the stairs together on their way to bed. 'Goodnight, Susie.'

151

'Goodnight, Peter.' Which of them paused at whose open door? It might have been either; it might have been both. Susie was looking up at him. His arms were round her, their bodies crushed together, two hungry people embracing hungrily; she could feel his erection. Old stuff. Henry would have seen the like often enough during his days at Ealing Studios.

In bed, as he was about to enter her, and she was certainly ready, to his surprise she stopped him.

'No?'

She switched on the bedside light and opened a drawer. There was a packet of rubbers inside with a tube of lubricating jelly. Rubbers seemed very old-fashioned to Alloway, and were known to inhibit pleasure, but if that was what she liked . . . She said, 'Kevin and I always use protection. He said we had to wait for kids until the business was established.' Peter said – almost said – just stopped himself from saying, 'There's a pill we use,' and managed instead to say, 'Right! Of course. Right!' and took a rubber from the packet, and she, to his surprise and intense pleasure, used her mouth to put it on him before switching the light off again.

Then he was inside her, deep inside her, with Susie holding him in, and Peter hardly daring to move for fear of coming too soon. In the darkness Susie said, 'Kevin's not going to come back, is he, not for a long time?'

Peter said, 'No, I don't think he is.'

'Take it off, then. Take that bloody thing off.' And Peter Alloway withdrew with considerable care, and allowed Susie to remove their protection.

Mission Accomplished

Cakehole had a little book, *The Countryman's Diary, 1939,* provided to the Auxunits by courtesy of Highworth Fertilisers. It was not really a diary but a forty-two-page handbook of useful information, such as how to blow up railway lines or an aeroplane on the ground, how to set booby-traps, and how to make an anti-personnel mine out of a cocoa tin filled with gelignite and buried in a biscuit tin packed with scrap metal or sharp flints. Cakehole had acquired all these skills and offered to teach the volunteers. They would not be immediately useful in assassinating the Reichsprotektor – that had to be done publicly and seen to be what it was – but they might come in handy later.

It had to be done publicly; the orders were clear on that point. The Reichsprotektor's death must not seem to be an accident or the private act of some deranged person satisfying an imaginary grudge. It was to be an execution by the Free Brits on behalf of their oppressed countrymen. It was to be done for show – to show the Americans what the British government-in-exile could do, to show the people of Britain, and by extension the peoples of other European countries, that oppression could not stand against the exercise of courage and will, to show the Germans that no one, even on the highest level, was safe from a people determined to be free.

That was it. Orders. And from the top, personally delivered. 'There's a hell of a lot depending on you two.' The Prime Minister had been sweating. Sinclair and Parry-Jones had thought this was because of the combination of a cashmere cardigan and central heating turned too high, but it was the weight of the occasion that had brought him out in perspiration.

153

Out of all the volunteers they had been chosen; it stood to reason that they must not be wasted. Therefore as much planning must be devoted to the getaway as to the act itself. The Operational Base beneath the outdoor privy would be useful.

The mice had been to see them at the cottage, no longer as mice but as men, one in his thirties, the other in his late forties, both educated men, well used to exercising authority. They had asked for delay, but there had already been too much delay. They had asked if there was really no way of getting in touch with Washington to warn the British government-in-exile of the likely consequences of the assassination, both to the population at large and to their own small organisation, which was nevertheless probably all the Resistance there was. They had again been told that there was no way. The Attack Group was not in communication with its masters. It had been given a job to do, and told to get on with it. The orders were clear.

The volunteers had asked the mice what they believed those likely consequences were likely to be. The mice had said that there was a worst scenario and a best scenario. The worst scenario would be wide-scale reprisals – the imposition of military law, mass arrests, hostage-taking, executions. That kind of thing had not been known in Europe for forty years, or in Britain at all, but it had happened, particularly in the East European countries where the populations were mainly Slav. And to the Jews, of course.

And the best scenario?

The best scenario would be that due process of law would be observed and the British police and MI5 left to find the assassins and bring them to trial. Probably the investigation would begin in that way, but if the police did not find the assassins quickly, the Germans would become impatient, would at first reinforce the investigation with their own people, and then proceed rapidly towards the measures the mice had already described, each leading naturally to the next. If the volunteers were prepared to give themselves up after carrying out the assassination, to declare themselves as members of the Free British Special Service Unit attached to the US Army and to insist that they had received no help whatever from any source within Britain, then that might ensure the best scenario. They would not be believed, but it would save face to blame the Americans. There would be a general tightening up, a number of people on the run might be caught and sent back to detention and others arrested, but the mice could live with that.

The volunteers told the mice that they were not prepared to give themselves up; there would still be work to do. If they were caught they would commit suicide so as not to be questioned. That was as far as they were prepared to go in obliging the mice.

Was it like that, was it as bald as that? No, they had argued as friends, had talked on into the evening with wine and bread, cheese and smoked goose which the mice had brought with them in a wicker picnic-hamper. Dorothy and Jack had been with them, and Carrie and Cakehole; it had been a proper Council of War. Real disagreement had been moderately expressed, with each side taking on board the other's commitments and points of view.

Sinclair and Parry-Jones stated this position, that they could not believe that the British people, or any free people, would willingly accept government in all important matters from the Council in Berlin, allowing foreigners to dictate the circumstances under which they lived.

The older mouse nodded and pursed his lips; he took the volunteers' point. The younger mouse, Stephen, pointed out that the people of Montana, of Manitoba, Spanish-speakers from Mexico and Panama, were governed from Washington and did not consider themselves unfree.

Different. Each state had its own government within the federation of the USNA, and each sent democratically elected congressmen and senators to Washington.

So did Britian. The provincial government was at Westminster and a small British contingent sat among the deputies in the Reichstag.

But not in the Council of State. It was the Council made the decisions, not the democratically elected deputies of the Reichstag. They were all Germans in the Council.

When had a Manitoban, when a Hawaiian, ever been elected president of the USNA? And there was no breaking away from the Union, the mouse called Stephen reminded them. The

War Between the States had been fought to settle precisely that point.

The problem, said the older mouse, was that the Present Emergency had made a difference; it had shown where power really lay. There was discontent now, but it needed to be harnessed, channelled, organised. Sabotage, strikes, refusal of co-operation in contentious areas, always pushing a little further, but never so far as to provoke a massively punitive response. Clogging the system, encouraging people gradually to take control of their own lives: that was the way. The volunteers had themselves said that there would be work for them after the assassination. That work remained to be done whether the assassination went ahead or not.

Cakehole made faces and shook his head. The Auxunits would not have pussyfooted around in such a way; they would have been wriggling under coils of barbed wire in the dark, blowing up petrol dumps. Cakehole was a great support to the volunteers. He understood about orders. The mice were civilians; they thought in terms of a continuum, of circumstances altering cases, of adapting to change. But Cakehole knew that, although one might be given discretion as to the means, ultimately orders were orders and must be obeyed.

Cakehole was the key. He had changed the balance of power, and everyone in that room knew it. Now they had Cakehole, the volunteers no longer needed the mice. At the end of the evening Dorothy shrugged, and Jack shook his head, and the mice went sadly away.

It was immediately obvious to the Permanent Secretary that the whole Re-education Programme had been the most gigantic cock-up. Nothing could be rescued from it; one could only tidy up after it. The problem was where to allocate responsibility.

Tidying up was simple. Those Re-eds who had already gone over the edge would be moved to high-security mental hospitals, the remainder to the new unit at Dartmoor, since they could not, for obvious reasons, be returned to the detention centres from which they had come. This might seem a little unfair, since the regime at Dartmoor would be stricter, but they had volunteered for re-education and there had been no guarantee of success. In any case, the regime at all the centres was in the process of being tightened up, and many more PUs than they were likely to find their way to Dartmoor.

Fairness! What a business it was! One did one's best. Nobody in government, nobody in the police or the prison service, believed that the detention of the PUs was anything but a mess, a mistake in danger of going out of control. All one could do was to make tactful representations to the Secretariat at Windsor, and the word was that these were having some effect; there was talk of instituting a gradual process of release on compassionate grounds, beginning with the older detainees. The Re-education Programme had been intended as a step in this direction, and it had gone horribly wrong.

Now there was the question of responsibility. One could not gloss over it: the shit had hit the fan. It would be convenient if that shit, instead of flying about generally and sticking to people who were under enough pressure already, could be piled neatly onto the faces of the personnel in charge of the programme on the ground – the two shrinks and the officer commanding the security guards.

Clearly they were to blame. Deterioration among the Re-eds should have been reported. The shrinks had reported it, but in their own impenetrable jargon, and the implication had been that they were dealing with it. And the deaths had been reported, of course – the suicides and the others – but not as a matter of high urgency; they had rung no alarm bells. One expects a few suicides at a detention centre.

Unfortunately the shrinks would say – he looked again at the Investigating Officer's report: *were* saying – that they had merely been operating the regime devised by the Working Party set up by government. Representatives of three ministries had served on that Working Party – Health, Education and the Home Office. It had seemed a good idea to spread the input. Now it was just spreading the shit.

Of course the Working Party had taken advice, but it had been the best advice – educationists, consultant psychiatrists, penologists, sociologists, bishops. No shit for them: nothing could be said against the quality of the advice without damaging public confidence in the

157

Great and the Good, and if that were to go then anarchy was bound to follow. How could it all have gone so wrong? He took off his spectacles and rubbed his right hand over his eyes. It would be a resigning matter for somebody. Damage limitation. In the end one's job consisted of that, always that and only that: anything else was flapdoodle.

Except that . . . his left hand now slid reflectively over the greasy skin at the side of his nose . . . except that it had not *all* gone wrong. There had been one man . . . Spectacles back on again and pages turned: the information came early in the report. One of the Re-eds had acutally been re-educated – re-educated and released. The name? – Pargeter, yes. Kevin Humphrey Pargeter. An address near Eastbourne, a telephone number. The Investigating Officer had been less than thorough. (Good! He was of no consequence and could safely be blamed.) He should have followed up this Pargeter man. Why had the programme worked for him and not for anyone else?

On impulse the Permanent Secretary picked up the telephone and asked his own secretary for an outside line. He dialled the Eastbourne number and heard the ringing tone . . . once, twice, thrice and then an answering machine cut in. A woman's voice. 'Susie and Peter are out at the moment. Do please leave a message, and speak after the tone.'

Carrie was dressed as a boy; that was the only touch of comic opera. Sinclair and Parry-Jones wore heavy boots, muddied cords bought at a market stall and ill-fitting British battledress blouses, left over from the war and still to be found in charity shops; the blouses were as near as they could get to uniform and also happened to be suitable wear for labourers employed by Highway Maintenance. Cakehole had come as he was.

The volunteers had travelled north with Cakehole by train, and stolen the lorry near Doncaster; they had been trained to steal unattended vehicles and took pride in showing off their skill. It was an old open lorry, suitable for their purposes but not an object of great value. Not even its owners, let alone the police, would consider its recovery a matter of high priority. They had driven it south by minor roads, broken into a pump at a wayside petrol-station at two in the morning to top it up with diesel, and taken the traffic cones, the lights and the generator from the unattended road-works on the B585 between Wellsborough and Market Bosworth. No need to steal petrol for the generator: they would not be using it for long.

There had only been room for two in the cab. Sinclair and Parry-Jones had taken turns to drive while Cakehole catnapped among the traffic cones in the back. They had avoided centres of population, kept clear of Oxford, skirted Thame and Princes Risborough, crossed the A40 and arrived back at the circle of gravel with its sign CARS HERE just after six a.m.

This was the tricky time. The lorry could not be concealed; it would be there all day. They unloaded the traffic cones and lights and hid them in Cakehole's Operational Base, and hid the generator in the kitchen under a plastic sheet. The lorry was now just a lorry, old and unremarkable, but they took turns to watch from an observation point in the woods to make sure that it was not noticed, and if it were, who noticed it. Carrie arrived during the afternoon, and was immediately placed on observation duty; Cakehole said it would occupy her mind during the waiting. Nobody but themselves and Juliet did come to the cottage. Nobody saw the lorry.

Up at dawn again. Costume parade. Then cones, lights, generator had been carried back to the lorry with a couple of shovels, a wheelbarrow and an empty barrel. They had been obliged to provide these from their own resources; such tools are not left on an unattended site for any gardener to steal. A pneumatic drill would have added verisimilitude and masked the noise of the shooting, but they could not have bought or borrowed one without the possibility of its being traced if it had to be abandoned. Shovels would do well enough, Cakehole said. Motorists were used to the sight of labourers leaning on shovels at the side of the road, and would not notice that there was no actual excavation going on; the attention of motorists was always on the lights, willing them to change from red to green or to remain green instead of changing back to red.

There should be *some* evidence of work, however. Since they lacked the equipment to dig the road up, they had better put something on it. Cakehole had given thought to this. They did not go directly to their chosen ground, but took a circuitous route which led them down a steep hill, one in six, where piles of grit had been left by the side of the road for use on winter ice. They stopped and shovelled grit into the lorry. Two piles of grit and a barrel judiciously arranged behind the cones would suggest re-surfacing.

Just after seven they reached the place they had chosen. It was ninety metres from a bend on the minor road between Hare Hatch and Waltham St Lawrence. Beyond the bend the road stretched clear for almost a kilometre. This was the road along which the Reichsprotektor was driven every morning in his green Mercedes convertible with a motor-cycle escort of two SS sergeants in front. His time of arrival varied – he was an uxorious man and liable to linger over breakfast – but had never, during all the days they had kept watch, been earlier than eight-thirty or later than nine-fifteen. Carrie would be standing at the bend, watching the approach. They would have about forty seconds from her signal.

Once the action began, there would be little time; the volunteers must be out and away at once. To their right there was a copse – in which the bicycles would be hidden with a change of clothing for themselves and Carrie, light casual summer clothes to wear when the job was over. They would walk on through the copse with their cycles, cross two fields and join a different road on the other side, two young men and a girl on a cycling holiday, who had not even heard the commotion. Cakehole would load the shovels, the empty barrel and the wheelbarrow into the lorry and use that for his own getaway: it would be abandoned in some distant lay-by later. The generator, lights, cones and grit would be left in situ; there was nothing to connect them with the Attack Group.

They unloaded the generator and shovelled the grit into piles under Cakehole's direction. Then Sinclair and Parry-Jones took the three bicycles over to the copse with a rucksack (also bought second-hand), leaving their weapons in the wheelbarrow. They hid the cycles and the rucksack inside an alcove of branches already constructed for this purpose. They had dug a pit two days previously for their labourers' gear and Carrie's, and there was a pile of earth to fill the pit and bracken to cover it. The rucksack contained their change of clothes. When it was empty it would carry the weapons.

Cakehole and Carrie put out the cones, the traffic lights and the barrel, and connected the lights to the generator. During this time two early-morning motorists passed, one in each direction, but took no particular notice. Sinclair and Parry-Jones returned. Cakehole started the generator. Everything was in position.

Arwen walked with Carrie to the bend in the road which was to be her look-out post. They reached it. There were tears in her eyes and his. She should say something, give him something, some word to keep, something more than 'Good Luck!' which was anyway supposed to bring bad luck. Was there a Welsh equivalent to 'Merde, alors!'? She said, 'Look after yourself.' Arwen said, 'We will be married, my dear love. We'll have lots of kids,' and Carrie said, 'I know.' They held each other, then Arwen broke away and returned to the roadworks, and Carrie took up her post, blinking back the tears and concentrating on the road ahead, though it was far too soon for the Mercedes.

A line of poplars and in the distance a railway at right angles to the road, with a tiny diesel engine and four carriages; it was the local commuters' train between Maidenhead and Reading. In another life, Arwen might have been on that train, with leather briefcase and a copy of *The Times*, wearing the cutest little bowler hat, and with the gold fountain pen she would have given him for his birthday in an inside pocket. Keep your eyes on the road, Carrie. No distractions, even this early, no going off into daydreams and fucking the whole enterprise up.

She had confined her breasts with a bandage and put on this blouson thing and boots and baggy trousers and a cap, and they had said she would pass. It was murder. Call it what you like, it had to be murder. How had she got herself into such a situation? Love, always love, led to the high drama and the trouble. No, that was not it; one drifted. They had taken Daddy away, and Grandad and Stanley, three generations of Baineses huddled in a police van, just for nothing, just for belonging to a sporting club, and no news came from them, and she had not been able to bear it, had needed to do something, whatever she could, or she would murder her mother, and one thing had led to another, and then Arwen – but nobody could blame Arwen. He was the ultimate best for her; everything had clicked between them. Please God, keep Arwen safe, whatever happens.

Time passed. Carrie's station was just around the bend; she would move back to give the signal. Cakehole sat on the back of the lorry, smoking an untipped cigarette, a Players Weight, heavy in tar; he was the gaffer and not required to engage in manual labour. Arwen and Sinclair leaned on their spades. Sometimes one of them would spread a little grit from one of the piles; Cakehole had told them that only one at a time must watch for Carrie because even preoccupied motorists might notice and wonder at two workmen staring persistently at a bend at the end of the road.

Cars arrived from both directions, waited if necessary at the lights, and continued on their journeys. It was commuter time, but this was not a commuters' road. So far – and during the previous days of reconnaissance – there had not been too many, never enough to cause a build-up of vehicles at either end of their line of cones. If that happened, they would have to abort the operation and come back the next day.

The lights were on a time-switch, but there was a manual override, which would be used when the action began. Eight forty-five. It could be any time within the next half hour. An elderly farm vehicle, filled with baled hay, lumbering on enormous tyres at five miles an hour, was approaching from the other direction. It would take forever to pass, forever to reach the bend. Cakehole switched the lights to green for the hay-wain, so that a three-wheeler coming the opposite way was forced to brake more suddenly than was prudent. The hay-wain moved past the line of cones like a mastodon heavy with premonitions of extinction. 'Go *on*, you bugger, go on!' Cakehole mouthed at it, willing it to burst into at least a trot. The driver wished them, 'Good morning!' and slowly the mastodon moved away up the road.

It reached the bend and disappeared. The three-wheeler had been given the green light and was gone already. Suddenly Carrie was there at the bend, waving. Arwen waved back. Her instructions were to go immediately to the copse and wait for them once she had given the signal and seen it acknowledged. Instead she remained where she was, staring back at them. Arwen said quietly, 'Go on. Go on,

Carrie. Please go on.' Cakehole pushed the flat of his hand in front of him, indicating the way she must go. Eight seconds. Then she was over the gate and belting across the field towards the trees. And nothing coming from the other direction, nothing to complicate the operation.

The motor-cycle escort swept round the bend, two sergeants of the Waffen SS in black and silver, two fighting machines, gloved and helmeted and armed for combat, the Mercedes some seventy metres behind them. Lights green for the motor-cycle escort. In no time at all they had reached and passed the traffic cones and were away down the road. Lights red for the Reichsprotektor.

At first it seemed as if the Mercedes would not stop; it would crash the lights. But a workman with a wheelbarrow had already stepped out into the road. The foot of the driver/bodyguard hit the brake, his hand hit the button of the horn. He was one of those chin-up, eyes-front, straight-backed drivers, a large arrogant man: the Reichsprotektor looked small next to him. He was shouting something which could not be understood because of the noise of the horn. The Reichsprotektor put a hand on his arm to calm him, and the workman turned to face the car.

The workman was a young man, not at all abashed to be delaying such important people. From his wheelbarrow he took a light machine-gun, and pointed it at the two men in the open car. His expression was of concentrated calculation. The Ingram Eleven fires twenty rounds a second, and there are only thirty rounds in the magazine, which must then be changed. To put both men out of action, his touch must be light.

There was a moment during which the two faces stared at him, utterly unable to understand what was happening. Only the glass of the windscreen was between them; it might or might not be bullet-proof. Since the hood of the Mercedes convertible was down on this sunny day, it was possible for those inside to stand up. The driver put his elbow on the top of the door beside him and began to rise in his seat, while his right hand reached towards his revolver.

Something terrible was about to happen, terrible in itself and with even more terrible consequences.

So far the patient, David Piper, had been only a receiver of impressions, emotions, pictures, messages. They had affected him, often painfully, but it had been a one-way communication. His mind had been blotting paper, soaking up what was sent to it but giving nothing back.

Now he must act. Those who sent the messages were in some way part of him, living inside his own consciousness; they were the people of a nightmare, going their own way, but because it was *his* nightmare he should be able to control or at least affect them. He had never tried to reach out towards them, never imagined he could, but now he must and would stop what was about to happen.

The gun jammed. Sinclair's finger was pressing the trigger, but it would not fire.

He could not believe it. The two men in the Mercedes could not believe it. Disbelief slowed down their response. Then the driver's hand reached the handle of his revolver and pulled it out of the holster.

From the side of the road, Parry-Jones rolled one grenade neatly under the car and lobbed the other into the back seat. Sinclair dropped the useless machine-gun and dived sideways into the ditch. Fatal indecision of the bodyguard. He could have attempted – probably ineffectually – to protect the Reichsprotektor with his own body, he could have shot Sinclair, he could have thrown himself into the back of the Mercedes, scrabbled for the grenade and lobbed it back before it exploded. Instead he tried to do all three at once. One! two! the Mercedes shuddered, buckled and caught fire. Bits of the bodyguard were spread over the road. The Reichsprotektor was thrown out in one piece like some unwanted pet animal.

But there was still the motor-cycle escort, both well down the road when they realised that the Mercedes was no longer behind them. They stopped to allow it to catch up. Then they heard the explosions. They did not lack courage and knew their duty; they came roaring to the rescue on their motor-bikes.

But these fighting machines, though their appearance was magnificent and daunting, had never actually done any fighting. If they had dismounted from their motor-bikes at a little distance from the roadworks, unslung their weapons and come at a run behind a spray of covering fire, they might have stood a chance. Instead, suddenly there were traffic cones, sent spinning by Cakehole, on the road in front of them. One came off his bike in a parabola and hit his head on the tarmac, the other crashed into the ditch, and both were finished off by Parry-Jones with the other Ingram.

'On your way!' Cakehole shouted. 'On your way! Quick!' and the volunteers were on their way, running towards the copse.

Sinclair had forgotten the jammed machine-gun, still lying where he had dropped it on the road. Did it matter? No, because it could not be traced to the cottage in the wood. Also, as an American weapon, it was evidence that the British government-in-exile had a long arm. Pity, though, just for a point of propaganda, to waste a gun which could probably be fixed and might be needed. Cakehole decided to pop the Ingram back into the wheelbarrow and take it home with the other gear.

But there was no time to tidy up. Already a tradesman's van, A. P. Harries Quality Waxes, was approaching from the direction of Windsor. Cakehole ran towards it, waving his arms.

The van stopped. The driver was an anxious middle-aged man, perhaps Mr Harries himself. 'What's the matter? Accident, is it?'

'Terrible! Terrible! Two soldiers come out of the hedge. Shot everyone. Terrible!'

'Soldiers?'

'Not ours. Funny uniform. You got to go for help. Ambulance or summing. They may not be dead. Drive through. We better take a look.'

'I can't. The light's red.'

'Don't be stupid. Emergency. Christ! my heart's thumping. I hope I survive this.'

The driver set the van in motion reluctantly and slowly: it was possible that he had never in his life crossed a red light. Cakehole walked in front. They stopped by the two SS sergeants, both clearly dead. The driver looked away. 'I haven't the stomach for this.'

'You're all there is.'

The Mercedes was still burning. Cakehole borrowed the van's fire extinguisher to dowse the blaze. He shook his head over the bits of

165

the SS captain who had been the Reichsprotektor's bodyguard. 'No point in an ambulance there,' he said. 'Cleaning-up job.'

Unfortunately the Reichsprotektor himself was still alive. He was unconscious, but breathing. There was some blood, but whether it was his own or the bodyguard's could not be known. Cakehole said, 'Have to get him to hospital.'

'You're not supposed to move them.'

'Only if they've broken their backs. He's not broken his back. You can't leave him laying here. Better take him to Reading. Or Slough? What you think?'

Always involve the other party in a decision: it is the first step in persuasion. The man who may have been Mr A. P. Harries gave the matter thought. 'Reading's closer.'

'You're right. Better get him in the van.'

'It's how to get there, isn't it? A4 or the way I came – B2034, the Windsor road – might be quicker for the hospital.'

'The B road.'

'I'll have to turn the van round, then. I'm facing the wrong direction.'

'Get him in first, turn it round after. You don't want to run over him by accident.' The Reichsprotektor's eyes flickered. Disaster if he regained consciousness now. Cakehole bent over him solicitously. 'Don't worry, sir. Take it easy. Don't try to speak. We're taking you to hospital; they'll soon put you to rights.' And to the driver, 'Get the back open quick.'

The driver opened the back of the van and began to make a space among the cardboard cartons of high quality waxes and polishes. It was crowded but it would do. Cakehole made a show of bustling about, moving cartons to make sure that none of them fell on the patient while the van was in motion. They made a pillow out of the driver's overcoat and some cleaning material, carried the Reichsprotektor to the van with great care, keeping him straight in case his back really was broken, and made him as comfortable as they could. During all this activity he did not speak, or even make any noises of pain, but his eyes were open. Cakehole said, 'Right! You drive straight there, quick as you can. I'll follow you in the lorry. There's a phone-box in the next village. I'll warn the hospital to expect you. There'll be a reward in this, I shouldn't wonder. You can tell he's important by the uniform.'

The driver returned to the front of the van. The Reichsprotektor's mouth opened and he made a small burping noise. Cakehole said, 'Can't allow this, you know,' and took his Fairbairn Field Service Knife from the concealed pocket in which he kept it. Fairbairn's own *Manual of Unarmed Combat*, on which Cakehole had been trained, recommended cutting an artery in the neck, with carefully drawn figures of German sentries (always obligingly looking the other way) to illustrate the technique, but Cakehole did not wish to risk the consequent effusion of blood. Instead he inserted the dagger into a less well recommended, but still viable, place below the ribs on the right where it would pierce the liver. He twisted the knife, withdrew it, wiped it on the cleaning materials they had placed below the Reichsprotektor's head, and replaced it in his pocket. He got out of the van and closed the back door. 'Drive on,' he said. 'And don't worry. They'll be expecting you.'

The van made its turn and drove past the roadworks towards the B2034. Cakehole returned to the lorry. Yes, better take the Ingram. Stupid to leave a weapon behind which could not be replaced; the empty cartridge cases would be evidence enough. He loaded the gear in the back of the lorry and set off towards Henley, stopping at the first convenient phone box to dial 999 and inform the Mengele Memorial Hospital at Reading of the imminent arrival of a German general in a poor state of health. Near the top of Remenham Hill he passed three cyclists, two young men and a young woman in light summer clothing, waved at them, but did not stop.

He arrived at the cottage, returned the wheelbarrow and shovels to the garden shed and the barrel to its usual position beneath a drainpipe to catch rainwater, hid the Ingram in the Operational Base below the privy, loaded his own bicycle onto the lorry, and set off north as far as he could travel before the supply of diesel ran out. He abandoned the lorry in a lay-by, cycled to the nearest railway station and put himself and his cycle on a train to Birmingham. There, amid all the bustle and crowds of Birmingham's New Street Station, he bought single tickets to Reading for himself and his bicycle, and from Reading he cycled home.

It had all gone splendidly.

Investigation

There were no witnesses, only Mr A. P. Harries who had driven the Reichsprotektor's body to hospital. Mr Harries had not seen the attack and only knew what he had been told by the old man, that two soldiers in funny uniforms had come out of the hedge. 'Funny': therefore not the uniforms of the Wehrmacht, but of a foreign army or perhaps some fancy dress which they had concocted for themselves.

Of course the old man may not have been telling the truth. He had kept his promise and telephoned the hospital, but had not reported the incident to the police, as he certainly should have done. Was this because he did not want to be involved, to be questioned and re-questioned for hours at a time, to be treated – as he was bound to be treated, as the unhappy Mr Harries was being treated – as a suspect until proved innocent? He would not have been the only witness wishing to avoid involvement. The first report of the incident had been received by the local police at roughly the time Mr Harries arrived at the Mengele Memorial Hospital. It had been from a caller who did not give his name, but gabbled his message and put the phone down immediately. That road was not busy but it was used. One could not know how many motorists had steered a slalom through the traffic cones, past the bodies and the burned-out car, and continued on their way, or simply turned round and found another road.

Well, it was natural for the public to wish not to be involved, but the old man was different. He had been on the spot when it happened. Was that because he was himself one of the gunmen, perhaps the only gunman? Mr Harries had seen a gun – some kind of machine-gun, he thought – but it had been lying in the road, where the old man would hardly have left it if it had been his. And it seemed unlikely that one old man, even with a machine-gun, could have killed the two SS sergeants (themselves armed with machine-guns), Captain Klein and the Reichsprotektor all by himself. The machine-gun which Mr Harries said he had seen had not remained on the road, but one could not be certain that it was the old man who had taken it away. Anyone who thought a machine-gun might come in useful could have taken it. Question: why had the machine-gun of the motor-cycle escort not also been taken?

The roadworks were part of it; they were bogus. Berkshire County Council's Department of Highway Maintenance reported no road-works on that road, and indeed the road had not been repaired; a little grit had been spread on the surface, and that was all. Mr Harries had not noticed any identifying marks on the lorry, and traffic cones are anonymous little objects, but the generator and lights were traced back to Leicestershire. So all the paraphernalia of the roadworks had been brought from Leicestershire by some person or persons unknown, among whom might have been the old man.

Unfortunately Mr Harries was not able to describe the old man in any helpful way. He was shown photographs of various politically unreliable old men, most of whom were already in detention, and recognised none of them, was given the assistance of photofit cards and a police artist to make a likeness and the likeness produced could have been that of almost any old man. He had been a common old man, Mr Harries said, a common labourer as one would expect of someone engaged in roadworks; he had used words in an uneducated way. That was as far as Mr Harries was able to go.

Empty cartridge cases – 9mm short cartridges of American manufacture – had been found on the road. Bullets matching these cartridges had been recovered from the bodies of the two sergeants. Splinters of metal had been found in the upholstery of the Mercedes and the bodies of Captain Klein and the Reichsprotektor. An expert in ballistics was of the opinion that the machine-gun was almost certainly an Ingram, Model 10 or 11, manufactured by the Military Armament Corporation of Powder Springs, Georgia. As for whatever had been used to blow up the car, from an examination of the surface of the road and of the bodywork of the vehicle it was determined that it was not a booby-trap or mine; two separate explosive objects had been thrown. A search of the area disclosed the pins of two pineapple grenades dropped by the hedge on one side of the road. One grenade is very like another, but almost certainly these were of American manufacture also.

Puzzlingly no bullets were recovered either from the Mercedes or its occupants. The machine-gun which had been seen lying on the road must have been used to kill the motor-cycle escort but had not been used on the occupants of the Mercedes. Why not? A light machine-gun is an inaccurate weapon but less so than a hand-grenade. Even more puzzlingly, what had actually killed the Reichsprotektor had not been a splinter of metal – Captain Klein had taken most of the blast – but an incision made by some knife or dagger.

Reconstruction of the crime: roadwork material had been brought from Leicestershire in a lorry by a group of not fewer than two, but almost certainly three terrorists, of whom the old man was probably one. A look-out had been posted at the bend to give warning of the approach. The Reichsprotektor's escort had been allowed through on a green light, which had been turned to red for the Mercedes. (Another puzzle: Why had the driver stopped? It would have been more natural to go straight through the light.) One of the terrorists, waiting at the side of the road, had removed the pins from two hand-grenades and thrown first one under the car, then the other into it, setting it on fire by rupturing both the fuel line and the petrol tank. When the two men of the escort returned to investigate, they had been shot with a machine-gun. The killer had then attacked the Reichsprotektor with a knife and he and the look-out had made their getaway (how?) leaving the old man behind (why?) to make his escape in the lorry.

Perhaps the use of the knife had some ritual significance. Only twenty-four cartridge cases had been found, so there would still have been ammunition in the clip of the machine-gun. A knife was a silent weapon, of course, but what was the point of silence by that time? Noise there had been already.

Noise there had been, but nobody had heard it. The nearest habitations were a couple of bungalows beside the road towards Windsor; they were round the bend, and so out of sight, but within eight hundred metres. Old age pensioners lived in both, therefore all perhaps were a little deaf, and they had been indoors having breakfast, but it was a summer day; the windows had been open. Nothing. If there had been a couple of bangs, they had not noticed. Twenty-four rounds had been fired from the machine-gun to finish off the escort. That would have been in two bursts, but each of less than a second, and the Ingram is fitted with a silencer as standard. All things considered, it was not surprising that four elderly people, tucking in to bread and cheese and sausage and coffee in kitchens sited at the rear of their houses, should have failed to notice that an assassination was going on just round the bend and down the road.

Fingerprints? The world and his dog had left their calling cards on those traffic cones, and the traffic lights and generator were not much better. There were fingerprints on the cartridge cases, however, and on the discarded pins of the two grenades. The computer did its best with them, but they did not match any prints in any of the records held by the police and the Security Services.

The investigative machinery went into laborious action. Sacks of material found in the ditches on both sides of the road were removed for sifting, but what could be made of a couple of stubs of Players Weights among so much else? Prints were obtained from everyone who had been working on the site between Wellsborough and Market Bosworth from which the equipment had been stolen, and the staff of Leicestershire's entire Department of Highway Maintenance were questioned and their dossiers examined for links to any group of political dissidents or to the criminal classes.

That was the Leicestershire connection and it did not seem likely to lead anywhere. Two clerks and a supervisor were found to have links – but only of kinship, not of friendship or interest, and distant in all three cases – with politically unreliable persons, but they had been nowhere near Windsor on the day of the incident, and the PUs had been behind bars, and the whereabouts of other members of the PUs' families was ascertained and none of them had been anywhere near Windsor either. The three were immediately dismissed from

Council employment and their identity cards endorsed to that effect but the only facts established were that some person or persons unknown, who did not necessarily live in Leicestershire, had on the night of 7th/8th July stolen equipment from roadworks in progress, leading to traffic congestion next morning when the theft had been reported, and enquiries began – to no great effect – by the local police.

Part of the problem was that the investigators had no experience of dealing with terrorism. In 1942, when the British surrendered, the people of Northern Ireland, faced with the choice of becoming part of Greater Germany, with no guarantees at all, or part of a United Ireland with guarantees of religious liberty and political autonomy, had embraced unification; orange had become an unfashionable colour. The Germans could, of course, have mopped up unified Ireland at any time, but the US government had let it be known that it would regard such a mopping up as a *casus belli* and there were easier fish to fry. Consequently the mopping up had been postponed, and an independent Ireland continued to exist, protected politically by the citizens of Boston and the New York City Police. The Irish Question had been solved and the IRA declined into a form of Friendly Society. There had been no terrorism in Britain for over sixty years.

Then there was the question of who was in charge of the investigation. The first report had been made to the Berkshire County Constabulary, which had sent a team to the incident, but asked Scotland Yard to take over. So the Criminal Investigation Department of Scotland Yard was involved, but so was Special Branch and so was MI5. There were so many investigating officers of the very highest rank that they fell over each other, and their various subordinates jockeyed for influence as quarrels broke out over whose computer should have access to which restricted data.

The Home Office, alarmed by the confusion, set up a co-ordinating Committee to report directly to the Cabinet, but this only made matters worse. From the beginning the Secretariat at Windsor had been asked whether anyone representing Central Government in Berlin should be invited to join the investigation, but the Acting Reichsprotektor, von Neustadt, had replied that Berlin did not, at this stage, wish to take any active part in what it regarded as entirely a matter for the British authorities, but that it would be watching progress with the greatest interest. The Prime Minister, the Home Secretary and the permanent officials of the Home Office found this reply distinctly ominous, and their disquiet was communicated downwards.

'I don't know much about the investigation itself,' said Stephen Grenfell to Sir Gervase Acland. 'That's all Top Secret. What's causing the chaps in my own Ministry to run about like headless chickens is what we tell the public.'

'You've said nothing so far. I've seen nothing.'

'Right. D-Notices. Nothing in the newspapers, nothing on radio or TV. So far. But we can't keep that up because the police need to question every motorist who used that road between seven and ten a.m. on 9th July, which means a public appeal for information, which means that we've got to say something.'

'Which will be?'

'Has already been. Today. It was on the One O'Clock News, and the late edition of the evening papers will have it. There was a shooting incident, an unsuccessful attempt to assassinate the Reichsprotektor, in which an officer of the SS and two NCOs were killed.'

'And Druckermann.'

'Minor injury.'

'How long is that going to hold?'

'Couple of weeks. He's recovering in hospital, doing well: we can fake some photographs. Then there'll be complications. He'll go back to Berlin for specialist treatment with a period of convalescence afterwards. Or he may have a heart attack under the anaesthetic. There'll be plenty of time for people to get used to von Neustadt.'

'The purpose of all this?'

'Public confidence. Save face. Confuse the enemy. It's known that American weapons were used. It's not known how they got into the country or who used them. It's thought that there may be an American hit-group at large. If so, our people don't want the Americans to know it's been successful.'

'Any hit-group would have reported success. You and I know that

Sinclair and Parry-Jones aren't in radio contact with Washington, but your people don't know that. How could they? Stephen, you're confusing me.'

'I told you: we're going to reassure the public. Photographs of Druckermann in hospital joking with the nurses, news footage – interviews with the consultants, family visits from Frau Druckermann and the kids, daily progress reports. Whatever the hit-group may have told Washington, they've been over-confident; they got it wrong. My Ministry intends the Yanks to believe that the group has made its strike and failed.'

In fact the Yanks, who had their own source in Berlin, already knew that the Reichsprotektor had been killed.

'What the fuck have those goons of yours been up to?' said the Head of the CIA to the Chief of the Imperial General Staff.

'I'm sorry, Joe. I can't talk to you right now. I'll get back to you within the hour.' The CIGS broke the connection. 'Now I've offended him. I'll have to apologise. Something's happened. He knows and we don't. How very embarrassing! What's the latest from the O & I Group in London?' There would be someone in the Operations Room, he supposed. With so little to do these days, it was not fully manned, but there would be someone sitting by the red telephone. The Head of Military Intelligence was away for a couple of days sorting out family problems: the nursing home they had found for his mother was threatening to discharge her for disruptive behaviour.

'The usual nothing, sir. Five days old.'

'Ah!'

These days Attlee and Cape seldom communicated with their masters in Washington because there never seemed to be anything to report. They had proceeded, as ordered, to London where Cape had found a job as a hospital porter and Attlee was selling insurance on commission. They had been asked for references and for their employment records, but, on Cape's inspiration, had replied that their instructions as Re-eds were to forget about their previous lives and to start all over again from Day One. They were sharing digs in Baron's Court, a twin-bedded room with communal breakfast, but dared not keep the radio and their weapons with them since there was no real privacy and the landlady cleaned the room, so it was back to left-luggage lockers, and their occasional radio contact was hugger-mugger with the door locked. Attlee was looking for another top-floor flat, but flats for two men sharing were hard to find: it was perfectly proper to share digs, but a flat suggested something more permanent which might indicate a homosexual attachment. They had not located the Attack Group, had heard nothing of any resistance movement, and had little time to make enquiries because just holding down a job was difficult enough and Cape's hours at the hospital were horrendous.

'And we've no way of getting in touch with them?' The CIGS knew there was no way. He was just speaking for something to say and to delay having to phone back. The lack of intelligence was infuriating, crippling: the whole Operations Room, a military machine in miniature, had been brought to a humiliating halt. They needed more men on the ground, and qualified volunteers were piling up at the training centre, but they could not be sent to Britain without the help of the Navy, which had been denied. The Operations Room was working on a scheme by which the O & I Groups made their own way south to South America, signed up as merchant sailors on ships bound for some British port and then jumped ship, but it all took time to arrange without CIA co-operation, especially since the weapons and radio equipment would not fit easily into a sailor's kitbag. 'It's quite obvious something's happened,' he said. 'Casey's rather cross about it for some reason.'

'It has to be the Attack Group, sir. They've made their strike. But why hasn't Attlee let us know? It must have been in all the media.'

'Do you think it would be that? I don't see how it could. Joe should have been ordering up the champagne. In fact, he's pissed off.'

He called back and was connected at once. Usually the CIA chaps liked to make a business of it, and the length of time taken by the business was an indication of whether one was in favour or not. The immediate connection should have been a good sign except that the Brits were so clearly out of favour. 'It seems there's been a temporary breakdown of communication, Joe,' the CIGS said.

'Are you telling me you don't know?'

'It seems not.'

'Are you telling me your people have stepped this far out of line and you don't even know?'

'Ah!'

'Don't keep saying "Ah": it's all you fucking Limeys ever say. And don't say you'll call me back. We're talking now. I want an explanation now.'

'You'd better tell me what's happened, I think.' But he knew what must have happened. The Attack Group had indeed made its strike, and the Yanks were angry because they had not been consulted or even warned. Joe's anger was only pique; it would not last long. But how did he know already when the Brits, with a team on the ground, did not?

'Your people have murdered Druckermann. The British aren't admitting it yet, they're still trying to cover it up, but it's happened.'

'Ah!'

'I may kill you, Victor.'

'Well, we were going to tell you about that.'

'You just said you didn't know.'

'We knew it was going to happen. Planned for it. For various unimportant reasons we didn't know it had already happened. Thank you for telling us.'

'You planned it? Intended it? You cunts! You pricks! You cretinous assholes! Oh, Christ! You were "going to tell us"! Don't you realise what you've done? This could mean war.'

'We're already at war, Joe.'

'We are not at war in any real sense. Nor do we intend to be: the Arabs do the fighting. Stirring up a bit of disaffection on the ground; that's one thing. It's a warning we could make life difficult at home, so maybe it'd be less trouble to pull out of the Gulf. Killing a German general – an SS general, fucking Druckermann, the latest fucking blue-eyed boy – that's different; that means retaliation. They're a vindictive bunch in the SS; they'll go over the top. We're liable to get a whole fucking swarm of hit-men landing all down the East Coast and homing in on the White House.'

'It's a risk one takes.'

177

'It is not a risk I take. So you'll apologise. It was a mistake, do you understand me? Your goons on the ground got out of hand and exceeded their orders. They will be disciplined; they will be appre-fucking-hended; they will be shot. And you people will crawl, Victor; you will fucking crawl; you will eat shit, you hear me? The President wants your assurance on that, and he wants it now.'

'I hear you, Joe. If the President wishes to talk to my Prime Minister about this, I'm sure the PM will be happy to meet with him, as he always is. As far as we're concerned at this HQ, I must tell you clearly – and I hope you hear *me*, Joe – that this was not a mistake, it was meant to happen, and it is our business, the British government's business, not yours. If we have to face retaliation from the Germans in consequence, we're quite capable of looking after ourselves.' Again he broke the connection. 'That told him.'

'Yes, sir. Very incisive. We don't actually have any contingency plans for defending this place. Do you want me to start working something out? And the homes, of course, the private residences. Technically I'm not sure how far we'd be allowed a military presence.'

'No, we'll probably have to eat a certain amount of dirt eventually. Drag it out a bit. The PM can do it. He sweats a lot; they like that.' His fingers drummed on the desk. 'What a bugger! Who'd have dreamed that would be their reaction? I genuinely thought they'd be delighted. Anyway it's done now, can't be undone; they'll have to live with it.'

Attlee saw the headlines in the evening papers as he caught the train at Dagenham. He was tired. A hard day out in the field and nothing to show for it; if he and Cape had to live on his commission, they would live very ill. As a naturally prudent person himself, he should have been good at selling insurance, but he found the frequent rejection dispiriting. Also he was expected to tell lies. This was called 'the positive approach': mere prudence was negative. Attlee greatly disliked telling lies for personal gain, and did it badly.

He bought an *Evening Standard*. There had been an attempt to murder the Reichsprotektor. So that was what Sinclair and Parry-Jones had been sent to do! It looked as if they had made rather a mess of it. He supposed that he had better stop at Victoria station and collect the radio. This would have to be reported as a matter of urgency. He wondered what the consequences would be. He and Cape had been ordered to give Sinclair and Parry-Jones support and assistance, but had not been able to find them – had not really tried, Washington suggested, but what did they know in the Operations Room about conditions on the ground? There would be a hunt. The *Standard* said the police had a number of clues and were vigorously pursuing their enquiries, but no clue could lead to Attlee and Cape; their documentation was now secure. The *Standard* said that the Mafia might be involved.

His briefcase was always heavy; there were so many coloured cards and charts to show people and a bound book of tables illustrating benefits for years ahead. With the suitcase containing the radio (also heavy) in his other hand, he looked like a refugee from the Dust Bowl. Back at the digs the kitchen door was open, the radio playing 'We'll Gather Lilacs' and the landlady hanging about the hall as usual. He wished her good evening and mounted the stairs. She watched him go, her gaze on the extra suitcase, which she had seen before, going in and out. Attlee supposed that she was on a retainer from the police to keep a watch on the doings of all her lodgers. Perhaps she was not even paid, but did it out of malice.

He could make the report himself, the operation of the radio transmitter being such a simple matter, and certainly Washington would be eager to have it. Yet it might be wiser to talk the situation over with Bernard first and get a little more and better information. It was bound to be the lead story on the TV News, and there was a coin-fed television set in their room as in all the rooms. Bernard was always so tired when he got back from the hospital: it was sometimes difficult even to drag him out to the ABC Café for a meal. Still, the thing must be done. They would watch the News, evaluate and then report.

Eating was not allowed in the room, but Attlee went out and bought sandwiches, smuggling them in sweatily under his shirt. The News was specially extended, with a great deal of on-the-spot reporting. There were pictures of the site of the ambush, and a kindly Chief Superintendent appealed to motorists for information. There were shocked reactions from the Prime Minister, the Home Secretary, the Archbishop of Canterbury, two generals, the Poet Laureate and the Director of the Confederation of British Industry, and there were expressions of sympathetic outrage from Berlin. There was a film clip of Frau Druckermann visiting her husband in hospital, where he sat propped up in bed among a bower of flowers and Get Well cards. One very large card from a primary school in Tolworth had been drawn and coloured by the pupils themselves. The Reichsprotektor wrote a thank-you in his own hand; viewers were shown the hand writing the message.

Well, it had to be done. Not much to evaluate. The attack had failed, but the attackers had escaped and were being hunted. If they were caught . . . well, that was the worrying aspect. As matters were, they could not be linked to the O & I Group, knew nothing about the cottage in the hills, nothing about the abbey, nothing about the new identity cards (what had they done with their own?), but they did know the names – Attlee, Cape, Alloway – and those were still the names on the new cards. They had been trained to resist interrogation, and anyway they had cyanide capsules and were expected to use them. Sinclair and Parry-Jones were good soldiers, trusted agents: they would not betray their country and their friends. But who would have expected Alloway to disappear as he had done, with no way of finding him? Attlee and Cape had not yet been able to bring themselves to tell the Operations Room about Alloway. They simply had not mentioned him, and nobody had asked.

If Sinclair and Parry-Jones were captured and did talk, there was no way Attlee and Cape could prevent it, or even know, since presumably the Security Services would act on the information first and tell the media afterwards. They would have to worry about that when it happened. Meanwhile it would be 1700 hours in Washington. Attlee opened the window and Cape prepared to transmit.

The arrival of an official letter addressed to Kevin Pargeter was nothing out of the ordinary. Once a name has been placed on a computer, there seems to be no easy way of removing it, and communications from the tax authorities, both local and national,

special discount offers from mail-order companies and free intro-
ductory copies of magazines attempting to reverse a decline in
circulation, unsolicited financial advice from accredited financial
advisers, offers of unsecured loans on favourable terms from
disinterested banks and building societies, charity appeals, requests
for biographical data from vanity publications, had all continued to
arrive at the address from which he had been taken away as a
politically unreliable person requiring protection from his outraged
fellow citizens.

This letter was a little different, but not alarmingly so. It was from
the Home Office, a Mr Harold Butterworth, requesting Kevin to get
in touch at his earliest convenience. The Home Office, of all offices,
ought to have known that Kevin was no longer at home and where he
really was, since it had put him there, but Susie knew that it is
common bureaucratic practice for one department of a government
ministry not to know what is happening in the others, so she and
Peter decided to ignore the letter; if the matter was important, Mr
Butterworth would write again. When, ten days later, he did so, but
still in general terms, something about how he would very much like
to have the benefit of Mr Pargeter's experience and that all
reasonable expenses would be paid, Susie wrote 'Not At Home' on
the letter, put it into the postage-free government envelope provided
for a reply, and returned it.

So Mr Butterworth, the officer investigating the cock-up at the
Re-education Centre, having already redrafted his report to place
responsibility firmly on the psychiatrists and the security officer at
the abbey, but being under instructions to find out why, when the
programme had failed spectacularly with every other Re-ed, it had
succeeded with just one, did as the Permanent Secretary had done,
dialled the Eastbourne number and received the same recorded
message. 'Something wrong here,' he said to the colleague with
whom he shared an office: he felt it in his water.

His letter had been courteous and firm – unspecific certainly,
because he had not wished to alarm Pargeter or to cause him to
prepare his replies, but making it clear that he was expected to attend
for interview. Instead the letter had been returned, 'Not At Home', a
flippant response, not at all appropriate from somebody who had

been taken into protective detention once and might easily be taken again. And now this – 'Susie and Peter are out at the moment.' He decided not to leave a message after the tone, but to visit Pargeter in person. He would ask the local police to make enquiries. It might be merely that the Pargeters had split up in consequence of the husband's incarceration, that the woman had refused to take him back on his release and was now playing silly games, but his water told him that there was more to it than that.

Of course Susie and Peter were not always out when the answering machine said so. Sometimes they were in the converted sauna working together on the off-line: Peter was beginning to develop a flair for editing. Sometimes they were out but not on business; they might be shopping together or walking the dog on the cliffs. Their relationship had already settled into something much more like marriage than adultery.

It was almost as if there never had been a Kevin; they certainly never spoke of him. Susie was temperamentally suited to being married, enjoyed the state and felt its present manifestation to be an improvement on what she had before: she had always – far more than Kevin – wanted marriage to be a partnership. Peter enjoyed the emotional security and being looked after. Both enjoyed the physicality of it, not just the sex but the hugs and the touching, the company. There was a difference in age, but it was not that important. For Peter it was like being married to one's mother, but not unpleasantly so: one had the advantages of both relationships. He had always been close to his mother, who was the fulcrum of the family.

Mr Butterworth took the train to Eastbourne. A police car and a uniformed sergeant were waiting for him at the station. The sergeant had little to tell Mr Butterworth but that little was more interesting than he knew. After her husband had been taken away, Mrs Pargeter had continued to run the business as best she could, and lately she had engaged a young assistant, Mr Alloway, some friend of her husband's from the West Country, who had moved into the house with her. Hanky-panky could be assumed, but that was her own business. A woman on her own needs consolation; her family was well liked in the town. A work permit had been obtained for the young man in the usual way, and his residency registered at the police station all as per normal. The number of the young man's identity card had been run through the computer when he registered, and before Mr Butterworth's arrival the sergeant had run it through again, and what had come up both times was 'Nothing Known' which is what automatically would come up if nothing criminal was known of the party in question.

'The West Country?

'It was a Gloucestershire registration, sir.'

'Did you see the card?'

'Not personally. The Desk Sergeant on duty made the entry. Card number. Details of the work permit. Place of residence.'

'And Mr Pargeter himself?'

'He's still away, isn't he?'

'Is he?'

'They're all still away, sir, all the PUs. I know the area. There's eighteen been taken in Eastbourne, twenty-three in Lewes, and they've none of them come back.'

'You don't approve?'

'Not for me to say.'

'I'd like you to come to the house with me if you will.'

Curious! Pargeter had not returned. Perhaps the psychiatric staff of the Re-education Centre had made a mistake in releasing him; perhaps he had fooled them and disappeared into some subversive underground immediately on his release. Those jokers had made so many mistakes that the possibility could not be ruled out. Clearly there must be an underground of some sort, even though one would never have believed it; those hit-people who had tried to assassinate the Reichsprotektor, whether they were Mafia or not, must have had some local support.

Mr Butterworth's water stirred again uneasily within him. The last thing one wanted would be to get mixed up in all that business. It would complicate his report, there was the risk of his being blamed for not acting more expeditiously, and it would be extremely time-consuming. Perhaps Pargeter had returned after all, found himself supplanted and gone away again immediately. That would be time-consuming also, because one still had to find him, but considerably less complicated.

'You're sure Mrs Pargeter will be at home?'

'Yes, sir. I asked them to stay in. Routine enquiry about the business, not worth them coming down the police station, not really a police matter at all, but you'd be grateful for an hour of their time.'

'Good.'

They drove out of the town in silence. Mr Butterworth said, 'The impression I have from you is that Mrs Pargeter is better liked than her husband.'

'Might be putting it too strong. She's local; her father's well known – charitable work, church affairs, local councillor and such. Pargeter's more . . . well, I don't know much about him really: he's from outside the area – they met at some Young Conservative function. Flash Harry. Sails a bit close to the wind, that's the general opinion. Gets above himself. Always leads to trouble: he'd no business joining a gentleman's club.'

Albion Awake. Membership concentrated in the South East, the South West and the Home Counties. A gentleman's club. Impossible to imagine it as the basis of a terrorist infrastructure. Pargeter too. Mr Butterworth had read the file. Pargeter was a joiner – Rotary, the Honourable Order of Water Rats, the lot: he had even applied to join the Nazi Party and been turned down. He was a conformist, not remotely subversive. On release he would have headed immediately for his home and his pathetic video business. Unless there was debt.

'Was he in debt, do you know?'

'Can't say, sir. Shouldn't think so. His missus seems to be doing fairly well. Anyway you'll see for yourself soon. I asked her to have the books ready.'

Peter had known when the Home Office letter arrived that he should cut and run. But where? And, as Susie said, there were so many letters. So he had waited for them to write again, and they had written again, and it had been clear to him that they were assuming that Pargeter had returned, but again Susie made so little of it that he had allowed himself to be reassured.

And now there was this man coming, and it seemed that all he wanted to do was look at the books, so perhaps there was nothing to worry about. If only he could have told Susie, if they could have concerted some kind of plan. *Look, I'm sorry, but there's something you ought to know; I murdered Kevin on the train.* It wouldn't do. She did know; there was something in her which knew, he was sure of it. But it could not be said, because if it were she would be the woman who had taken her husband's murderer into her bed.

Mr Butterworth said, 'You haven't heard from your husband at all?'

'They're not allowed letters.'

'No, they're not.' In fact it varied. The English, except in compassionate cases, were not allowed to communicate with their families; many of the Welsh and Scots were. It was the difference between being wilfully political and sentimentally nationalist. 'A gentleman's club.' Even the police disapproved. Locking these people up had to have been a mistake. Except, of course, that with the attempt on the Reichsprotektor everything had changed.

Peter waited for the man to say, 'Not even when he was released?' How would Susie reply, how would she take it? She had not introduced him as the man who had known Kevin in the Re-education Centre; she had said, 'This is my husband's associate, Mr Alloway,' as she always did. Even unprepared, even with no plan at all, there was a fifty per cent chance that she would protect him, and then, when they were alone together, he would explain.

'Mrs Pargeter, your husband was released from protective detention on 4th May. Didn't he come straight home?'

Only the smallest hesitation. She did not look at Peter. No change in the level of tension in her voice. 'No.'

'Didn't you know he had been released?'

'No.'

'He hasn't communicated with you in any way since 4th May? Not even anonymously?'

'How would he do that?'

'Some printed message in the third person? You have a fax machine, I see. Or even a telephone call by some third party?'

'Nothing like that.'

'Nobody has come to you since 4th May with some message from or about your husband?'

This is the moment. Peter had arrived on the day after. *I'm Peter Alloway. I've come to give you news of Kevin.*

'No.'

'Do you have a joint bank account?'

'Yes. I couldn't operate otherwise.'

'Has it been used by anyone but yourself in the last two months? Or the credit card account?'

'Not as far as I know. I haven't had the June statements yet.'

Peter was home; he was home. There would be a lot to explain after they had gone, and honesty would be the only way, but he could do it because she was on his side and that was all that mattered.

'Mrs Pargeter, I have to find your husband; it's most important that I do.' The words 'Otherwise I cannot complete my report and am up Shit Creek without a paddle' remained unuttered. It was not just the report; there were questions of national security at issue. One had to be certain that this disappearance was no more than a matter of money or sex and anyway one had to talk to the man. He had better ask her about money; the books showed at first glance a problem of liquidity in the early part of the year, but the situation had improved since the arrival of this man Alloway. He had better ask her about other women.

A scenario formed suddenly in the front of his mind – a cheap novelettish scenario, but it would explain everything. There was no other woman. Alloway was the other man. They had arranged for him to join her from the West Country, and just before he did so, her husband suddenly arrived on release. She had murdered Pargeter, disposed of the body, and the new partner had arrived, knowing nothing of what had occurred. Mr Butterworth closed his eyes, and pictures formed behind the lids. A frantic, frightened woman, her nightie muddied and torn, sweat running down the sides of her cheeks and neck, digging the kitchen garden at midnight. A locked wardrobe which had once held her husband's clothes and now hid his body. Floorboards creaking where they had been pulled up and replaced. An emanation of rotting flesh slowly filling the house. A cleaver, a mincing-machine, a knife with a stained blade clattering into the kitchen sink, and a pool of dark blood spreading over the lino tiles. Or, again at night, perhaps not long before dawn and the tide full, a woman drags the naked body of a dead man by the heels, the head bumping against tussocks of rough grass, only the sheep to see. Then the long fall and the splash as it is bundled over Beachy Head.

Up to now, he had been concerned only with routine irregularities in the Civil Service, but it was clear that he had a genius for this sort of thing. Beside him the police sergeant cleared his throat. Nothing as exciting or creative as Mr Butterworth's pictures had formed in the sergeant's mind, but his memory had been at work. Early May . . . that was the trigger. There had been a general Missing Persons enquiry addressed to every police force. A man in his forties, wearing knickerbockers, had been found dead on a train. Had there been a photograph of the face of the corpse, over-made-up? – they all looked Chinese to the sergeant. The enquiry had been routinely dealt with. There had been no missing person of that age on the register. A report to that effect had been made and the enquiry forgotten. Until now.

'Excuse me, sir. Would you object if I was to ask Mrs Pargeter a few questions?'

The man was trying to get into the act. He must have sensed Mr Butterworth's mind racing, imagination and logic carrying him forward like yoked racehorses. Perhaps the police presence had been a mistake – except that one would need him when, under remorseless cross-examination, the woman broke down in tears and confessed. 'By all means, go ahead.'

'Do you remember what Mr Pargeter was wearing when he was taken into protective detention?'

'Don't *you* remember?'

'I wasn't there, madam.'

Peter Alloway thought, *This isn't happening. It mustn't be happening. Can't be allowed.*

'I wasn't there either. You picked him up at the golf club. We never had a chance to say goodbye. It was the Admiral's Cup. Mixed doubles. I don't play golf. A policewoman came round afterwards and told me to pack a suitcase for him.'

Peter Alloway said, 'Would you excuse me a moment? A call of nature.' It was one of those peculiar British expressions he had been taught at the training centre. He had last used it, he remembered, to Kevin Pargeter in the buffet of Gloucester station.

As Peter left the office, he heard the sergeant say, 'And when he went off to the golf club that morning, Mrs Pargeter, the morning he was arrested, do you recall what he was wearing then?'

Peter Alloway walked easily across the lawn and into the house. It was just like the time at the railway station; he must not be seen to hurry. He went upstairs and into the bathroom, locked the door, lowered his trousers and sat on the john. There was no way out that he could see. If he had gone instead to his bedroom, taken his rucksack from the cupboard and the Ingram from his rucksack with a couple of clips of ammunition, made his approach back through the garden as silently as he had been taught, and shot the two of them where they sat together on the functional sofa, that would solve nothing. Wherever he tried to go, he would soon be caught, and Susie would be involved as an accessory; he would not have that.

He undid the top two buttons of his shirt and pulled out the heart-shaped locket to let it hang free. He could hear the cyanide capsule rattle inside it. Susie had asked him about the locket more than once. He had told her it was a keepsake from someone who had once been very important to him.

There was so little time. He must concentrate. What was there he should do first? It would be bad, very bad, for Susie: she would be talked about all over the town, which she hated, but she had put up with that before when they took Kevin away, and there was no way they could make her responsible now for Kevin's death. He wanted to write, 'I love you, Susie,' on the toilet roll, but had no pen. Well, she knew he loved her.

There was the forged identity card, issued at the abbey. The monks must not suffer: Father Philip and the abbot must not suffer. He had intended to go back there and ask them to accept him as a novice, except that he had lost his vocation when he took up with Susie. Still there must be nothing to lead the police back to the monks, and apart from this card, there was nothing. It was small and of thick cardboard in a plastic cover. Because he did not smoke, he had no matches to burn it. He took it out of the cover, tore it in two at the join, then tore the pieces once and then again, but could tear no smaller. The pieces of card were still too large and would float; they could not safely be flushed down the john. He removed the top of the cistern and put the pieces inside. Nobody would think of looking there, and if Susie found them, she would destroy them. He took the capsule out of the locket. It looked like medicine.

He could hear someone heavy-footed come out of the kitchen and into the hall below. That would be the sergeant. No policeman, if he had any sense, would tackle a trained Free British volunteer alone, but the sergeant did not know yet that Alloway was a Free British volunteer. Would they connect him with the attack on the Reichsprotektor? That would have been Sinclair and Parry-Jones – silly sods, they had fucked up – nothing to do with Alloway. He put the capsule into his mouth. The volunteers had been told not to swallow it, because there was the risk that one might be forced to vomit it up again. He must bite. It would be immediate. Three hundred milligrams were enough to kill a man, and each capsule contained five hundred. That would be half a gram. How much was that? Starting with a kilogram as 2.2 pounds, he began to try to do conversion tables in his head. The heavy feet were mounting the stairs. 'Mr Alloway?' He bit into the capsule.

It hurt horribly. Nobody had warned him it would hurt. Violent burning pain, knives in his throat, the world whirling, consciousness but somehow not sensation blocking out, his body jerking, his mouth wide trying to suck in air – the pain! *It is not supposed to be like this.* His bowels moved, and he died. In the mind of the patient, David Piper, a point of light went out.

So the two investigations came together, and matters did not look good for the monks.

First, it was clear that Alloway had been an American agent: the Ingram machine-gun, ammunition and plastic explosive found in his room proved that. The torn identity card was not discovered in the cistern of the WC because nobody looked for it. The assumption was that he had managed to flush it down the toilet or that he had burned it before Mr Butterworth's arrival, but that was of no importance since the number was registered at the police station and could be traced back to the issuing authority.

The number was so traced. It was one of a series allotted to the security officer at the Re-education Centre. Only one of this series had been issued and that was to Kevin Humphrey Pargeter on 4th May.

It was now easy to identify the dead man on the train as Pargeter. Dental records were hardly necessary. Both Mrs Pargeter and the re-educational authorities were able to make a positive identification of the man and his knickerbockers: the mortuary tray in Bristol would now be available for some other corpse. Alloway must have murdered Pargeter on the train and stolen his documentation.

That would be how these underground American agents operated. They were landed on a deserted coast, made their way inland, got into conversation at some railway station or pub with a stranger, gained his confidence, found out as much as possible about him, then murdered him and took over his identity. Perhaps the message on the mirror was not a lie; perhaps Pargeter had indeed harboured homosexual tendencies, and Alloway had taken advantage of that. The investigating authorities knew that homosexuality was rife and legalised in the USNA. An agent would think nothing of prostituting his body to gain a cover, as was proved by the fact that Alloway had also seduced Pargeter's wife, a woman sixteen years older than himself.

The flaw in this theory was that it assumed that the agent would have the skill and facilities to alter both the name and the photograph on the identity card he had stolen. It was not just a matter of lifting the photograph off to replace it and scraping out the old name with a blade. The stamp of the office of issue went across both the photograph and the card: a new stamp would have had to be fabricated, or the original stolen, and a match made exactly. Also the last two digits of the card issued to Pargeter differed from that which Alloway had registered at the Eastbourne police station.

A total of fifty cards had been allotted to the security officer at the abbey, since it had been anticipated that, once the scheme was under way, a continuous flow of Re-eds would be returned to the community. The first had been issued to Pargeter. The investigators examined the remaining cards in the series. Three were missing; one was the card registered by Alloway and there were two others.

The cards had been kept in the office safe of the abbey. Only six people – three lay and three clerical – knew the combination. Had the security officer counted the cards when he received them, or merely checked the top and bottom? He could not remember. He had kept them secure without paying any other attention to them until the time came to use one. The possibility remained that three cards might have been abstracted from the series before the security officer ever received them.

A prolonged investigation of the discrepancy was rendered unnecessary by the fact that the Rule of Saint Benedict forbids its followers to lie. Unfortunately the main body of the monks had only known the Christian names of the strangers they had sheltered, and the abbot was unable to remember exactly what names he had entered on the identity cards, but the investigators were able to piece together general descriptions of the three men – one of them Alloway and therefore now dead – and knew the serial numbers of the cards. They should be able to track down the other two.

Should is not the same as could. Every day, at police stations all over the country, the registrations of overnight residents were reported by hotels and lodging houses, employers registered their employees and the self-employed registered themselves, universities and polytechnics registered students and coroners registered deaths. Thousands of registrations. Every day. These registrations were kept, as one might expect, in registers at the various police stations, to be consulted if need arose. To transfer them all onto a central computer would clog the system: only those with a criminal record made it to the central computer. It was easy to track suspect documentation back to its source, but nobody had ever tried or needed to try to go the other way, from source to suspect. Nevertheless it could be done. Every police station in Britain was instructed to check its registrations since the beginning of May; the two numbers were bound to show up.

Meanwhile the authorities were spared the embarrassment of having to take a whole chapter of Benedictine monks into custody by the fact that the abbey was, practically speaking, a detention centre already, so the security guards were reprimanded and replaced, the two psychiatrists sent off to work in a geriatric hospital, and the monks continued to be confined to the premises in which they had already chosen to confine themselves.

Cape and Attlee were luckier than the monks. Anything to do with the events of 9th July was subject to clearance from the Ministry of Information, but there was no such bar on news about the Cheltenham Flyer Murder (as the newspapers called it) and the Chief Detective Inspector in charge of the case had been stalled for so long, and chafing at it, that he was glad now that he had a success to boast about, to be able to chat off the record with his old friend, the Chief Crime Reporter of the *Daily Mirror*.

The news of Alloway's suicide was censored almost as soon as it was reported, but this time the report came first, the censorship afterwards. Cape saw the picture at work. He and Attlee read the news story together that evening, knew that their identity cards would soon be linked with his, and were out of the Baron's Court digs within an hour and heading west. They were in great danger, they had nothing to show if they were challenged, but at least they were a step ahead.

Three agents, one dead and two to find. Was this the team which had murdered the Reichsprotektor? It seemed unlikely. Alloway could not have taken any part in the murder. On the morning of 9th July – all day in fact – he and Susie had been working in Eastbourne at the Old Harbour and the Butterfly Museum, shooting promotional material for the Tourist Board. That would not rule out the other two as participants, along with the mysterious old man, but in that case what had Alloway's role been? He seemed to have had no contact with any other agent or undercover group since leaving the abbey in company with his two fellows. No strangers, either young or old, had come visiting the Pargeter house over the last three months. It was not isolated; there were three other houses in that small group of desirable residences on National Trust land near Beachy Head. Strangers would have been noticed, as any visitors were noticed, as Alloway's own arrival had been noticed. There must be more than one team. How many more? The investigating authorities had to face the horrifying possibility that Britain had, over the past months, been flooded with armed undercover American agents.

This directed attention once more to the list of names which had been found in the back pocket of Pargeter's knickerbockers. The Alloways of Lidlicote had not been able to identify the dead man in Bristol. Brought a longer journey this time but in less friendly company, they were not able to identify the corpse of Peter Alloway either, but they knew who he must be and that it would have been easy for him to have compiled a list, though why he should have given it to (and left it with) his victim was an element nobody could explain. This time they were not returned to their homes but to a police cell for further questioning. Matters were not looking good for the Alloways either.

Matters were not looking good, now the authorities were forced to think in this way, for any British family with connections among the Free Brits of the USNA. The Leicestershire connection had led nowhere. The Free British connection might lead anywhere. The investigation could be a nightmare.

Sinclair and Parry-Jones, safely back in their cottage in the woods, suffered from a strong sense of anti-climax. They had done what they had been sent to do, carried it off brilliantly, and the British people showed no propensity to rise in arms and seemed to regard the attempt by Yankee hit-men to murder the Reichsprotektor as not having much to do with them except as an item of interest in the newspapers and on TV.

This detachment was vexing to the volunteers, but it had this advantage, that if the Ministry of Information had not played down the murder, and had played up the probability of arson, bombs, the poisoning of wells and the general loss of life to be expected in a programme of indiscriminate terror, the presence of two young men, living on their own in an isolated cottage, might have been reported. As it was the villagers knew that the lads from Devon were convalescents who had taken Mrs Brooking's cottage for the summer because of the healthy air of the Chilterns, that one of them had a girlfriend who visited him regular and both were friends of Cakehole's.

What were they to do next? It was possible that an important element had been left out of the plan. The British people did not know that Free British volunteers had done the deed on their behalf. All this disinformation about the Mafia was muddying the waters. There should have been a signature on the job. It occurred to Sinclair that, if they had indeed been sent on a suicide mission as the mice had suggested and they themselves refused to believe, if they had been captured or killed during the attempt, then the signature would have been there for all to see: it was possible that they had succeeded too well to please their masters. He did not communicate this thought to Arwen.

It was also vexing that the news media should continue with the pretence that the assassination had failed, and that the Reichs-protektor was not dead. If it had not been for Cakehole, that would indeed have been the case; the Attack Group, highly trained and motivated as they were, would nevertheless have fucked up because of the jammed Ingram. How could that have happened with a gun meticulously maintained? Since Cakehole had brought the Ingram back, Sinclair had stripped it down, examined every part, taken a risk by test-firing it in the woods near the cottage, and there appeared to be nothing wrong with it. One could become paranoid under pressure. Was it possible that the Operations Group had jinxed the Ingram?

Parry-Jones talked about hit-and-run tactics and Cakehole supported him. The older mouse had suggested that there might be a role for the volunteers in organising discontent. He had made the suggestion as if it were some kind of treat, a reward for not going through with the assassination, but did he have something definite in mind? While Arwen went off with Carrie to take a look at the steel works at Corby as a potential target, Sinclair cycled to Oxford and met the older mouse outside the Botanical Gardens.

'We'll stroll for a while. Then I'd like to take you somewhere.'

The older mouse paid for them to go in and bought Sinclair an illustrated history and guide. They walked in the gardens, the older man and the young, like teacher and pupil; they walked by the river. The mouse said, 'You know one of your colleagues has been found?'

A trick? A test? What? Sinclair said, 'There was nothing about it in the papers.'

'The *Daily Mirror*. Just a report and then it was sat on. Someone

194

called Peter Alloway. He'd murdered a man in a train, then set up house with the man's wife.'

'Doesn't sound much like Peter.'

'He killed himself when he was discovered. There was nothing in the news report to link him with your Free British Special Service Unit.'

'But you know.'

'Yes. You've never mentioned him.'

'No.'

'Or any others.'

'No.'

'There has to be some trust, Ian.'

It was true; there had to be some trust. Sinclair doubted whether it would extend to his being told how the mouse knew so much about Alloway when the news had been so efficiently suppressed. However. 'There were two others with Peter,' he said. 'It was a group of three; there may be more groups by now. They do have radio contact with Washington, but we've no way of getting in touch with them, or they with us.'

'Very wise.'

'They'll have reported what's been in the newspapers. Washington will think we failed.'

They sat on the bank and watched the river. Term was over. The Cherwell was crowded with parties in punts, but these, the older mouse said, were all townies and tourists; they had no grace and no technique in punting and some were positively dangerous. Also, since this was Oxford, they punted from the wrong end. Sinclair had never seen a punt before; it did not seem to be an efficient method of transport, either end being, as far as he could tell, equally impractical.

He said, 'The question is, what happens next?'

'Are you asking me to tell you what to do?'

'We're asking for advice.'

'Depends on what objective you want to achieve. Didn't your masters give you any other targets?'

'You know they didn't.'

'And you really have no contact with them – by any means? I do find that odd.'

195

'Please don't make a meal of it, Gervase. We know what you think. Let's get back to objectives. Suppose our objective was simply to damage the war effort?'

'Hard to do. There's no line of communication to cut: we're out on the edge in Britain. This is an enormous empire and what's in the Gulf is a fraction of the resources available. Armaments are produced all over Europe, far more than one would need to fight anything smaller than Armageddon. Take out a factory, blow up a train, and you make no practical difference. And the moment you start killing our own people – even the police if they're British police – you might as well go home.'

'Electronics?'

'Not here. Very little here. You forget the Brain Drain. Over the last thirty years all the important and highly paid work has been done in Germany, and all the high flyers have gone to where the money is. I don't think that was planned; it just happened. Once upon a time all the talent in Britain found its way to London, because that was where the money and fame were. Now we're part of a much larger unit and it drifts to Berlin. Let's walk back.'

They walked in silence for a while. Sinclair chewed his lip. 'Suppose we change the objective? Specifically anti-German action? Force people to remember what side they're on?'

'Germany or the USNA?'

'German or British. There's still a German Army in Britain. We're still an occupied country.'

'You don't mean the Wehrmacht? That's integrated – soldiers from all over the Empire; the Germans are a minority.'

'I mean the SS.'

'One division in the whole country – mainly ceremonial duties. Headquarters at Osterley Park. Well, it would certainly cause a fuss, and you're right: it would remind people. You feel you should take on the SS? Just the two of you?'

'And Cakehole. And anyone else who wanted to join us.'

'And you have two light machine-guns, several grenades and a small quantity of plastic explosive? Plus Cakehole's collection. I don't know how reliable his own store of explosives will be after fifty years, but at least it's not nitro-glycerine or your little hideaway would have been plastered over the surrounding countryside long ago. Very embarrassing if someone happened to be sitting on the outside loo reading Trollope at the time.'

'I said, "And anyone else who . . .".'

'I heard you. You've never asked about our organisation, Ian, not for any details, because you knew you wouldn't be told. You know roughly what we do?'

'Look after people on the run.'

'PUs. Right. That's all we do. The total number of our group is fifteen people, of whom you have already met five. I think there may be other groups doing the same thing, but I don't know for sure. We have a limited access to part-time helpers, who may assist us in limited ways – your identity documents, for instance – but prefer not to ask questions. We have no weapons.'

'You said you wanted to take me somewhere.'

'Show you something. We'll go by car. Leave your cycle where it is. This is Oxford: it won't be stolen.'

'If it is, I can't get home.'

'If it is, you borrow someone else's.'

They crossed the Plain and walked towards Saint Hilda's, where the mouse had left his car.

'Where do you get the petrol?'

'I have a source. I don't abuse it. We'll take the scenic route.'

They drove through the centre of the city, the mouse pointing out historic landmarks all the way and discoursing on the superior attractions of his own university. They drove through Summertown and Kidlington and north along the A423, turning right at Hopcroft's Holt, left through the Heyfords towards Fritwell, then right through an open gate on which there was a sign reading:

ALLHALLOWS COMMUNITY FELLOWSHIP
COUNTRY CRAFTS AND HERBS
ORGANIC FRUITS AND SEASONAL VEDGE
CALL AND SHARE

The dusty track must have been almost impassable in winter. They drove through two fields, and stopped at an old farmhouse to which accretions had been made over three centuries, of which the latest and already most decayed was a clutch of pre-fabricated bungalows in what might once have been an orchard. Chickens were picking amongst the pre-fabs, and in the front garden, which had been planted with flowers and vegetables all mixed in together, there was a young man with a hoe, who turned towards the car and favoured its occupants with a smile of singular sweetness. Sinclair had seen that smile before. Only those afflicted with Down's Syndrome smiled like that. 'I'm a trustee here,' the older mouse said.

They left the car and walked towards the house. There was already a woman, middle-aged and wearing a kitchen apron, standing in the open door to greet them. 'If you've come for lunch you'll have to get it yourself. It's Eat As You Stand today, cheese and salads mainly. Can't spare the time for real food; we're making jam.' Sinclair could see through the window that there was a group of four at the kitchen table, one in a wheelchair, hulling gooseberries from a wicker trug.

'Perry and Irene?'

'In the Studio.' A moment during which Sinclair watched her repressing curiosity. 'I'll get back to my lot.'

The older mouse knew where to go. The Studio was a converted barn next to the pig-sty: the farm had more barns than were needed for hay. Downstairs handicapped members of the Allhallows Community wove cloth in long strips on a wooden loom, and the strips were cut up to make shoulder-bags and decorative wall-hangings. Coloured beads were sewn onto canvas to make covers for cushions and dried rushes were transformed into useful matting or the seats of wooden chairs. The frames of the chairs were made upstairs, together with a range of educational wooden toys, salad bowls, trays and platters of various sizes. The barn was airy but had no windows, and although the doors at both ends and on both floors had been opened on this sunny summer day, the mingled stench of pig-shit, fish-glue and human sweat, together with the sounds of hammer, saw and drill and the uninhibited chat and laughter of the workers were a bit of a facer to anyone unused to them.

There was a grey-haired woman sitting cross-legged on the floor sewing remnants of all sorts of cloth – shot silk, brocade, satin and plush, wool, linen, even what looked like dyed hessian – into a patchwork coverlet. Beside her a child, also cross-legged, picked through the box of remnants like a monkey looking for lice, and the woman took whatever she was given in the order of giving and used it. She looked up and smiled at the older mouse, but did not speak.

The mouse said, 'Perry?'

'Upstairs. Trouble?'

'No.'

The woman had stopped sewing for a moment, and the child by her side plucked at her arm to tell her to get on with it. Now Sinclair saw that the child was not a child but a tiny adult whose face was hatched all over with lines, particularly round the eyes which were bright and liquid but expressive mainly of fear. The woman stroked the hand on her arm and the monkey-child nestled into her side. The woman motioned to Sinclair to move on; it was his attention which was causing the fear. The mouse was already climbing the open stair to the upper floor and Sinclair followed.

Upstairs there was a group of men in overalls. They had large flat hands and their mouths hung open. They looked like earthenware figures made from a mould which has worn thin, so that all the features lack definition. Their attention was on an older man, bald and stout and sweating, self-interrupted in the demonstration of how to make a dovetail joint. 'Oh God! God!' he said. 'Heard you down below. Oh, God!'

'Then you heard me say, "No trouble." '

'Oh God! I like it here.' He wiped his face with the back of his arm; it looked as if he were flinching away from a blow. 'Like it here. Not doing any harm. Good. Doing good. Irene more so. No trouble to anyone.'

'I know. Everyone knows. I brought Dorothy's nephew to meet you. Ian, this is Perry.'

Sinclair said, 'Glad to meet you, Perry.'

'Is he coming here? There's no room. We're overcrowded.'

'No, he's not coming. I just wanted him to meet you.'

'Why?'

'To see for himself that you're happy here. To see that you're doing useful work. Valuable work.'

Without removing his attention totally from the mouse, the sweating man said to Sinclair, 'I do the accounts too, you know. I keep all the books and work in the Craft Shop.'

199

'I'm very impressed.'

'That's all right, then.' And to the mouse, 'There's really no room at all for any extra. I speak as I find.'

Downstairs the mouse said to Irene, 'Gave him a bit of a shock, I'm afraid. Sorry.'

'He's still rather jumpy.'

'Yes, I know. Sorry.'

'Shall we see you again?'

'Not for a while.'

As they returned to the car, having refused the Eat As You Stand lunch, Sinclair said, 'What was all that about?'

'Told you. Wanted you to see for yourself.'

'And what have I seen?'

'You've seen Perry.'

'Rather a long way to come for a short visit.'

'Knowledge is worth a journey.'

'Knowledge of what? You may have to interpret.'

'Perry is a PU. He was the Marketing Manager of a firm making sports equipment; they were very big in ski-wear. Irene is his wife. These days when the police come for somebody, they do it at three in the morning, the way it used to be done in the fifties, but at the beginning of the Emergency the Security Forces had got out of the habit of that sort of thing: they came at drinks time and Perry was away at some kind of function. Irene's a very sensible, competent woman. She put them off, told them he'd come in to the police station next morning, managed to reach him to warn him, sat tight herself but set him running – only contact by public telephone, and by God he needed contact; he has no mind of his own. She was close to giving up when she came to my Surgery –'

'You're a doctor?'

Silence. Then the mouse said, 'Careless of me! You could say so. A sort of doctor. Anyway she got in touch. I collected him, found him a place here, and when we thought it was safe, she joined him.'

'Why here?'

'Most people are uncomfortable with the mentally ill, don't like to be near them, so they don't pry. Irene and Perry are both registered as mentally handicapped, but in fact, as you've noticed,

200

they work as members of staff. And Perry's quite right; there is no more room.'

'Interesting, but I'm not sure it amounts to an interpretation.'

'You think – still think – that there's a body of people, PUs on the run, who could be used to do Resistance work: you want to organise a secret army, a battalion of Cakeholes. There isn't a battalion. The PUs aren't like that. Cakehole is unique. I wanted you to see the kind of work we do and the kind of people we're helping – frightened people, mostly middle class and middle-aged, who still don't understand what they did to upset the police because they're used to thinking that the police are on their side.'

'I could use Irene.'

'She's like Cakehole. There's only one of her. Unhappily she's decided to devote herself to Perry.'

'What else have you got to suggest?'

'The problem with your lot in Washington is that they're still fighting the last war. Nobody's going to rise in righteous anger because of something that happened fifty years ago. People don't think they're living under an occupying army because they aren't: people don't think like that at all because the police, the prison service, tax inspectors, customs officers – they're all British. Yet you're right. Control is in Berlin. We don't control our own lives: our people have got to be made to realise that. Locking up the PUs was a mistake. Most people in government know it, but Drucker-mann wouldn't be told: he went ahead and did it. There's been a gradual move towards letting them out again – they called it Re-education – but it's gone wrong. Your friend Alloway seems to have been mixed up in that somehow, but I don't know the details. And what with that, and a minor break-out in Scotland, and Drucker-mann's murder by undercover American agents –'

'By Free British –'

'Yes. Right. We know that; they don't. And now another agent – the dead man in Eastbourne –'

'What the fuck was he doing in Eastbourne?'

'– and God knows how many others, all of whom must be getting cover and support from somewhere –'

'Do you believe it? I don't believe it.'

'There's been a change of attitude. The regime at the detention centres is being toughened up, extra prison officers drafted in, no visits, no letters, no recreational activities, and anyone who gives trouble transferred to the top security prison on Dartmoor.'

'Then we have to strike again. Hardly matters where. Keep them rattled.'

'We have to find a way of telling people. Friends and relations of the PUs already know, and if we're careful we can recruit them, but a lot of them are afraid because they're in a minority. What we need, what we badly need, what could be run perfectly well from Cakehole's hideaway because we can move in the equipment, is an underground newspaper and couriers to distribute it.'

'Freedom Radio?'

'Too easy to trace, and listeners have to know the frequency. Posters. Broadsheets. Facts which can be checked. Questions which aren't being answered. When enough people know, then we can begin to organise action. Industrial to begin with. Blowing up Osterley Park comes a long way down the line.'

'You said there'd been a break-out?'

'Just the one. A tunnel. Took months to dig, I gather, and most of the PUs who escaped were rounded up in a couple of days. There have been no break-outs since.'

'We could organise something. Dartmoor, you said – where is that exactly? A co-ordinated attack. Wouldn't need many. Once you begin to release the prisoners you've got reinforcements. Arm them with weapons taken from the guards.'

The mouse grinned. 'What a child you are! Do the first job first, Ian. One Cakehole is enough.'

The woman in the slate-mine had also said they were children. That was okay. They had liked and trusted her, and for her children were important people. Sinclair suspected that the same might be true of the older mouse. 'A sort of doctor' – probably meant he was a psychotherapist. They returned to Oxford in amicable silence and recovered Sinclair's bicycle from outside the Porters' Lodge at Magdalen. Sinclair said, 'Are you married?'

'You mean, have I children of my own? As it happens, yes. My wife and I don't communicate, however.'

Susie Pargeter returned home after forty-eight hours in the police station to find the kitchen covered in dog-shit, cushions chewed, curtains pulled down and Delphine, her King Charles Spaniel, in a state of such hysteria – reproach and welcome all mixed up together and fighting for dominance – that she bit Susie's hand before lathering it with apologetic saliva. The police had warned Susie that she might be away for a while, so she had put down food and water, but had been too shocked and embarrassed to ask her neighbours to keep an eye on Delphine or even to take her in, and anyway the dog would not have stayed with them. She washed the bitten hand under the kitchen tap, and poured on disinfectant. It was hardly a bite, really only a nip; there was no call for anti-tetanus or any of that rubbish.

It had been frightening at the police station and also very boring. She had told the same story over and over again to a series of different people, each more important than the last, until it had begun to seem unlikely even to herself. When she herself had ceased to believe it, even though she knew it was the truth, they had released her, and she had made her own way home, walking the three miles because she had no money with her for a taxi.

She was tired. She would clean up later. She took Delphine out into the garden, sat down on the bench beneath the walnut tree and went immediately to sleep while Delphine re-asserted her territorial rights on bush and fence. That done, the dog returned to her mistress, jumped up onto the bench, put her head on Susie's lap, and so the two remained for the rest of the afternoon.

Susie woke as the shadows reached the end of the lawn. She was still tired but it was a different tiredness, a sort of deadness. Dead. Kevin dead, Peter dead, the business up the spout and people talking about her all over town. Daddy would have to resign from all his committees, and she would be blamed. Although decent people would shun her, she would not lack for company; she would be harried by reporters wherever she went – fawning crocodiles, pretending sympathy as they dug for filth; her photograph would be in every newspaper and on the television for the public to mock or pity. It did not occur to Susie that, if this were going to happen, it would be happening already, that the reporters would have been in force outside the police station, and there would have been no difficulty in getting a lift home.

Meanwhile there was the house to be cleaned. She scrubbed floors, dusted, hoovered, tidied. It took for ever, and perfection could not easily be achieved by artificial light. When she had finished she ate two poached eggs on toast with a mug of cocoa, set the alarm for five-thirty and went to bed. Delphine, refusing her basket in the kitchen, went with her.

A fine, fresh morning with nobody about. She considered a bath, but there would not be time. Instead she washed and cleaned her teeth with extra care and dressed in jeans, trainers and a clean check shirt. She had used Peter's toothbrush and took a pair of his underpants in her pocket for comfort, nothing of Kevin's. She walked out with the dog in the early morning, as so often before, over the National Trust's springy turf to the chalk cliffs.

She would have to pick Delphine up and hold her to be sure they went over together. It was so far down, it would not hurt either of them, and if it did, it would not be for long. She called the dog, picked her up and held her: Delphine licked her nose. She could not stand at the edge because Delphine might get excitable, wriggle out of her grasp and fall alone; that would not be fair. She would have to take a run at it. Delphine was beginning to be excitable already. Susie tightened her grip. It was just a run and then over; she had better not shut her eyes in case she tripped before reaching the edge. Oh Christ, let Delphine be killed at once without pain. If anyone had to suffer, let it be she, because somehow, without knowing why or what she had done wrong, it was her fault, must be, Susie Pargeter to blame.

Delphine had caught the gush of feeling and had begun to be frightened: dogs were quick like that. Perhaps if Susie were to put her down, just leave her on the cliff-top, someone would find her and give her a good home. She put Delphine down and the dog ran off a little way and squatted to piss. Susie moved closer to the edge. No need now to take a run. She could stand on the edge, shut her eyes and sway.

She was there, almost there, as close to the edge as she could get. It would not be difficult; she could feel the drop pulling at her already. She felt in the pocket of her jeans and took out Peter's underpants, clutching them in both hands held tight against her chest. Peter had loved big tits, had buried his head between them, nuzzled them, nipped and licked at the nipples. Peter . . .

But there was something else to be taken into the reckoning. It came to Susie very strongly that there was something else.

It was far too soon, far far too soon for any positive indication, but she had to consider that she and Peter had never, not once, not even that first time, used protection; that Peter had been young and healthy, and that she herself wanted, did most sincerely and desperately want a child, and that must make a difference. That hadn't been the reason she had made love but it did mean that she had been in a receptive state of mind. She was not too old. Thirty-eight was by no means too old.

Peter was dead. There was no doubt of it. They had not allowed her to see him, but they had taken his body away in a plastic bag. The only part of Peter which might be alive would be inside her body, if only as a tiny fertilised egg no larger than a pin-point. It must be there and was; she would not kill it.

It came to Susie Pargeter that you have to give something to get something; nothing is for free. Why should she care about intrusive reporters and neighbours who looked the other way, when she had something so much better? Let Daddy's committees go hang: he would have to learn to be a grandfather instead. 'Del!' Susie said, 'Come on! Walkie's over. We're going home.'

Cakehole woke them early; Cakehole was always up betimes. 'Up! Shift! Into the Base and stay there! Carrie too. Take all your gear and your cycles.' Sinclair and Parry-Jones were already out of bed and dressing. They had been trained to unquestioning obedience in an emergency; Carrie might take a little longer. Cakehole said, 'As far as anyone will know, you left last night for an unknown destination. Juliet's downstairs, cleaning up.'

He had brought a selection of newspapers, the *Mirror*, *News Chronicle* and *The Times*. Across the front page of each were photographs, head and shoulders, of five young men in British Army battledress with their names beneath – Peter Alloway, David Attlee, Bernard Cape, Arwen Parry-Jones and Ian Sinclair. Only the British government-in-exile could have provided those names and photographs and the news report confirmed that it had.

Retribution

Cakehole was walking a knife edge and he knew it.

First, the two lads must be believed to have left hurriedly by bicycle at night. This must be reported and the interior of the cottage arranged in a way which would support the report – the beds unmade, items of clothing, toiletries and food left in disarray, burned papers in the grate of the sitting-room fireplace. All this must be done quickly by Cakehole and Juliet working together, must be finished before the morning had properly begun in case anyone came looking. Then Juliet would report the departure to Mrs Brooking, Cakehole go immediately to Bobby the policeman, who would make his own report by telephone afterwards.

And the search would begin. Photographs had been published in the newspapers already and would be on TV by noon. There would be posters and hand-bills. Trains would be stopped between stations, and armed Transport Police would interview the passengers. There would be road blocks on the main roads. Squad cars would patrol the by-ways. They would find – well, maybe they would find the other two lads: Cakehole could do nothing about that. They would not find Sinclair and Parry-Jones, who would be lying low as once the lads of the Auxunit would have lain low. So far so good.

But Cakehole himself was at risk. He had been a friend to the two young men, known to be, had taken them under his wing, been often in their company. He would be shocked and appalled, of course, by their duplicity, betrayed, deeply hurt; he had believed them to be what they had said they were, two good lads, farm-workers from Devon, recovering from TB. That would hold for

Bobby, but not much further, probably no longer than it took Bobby to get on the phone to his Section Sergeant, certainly no longer than it took the Section Sergeant to talk to Division. Minutes not hours. Too many questions. If Sinclair and Parry-Jones had been involved in the attack on the Reichsprotektor, then who was the old man? The police would require Cakehole to assist them with their enquiries, and once they had him, they would keep him. He had better go to ground as well and the sooner the safer, but again must seem to have left the village.

And there was Juliet. What was he to do with Juliet?

'You'll have to go to your Aunty Bet,' he said.

'Well, I shan't.'

Juliet disliked her Aunty Bet, who had married into butchery, and her dislike was returned. What Aunty Bet disliked about Juliet was her directness, her clear-sightedness, her disconcerting innocence: the girl had got above herself, and Bet knew when it had begun, at the christening when she had been given that bloody silly name. What Juliet disliked about her aunty and uncle was that they smelled of raw meat.

'It's the lesser of two evils, girl. Bet's all right when you get used to her. I can't keep you with me. I'm going to have to disappear.'

'Into the Base?'

'Eventually. Take off somewhere else, then work my way back. I'll warn the lads. Might shoot me else, arriving unexpected.'

'Can't stay there for ever.'

'Till the hunt dies down. Then find somewhere else.'

'Better if I go with you.'

'Don't be bloody stupid.'

'Stands to reason. Safer. First, you can't stay in the Base for ever, and once it comes to moving out, there's places I can go where you and the boys couldn't. Even Carrie couldn't. Nobody's going to suspect someone my age. Second, once you've done your disappearing trick, whether I'm at Bet's or not makes no difference. They're bound to question me, and I'm only young; they might make me tell. About the Base. Everything. I know too much. Don't take those gloves off. We've still got the bathroom to do.'

She was right. Juliet was always right in practical matters. He looked at his watch. No point in an argument which would only take up time. 'You finish here, phone Mrs Brooking and get back home. I'll talk to Bobby.'

'What if he keeps you? Arrests you?'

'He couldn't hold me, girl. Not Bobby on his own. If I'm not back within the hour – say ninety minutes – and you've heard nothing, go to the Base yourself.'

'Be careful, grandad.'

'You know me, girl. Charm the birds off the trees if I have to.'

'What it is,' he said to Bobby, 'It's Juliet; that's *my* worry. I'm not stupid. I know I'll have to go in for questioning. I was deceived in those boys; we all were, but me most because I saw more of them. What were we to think? – both of 'em speaking perfect English and one with an English girlfriend – nice girl – Carrie – you met her.' Bobby nodded. Fair is fair. He had met her and been deceived along with all the rest. 'Makes no difference: what's done is done,' Cakehole said. 'They'll keep me in – it's an intelligence matter, bound to be – drain me dry, debriefing it's called, find out things I don't even know I know. But it all takes time, and meanwhile Juliet's on her own. I tell you, I'm worried sick.'

'Isn't there anyone she can go to?'

'Right. Her Aunty Bet in Kettering. You've hit it. Problem is, they don't get on.'

'It'd only be for a while.'

'How long a while? You're right: stupid question. Who's to tell?'

'Want me to speak to her? Reassure her, like?'

'What would you say?'

'I'd have to think of something.'

'She's very sharp. Very quick in her mind. You can't deceive her.'

It was true, known to be by all the village: if anyone tried to lie to Juliet, she saw straight through. Bobby wrinkled his nose and chewed his upper lip. He would have to find a way to reassure the girl without telling actual lies. 'Tell you what,' Cakehole said, 'I'll put her on the train myself. Kill two birds with one stone.'

'How'd you mean?'

'Get a suitcase packed for her straight away. Phone Bet to expect her. Say it's only for a while, indeterminate period of time; say that in

Juliet's presence so she knows she's coming back. Catch the eleven-thirty bus to Marlow, stops at the railway station. Buy her ticket, put her on the train, see it leave. Then go round the police station, only two minutes' walk – sub-divisional HQ in Marlow, isn't it, Superintendent Heneage? Tell them you sent me. How's that strike you?'

'It's very civic-minded, I suppose.'

'Made a mistake. I should pay for it.'

'I'd have to come with you.'

'Why?'

'Make sure.'

'Bobby, you know me. You've known me all your life. You said yourself, I'm civic-minded.'

'Don't you want me to come?'

Cakehole looked at him. He did not wish Bobby to come. He wished very much, for both their sakes, that Bobby would not accompany Juliet and himself to Marlow. 'Shows a lack of trust, Bobby,' he said. 'I put it no higher.'

'Procedure. Has to be followed.'

'Okay. You can pay the bus fares if you're going to make it official.'

They caught the eleven-thirty bus to Marlow, the three of them, Juliet with a suitcase which Cakehole had packed for both, though all it contained of his were spare socks and underwear and a cut-throat razor; he did not need a toothbrush since his teeth were not his own. On top of the clothing and toiletries he had packed four strong plastic bags, and in the secret pocket of his jacket he carried his Fairbairn dagger and all the money they had in the house. He wished there were more. They would need ready money when they left the Base; the volunteers had very little with them and would no longer be able to use their post office savings books. He wished he were able to get off the bus before the railway station, visit the bank and use his credit card, but he must do nothing to make Bobby suspicious.

They stood together on the station platform, Bobby at a little distance. Juliet looked up at her grandfather. So forlorn. Bobby wanted to say, 'It's all right, girl. Don't you worry. You'll be together again soon enough,' but thought it might be taken as putting himself forward. A station announcement informed them that the train would be delayed by ten minutes owing to the failure of a signal outside Maidenhead. Cakehole shifted uneasily from one foot to another and looked at Bobby. 'Got to go to the Gents. Bladder always lets me down if I'm in a bit of a state. Emotional. There's plenty of time, with the train late.'

'I better come with you.'

'You don't want to watch me piss, for Christ's sake? Have a little consideration.'

'Sorry.'

But Bobby came with him to the Gents, as Cakehole had known he would. 'Back soon,' he said to Juliet.

The Gents was empty. Cakehole had been watching, to be sure that it would be. It was one of those, only found on the smaller railway stations, which had a proper door that closed, shutting the people inside away from the platform. Bobby did not remain by the door, but came all the way to the urinal. 'Might as well join you.'

Cakehole had the Fairbairn dagger, and it was handy, but he would do better not to use it, partly because getting it from his pocket would allow a moment of warning during which Bobby might cry out and partly because of the blood. Like the volunteers, he had been taught how to kill with his bare hands. It had been over fifty years ago, but there are some skills one does not forget.

Standing next to him, willy in hand, whistling as he pissed, Bobby never stood a chance. Cakehole most sincerely wished that there had been a little more variety in the Auxunits' training, that some distinction had been made between the degrees of violence, that some special blow in a special place would allow him to knock Bobby out for a couple of hours and leave him none the worse, but his instructors had disapproved of that kind of thing as being bound to lead to complications. It had been all or nothing with the Auxunits. Cakehole's instructors had not anticipated that he would be required to silence a village policeman, a decent and humane man whom he had known and liked for many years. He had not been trained to resist emotionally the expression in the eyes of such a victim as he died.

Nevertheless the training held; it was efficiently done. Cakehole dragged Bobby's body into the cabinet of the WC, locked the door from the inside, climbed back over it, and joined his grand-daughter on the platform shortly before the train arrived. It was a diesel of three carriages and with very few passengers at that time of day, so that they were easily able to find a non-smoking section empty.

The train approached Bourne End. It would stop, as it always stopped, at the signal a quarter of a mile outside the station. The elderly carriages of the little local train had doors on both sides between every pair of facing seats. Cakehole opened the door beside them, threw out the suitcase, jumped after it and was ready to catch Juliet as she jumped after him. Nobody on the train saw them go.

'Where now?'

'Lie up till dark.'

Easier to say than to do, since they were in commuter country. An old man and a teenage girl with a suitcase made an easy mark, and it was possible that some house-bound wife, some child, some old biddy waiting for death in a granny-flat had seen them leave the train. But Bobby's body would not be discovered for several hours and they had time before a search would start. They would have to get rid of the suitcase, but that had been allowed for: they transferred its contents into the four plastic bags before piling rubbish on it to make a bonfire behind bushes on a patch of waste ground. Then they walked. They left the houses behind and came to fields. They crossed the fields and came to woodland. They lay up in the woods until dark and then returned across country to the gamekeeper's cottage and the Operational Base, where they were expected and made welcome.

It was torture to Attlee not being allowed to shave. Not allowed: Cape had forbidden it. They were vagrants and must look the part, with shaggy hair and beards dyed with henna bought from the Natural Health Supermarket in Machynlleth, which Cape had visited at great risk, mingling with the tourists. Leadership of the O & I Group seemed to have passed to Cape, who was not, in Attlee's opinion, fit to exercise it, being given to wild ideas and acting on impulse. But Nature abhors a vacuum, and Attlee's own qualities of leadership hardly existed these days, being so diminished by indecision and doubt.

His mind could not settle even on the necessary object of survival, but kept going over and over the same ground, trying to find a reason why their own government, their own people, First Family people, should have betrayed them to the enemy. He would not, could not snap out of it; he was, as Cape pointed out, a typical case of someone whose capacity for action was being destroyed by bereavement. He was like a husband whose wife has suddenly gone off with someone else. Cape kept expecting him to say, 'She didn't have to do this. We could have worked something out.'

What he did say, and very often, was, 'They must have had a reason. A compelling reason. If we knew what it was, we'd know what to do.' If there was a reason who gave a fuck for it, when they still had to deal with the consequences? Answer: Attlee gave a fuck, and it was just about all he was capable of giving.

When the news had broken, they still had the radio. Though they were already on the run, and must travel light, and their weapons took up weight and space, they had not even considered dumping it. They had taken risks to keep it with them. In rain they had wrapped their own jackets round it to protect its delicate components from wet. They had no access to houses with power points these days, not even to a deserted holiday let, now that the Welsh mountains abounded with summer visitors; yet they had managed to report regularly to the Operations Room in Washington, partly because it was their duty and partly because the only hope they had of getting out of this bloody country was that eventually a submarine would be sent to pick them up. It had not occurred, even to the prudent and cost-conscious Lieutenant Attlee, that on the scale of strategic values, their own lives would weigh much less heavily than the trouble and expense of recovering them.

And they had received no warning of what the British government-in-exile was about to do. They had been talking to Washington two nights before, talking to Steve, the Duty Officer in the Operations Room, and he had said nothing at all, not even a hint. For some reason Washington must want them to be caught. That much was clear to Attlee and the cause of all his indecision.

Vagrants do not usually buy newspapers, so they had used papers thrown away in trash cans or left on seats when compiling their

Intelligence Reports. Just as well. What if either had bought a paper that morning, had stood in front of some news vendor's stall where piles of dailies were displayed, uncrumpled and unstained, each folded to display the five confident faces spread across every front page?

Attlee imagined the scene, saw himself staring at the photographs and the names beneath, unable just to take a paper, pay for it and move on, puzzling and alarming the news vendor, who would follow the direction of his customer's gaze, then look from photograph to face and back again as suspicion grew. Behind Attlee there would by now be a queue of people, impatient to buy a paper and move on, but already sensing a drama. Hairy and hennaed as he was, he would know he had been rumbled; he would lower his head and lurch away, breaking into a clumsy run as the people followed crying, 'Stop that man!' The scene had never happened; they had absorbed the shock in private and a day late. But in the chilly hours between three and six in the morning when he lay awake, Lieutenant Attlee imagined it.

That night they broke into a Tourist Information Centre sited beside a main road, deserted but frequently illuminated without warning by the headlights of passing cars. There was a window at the back, but it did not face in the direction of the satellite. Only the front window would do, and for a long three seconds anyone standing at it would be brightly lit. Well, the risk had to be taken. Drivers should be watching the road in front of them. Why should they stop for something they thought they saw briefly in the window of Tourist Information?

Attlee's whole body shook. The cars seemed to follow each other without remission, each one a searchlight. Okay, they did not stop; they did not have to; it would be easy to report a suspicious presence to the police by mobile telephone. And then sure enough there would be a car that stopped, a car with a siren and a blue light, and no quick way out of that Information Centre, not when they were lumbered with two rucksacks and the fucking radio.

Yet they followed the procedure correctly, heard, as so often before, the ringing tone of the red telephone in the Operations Room, but nobody answered. They let it ring longer than was wise, because they could not believe what was happening. But the message was clear. They had been written off. Nobody in Washington any longer wanted to know about David Attlee and Bernard Cape.

The radio, weighted with a stone, was now at the bottom of stagnant water in an abandoned quarry, all its expensive state-of-the-art components broken and rusting. This was not pique; the volunteers were trained professionals, above pique and all forms of petty emotionalism. They had made a professional decision to jettison a piece of equipment for which there was no longer a use. Clearly it would be dangerous, Cape said, to keep a contact with people who had already ratted on them once and might again.

The two Ingram machine-guns and the grenades were also heavy and inconvenient to carry about, and certainly they hoped never to have to use them. The O & I Group was no longer concerned with either organisation or intelligence: the name of the game was now survival. Nevertheless the volunteers did not feel able to get rid of the weapons and leave themselves naked to their enemies.

They were in a bad way, no doubt of that, but matters could only get better, Cape said. The newspapers had published their photographs once, and might be required to do so again as a reminder – would certainly do so if Sinclair and Parry-Jones were caught – but if they could get safely through these first few weeks, they would become old news, recycled, used to start bonfires or line a kitchen shelf. The posters would age; moustaches and Vandyke beards would be inked onto the volunteers' yellowing faces, stick-bodies with exaggerated genitalia would be added and finally the posters would be pasted over with other posters.

Meanwhile each day of vagrancy would make its own alterations to the appearance and bearing of meticulous Lieutenant Attlee, of debonair Sergeant Cape: they would less and less resemble those photographs, which even now they did not much resemble. They would last out the summer, living mainly in the open. When winter came there would be empty holiday cottages again in Snowdonia, and if they continued to be prudent with money, they would not need jobs.

It was not easy but it was possible to live without documentation: they had already proved it. The Present Emergency would not last for ever. They had only to wait, and then, when better times came, to find their own way home to the good old USNA. And when they did, Lieutenant Attlee would have a word or two to say to the people in the Operations Room in Washington.

Stephen Grenfell, working at the Ministry of Information, did get a little warning, and a contingency plan was put into operation.

Sinclair and Parry-Jones had lived with Dorothy's family as her nephews; neighbours had noticed them and might be expected to remember two such handsome and affable young men. They had been gone two months, and faces fade in the memory, but the risk was too great. On the night before the photographs were released to the media, Dorothy and Jack and their daughter Sally packed themselves and their luggage into Jack's old blue van and drove to a lock-up garage. There they transferred into the DKW which, back in March, had brought Sinclair and Parry-Jones to London, and were driven to another of the Allhallows Communities, this one near Loughborough. The blue van was resprayed, given a new number plate, its chassis number obliterated, and was sold at a car auction later in the week. Dorothy was unhappy to leave her patients, but they would have been left anyway if she had been arrested. Her colleagues would cover for her and the Association would hire another District Nurse to replace her when they realised that she would not be coming back.

The identity card numbers of the bogus nephews, Ian and Arwen Sinclair, which were on record at the police station in Battersea as well as in Bobby's ledger, could be traced back to the office of issue. Cards with those numbers had been issued in Barnstaple in 1969 to infants still alive, one a young fisherman of Appledore, the other a lady assistant in a greengrocer's shop. Both endured prolonged interrogation – the investigating authorities had to be seen to be doing something – but neither could be connected in any way with Dorothy's own family in Kingscott (who were also interrogated), or with the murder of the Reichsprotektor or with whatever criminal elements might have forged the cards. Forged identity cards good enough to pass a cursory inspection at a police station or post office were not unknown, and the police were able to pull in for

216

questioning a fair number of those who had in the past confected such forgeries, and it all took time and led nowhere.

It was extremely embarrassing. A senior German general, the appointed representative of the Council of State in Berlin, had been murdered – though one could not yet tell the public so: officially he was enjoying a period of convalescence at a hunting lodge in the Black Forest. The investigating authorities in Berlin had been provided, through diplomatic channels in Berlin, with the names and photographs of American agents, two almost certainly directly concerned with the murder, two in suppport. And they could none of them be found.

Two had lived as members of family with a District Nurse in Battersea, and she and her own husband and daughter could not now be found. One of the two 'nephews' had formed an irregular relationship with a young woman named (it was thought) Carrie (surname not known), and she could not be found. They had made a friend in the village, an old man, Henry Simnel, living with his grand-daughter. An old man of similar appearance had almost certainly been part of the murder gang, and Simnel himself had since murdered a policeman, and he could not be found and his grand-daughter could not be found.

How could so many people have disappeared without considerable underground support? The girl Carrie, for instance. Where had she come from? The number of her identity card had not been recorded by the village policeman, because she had not actually resided with her paramour as a living-in lover, but only visited: they had been observed laughing together in church. She must have had another residence, other employment. How and where had she met this agent? Enquiries in Battersea were fruitless. Carrie: it was not a common name. The village people had provided descriptions of a sort, but once again the photofit could have been anybody. Why had nobody taken snapshots?

The public was to blame. Appeals had been made to it, essential information provided to it, and it had provided nothing in return. That the Reichsprotektor's death was a secret should have made no difference. This was still a case of murder: an SS officer and two sergeants had been killed. The widow of the SS captain, Klein, appeared on television weeping in black watered silk, but was not thought to have made a good impression.

A few members of the public had come forward with reported sightings, almost all mistaken, but in general the public was lethargic, not actively co-operative, interested only as one might be interested in a detective story on TV. The British seemed to regard the whole affair as not being anything to do with them. How could one explain that to Berlin?

Mr Goronwy Watkyns of Abersoch left his van in a lay-by near the junction with the main road and cycled three miles in the dark to the hotel on the cliffs. Megan and Hastings took the train to Pwllheli, then a bus to the Happy Homemakers Holiday Park at Llanast Ymwelyr, arriving late in the afternoon. There were still some hours of sunlight to go. They had brought with them in a bag white panama hats and brightly striped blazers, as favoured by seaside photographers, and put them on behind a sand dune. Thus clothed they played a couple of rounds of Krazy Golf, treated themselves to refreshing ices of pig fat whipped up with cocoa substitute, mingled with the holiday-makers until dusk, then set off along the beach together, hand in hand, as if looking for some private place to settle.

It was well dark by the time they reached the cliff path below the hotel. They climbed it carefully and met Mr Goronwy Watkyns by the rustic feature at the bottom of the garden.

They entered the hotel by the back door and found the landlady at a desk in her private apartments, counting the bar takings into a cash-box. There were five families staying, more than half the rooms occupied, not a bad week for the end of the season.

'Good evening, Mrs Phillips,' Mr Watkyns said. 'Sorry to burst in on you so late. I would have telephoned but there's a fault on the line.'

She must have been surprised to see them, but did not show it. 'I can't take anyone else. The season's not over yet. It was a one-off, that arrangement.'

'That's not the agenda. Council of War, I thought, best thing – you've seen the papers? Quite a to-do in my opinion, requiring the most careful consideration by all parties concerned. Megan and Hastings happened to be in the vicinity so I brought them with me.'

'If you want a drink, the bar's closed but I could get you something.'

'Don't disturb yourself: it's of no consequence.' A look between Megan and Mr Watkyns, the same thought occurring to both. The landlady did not need to visit the bar to get them a drink; she was bound to have a bottle of something in her own kitchen. She suspected trouble and was anxious to get out of the room. For help? But there was none: the staff did not live in. There would be nobody in the hotel at this hour but the guests and they, being families with young children, had not lingered in the bar, but gone upstairs to bed early. 'Gawain and the girls gone home, have they?'

'I don't know what there is to discuss. Let them print all the photos they like, there's no connection, can't be. They were never seen, those two. There was nobody else in the hotel, and they kept to their own rooms until Trefor took them away. No staff to observe them, being as it's only seasonal employment, laid off in winter. I waited on them myself, hand and foot. It was you got Brynfor in, over the language question. I imagine he's to be trusted.'

'Totally.'

'I've never had any trouble with the police.'

'Nor ever likely to have; that's our sincere expectation. You've made a fine place here. It does you credit.'

During the high season many of the glass animals, the china ornaments and the little pillows of fine net embroidered with pink roses and embellished with blue velvet bows, which were a speciality of the hotel, were pulled out of the rooms occupied by families with small children and into the landlady's own living-room, which became something between a boudoir and a gift-shop in consequence. It was difficult to sit down without crushing a rose or to move one's hand without knocking over an ornament. Megan said, 'You won't object if I clear a space for Hastings to sit?'

She picked up a couple of the larger pillows, six inches by four, and Hastings sat uncomfortably on the space cleared for him, his legs pressed together and his hands on his knees. Megan moved vaguely about the room, looking for somewhere to put the pillows down which was not occupied by little pillows already. Mr Goronwy Watkyns said, 'Our problem is, do you see, that you are the weakest link in the chain, Mrs Phillips. What we have to discuss is the degree of that weakness and what we must do to protect ourselves against it.'

Megan, still moving vaguely, one pillow in each hand, was now behind the landlady where the window was uncurtained. 'There's room here on the window-seat if I move things up a bit.'

'Anywhere, anywhere.'

'I'll draw the curtains while I'm at it.' Megan drew the curtains, but without letting go of the little pillows. Then she moved swiftly forwards and pulled the landlady's chair back and down. The landlady opened her mouth to scream as she felt herself falling, and Megan jammed one pillow into her open mouth, the other over her nostrils. The landlady fell backwards and Hastings was on her like a terrier. Megan said, 'More. Something bigger. Cushion.'

A tapestry cushion had fallen off the landlady's chair when she went over. Mr Watkyns picked it up and passed it to Megan who used it to replace the little net pillow over the landlady's nose. Then she knelt on the cushion and heard the back of the chair break. There was now no need for the pillow which had been stopping the landlady's mouth. She had already bitten clean through it and her mouth and the top of her throat had filled with a mixture of cotton waste and small curls of foam rubber. 'If it was a question of post-mortem forensic,' Hastings said, 'I'm not sure we could get away with accidental death.'

'There won't be a post-mortem. She won't be found.'

After some while the landlady's legs ceased to kick, and then even to twitch. Hastings said, 'Not wishing to be previous . . .'

'Give it a little longer.'

So they gave it a little longer. Then Megan stood up, the cushion was removed and Mr Goronwy Watkyns pronounced the landlady dead.

Megan said, 'They're bound to offer a reward soon: they'll use the carrot before the stick. She'd have talked before we could get to her. Is there a black plastic bag in the kitchen?'

Two months had passed since the Reichsprotektor's murder, three weeks since the publication of the photographs, and so far the investigation had succeeded in establishing only a series of negatives. The firm of efficiency experts appointed by the co-ordinating committee to investigate the investigation reported that this seemed to be par for the course. It was all information and classification with the police. Without reliable informants they could not function. And in this case, although there was a great deal of miscellaneous information, all of which required classification, computerisation and evaluation, there were no informants of any consequence, none who was in the know.

The Alloways had been questioned many times. Their houses had been searched, their bank accounts and private papers had been examined. They knew nothing. They had exchanged cards with Peter's family at Christmas, occasional letters, photographs, a small piece of wedding cake in a box, had not kept copies or any record of what was sent, had thrown away most of what had been received. 'Why did you destroy the letters?' 'We didn't think they were important.' 'Who is this man?' 'It says on the back. Gavin, fishing.' Nothing. Two other families living in the village had been discovered to have distant relations in the USNA, and been as rigorously interrogated to as little effect. And the monks had been questioned again, although it was clear that they had told the truth from the beginning, and the abbot and Father Theodemar had each undergone three days of solitary confinement at a Safe House in Ongar, and all for nothing.

Four enemy agents at large with six civilian supporters, two of whom were teenage girls. Good photographs of all except the young woman, Carrie, who was still something of an unknown quantity. They might be in almost any combination, but would probably be in four groups, the two who had been in the abbey and then in London together, the old man and his grand-daughter together, the two who had masqueraded as farm labourers and the young woman together, the District Nurse and her family together.

Unless they had obtained fresh forged documentation (which had to be a possibility), the numbers of the identity documents of all but Carrie were known, and had been supplied to every rooming-house, every employer of casual labour, every police station, every town hall.

221

Posters were still on display at places of public resort, were regularly renewed as they were defaced, and defacement itself made a punishable offence. Why did nobody come forward? The fugitives would need food and shelter: they must come into contact with other people sometimes. Of course they would have altered their appearances, the men grown beards and moustaches, the women changed the style and colour of their hair and make-up, the teenage girls been dyed or padded, dressed up or down to make them seem older or younger. Perhaps they had all used padding, and the police should be searching for a bunch of fatties.

The efficiency experts suggested that, if the fugitives had changed their appearances and bought food only at busy kaufhäuser with no personal service and a queue of self-obsessed strangers at every check-out, they were unlikely to be noticed. There were already spot-checks on roads and railways; even the narrow-boats on canals had been searched. But no spot-checks at kaufhäuser. They should be tried. For a morning, an afternoon, at kaufhäuser all over the country, randomly selected, a unit of at least three armed policemen with back-up readily available should stand at the exits, examining every identity card, comparing every face with the photographs provided.

It was tried, and provoked a hostile public reaction. Most people for most of the time did carry their identity cards as the law required, but many sometimes forgot, and it did not need many to forget, only a few, to clog up the exits of the kaufhäuser. If to these few were added every man with facial hair and any woman over-made-up and with a suspiciously ample figure, the unit of police – armed or no, back-up or no – was soon in trouble. Shoppers who, on busy days, had already been waiting in a check-out queue for twenty minutes, now found another queue stretching all the way to the exit doors, or that they could not actually leave the check-outs at all because of the crush, so that behind them further queues built up, filling the aisles and preventing those still trying to shop from getting at what they wanted.

The patience of these shoppers soon became exhausted. First they complained – to each other, to the check-out ladies, then generally into the already fetid air. Then someone – one could not tell who, someone at the back – would begin to push, and soon the whole mass would be in surging movement, children crushed, women screaming, plate glass broken. In towns and cities all over the country there were injuries, many severe, a few fatal, mostly to the young, the old and the disabled, but policemen were also knocked over and trampled. Spot-checks in kaufhäuser were stopped and the efficiency experts paid off.

The authorities were late in offering a reward, because they thought at first that public spirit would be enough, but eventually a substantial reward was offered for information leading to the apprehension of the American agents and those assisting them. Again the consequence was unfortunate. Members of the public did come forward to claim the reward. Most of what they had to tell was mistaken or irrelevant and, even when it was not, it invariably referred to periods of time before the disappearance of the wanted persons, confirmed what was already known, and was of no practical use in catching them now. Yet those who had come forward expected to be rewarded, and when the words 'leading to the apprehension of' were pointed out to them, they went away grumbling, and complained to local MPs and to the newspapers that they had been cheated: the 'Old Codgers' in the *Daily Mirror* received a particularly large number of these complaints. At present this was no more than an irritation to the authorities, but, as the permanent officials pointed out, as soon as any of the wanted persons *were* apprehended, there would be a multitude of claimants and litigation was likely to drag on for months.

It was obvious to anyone in the know that Berlin would not hold off for ever. All the provincial governments, even of the German-speaking provinces, had become a little worried about the Council of State: the word was that the hardliners had taken over. Hardliners would not accept the reasonable excuses of the co-ordinating committee in charge of the investigation, would not attempt to understand the problems involved, would insist on some success to show, ASAP and PBQ, and it would have to be the genuine article – capture, confession and execution: suicide in the WC would not do. So far the British had been lucky. The attention of the Council, and particularly the hardliners, had been fully occupied with what the

German generals themselves called 'Operation Desert Storm' and their Iraqi allies, 'The Mother of Battles'.

This was itself the creation of the hardliners who had grown sick of stalemate. Balance is a tricky thing. It was not that the ratio of military to civilians within the Council had changed, but that one general had died and another retired, and their replacements were not experienced veterans but Young Turks, mere children in their early sixties who had been too young for the war of 1939–42 and had only participated as junior officers in the limited mopping-up operations which followed it. They were the new face of the German High Command. They lacked battle experience, knew they lacked it and were determined to make up the lack. Add to them a commander in the field who believed himself to be the spiritual heir of Rommel, and trouble was bound to come.

It did. The battle began with the most elegant panzer deployment. The Allies were quite outplayed, chased off the ground. It was a bumping pitch and a blinding light. Wickets tumbled; own-goals abounded. American and Japanese tanks burned like discarded toys on a bonfire.

Of course action of this sort requires a command of the air. At first the Germans had it. The Allied air forces, operating under separate commands, were badly mauled by the Luftwaffe, but between them the Americans and Japanese had the greater resources. Hurt pride and mutual recrimination slowed the process, but in time they were able to get their act together, and they secured parity and then superiority. Rommel had never had to face an enemy able to strafe his tanks at will and drop troops at will on his line of communication; it proved too much for his spiritual heir. The burning tanks were now German, the elegant deployment an undignified scuttle.

At the end of it all, soldiers who had been taught that they could never be defeated had been defeated, pilots who had believed that combat was merely what one trained for, that one would never actually be shot down, had been shot down, and the total losses of the forces of the Three Empires were almost as great in men as those of the Arab infantry (who had hardly been engaged), and much greater in material.

To make matters worse, five journalists had been killed during the course of the action; they had strayed too close and been mistaken for participants. One was a photo-journalist of international stature. His photographs, taken during the civil war in Uganda, of children impaled on stakes and prisoners shot during interrogation so that their brains spattered the uniform of the jovial officer who had ordered the shooting, had been greatly admired and widely syndicated. The death of this man caused much indignation among the world's press.

Operation Desert Storm had taken up the attention of the Council of State for three weeks: the progress of the investigation in Britain was not even a sideshow to it. Now that it was over, and had failed, the balance of power did not immediately shift back. Too many faces needed saving.

In any case Druckermann's murder was a military matter. If the British civilian authorities could not deal with it, then German civilians were not going to tell them how: the military must do it. There were, if one looked back far enough, recognised and approved procedures, employed during the 1939–42 war and in Eastern Europe thereafter, for dealing with disloyal civilian populations which shielded and supported assassins, saboteurs and other enemies of the state. It was simply a matter of making a public example of selected disloyal elements in order to recall the rest of the population to a proper sense of duty.

Of them all it was Cakehole who found it hardest to endure life underground in the Base. He had overseen the making of it, he had maintained it, but of course he had never actually had to live in it. Cakehole was an active man. He could not abide to be idle.

For the first couple of days there had been plenty for him to do, getting the whole place shipshape, checking over all the stores and clearing the emergency exit. This was a tunnel which ran for four hundred metres downhill, following the slope of the woods and ending in a dry bank behind a boulder and a curtain of moss and vegetation: the boulder was massive but had been arranged so that it could easily be moved, from inside or out, if one knew how. The tunnel had not been maintained as meticulously as the Base, seldom even entered during the last thirty years, and in places the roots of trees had pushed through the walls and in other places the roof was not secure. Also the boulder had settled and could no longer be easily moved, whether one knew how or not, which was just as well since foxes had made an earth in the bank and had attracted the attention of the Hunt.

Cakehole had gone at the tunnel, and soon had it to rights again, clear and dry, the camouflage of the exit renewed and the boulder again responsive to those in the know. He had used it at night, had set snares for rabbits at the edge of the woods, knocked pigeons out of the trees and made a careful inspection of the outside of the cottage so as to be sure that the police were not keeping it under observation. Cakehole came alive during the dark hours when he could get out, but by day he moped and brooded. Not that it seemed like day, since their only light was from the paraffin lamps.

Sinclair and Parry-Jones were not troubled by the compulsory idleness. Both had been through Graduate School and both were accustomed to periods of purely cerebral activity. Parry-Jones had brought with him to Britain a paperback Welsh edition of *The Mabinogion* and a photostat of his own translation, and now returned to polishing up his version of the story of Geraint, son of Erbin. Sinclair began an analytical study of the character and institutions of the British insofar as he had been able to observe them: he hoped it would be useful in removing misapprehensions in Washington.

As for their having been betrayed by those who had sent them, well . . . it had happened; they had to adjust to that. Possibly they were being sacrificed for obscure political reasons. Possibly, as the mice believed, they had never been intended to survive the success of their mission. Equally there might have been a break-in; there might have been a leak; there might have been some intrepid investigative reporter getting to the bottom of the mysterious goings-on in Dutchess County.

Carrie and Juliet were sufficiently occupied in performing the traditional tasks of women in both the German and Japanese empires; they ministered to their menfolk. They cooked and laundered and mended. Of these tasks only mending could easily be performed in the confined space.

226

Cooking was more complicated than either had expected. There was a sufficiency of tinned and dried food, supplemented by the rabbits, pigeons, pheasant and the occasional squirrel provided by Cakehole, who considerately degutted them before bringing them home, but Carrie, though she had been brought up in the country, had never plucked a pigeon or skinned a squirrel in her life, nor had these skills been part of the Domestic Science syllabus at Juliet's school.

As for the laundry, there were a hundred and fifty gallons in the water tank, but the lads of the Auxunit had not anticipated washing themselves very often or their underclothes at all. A hundred and fifty gallons would not last long for five people trying to live a normal life; just flushing the loo seemed to use up so many buckets. For the time being the tank was not used, and water was brought cautiously by Cakehole at night from the stand-pipe behind the cottage, but undies were difficult to dry over a paraffin cooker – and how long would the paraffin last with the lamps going all day? Also the Auxunit's store cupboard had no provision of sanitary towels. However, they coped. It was traditional that women should.

Sinclair and Parry-Jones no longer wondered what the Attack Group should do next. They should do nothing. Their cover gone, escape was their only remaining duty. Cakehole itched for action, to be out there every night blowing up a barracks or derailing a train, but such action, Sinclair told him, was inappropriate now: they must not draw attention to themselves. Since they were believed to have left the district on the very night before the photographs were published, they should stay where they were, the longer the better, while first the hunt went elsewhere, then ran out of steam. When the check-points had been dismantled, the mobile patrols returned to normal police duties, the whole operation scaled down to five men and a filing cabinet, then they would move, mainly by night, get to the coast, steal a boat and escape to Ireland. To pluck a figure out of the air, one might give it four months, but since cross-country travel would not be easy in January, and the Irish Sea would be stormy, they had better wait until early in the summer, and remain in the base until May '93.

Cakehole said that by May '93 he would certainly have gone off his rocker. Sinclair, always reasonable in discussion, replied that this was an element they would have to take into serious consideration.

Carrie wished to say that if she were cooped up this close to Arwen for eight months, always in company, never able to make love or even to hold hands and cuddle without embarrassment, she would go off her rocker even more certainly than Cakehole. She could not live entirely in public for eight months; nobody could; it was against nature. She wished to say this but could not, because clearly it was a personal and not a strategic consideration.

Perhaps Arwen would be able to make the point privately to Sinclair. She had noticed that he had looked worried at the eight months figure, just as she noticed everything about Arwen, and a lot of good it was doing her. But there was no privacy in the Base. Arwen could no more talk over plans privately with Ian than she could with Arwen; it all had to be this bloody group discussion, which Ian dominated, being the most articulate and logical. If she could only find a way of getting Arwen on his own, he might be able to think up a good strategic reason for leaving sooner. She wondered whether Cakehole would ever allow anyone else to use the emergency tunnel. She had never set a rabbit-snare, but she could learn and so could Arwen. If only Cakehole would let them go rabbiting together, it might relieve the pressure.

Juliet knew that if she never saw the daylight again she would certainly die.

Cakehole agreed with Sinclair that January would be a bad month in which to travel or steal a boat. It was also likely to be a bad month within the Base. Food would have run out, and supplementing it would be much more difficult than in summer. If there was snow, he would not be able to get out at all, even to fetch water, because he would leave tracks. The paraffin would also be gone, leaving them without light or heat at the coldest time of the year.

Sinclair said, 'How did your Auxunit expect to manage? The Germans would still have been occupying Britain.'

'We'd have managed somehow. We'd have had to.'

'Then we'll manage if *we* have to.'

Cakehole said, 'The Auxunits weren't meant to be a permanent fighting force. The Germans were going to invade in summer. We were supposed to cause trouble behind the lines. The army would have regrouped in the north, and pushed them back. It would have been all over by January.' It was true, but cost him something to admit; the Auxunits had considered themselves a cut above the army.

So they agreed to keep their options open for a fortnight, and see how things went. They would probably have remained open for longer than that, as Sinclair hoped, maybe even until winter when it would have been too late to leave, but for two misfortunes. The first was the arrival at the cottage of a young man and woman, apparently husband and wife, whom Cakehole believed to be undercover police or security; he had spent a night in the back garden and heard them taking up floorboards. The second was that Cakehole's snares were found, and a watch set over them.

It was not the rabbits. No landowner would mind a poacher taking rabbits, which were vermin, but someone who poached rabbits would also be poaching pheasants, which were both sport and income. There was no danger that the watchers would catch Cakehole, who could walk rings round any gamekeeper in the dark and take the rabbits too, but if he did do so he would provoke a search, and the emergency exit might be discovered.

Tenants in the cottage using the outdoor privy, and gamekeepers in the woods looking for poachers. The lads of the Auxunit, with nowhere else to go, might have sat tight, killed those who got too close and, when trapped, gone down fighting. But their girlfriends, their grand-daughters, would not have been in the Operational Base with them. Even Sinclair agreed it was time to move.

The Acting Reichsprotektor, von Neustadt, had come back from Berlin. 'Nothing's changed essentially,' he said to the Prime Minister of the British provincial government. 'It's a purely British matter: they're still solid on that. But the general feeling – particularly the feeling of the military – Druckermann was one of them, you know, one of their own; it's very awkward.' He bit his upper lip, shook his head, and seemed about to go into a reverie.

'The general feeling?'

'How can I sum it up? "After the carrot, the stick" – something like that, something gnomic, eh? After the carrot, the stick. It's only a recommendation of course.'

'It's only a recommendation, of course,' the Prime Minister said to the Cabinet Committee. 'Berlin's position hasn't changed. It's a local matter, entirely up to us to deal with; he emphasised that.'

The five members of the Committee on Internal Security sat at one end of the table with the Cabinet Secretary. Their six advisers sat at the other. Twelve altogether, all men. There were guards outside the room, which had been swept for listening devices. The investigation had been getting nowhere for too long. It had been made clear that they were expected to come to a decision leading to positive action.

The Secretary to the Cabinet regarded his position as analogous to that of the Clerk of a Magistrates' Court. It was his business to put the silly buggers right on matters of law. 'With respect, Prime Minister,' he said, 'it's not entirely a local matter. If Berlin wishes to instruct us, they have jurisdiction.' He meant that if only Berlin would take over, the British Cabinet would be off the hook. 'General Druckermann was a senior German officer, representing the Imperial Government. And infiltration by enemy agents into any part of the Empire must involve the security of the Empire as a whole.'

'Oh, it must; it does.' The Prime Minister so disliked this kind of thing. So much of it was just guarding one's back. 'Nevertheless Berlin has complete confidence in our ability to deal with it. Von Neustadt wanted us to be clear on that. A purely British responsibility.' They were all looking at him. He wished they wouldn't all look at him. 'All Berlin asks is to be kept informed.'

'Well, they are being informed.'

'Yes. They are. I think the implication is that they'd like to be more informed. More information. They'd like us to have more and better information so that they can be better informed.' Silence. 'Information of action on our part. Definite action.' Silence. 'Definite and positive action. I think the feeling in Berlin is that some of the information we've given them may have been unduly negative. Von Neustadt thinks they might like to be informed of some definite and positive action which the military members of the Council would consider appropriate.'

All heads turned towards General Allenby, who had been nominated by the Wehrmacht to serve as the Military Adviser to the Committee. He was not the most senior general officer stationed in Britain, and his military experience had been mainly in engineering and transport, but Berlin had insisted that, in this purely British matter, only a general officer of British birth would do to advise the British Cabinet on questions of Internal Security. 'Search me,' said General Allenby.

'Exactly what did von Neustadt say?'

'I wrote it down. "After the carrot, the stick." Of course it's only a recommendation. He emphasised that.'

'His own recommendation?'

'I got the impression it might be Berlin's recommendation.'

'Did he say what sort of stick?'

'He said it's a purely British matter.'

The Home Secretary said, 'I think the police have a point they want to make here.'

The Commissioner of the Metropolitan Police, a thoughtful, worried man, was still recovering from surgery to remove a tumour from his bowel. His said, 'Berlin should know as well as we do: these enquiries take time. There was that mulitiple murderer in Frankfurt – kidnapped little girls from the Children's Hospital, cut them up and sold them for cat food. It took three years of patient police work to catch that man, even with a very positive response from the public. But they got him in the end.'

'I don't think there's much mileage in reminding them of that, Commissioner; I really don't. I think it might be counter-productive to make that sort of point to Berlin at this moment in time.'

The Head of MI5 said, 'If you'll allow me, Prime Minister, there are aspects we have to face. These people have been aided and supported by members of the public since they landed on the Welsh coast in February. Three of them got to that abbey in Gloucestershire. How? How did they know about the abbey? How did they know the monks would take them in? One of those three, a man named Alloway, had family connections in Berkshire, not far from Harwell, the Genetic Research Institute. You'd think he'd go straight to them, but no: he avoided Berkshire. Instead he went to

London, stayed in a hotel in North Kensington, went out that evening, nobody knows where – except that one member of the Alloway family lives in *South* Kensington. Next morning he was off again – where? – to Eastbourne. Why? We're told that it was because a man he'd met – and murdered – a small-time businessman, a PU under detention at that same abbey – had his home there. Alloway arrived and was accepted without question by the wife – almost as if she were expecting him, but we're told they'd never met before, yet she sheltered him and he became her lover. And we're asked to believe it. Berlin is asked to believe it.'

The Commissioner said, 'I do believe it. We've checked every part of it. He never met his family, and as for the second cousin in South Kensington – Piers Alloway – he and his wife were out to dinner that night.'

'Two of them – Sinclair and Jones – came directly to London. How? Sure, they had money, but they knew nothing about the British way of life; they must have given themselves away every time they opened their mouths. Somebody hid them in Wales; therefore somebody knew they were coming – met them on the beach probably – and that somebody arranged transport to London. Somebody introduced them to the District Nurse and to this other slag, who calls herself Carrie and whose real name somebody must know. Somebody provided them with forged identity cards; somebody suggested they answer an advertisement in *The Times* by Mrs Whassername, who just so happens to own a cottage outside a village in which – guess what? – dear old Mr Simnel lives, and the first thing this Simnel does is assist them to find a lorry, steal roadworks equipment –'

'We don't know that.'

'We do know it. We can't prove it because nobody's talking, but we do know it.'

'We've interrogated everyone connected with the roadworks, everyone who knew Simnel and his grand-daughter, Mrs Brooking and her family, every friend, neighbour and family connection of the District Nurse in London and Devonshire, every member of the Alloway family and the people of Lidlicote, the Eastbourne woman and her family, the monks, the landlady in Gloucester, all those and more, not once but many times. Every statement has been checked and counter-checked. Your own people have been involved; you've seen the transcripts.'

'Look at the whole picture: that's what Berlin is doing. What you see is a network already in place, been in place for years, a network of sleepers.'

'We've offered a reward.'

'They're laughing at us.'

The Home Secretary said, 'I'd no idea you feel so strongly about this, Rupert.'

The Head of MI5's strong feelings had probably begun to come on during the meeting: he had supported and suggested many of the measures so far taken and his people had done much of the questioning. What he was doing now was getting out from under and they all knew it. In a moment he would ask for his advice to be minuted.

The Deputy Prime Minister wished to be thought the strong man of the Cabinet. When the nation tired of weaklings it would turn to him. He said, 'What Rupert means is that we've been playing this with kid gloves for too long. "After the carrot, the stick." Quite right.'

'Make an example?'

'There are people with information. Must be. We've got to frighten them into the open.'

The Home Secretary said, 'The only people positively proved to have committed an offence are the monks, and even there . . .'

'You don't imagine stringing up a couple of monks will do it?'

At both ends of the table faces went blank. Then the Home Secretary said, 'I don't think anyone suggested stringing them up.'

'What's the Council in Berlin suggesting?'

'Berlin,' the Prime Minister said, 'is suggesting that this is an entirely British matter.'

'Right. They won't take our chestnuts out of the fire. Why should they? We have to do it ourselves.'

It was a pity about the Deputy Prime Minister. Some day, when it was safe, he would have to go. The Prime Minister said, 'There'd be trouble with the Vatican if we were to hang a couple of Benedictine monks. Back in the fifties that wouldn't have mattered, but I don't think Berlin would care for it at the moment.'

The Deputy Prime Minister said, 'Anyway two wouldn't be enough.'

A voice down the table: 'Enough for what?'

The Prime Minister said, 'That's rather the crux, isn't it? Enough to frighten people into talking or enough to please the military in Berlin?' No reply. Why did they always wait for him to give a lead? He said, 'I suppose, both. If we're honest.'

The Home Secretary said, 'If we're talking about making an example, just who are we expected to make an example of? It can't be the people who've been supporting these agents because we don't know who they are. It can't be the people who've failed to come forward with useful information because we don't know who they are either. It can't be the PUs because the one thing we bloody do know is that none of them took part in the assassination because they were all locked up at the time and had been for months.' The Home Secretary had lost his temper. The Commissioner of the Metropolitan Police and General Allenby were nodding their heads in agreement. The Deputy PM and Head of MI5 were shaking theirs. Nobody else gave any indication either way. 'What kind of crazy game do we think we're playing?' he said, 'Trying to second-guess a bunch of pig-ignorant generals in Berlin?'

He had gone too far, always did, overplayed his hand; he knew it, they knew it. He was the most able, had the ear and confidence of the House, even journalists respected him. He could not be left out of any Conservative Cabinet, but when it came to matters of principle he always went too far, which was why he would never be Prime Minister.

The Minister of Information said, 'I'm just a media man. I don't do diplomacy; I don't do abstract justice; my job is communicating with the public. We have to make a statement to secure a desired effect. What's the effect? – The Public comes forward with information. What's the problem? – Apathy. How do we solve it? – By making the public realise how serious this business is. Am I right?'

Heads nodded all round the table. They nodded guardedly, but they nodded. The Minister of Information continued, 'Only a strong statement makes a strong effect. Hang a couple of monks? – That's a strong statement but it's the wrong effect: the religious element makes martyrs of them, and all you get is public sympathy for the wrong side. If there's general agreement round this table that some sort of example should be made . . .' He looked around the room. Fewer heads nodded this time. It was not really general agreement, but they did not know what else to do. 'Then we can forget about pleasing Berlin; it's nothing to do with that. We have to show the public that this thing is serious. When the enemy uses terror tactics, even silence is a crime. The whole community has to fight it together. Our example would have to make that strong a statement to make that strong an effect.'

The PM said, 'How do you deal with Julian's point. That there isn't anyone to make an example of?'

'First, we mustn't think in terms of any*one*. One person, two, even three – they don't make a really strong example. Just think how many people are killed on the roads every week. A strong statement has to reach every home, every community. You have to fight terror with terror, and you can only do it once – if you don't succeed first time, people get used to it. Second, the public isn't concerned with finicking points of law. What we have to get across is that there are people in Britain who've been assisting these terrorists and who still are assisting them. We have to persude Joe Public to look about, each man at his neighbour and his neighbour's neighbour, and denounce anyone he suspects. Suspicion is enough. Just name the names; the police will get the proof. But to produce that strong effect, Prime Minister, to roll up the network, our strong example would have to be of a whole group of people – a cross-section, a small community – whom we can *reasonably suspect* of having helped these men. We can't afford to wait for proof. We need the strong effect now.'

The Home Secretary said, 'That's outrageous.'

'I agree with you. Speaking as a civilised human being, I entirely agree. But speaking as a member of Cabinet, my responsibility is to consider the welfare of all our people in the fight against terrorism, and speaking for my own Ministry I'm saying that if you want to frighten people into coming forward –'

'We don't know there is a network of helpers. There's no proof at all, only suspicion.'

'Exactly. Reasonable suspicion, my point exactly. But I'm not making a formal proposition at this stage; I'm simply putting forward a point for discussion. You have to allow me my own expertise, Julian. Obviously if there *was* a question of obliging the military in Berlin, then this could also be a way to do it, and a way the public would easily understand – how many lives is a Reichsprotektor's life worth? But I'm not suggesting that. All I'm saying is that if a strong effect is needed, then only a strong statement will get it.'

The Deputy PM said, 'A community?'

'A small community. And reasonable grounds for suspicion. I agree with Julian that the PUs won't do. I'm afraid our record there isn't of the best.'

The Deputy PM spoke down the table. 'Any suggestions?'

The Metropolitan Commissioner looked down at his hands. The Head of MI5 said, 'Three villages for a start. There's this place in Devon where the District Nurse came from. These Devon villagers, they're all clannish, must have known something. And of course the village in the Chilterns where the old man lived. Reasonable grounds for suspicion there. And there's the Alloways. Direct family connection, and most of them living in the same locality. And there's another group in that village, come to think of it, with cousins in Indianapolis.'

The Minister of Information said, 'From the professional point of view, a village is ideal. Ideal size. Ideal cross-section. Any village would do.'

'Hadn't you better put a stop to this, Henry?' the Home Secretary said privately to the Prime Minister.

'We have to do something. I'm only taking advice.'

The Home Secretary stood up and said, 'You'll have my resignation by motor-cycle messenger this evening.'

'Julian, I do wish you wouldn't.' But of course the gesture had been made. 'You will remember when it comes to writing the letter, that you're still bound by the Official Secrets Act?'

The Lord President of the Council said, 'Hang on, Julian. I've got something to say.'

The Lord President had come to the Cabinet through the Whips' Office. If he chose to speak, his colleagues listened. He looked round the table. His hair was short and had been sandy; now there were crushed sea-shells among the sand. He wore bank manager's spectacles of thick plastic with heavy black frames, and a bank manager's moustache, clipped close. When he looked at you, you knew the amount of your overdraft. Of the men at the table only General Allenby could meet his gaze; the others looked down and some of them doodled or pretended to make notes.

He said, 'We all know this sort of thing has happened. Not here, not anywhere for many years, but it has been done. If we don't do it ourselves, it may be done for us. And if Berlin does it, if the Wehrmacht does it, if the bloody SS does it, there'll be demonstrations, riots, God knows what – more lives lost, certainly. Our whole movement towards independence within the Empire, all the ground we've gained, will go right back to first base. We're talking about damage limitation here. It has to be done as surgically as possible, as cleanly as possible, as humanely as possible and still make its effect. There's no question of executing a whole village community, whatever they may or may not be hiding; we're not barbarians. Just the men will do. And then bulldoze the houses: that hurts nobody.'

There was a silence. Then the Home Secretary sat down again and slowly, unhappily, General Allenby nodded.

Stephen Grenfell said, 'They seem to have jumped from the best possible to the worst possible option with no intervening stages.'

'When will it happen?'

'Soon.'

Both men sat in silence for a while. Then Grenfell said, 'There's nothing we can do, Gervase. No warning. No way of saving them.'

'Then I have to be there.'

'I may be able to arrange it.'

The Strong Example

At five-thirty p.m. on Wednesday 23rd September, the telephone rang in the public box which was on the edge of the village green opposite Heritage Antiques and the Walnut Tree, where Main Street met Peacock Lane in the village of Lidlicote. It rang three times and then stopped. Mrs Gambon, who was on her way to the sub-post office, which was also the village shop and took in dry cleaning, heard it, lingered for a moment wondering whether she should answer it, then continued on her way.

'The phone's just rung in the phone box.'

'Just rang in here, didn't it? Stopped before I could get to it.'

'Rang three times. I was going to answer. See who it was. But it stopped.'

'Same in here. Stopped.'

'There's a funny thing, then.'

'World's full of them.'

Mrs Gambon picked up a packet of gravy browning from the counter and put it down again. 'I only come in for the cat,' she said. 'Simultaneous, was it, then?'

'Don't know, do I? I only heard it in here. Wrong number, I expect.'

'Thass right.'

In Doctor Dart's surgery his receptionist had come to the same conclusion. The phone was right next to her, but she always let it ring for a little while to give people a chance to change their minds, and it had stopped just before she picked it up. There were two patients waiting, old Jim Lester (twenty Woodbines a day since

239

puberty) whose leg-ulcers required dressing, and Lily Passmore who had missed the ante-natal clinic at Harwell on Monday and thought she could make it up by the expense of a private visit. Jim was the five-fifteen appointment, Lily the five thirty-five. Doctor Dart was running late, but no more so than usual.

'No peace for the wicked,' said the receptionist. 'It'll ring again in a moment.' But it did not ring again.

In the Walnut Tree, Katrina Masterson was sitting right by the phone, and picked it up at once, since they were not fully booked that evening and it might be a party for dinner. The Walnut Tree was in *The Good Food Guide*, highly commended for traditional English cooking, served in an unfussy but friendly atmosphere, and a sensibly restricted wine list imaginatively put together. 'Walnut Tree,' she said, 'How can I help you?' and the telephone burped at her, made that high-pitched whining noise which always means, in telephones, televisions and radios, that something has gone wrong which it will cost money to repair, and then went dead altogether. This was extremely worrying for a family of hard-working people in the catering trade who depended on the phone for their livelihood. She would have to go to the box by the green to phone the engineers and report the fault, but nobody would come out until tomorrow to repair it.

The telephone rang at five-thirty that evening all over Lidlicote wherever there was a phone, rang three times and stopped, and most people did not reach it in time to answer it, and those who did found that it went dead. Several villagers went out to the public box to report it, where they found neighbours with the same intention, but the public phone was out of order also, so they concluded that there must be a fault in the Exchange, and that the engineers would probably already know about it. But if the phones were still off in the morning, somebody would have to go over to the next village, or Jim, Robert, Henry, Peter, Stephen would get his secretary to report it from the office.

There were two school buses, one for the Technical School at Wantage, the other from the Grammar School at Newbury. They did not come into the village, but picked up the Lidlicote children and put them down a couple of kilometres away at the junction with the B4494. The children walked the rest of the way, which was not pleasant in snow or fog, but they were all over eleven years old; the younger children went to the Primary School in the village itself. It was a long school day for the older children, who left the village at a quarter past eight and returned at a quarter to six. If they were involved in extra-curricular activities like the school play or the Von Schirach Youth Group, special arrangements had to be made.

There were no special activities at the Grammar School that Wednesday; the autumn term had only just begun. The four Lidlicote children, Gareth and Lydia Halliday, Simon Hatcher and Grace Powell, left the bus and began to walk up the hill to the village. There was an obstacle in the road. They knew what it was, had seen such a thing on television often; it was a road block. There was a police car by it, as one would expect, with a couple of uniformed policemen, but also two large army lorries, one empty, and soldiers were being hustled out of the second. A Hauptfeldwebel – Gareth recognised the badge – was barking at the soldiers, herding them at the double through a gate at the side of the road and into the field where bullocks from Manor Farm had retreated uphill before them and gathered in a clump at the top. The soldiers did not look very happy or very used to what they were doing. One fell over a molehill and landed in a cow-pat, to the Hauptfeldwebel's fury; he was not permitted to return to the truck, but told to get on with it (whatever 'it' might be), smelly and dirty as he was. All the soldiers had rifles, and there was a young officer with a revolver in a holster on his belt talking to the policemen at the road block, and more soldiers in the field on the other side of the road.

'What's up?' Simon said to one of the policemen at the road block.

'Police business. Nothing for you to bother your head about,' and the young officer said, 'Exercises. Just night exercises. Manoeuvres.'

The children would have liked to linger and watch, but it was clear that they were not welcome, so they walked on slowly together up the road. Their parents might know what was up: if it really was some sort of army exercise outside the village, then the Parish Council would have been given advance warning. Or the kids from the Technical College, who were usually home before them, might know.

241

'Someone escaped from Reading Gaol, I expect,' Simon said. 'Some rapist. Psychopath. Violent anyway. Probably that weirdo who ripped up the horses on Lambourn Downs. Soldiers won't catch him on their own. They'll have to use dogs.' He did not really believe it. It probably was just night exercises as they said, nothing exciting at all, nothing to be part of, but one could hope.

What was odd, Gareth said, was that the Hauptfeldwebel had sworn at the soldier in English, and the soldier had obviously understood him. Usually the language of the Army was German. Gareth was older than the other three, a sixth-former, almost eighteen. He would be doing his own military service soon, and was thinking about making a career in the Wehrmacht, so he was interested in such matters.

The posting of General Allenby as military adviser to the Cabinet Committee was now seen to be judicious. He was a specialist officer, had begun his military career as an Engineer and had moved onwards and upwards with the Transport Corps. Operation Strong Example was primarily a problem of transport, of organisation and transport. Why? – Because it was a purely British matter. The British provincial government had ordered it, and British personnel must carry it out. But which British personnel? The police were not equipped to handle it, psychologically or in any other way. Prison officers could not do it: they were accustomed to capital punishment for murder, but had never been required to administer it themselves, and clearly execution on such a scale would be beyond the capability of the public hangman. This was one for the Army, but the Army was not British.

The Wehrmacht was not organised on national lines: its obedience was to the Empire, to the Reich, in effect to Berlin. Every unit was a mixture of nationalities – German, French, Italian, British, Dutch, Scandinavian, Iberians, Georgians and Armenians, Balts and Bohemians, Moravians and Slovaks, Hungarians, Romanians, Croats and Serbs and so many more, all mixed up together. For the period of their military service, soldiers were trained and stationed away from the province in which they had been born, saw few of their own countrymen and were discouraged from association with those they did see. The Wehrmacht was organised like the legions of Imperial Rome, only more thoroughly integrated and without the support of untrustworthy allied cavalry.

Before the Army could function in this purely British matter much disentanglement would have to be done. Soldiers born in Britain would have to be temporarily removed from their units and shipped back to be remustered *ad hoc* as one purely British battalion. And the disentanglers would have to ensure that no soldiers born or reared within fifty miles of Lidlicote were among them.

Could a firing squad be formed from such a scratched-together group? Almost certainly not: such soldiers would have no *esprit de corps* at all and could not be trusted to do the job professionally. One must look elsewhere. The most trustworthy, highly trained and mutually reliant soldiers were the SS, who were not conscripts but dedicated professional soldiers. Unfortunately the SS units were almost entirely German, and therefore quite out of the picture. However, the four soldiers who had been killed – Obergruppen-führer Druckermann, Captain Klein and the two sergeants – had all been members of the SS, so some sort of SS presence in the operation might be considered appropriate.

'*Almost* entirely German.' The solution lay in that 'almost'. During the 39–42 war, for reasons of propaganda, a number of divisions of the SS had been formed of ideologically committed foreigners who volunteered for the service. The 5th Wiking Division consisted of Scandinavian volunteers, the 33rd Charlemagne of French and a rag, tag and bobtail of disaffected British prisoners of war were recruited into what began as the British Free Corps and later became the William Joyce Company of the 23rd Nederland Division. These token units, although much diminished, still existed. The William Joyce Company was employed in ceremonial duties in Berlin. It seemed to General Allenby that it made excellent sense to form the firing squad from soldiers of the William Joyce Company.

So it was arranged. A detachment of twenty experienced men – ten to do the business and ten in reserve – under the command of Standartenführer Hawkins, had been assigned to the operation. Since a firing squad cannot efficiently be manned by soldiers who, when it comes to the point, are unwilling to fire, the men had been told that they were to execute traitors who had given shelter to the murderers of Obergruppenführer Druckermann, that it would not be pleasant but, for the honour of the service, the execution must be carried out in a soldierly manner by skilled marksmen who would dispose of the condemned men humanely with no mess. All had volunteered. They had been flown to London, taken to visit the tomb of William Joyce in Westminster Abbey, and had been billeted at the SS Barracks in Osterley. They would proceed at first light by military transport to Lidlicote to rendezvous with the battalion sealing off the village.

This battalion, the scratched-together battalion of men disentangled from other units, did not consist of experienced men. The soldiers had been collected from various sources, but preference had been given to the Pioneer Corps, the Service Corps and to troops still under basic training. Most were conscripts aged between eighteen and twenty. Inexperience and ignorance were the criteria here. Experienced infantrymen, if they discovered that they were assisting at a mass execution, might be unhappy about it. Inexperienced men would be more concerned with getting the details right and avoiding the disapprobation of their officers than with the nature of the action itself. They had been told nothing about the object of the exercise, only that they must let nobody through their lines and that any civilian who attempted to get past was to be held until the arrival of an officer, or, if he would not stop on command, shot. They were, objectively considered, an extremely shoddy lot of soldiers, but General Allenby believed that they would be sufficient to the purpose.

Now they were spread out all round the village, two kilometres away and out of direct view. This was their First Position; the tapes had been laid during the afternoon. There were road blocks on all three roads, manned by the police with the soldiers' officers in attendance. The officers were rather a shoddy lot also, but not so stupid that they could not guess that something unpleasant was up. The police did not know what was to be done in the morning or that anyone attempting to force a way out of the village would be shot. All the police had been told was that they were to assist the military in a night exercise, controlling the public. Only *bona fide* residents of Lidlicote were to be allowed access to the village, and only those who were not residents were to be allowed out.

Six o'clock. Village men and some women who worked in Oxford, Newbury, Didcot, Wantage, Marlborough and Reading were coming home. Harry Peace and Paul Hatcher, boffins from the Genetic Research Institute at Harwell, sharing a car because Paul had injured his wrist, were stopped at the road block and allowed through. Anthony Cladding, Von Ribbentrop Professor of Applied Aesthetics at Oxford, was dining in college and would be home later if he did not decide to stop over. It would be better for him if he did so decide.

No contingency plan had been made for villagers on holiday, in hospital or spending the night away: General Allenby assumed that this was a question which would sort itself out. The Alloways were another kettle of fish; they had a direct link to the terrorists. Piers Alloway and his wife would be taken from their flat in Onslow Square during the night to Paddington Green police station, from which Piers would be brought to Lidlicote to be shot with the others. Other Alloways living further away would be held in detention and a decision made in due time about what to do with them. It rather depended on what happened as a result of the Lidlicote operation.

The soldiers were stationed singly with five metres between each. That was a sufficient interval during the remaining hours of daylight, but when the sun set they would move to their Second Position just under a kilometre away from the village, which would bring them closer together. The line would not be broken for a meal or toilet purposes. Each man had been supplied with bread, cheese, sausage and an apple, there was water in their canteens and they would have to piss and shit where they stood. The only worry was whether, if any alarmed villager did attempt to escape through the fields, the soldiers would get into a muddle and shoot each other.

Luckily there was very little cover. The fields were large. Hedges had been grubbed out shortly after the war to open the land for the plough, and these new fields were divided only by fences of barbed wire strung between wooden posts. In those under cultivation, the wheat and barley had already been harvested, leaving a stubble which the soldiers found inconvenient and hard on the feet, but it would hide nobody. Sheep had been let into one of the harvested fields to glean, and there were more sheep in the fields left to grass, and the Manor Farm bullocks in two others, and Jim Shepherd's herd of pigs with their portable triangular shelters in a third.

Perhaps these shelters should have been moved out of the way; a small man could hide in a shelter with the pigs if he could reach it. Too late now. It would confuse the soldiers; those stationed in the pig-field had better be instructed to lift each shelter as they reached it and look beneath. Meanwhile a decision had to be taken whether to drive the various animals back towards the village as the line moved in or allow them through the cordon under supervision. Some of the soldiers, city-bred lads, were already nervous of the bullocks, and they were likely to become more so after dark. The battalion commander gave the order and the line moved forwards, parting to allow the bullocks to be driven through it to the bottom of the hill.

Six forty-five. A car turned off the B4494 and was stopped at the road block. The people inside were a party for dinner at the Walnut Tree, arriving early so as to be able to enjoy drinks in the garden in the warm September dusk. They were turned back, protesting. They should have been warned; it was an anniversary; the soldiers had no right to inconvenience the public in such a way with their night exercises, after one had put on one's glad rags and driven from Hungerford. The driver, a man of some influence in Hungerford, wrote down the names of those in charge and said he would report it.

People driving out for dinner at a restaurant were not a problem. Dinner guests at private houses were another matter.

Two dinner parties had been arranged for that evening, one at the Garlands, one at the Gills. Lidlicote people were well-heeled; they gave dinner parties. Some of the guests were related to their hosts; some were close friends. They did not understand why the presence of the Army on night exercises in fields outside the village should prevent their keeping a social engagement. They showed a disposition to argue; they asked unanswerable questions. 'Why can't we? We won't be in anyone's way. We're simply going to my uncle's house for dinner and we'll be leaving before midnight.' They demanded reasons, and the police had no reasons because they themselves had not been given reasons. 'Well, do my aunt and uncle know what's happening? For Christ's sake, man, we're expected. If they'd known they would have phoned, wouldn't they, and warned us not to come?' Obviously the villagers did not know that their guests were being turned away, just as the guests did not know that the village telephones were not working. 'Look, I'll just go on to the house, tell them what's happening and come back. You can send someone with me if you like.'

It became extremely messy, the Gills' dinner guests and the Garlands' dinner guests all mixed up, and four senior citizens, crowded together in a three-wheeler bound for a Whist Drive in Lidlicote Village Hall, and other cars arriving, containing genuine villagers getting home from work and having to be allowed through the road block ('Well, if they can go, surely we can go?'), and finally the army officers had to intervene. Hands resting on their revolvers, chins raised high above the metal braid of their uniform collars, they embodied authority. They reminded the angry dinner guests that there was a war on, and that interference with the military in the performance of their duty was a form of treason and liable to trial and summary punishment in a military court, and the dinner guests went grumbling away.

It was nonsense, of course, and both sides knew it. There was a war but it was far away, and military law had not been imposed in any of the German provinces. The dinner guests would talk, were bound to; it would get about. The purely British officers of the hotch-potch battalion did not like what little they had been told about this operation, but wished they had been told more.

There was talk in the village, as there was bound to be, but no apprehension of danger. The talk was all of the inconvenience, how they should have been warned of these night exercises in order to rearrange their social commitments. With the telephones all out of order, the villagers visited each others' houses to grumble together, congregating particularly in the homes of those who were parish councillors and in the Walnut Tree to commiserate with Harry and Katrina, who were not merely being inconvenienced but actually losing money: Justin, the younger of the two Alloway solicitors, was reasonably confident that compensation would have to be paid. When it was clear that the dinner-guests were not going to arrive, the Garlands invited neighbours to help them eat up all the food: the Gills preferred to use their freezer. Many children asked to be allowed to watch the exercises, but the word was that the soldiers were armed, so the parents refused.

At eight o'clock, when it was well dark, the soldiers moved to Position Two. Most of the farm animals were now outside their perimeter. Nobody was found to be hiding under the pig-shelters.

The road blocks remained in position to deal with any villagers still to arrive home, any late bookings at the Walnut Tree and with those who had arrived early at the Whist Drive and now wished to leave. The policemen were replaced at midnight by other policemen: the army officers remained at post.

At twelve-thirty, the Von Ribbentrop Professor of Applied Aesthetics returned from dinner in college, to find his secretary-companion, Mark Auster, watching the late-night movie on television. They heated milk for Ovaltine, drank it and went to bed.

The Head of MI5 arrived by Rolls Royce at two in the morning, followed by two Austin Twelves containing eight of his field officers. They were waved through the road block and drove on side-lights past the perimeter of Position Two to a point just outside the village where a white gate beside the road opened onto firm pasture. This had been selected as the Operational Command Post by an advance party masquerading as county surveyors. The driver of the Rolls opened the gate, and all three cars were driven into the field, where they were parked and the lights switched off.

At two-fifteen General Allenby arrived in his command vehicle. Oberstleutnant Gillman, the battalion commander, was waiting for him at the road block. The command vehicle, with its kitchen area, chemical toilet, central table and sofa-bunks, would have been immediately recognised by the Happy Holidaymakers of Llanast Ymwelyr as a motor home, except that its body was armoured and its radio capable of receiving more than the Light Programme. Gillman joined the general and his ADC inside the vehicle. At the Command Post they were joined by the Head of MI5 and one of his officers.

'The immediate job is to get all the people out of the houses,' the general said. 'Start at this end of the village and do only two houses at a time, so as not to alarm the others. No panic. Bound to be agitation, but keep it under control, eh? Separate them as we get them out, men one way, women and children another, both to be kept in a secure environment.'

The Head of MI5 said, 'There's a cellar at the Manor Farm. Restricted access, very easily guarded. There's only one entrance, outside from the farmyard and down a flight of steps. Nothing much in it but straw and sacks and a pile of smokeless fuel. Ideal for the men. Take about eighty.'

'How many men are there?'

'Eighty adults on the register. They're not all here, of course. Three away at college, two doing army service, two still on holiday, one in hospital. I don't know how many you've checked in at the road blocks.'

Gillman said, 'Fifty-one,' and to the general, 'May I ask the object of all this, sir?'

The Head of MI5 disliked being interrupted and disapproved of questions about the object of anything. Like many civilians he had an exaggerated respect for orders. 'Women and children in the church, we thought. It's at the opposite end of the village, and again the access is restricted.'

General Allenby said, 'Excellent! Very thorough advance preparation by your people,' and to the battalion commander, 'One step at a time, eh, Gillman? There's always the possibility you may not have to take more than one.' The Head of MI5 narrowed his lips and sucked in his cheeks, and the general said, 'I don't know why you should be so prune-faced, Phibbs.' He had been sitting next to the fellow at Cabinet Committee for several weeks but was damned if he was going to call him Rupert. 'You can't be looking forward to it. Anyway I've no authority as of now to go any further than separating the men and women under secure conditions. The order to proceed thereafter has to come from a member of Cabinet.'

'You've no authority because you've refused it; that's the only reason.'

'Right. I've refused it. Interesting that you should know that.'

249

Mr Phibbs' subordinate, the very officer who had been in charge of the advance party, thought *No love lost there.* If this operation were to go wrong, somebody would have to carry the can. He wondered whether his Chief might be putting himself too conspicuously on the line.

What General Allenby had said at a private meeting with the Prime Minister had been this: 'I need someone with the authority to call it off. I *require* someone – do you understand me? – with the authority to put a stop to it at any time. I haven't the authority to do that myself, and I will not proceed without the presence of someone who has.'

Consequently the Deputy PM would be attending on behalf of the Cabinet: he had volunteered. He would be arriving soon after the firing squad. Officially his presence was to ensure that the operation was carried out in an orderly manner and, as they had agreed, as cleanly and humanely as possible. For the same reason a film unit from the Central Office of Information would make a record of the execution, a print of which would be sent to Berlin. None of those concerned was sure what 'cleanly' meant in this context, but they found it was a word they could not do without.

Politicians! the general thought, *What a crew! What a bloodthirsty amateur shambolic crew!* 'Do your people have up-to-date lists for each house?' he said to Phibbs.

'Of course.'

The general turned back to Oberstleutnant Gillman. 'I'd like this part of the operation completed within two hours. Mr Phibbs' people will show you the cellar and the church. I suggest detachments of six men under an NCO to guard each secure area, another eight for each house. You were asked to keep a platoon of experienced men out of the line as a reserve.'

'That's been done, sir.'

'One officer from MI5 will accompany each detachment to check the occupants against his list. No time to be allowed – no arguments, no explanations, no appeals. Your men to speak only German throughout; that should cut down the chat. Male adults to be taken to the cellar immediately under a two-man escort – bare feet and underclothes, no time to dress; keep them disorientated and they won't try to make a run for it. Women to be allowed to dress and to dress the children before proceeding under escort to the church, but no hanging about. Again a two-man escort. Escorts to return immediately they've handed the prisoners over. Meanwhile the remaining four men and the MI5 officer have already gone on to the next house. Sorry to give you this in such detail. Doing your job for you – very bad form – but under the circumstances . . .'

'German, sir?'

'Better language for this sort of thing. "Raus! Raus!" Carries conviction, and it'll help with the disorientation. Not many of the village people speak German, I imagine, and certainly not fluently.'

'What about Mr Phibbs' people?'

The Head of MI5 said, 'They don't talk much.'

'Raus! Raus!' They did not know what was happening, could not tell what it was all about.

Old Jim Lester was hustled away, wearing only his combs and in bare feet. He tried to tell them about the ulcers on his legs, but they did not seem to understand. They had blackened faces and carried guns. They picked him up, each with an arm under one of his elbows, took him to Manor Farm at a run and slung him down the steps into the cellar against a pile of Coalite. He asked them about Ellen, what was happening to Ellen, but they did not answer.

It was cold in the cellar and dark and the floor was damp. They had lighted a Tilley lamp outside and made a small fire and there were soldiers standing around it, so he went to the open door to complain, but a soldier pushed him back with the butt of a rifle, and spoke harshly to him in a foreign language, the sense of which seemed to be that he should stay where he was and be quiet. Behind the soldier, he could see, they were bringing in John Oade, his next-door neighbour, and his son Peter, both also only half dressed. Peter was simple, which was why he still lived at home with John and Annie.

A voice spoke out of the darkness from against the wall of the cellar. It was Mr Kingston, the farm manager. He said, 'Doesn't seem to do much good talking to them, Jim. We don't know what's happening, but I imagine we'll find out. Something to do with the exercise maybe: something gone wrong. Are you hurt at all?'

251

Jim thanked Mr Kingston and said that he was not hurt. Mr Kingston told him to turn away from the door and look only inside the cellar, and he would find he could see a little as his eyes grew used to the dark. It was true. There were several men in the cellar: all three of the hands who lived in the farm cottages and Mrs Kingston's brother, Mr Freeland, who was on holiday from where he worked near Bristol. Mr Freeland had hurt his forehead and Mr Kingston his arm. They were joined by John Oade and Peter who were unhurt – though John was indignant – and then Billy Wilsher was pushed in, Jim's neighbour from the other side, known to be light-fingered and had done time. 'Here's a fine go!' Billy said, 'Puts me in mind of the Scrubs. What you been up to, Jimmy?'

The Manor Farm was no longer owned by the Manor, but had been bought by a chain of food stores, Qualitäts Lebensmittel, which owned farms all over the Empire, all managed to the same system of quality control. The Manor itself was something of an embarrasment to the village. The Denford family had lived there since the early eighteenth century – which was itself off-putting since most of the villagers were newcomers – but they had fallen into genteel poverty: the fabric of the house was in poor repair and the grounds not kept up as they should be. National Gardens Day passed Lidlicote Manor by, when every other village garden of a suitable size was bright with visitors in summer clothing, all of whom had paid their two marks fifty to the Nurses' Fund. Now, as Sir Charles Denford was pushed down the steps, it could be seen by the light of the Tilley lamp outside that he had been allowed to put on a woollen dressing-gown over his pyjamas, which was a mark of privilege resented by those already in the cellar. 'What's going on?' he said. 'These buggers don't answer.'

None of the men in the cellar had any idea what was going on. The street-lamps had been switched off, as they always were at midnight, but there was a clear sky and a quarter moon, and as they were hustled towards Manor Farm they had seen women and children from other houses, more warmly dressed, being hustled the other way. They were confused and cold, and all of them were frightened but trying not to show it. More and more men in their underclothes were pushed down the stairs, and as the cellar grew fuller it warmed up a little, but the fear and confusion persisted.

The soldiers and MI5 agents were already discovering difficulties not covered by their orders. First there were people like the obstreperous Mr Freeland, who were visitors not villagers and therefore not on the list, but who could not be left in houses otherwise emptied or they might get up to mischief by raising the alarm or some such behaviour. The solution was to treat them like villagers for the time being, and sort them out in the morning, but it was bound to cause trouble. Unlike the soldiers, the MI5 people knew what was to happen in the morning, and did not relish the problems of organisation it would cause. This was one of the jobs they would cheerfully have relinquished to Special Branch, but that bugger Phibbs was in a power struggle and took his people with him.

Then there were the pets. Budgies and hamsters could be left in their cages, ponies in the paddock and cats to look after themselves, but dogs were a problem. First they barked, which was a risk of general disturbance, then they tried to accompany their owners to church or cellar; the stupid animals seemed to imagine that they were going for walkies in the middle of the night. Since they would be shot or otherwise disposed of in the morning anyway, the obvious course would be to shoot them immediately, but this was likely to lead to distress – and therefore noise – among the children, and the shots would themselves be noisy, causing a general alarm while it was still important to keep everything softly softly.

So most of the dogs were locked in kitchens, if possible by their owners. A few exceptions, where the dogs were unduly persistent or the children hysterical, were allowed to accompany the family to the church. The dogs left in kitchens howled and the dogs accompanying families got underfoot. You could not win with dogs.

One of these exceptional dogs was Nell, a golden labrador, solidly built and half the height of a man. She was the Hatcher dog, twelve years old, the same age as Simon: she had been brought up with him and would not leave him or his eight-year-old brother, Jamie. When Paul Hatcher was taken away, in boxer shorts and pyjama top, trying to persuade his German-speaking escort to be careful of his broken wrist, his wife Harriet made a token attempt to persuade Nell to stay in the kitchen, but Nell could smell the fear and refused. She put back her ears, bared her teeth and snarled at the soldiers, and Harriet said, 'She's a very gentle dog really but I wouldn't upset her if I were you,' so permission was given for Nell to accompany them. But Nell was not fooled. She knew well enough that there was no element of walkies in what was happening, and she kept close to the boys.

Harriet was not fooled either. Her children were in danger: the whole family was, but Paul had already been taken away and she could not help him. As they were leaving the house, she said to Simon, 'What's the best place for Brer Rabbit at a time like this?'

'Briar patch.'

'What's that?' said the MI5 officer. 'What?'

'It's a children's story. Brer Rabbit and Brer Fox. "Born and bred in a briar patch." Don't you know it?'

'Just keep the talking down.'

Had Simon understood? The Briar Patch was his own secret hiding place, across two fields in gorse at Farley Edge. Even Jamie had been there rarely, Harriet only once as a privilege on her birthday.

Simon said, 'Would all the rabbits go?'

'The little ones would.'

'Keep the talking down, I said. You're only going to the church with the other families. Plenty of time for children's stories when you get there.' They were outside the Gills' house, and he turned in at the gate with his four soldiers. The Gills' outside light came on as the sensor picked them up. That left only two soldiers escorting Harriet and her children, and about a hundred and fifty yards before they reached the church.

Butchery Lane was coming up on the left, narrow and going nowhere: there was no longer a butcher's shop in the village. Once the lane had led to the abattoir, which had long since been converted to a desirable family residence. There was a field beyond, and a stile to the field. No street lamps. If only a cloud would come over the moon! She touched Simon's shoulder. Good boy! He grabbed Jamie's arm and began to run, and Harriet launched herself at the nearest soldier, both arms round him as if in an embrace. The other soldier stopped, startled, unsure whether to help his comrade or chase the boys, and Nell knocked him over. Harriet's soldier pushed her away and struck at her with his rifle. Nell bit his wrist, then bounded off down the lane after Simon and Jamie.

'Good Nell, good dog!' Harriet shouted. 'Look after them.'

'Stupid bitch!' the soldier said, forgetting that he had been ordered to speak only German. What did she think she was doing? He could easily get rabies; it would have to be reported. As for the kids, the soldiers on the perimeter would pick them up; it would give them something to do.

So it was that soldiers, spread out in a line two metres aparts at the bottom of a field, nervous and inexperienced and unsure what they were supposed to be doing beyond their immediate orders to let nobody pass, saw – heard – were conscious of – three figures, already dangerously close, running towards them in the dark. One of these figures was not human – an animal – enormous – slavering – the Hound of the Baskervilles trained up for war. The other two were smaller, possibly Japanese; they made horrible panting and gasping sounds as they ran. The soldiers had been told to halt anyone coming from the village and to refer to their officers, but these two and their animal were already attacking them.

The soldiers' fire was ragged: nobody later was able to say who had fired first. All down the line they fired and fired again, hitting the animal first since it was the largest of the three and most to be feared. When the animal fell, the two Japanese ran to it, crying out in high childish voices, 'Kneel! Kneel!', and then they were easy to hit, even in the dark, and they cried out again, but in pain now, and then they were silent. The soldiers let off several more rounds, just to be sure, and then an NCO, a corporal, went out to take a look at the bodies.

He returned to the line carrying a child, a little boy. The child was not dead, but dying, blood pouring from a wound in its throat. The corporal ran with the child in his arms to the road block, to his officer and the police, but the child was dead by the time he arrived. One of the policemen took the body from him, and his officer went with him back to the line to get the other. 'What the fuck's going on up there?' the policeman said.

The noise of the shooting had been heard in the village, and lights were coming on in every house not already visited. The men in the cellar heard it, and the women in the church banged on the heavy door of wood and iron. Harriet heard it.

General Allenby and Oberstleutnant Gillman heard it in the command vehicle, and soon afterwards the report came in from the road block. Allenby said, 'We've lost the element of surprise, I'm afraid. Things might get a bit messy. Find a way to turn the street-lamps on, and bring your perimeter force right up to the outskirts of the village. You may need to reinforce the detachments which are going into the houses – do as many at a time now as you can. And perhaps you'd better take the men who actually shot the children out of the line; they won't be good for much. Meanwhile none of the police at the road blocks is to go off duty until I say so. There's going to be a problem of news management, I'm afraid, rather earlier than expected.'

There were electric lights in the church, some warmth and much more space than in the cellar, and the guards had been chosen for qualities of humanity; two were Education Corps, two medical orderlies, one a cost clerk and one a cook. All the women were distressed and the children confused and that did no good to anyone, the cook said; they needed occupation. There were teabags, mugs, powdered milk, packets of biscuits and an electric kettle in the vestry, so they had a brew-up, with communion wine for those that fancied it. The pews were uncomfortable, but couches could be made for the younger children out of embroidered hassocks pushed together. So a crèche was made in the gallery, where the lights could be switched out, and some mothers and older children left to look after the little ones while the other mothers gathered in the main body of the church to try to make sense of the situation.

They could get little sense from the guards. Only the cook was prepared to speak a little English and for all other communication they had to rely on those older children who studied German as a second language at school. Though they could get nothing out of the soldiers about their menfolk, they managed to understand that neither they nor their children would be harmed, and that more would be explained by the officers in the morning. The soldiers did not know that the women would not be harmed – they knew no more than the women themselves what was happening or why – but judged it prudent to offer this reassurance.

Many of the younger women were unused to the church and ill at ease there. A few of the older newcomers were regular attenders, along with those of the old villagers who used church-attendance as a way of asserting their separate identity, but the congregation seldom exceeded thirty; the younger newcomers went at Christmas and Easter if they were not busy entertaining guests. It seemed appropriate to pray, but there was no priest to lead them; the vicar served four churches and, luckily for him, lived in another village. So Janet Alloway led the prayers; as a Justice of the Peace, she was as near as they could get to sanctity. *Our Father, Which art in Heaven* . . . that was safe and also well enough known for everyone to join in . . . *Lighten our darkness, we beseech Thee, oh Lord* . . . and then Janet, to a general, deeply felt but unspoken approval, launched into a prayer of her own devising in which she asked the Almighty to let them know soon what was happening and to have a special care for their menfolk and children.

After that it seemed natural for Grace of the post office to go to the harmonium which did duty for the organ (there being no organist in any of the four villages), and begin to play hymns. *Eternal Father, Strong to save, Whose arm hath bound the restless wave* . . . it might not have been entirely appropriate to their situation, but the tune was comforting, and most of them knew some of the words. After a faltering start the voices of the women grew stronger and filled the church.

It was a clear night. The sound carried. Faintly the men in the cellar could hear the women singing in the church. It was their first communication of any kind since they had been separated, a way to tell each other across the length of the village that they were alive; it was a way to communicate love and concern and longing. *Eternal Father, Strong to save* . . . the men also knew the tune and some of the words and those they did not know they could la-la. First one, then another, then all the men began to sing, pushing the words up the steps of the cellar, into the farmyard, out towards the church, towards the women and children to tell them . . . what? . . . anything . . . that they were there, thinking of them, loving them, wanting to be with them, *Oh hear us when we cry to Thee*, the men sang strongly in unison, *for those in peril on the sea*.

Vehicles in motion along the road to Lidlicote. Headlamps on full beam slicing into the dark hillsides of the Berkshire Downs, army lorries on dipped beam like the eyes of enormous fish moving through the early morning mists between Osterley Park and Slough. At different times, from different starting points and for different reasons, the different vehicles began their journey.

Piers Alloway was taken from a police cell and put into a police van. This was the first of the vehicles to arrive at the village, and it departed soon after its arrival. He was made to remove his shoes and socks in the farmyard, but otherwise allowed the clothes he stood up in; his belt, jacket and the contents of his pockets had already been taken from him in the police station.

When Piers was brought in, the village men knew for certain that something was very badly up, and that the village was being punished. Walter Alloway, as the head of his family, apologised formally to his companions in the cellar. There could be no other reason for what was happening than the presence within the village community of the kinsfolk of a dead terrorist. He told them what they already knew – what the authorities already knew – that none of the Lidlicote Alloways had met the man, and had not even known of his presence in Britain. Nevertheless he and his family asked forgiveness of the men in the cellar. Leonard Garland said, 'Surely they can't send *all* of us into detention? Not the old people and the kids?'

The COI Film Unit set off in a van from SE1. The unit was of minimum size, a camera operator and a sound recordist, both freelance. The camera operator had been brought out of retirement for the job. He had covered the tribal wars in Somalia and Senegal, and was said to have a strong stomach. The sound recordist was less experienced and not much was known about his stomach. He suffered from psoriasis, and it was his practice outside his own home to cover his face with a balaclava of navy blue wool with a peak, which made him look like a bank-robber. They were clearly a scratch couple but the job did not require a high degree of skill.

Mr Grenfell of the Ministry of Information briefed the unit. The film was being made only for record. It would never be seen by the public: no clips would be shown by the BBC Television News or in the cinema by Movietone. It would be shot in black and white using a single camera. There would be no fancy shots, only natural light, no camera movement beyond what was appropriate to a fixed camera operating from a tripod, and only the one set-up. The unit would make its own way to the location, using the map provided, and would report on arrival, no later than 0600 hours, to the OC Troops, Oberstleutnant Gillman. Any questions so far?

No questions so far.

Oberstleutnant Gillman would show them where the execution was to be carried out, and would assist the operator to choose a camera-position which would allow him to film the conduct and demeanour both of the firing squad and the condemned men. Sound would be recorded from behind the camera. Members of the unit would not draw any attention to themselves or attempt to interfere in any way. They would be subject to military law and the operation was covered by the Official Secrets Act. 'Just remember that you're being paid double time for a nasty job in unsocial hours,' Mr Grenfell said. 'So keep your heads down and your mouths shut and don't trip over the furniture.'

The COI van was the second vehicle to arrive. It was stopped at the road block, where the members of the unit were instructed to leave the cab and get into the back of the van, which was then driven by a military driver to the Command Post. There was a window in the back door; they could see out. They were driven through a cordon of soldiers and then off the road into a field, and instructed to remain where they were until summoned.

The camera operator had brought with him a canvas holdall containing two dozen bottles of Pilsner of which six were now empty. He complained that if he were not allowed to take a leak he would be no use to anyone, so he and the sound recordist were permitted to piss side by side into the hedge under military supervision. It was hardly dawn; there was nothing to see but a motor home and a few parked cars, nothing to hear but the dawn chorus. 'I'm a beer person, me,' said the camera operator to the sound recordist as they pissed, 'For medical reasons mostly; I find it answers best. Most camera crew, as you well know, they're all for schnapps, can't live without it, dropped like flies in Africa. I stick to beer. It has its disadvantages, but it washes out the toxins.' The sound recordist replied that, with his condition, he was hardly allowed alcohol at all.

Shortly afterwards three coaches and a minibus arrived from Reading and were directed to wait near the church. A tall army officer with a moustache came out of the motor home, followed by a middle-aged man in a suit who carried a clipboard. The officer came over to the van and the back door was opened for him. 'Heard you'd arrived,' he said. 'Gillman. Be with you soon. Are you sure you're comfortable in here?'

They told him they were not comfortable.

'Don't see why you shouldn't sit in the front. No point in secrecy. You know what's happening.' He spoke to the soldier guarding the van, and went away towards the church, the man in the suit running to keep up.

The coaches were to take the women and children away to detention before the men were shot, the minibus for those who were not Lidlicote people at all and would be kept under wraps at a holding unit for a few hours before being returned to their homes. It was not an ideal arrangement; nothing about this Lidlicote business was ideal in Gillman's opinion. A decision had been taken that the women and children should go different ways, the women to detention centres, the children to juvenile offenders' units. Easy enough: there was a legal definition of a juvenile, a child under the age of eighteen. But one could not consign an infant to such a unit. Infants would have to remain with their mothers, but what was an infant? There had been no time to set up a panel of child psychologists and educationists to answer this question and anyway the whole operation was under wraps. The Cabinet Secretary had, without giving away the context of his enquiry, asked his wife how she would define an infant. Answer: an infant is under five years old.

First thing: check with this man Phibbs that all the women in the church belonged to the village, and keep back any visitors for the minibus. Then tell the women where they would be going, and that it would not be for ever, only for the duration of the Present Emergency, and explain that their menfolk would be sent elsewhere.

Direct the women and infants each to a particular seat in a particular coach, and the juveniles into another coach, keeping everything as low-key as possible, very much as if it were an ordinary village outing and the older children were travelling separately. Lock the doors of the coaches once the passengers had embussed. All three coaches would leave the village together, and the women would not realise that they were being separated until the juveniles' coach went another way.

So much for the plan. It could not have been expected to work entirely smoothly, and did not. The women with infants were quiet enough because they were afraid for their infants, and the older village women were used to being told what to do. But three of the younger women left the line, tried to get to the cellar to be with their husbands, and had to be physically restrained. Mrs Hatcher was with them. She was the mother whose two children were missing: one had to assume that they were the two kiddies who had been shot, though of course she did not know that. She became hysterical, and the physical restraint went further than intended, requiring bandaging and a sedative injection before they could get her on the coach. This unsettled the other women.

The coaches drove in convoy down Peacock Lane. They would be together for an hour before one turned left towards Andover, the others right towards Devizes. Meanwhile two army lorries were climbing the hill to Lidlicote. They were directed to the Command Post and parked in the field. An officer in black and silver left his seat in the cab of the first vehicle and walked, with the confident ease which comes of a long experience of ceremonial duties, to the command vehicle.

Phibbs had gone ahead to the cellar to sort out the men. Oberstleutnant Gillman took his time, trying to decide what he should say to them. How could he get it through to them that they should not make a fuss, but accept the unpleasant necessity and endure it manfully? Sir Walter Raleigh came to mind: politeness to one's executioner was the mark of an aristocrat. There must be a way of putting it to the villagers which would promote a kind of co-operation, a pride in dying well, sort of Bishop Latimer kind of thing. *Be of good comfort, Master Ridley, and play the man, for by God's*

grace we shall this day light such a candle as shall never be put out.
Perhaps that was not quite it, but that was the spirit of it. He arrived
in the farmyard to find Phibbs in angry altercation with one of the
prisoners and the guards standing by looking helpless.

'You said eighteen and over. He's not eighteen yet.'

'Then why is he in here with you?'

'I don't know why he's here. I didn't bring him here. We were both
brought here.'

'He looks eighteen to me. Every bit. His balls have dropped; he's
taller than you are. You're trying it on.'

'You've got a list, haven't you?'

'You don't seem to understand: you've already been sorted. The
agent who came with the soldiers had a list.'

'He never consulted it. Gareth Halliday. Look him up. If he was
eighteen he wouldn't be living at home: he'd be doing his army
service.'

'Not necessarily. University applicants get deferment.'

Other men in the cellar joined Gareth's father in protest. The village
people knew how old they were and how old their children were.
Reluctantly the Head of MI5 consulted his list. '6th December 1974.'

'Thank you.'

'Only two months under. It's extremely inconvenient. The
juveniles' bus has already left.'

Gareth said, 'Where's my mother?'

'With the other women. Her bus has gone as well.' He turned to
Gillman. 'I don't know what we're going to do here. This male seems
to be under eighteen.'

'The minibus can take him. Get him over there, please, along
with the other two, and instruct the driver accordingly. Mr Freeland,
Mr Haigh, you'll find your wives waiting for you outside the church.
The soldiers will take you. Thank you, Mr Phibbs.'

Mr Haigh was half of a honeymoon couple who had been staying
at the Walnut Tree. Although frightened and confused, he was
unwilling to leave without at least making an attempt to help.
'Harry,' he said to Mr Masterson, 'is there anyone you'd like me to
tell? Solicitor or somebody?' but one of the guards said, 'Come
along! You heard the officer,' and took him away.

As the two visitors and the juvenile were taken up Main Street towards the church, the next lot of vehicles arrived; the bulldozers and the JCB. That left only the Deputy Prime Minister to come. Oberstleutnant Gillman remained in the cellar to explain the situation to the men of Lidlicote. It was already day, and although not much light came through the open door, it was enough for him to see the faces, all turned towards him.

'Well,' he said, 'I dare say you're wondering what this is all about.'

When the Oberstleutnant left the cellar the door was closed behind him and locked from the outside. He said it was to give the men privacy and time to get right with God and all that, but his real intention was that, confined in darkness, they should become more docile so as to make the unpleasant job ahead a little easier for all concerned.

Old Jim Lester began to cry. The ulcers on his legs were hurting, he was cold and he was frightened and he wanted his wife. Someone said, 'We ought to pray, I suppose.'

But there was no parson, no priest, no Methodist minister, no one to comfort them in a religious way. They said the Lord's Prayer together and that passed the time and helped them to feel a little better, but there was still something missing. Then Billy Wilsher said, 'Duncan's a reverend.' Duncan Lester was old Jim's nephew who worked on the pig-farm; he was a lay-preacher at the chapel in a neighbouring village, respected among the old villagers as a good Christian, always ready to give a helping hand to those in trouble.

'No, I'm not.'

'You do preaching.'

'When I'm called. Doesn't make me a reverend.'

Mr Gill said, 'Duncan, I need to confess.' This was astounding to the new villagers in the cellar. The Gills were not Roman Catholics and did not even go often to the parish church. Mr Gill said, 'I need to confess my sins to God and be absolved before they shoot me. Any man of God can do that; you don't have to be a priest. God gives grace to anyone in an emergency: they taught us that at school. I'm sorry to embarrass you. I wouldn't ask if there wasn't a need. There may be others who feel the same way.'

Billy Wilsher said, 'That's idolatry.'

The men in the cellar could hear that Duncan was troubled. He said, 'I do consolation sometimes. Have done. Visit the dying, just to be someone there. Talk to them a bit about the life everlasting. I could do that if you like. See what the Lord puts it into my head to utter. Might help.'

'I'm sorry. It's not enough. I need to confess my sins in private and be absolved.'

Another voice, an educated voice, Duncan could not be sure whose, said, 'I'd like to confess as well, please, Duncan. I'm sorry to put this on you but there doesn't seem to be anyone else.'

There was a silence. Then Duncan said, 'All right, Mr Gill, I'll do my best for you. We better go over by the Coalite, get a little privacy. Everyone move away, please, as far as you can. I'll do anyone else after, in turn; you just have to say.'

They knew where the pile of smokeless fuel was; they had seen it as they were brought in. Duncan and Mr Gill could be heard making their way to it through the others, and the men lying against it were heard moving away. Then the men in the cellar heard Mr Gill say, 'Forgive me, Duncan, in God's name, for I have sinned,' and then there was a whispering, sometimes interrupted by tears, which continued for a long time, and then Duncan saying, 'He won't mind that, don't you worry; the Good Lord won't mind that. That's why they call it the Mercy Seat. There'll be no objection to that.'

At eight-thirty the Deputy Prime Minister arrived. Much work had been done by then.

Together General Allenby, Oberstleutnant Gillman and Standartenführer Hawkins had chosen an execution ground. This had not taken long; the place had chosen itself. First, the ground had to be open for a good field of fire. Therefore, unless they used the village green or the lawn of the Manor, it had to be outside the village. Second, since the men would still be in bare feet, and would be blindfolded and their hands tied behind them, so that their progress would be slow and difficult, it should not be far from the cellar. Third, there should be a stout wall behind the men, at least three and a half metres in height and of a smooth surface in case of ricochets. Fourth, the ground should be soft enough for a deep trench to be dug between the men and the wall, so that after they had been shot they could be thrown into the trench to make room for the next batch.

Few areas fitted all these criteria, but there was a barn at the far end of the farmyard opposite the cellar with a field of cabbages behind it. The back wall of that barn should do well. The cabbages would be a hazard, since one wouldn't want the men to be falling over them on their way to execution, but the bulldozers, brought in to flatten the village houses and other buildings, ought to be able to deal with a few cabbages and take no time about it.

The bulldozers flattened the field while the JCB dug a trench in front of the wall. Standartenführer Hawkins paced the ground, and stood for a moment in thought, estimating a distance. If the soldiers of the firing squad were too close, there was a danger that they might become emotionally involved in what they were doing; the execution would lose its quality of detachment and disinterest. If they were too far away they might miss. He made his decision, and a tape was put down on the flattened field.

The men would be shot in groups of five. This arrangement would provide every two men of the firing squad with one target, and would also, on the MI5 assumption that there would be eighty altogether, divide neatly into sixteen batches. In fact, when the eight absentees were deducted and Piers Alloway added, there were only seventy-three, a vexing total which would not divide into equal groups of any number. Well, there would have to be fourteen groups of five and one of three.

The posts had been brought from London, thick wooden posts two and a half metres tall. They were dug into the ground in front of the trench, three-quarters of a metre below ground, one and three-quarters above. The men would be tied to these posts at chest and knees to hold them upright and inhibit struggling, so that the men of the firing squad would be provided with motionless targets and there would be no need for Standartenführer Hawkins to finish anyone off with his revolver – though of course he would be ready to do so if required.

Why should the men be brought blindfold from the cellar instead of being blindfolded at the place of execution? Because, being only civilians, when they saw what was before them they might try to run, and although they would not be able to run far in bare feet, the business of catching them and bringing them back might add an element of farce to what should be a solemn occasion. Blindfolds and ties had not been brought from outside, because it had been rightly assumed that there would be plenty of suitable material in the empty houses. Fresh ties would probably be needed for each prisoner because those at the chest would be damaged by gunfire and those at the knee soiled as the prisoners opened their bowels. That would be seventy-three blindfolds and a hundred and forty-six ties. The men who had been guarding the church were set to collect curtains for the blindfolds and sheets for the ties and to cut them into suitable lengths.

A position was chosen for the film unit. The camera would be sited to one side of the action, about two-thirds of the distance from the wall, facing the direction from which the condemned men would approach. This would allow the operator to film the arrival of the men and the process of securing them to the posts. He would then pan to the firing squad as they prepared to fire, and then did fire, and would pan back to record the result, five dead men who had died instantly. If by mischance there were any need to finish someone off in a merciful manner, that would be filmed as well with nothing shirked, though from a distance. The sound recordist, located behind the camera, would find it difficult to maintain a level between gunfire and human voices, but it could be managed.

The soldiers at the perimeter were sent back to Position One to keep outsiders well away from the village. There was no reason for these soldiers to witness the execution and it would be better for their own morale and for that of their fellows when they were returned to their units that they did not. Catering vans had by now arrived at all three road blocks, and the police and soldiers breakfasted in batches on bacon rolls and hot coffee.

The preparations were explained in detail to the Deputy PM and he was formally introduced to Oberstleutnant Gillman and Standartenführer Hawkins. He seemed jumpy. 'Hadn't we better get on with it?'

General Allenby nodded to his ADC, who took a small notebook and a ballpoint pen from his pocket. He said, 'The situation is not irreversible, Deputy Prime Minister. We could send the men to a detention centre. It would still be a strong example.'

'Cabinet decision.'

So the order was given to proceed.

The beginning went well enough. Since the men were being shot alphabetically, the Alloways made up four-fifths of the first batch. They gave no trouble. The Alloways wanted to die. They had tried to tell the gentleman from MI5 and then the Oberstleutnant that none of their fellow-villagers had any connection, even by blood, with any undercover agent, and that nobody had been concealing information because there was none to conceal. Three of them were lawyers, and had invoked the law. It had done no good; they had been unable to save even the old-age pensioners and the mentally handicapped Peter. They were ashamed. They walked as steadily as they could, allowed themselves to be tied to the posts without protest, held themselves still, were killed cleanly and their bodies thrown into the trench.

The second batch did not do quite as well, since one of them was overcome with fear and could not support himself. It had been decided that, instead of Gillman's men, those members of the William Joyce Company who were being held in reserve should secure the prisoners to the posts; it would involve the whole group and present a better appearance. This fear-stricken fellow had to be held up against the post as the ties were put over his chest and knees, and vomited over the soldier who was supporting him, which took one of the detachment immediately out of action since there were no spare uniforms. However, the shooting itself was properly done and the bodies disposed of. Sixty-three to go.

General Allenby was watching the Deputy PM, but although he swallowed more often than usual, he seemed to be otherwise unaffected. Nobody looked at the film unit, but the sound recordist, who had little to do since his microphone was in a fixed position, was watching the camera operator, who was working without his jacket and had broken into a profuse sweat. Perhaps the man always sweated when he worked, but it seemed odd so early in the day. The sound recordist was keeping himself under tight control. The physical effect of this was that his jaws were clamped together and his hands like claws. When it came to putting in a new reel of tape he would need to be careful.

Trouble began with the third batch. Professor Anthony Cladding had seen his friend Mark taken away among the second group and had heard the firing. There was nothing to be done. Let them get it over with; it had to be endured. There was an emptiness in his mind, situated behind the eyes, an inability to form coherent thought. It would not do to blub.

Duncan had heard the confessions of twenty men. Now he stood beside the door, and as each man went out and up the stairs he would say, 'May God be with you, brother,' and the man would put his arms round Duncan, or touch him, and go on. 'God be with *you*, Duncan,' Anthony Cladding said, hugged him tight, as he had not hugged Mark when he went, and walked up the cellar stairs to where the guards were waiting.

The blindfold was of maroon velour, not a hood but tied at the back of the head; it was curtain material, one of those hideous swagged things in the dining-room of the Walnut Tree. They tied his hands behind him and he walked, with some assistance from the guard, across the muck, protuberant stones and bits of metal of the farmyard and onto soil in which vegetable matter had been crushed. He came to a place where there was a stench of vomit and of something sweetish which he took to be blood. Whose? Mark's? For a moment there was nobody holding him. He resisted a sudden impulse to reach down, put his hand to the blood and smear it across his mouth. Even to resist such an impulse was to tense his body, a very small movement, but sudden. As if in response a hand grabbed at him, he reacted away and slipped on the blood and vomit underfoot. With his hands tied, he could not prevent himself from falling. He lifted his face from the mud and the blindfold came off.

Anthony Cladding looked across at the firing squad and the small group of important people standing a little to one side, and saw the Deputy Prime Minister. 'Guy,' he shouted, 'What's happening here? What the fuck do you think you're doing here?' Then the soldier in charge of him picked him up, replaced the blindfold and tied it much more tightly so that it would not slip again, and pushed him back against the post while someone else began to tie bits of sheeting round his chest and knees. But the Von Ribbentrop Professor of Applied Aesthetics at the University of Oxford continued to shout, 'Guy! Guy!' until another bandage stopped his mouth.

The Deputy Prime Minister covered his eyes with his hands and turned away. They were all looking at him, even the soldiers and the people from the COI. He must find somewhere private to recover his composure; he would sit in the car for a while.

General Allenby stopped him. 'No. Stay.'

'You don't need me here.'

'We do.'

'Tell me when it's over. I approve your actions.'

'You will stay and you will watch until we are finished,' the general said, 'or else you personally will abort the operation.'

The two men stared at each other. It would not be forgotten. The Deputy Prime Minister said, 'I want the film from that fucking camera. I want it before anybody else sees it. I want it edited,' and turned back to watch the execution, not noticing that the sound recordist, who had himself served with Anthony Cladding on a Committee of Enquiry into the Wider Dissemination of Music and the Arts, was weeping also behind the cover of his balaclava.

The incident had a bad effect, no doubt of that. When the order was given to aim and fire, rifles were seen to waver. The soldiers were using the standard infantry automatic rifle, the Heckler & Koch G3A3, which fires three-round bursts, so there was no excuse for failure, yet Standartenführer Hawkins was obliged to administer the *coup de grâce* to two bodies still twitching against the posts. The four marksmen reckoned to be responsible were replaced by four from the reserve, at first to their relief until they discovered that they must replace their replacers in fastening the condemned men to posts which had already become soiled with blood and shit.

General Allenby said to the Deputy Prime Minister, 'You never told me you knew one of these people.'

'Long time ago. Lost touch.'

'His name was on the list.'

'I never looked at the list.' No member of the Cabinet Committee

269

had looked at the list. That was not the point of the operation. General Allenby had not looked at it. Only the MI5 people, who had prepared it, had actually read it.

The camera operator, already red in the face and sweating profusely, now began to belch. At first the belches were controlled, hardly more than burps, covered with a hand and a 'Scuse me, scuse me', but soon they began to burst forth as if he had taken a large dose of sodium bicarbonate against acid indigestion, and then they became retches, and he set himself in clumsy motion, head down, blundering away from the camera position.

'Stop that man!'

'Don't shoot! He's ill.' Already the camera operator was on his knees, spewing out a mixture of bile and Pilsner. The sound recordist went to him. 'What's up, Charlie?'

The camera operator, who had nothing left in that once strong stomach to bring up, had fallen back into a sitting position. 'Food poisoning.'

'We've got to go through with it. They warned us what would be happening. We agreed to do it, Charlie.' The sound recordist's own face was still wet with tears, but they had been soaked up by the balaclava. 'You were in Africa.'

'They were blackies in Africa. Used to it.' The sound recordist put out a hand and helped him to his feet. 'Little kids. Women. Savages there. Had to shut my eyes sometimes. Bloody odd footage I shot out there.'

The sound recordist said quietly, 'We've got to get it right here, Charlie. We're making the only record there is. It'll be needed. Remember that.'

'Ah!' The camera operator took the thought, and nodded. 'Right. Better get on with it, then.'

Standartenführer Hawkins was waiting by the camera. 'What's the matter with him?'

'Something he picked up in Africa. It's recurrent, I think.'

'It's unmanly behaviour and it slows up the operation. We're already behind the clock.'

The sound recordist said it would not happen again.

'Can you operate this thing if it does?' The sound recordist said that he could not. The camera operator looked into his eye-piece and framed up a group of soldiers throwing bodies into a trench, and Standartenführer Hawkins returned to his position by the firing squad.

Not long afterwards the timetable for Operation Strong Example went to pieces completely. It happened after the Lesters, old Jim and Duncan, were taken to be shot. The Feldwebel in charge of the guards at the cellar had known there would be trouble. He had been tempted to alter the order in which the men were being taken so as to leave Duncan to the last, because it was clear that his presence and example calmed the men and put a bit of spunk into most of them, but he had no authority to make the alteration on his own and was reluctant to ask in case he were thought to be putting himself forward. With Duncan gone, undesirable elements in the cellar took over.

'The men refuse to come out, sir.'

'Don't they understand the situation? It's all been explained.'

'They understand it, sir. They refuse to accept it.'

'You'd better use compulsion, then. Do you need reinforcement?'

'Wouldn't do any good, sir. I have tried to use compulsion. The problem is, sir, with the steps to the cellar being so narrow and just the one door, sir, it's the same for my men getting in as for them coming out. There's only room for one at a time and it's dark in there. I've had two men set on, sir, and disarmed.'

'Disarmed! Good god, Feldwebel, that's a court martial matter. Were your people injured?'

'Not to mention, sir. The men aren't violent; they just refuse to come out. Can't see the point if they're going to be shot anyway.'

'Have they tried to use the rifles they took?'

'Threatened, sir, but only in self-defence. One of them also asked for a solicitor.'

The Head of MI5 said, 'We're not going through that again. We've been through that.' All the officers turned to look at him, and General Allenby said, 'I think we might begin by losing you, Mr Phibbs. I find your presence distracting. Take your people and bugger off. There's nothing for you to do here now.' The head of MI5 looked towards the Deputy Prime Minister for support, but did not receive it, and the Feldwebel in charge of the guard at the cellar wondered how much longer he could continue to stand to attention without beginning to sway.

Proceedings had become extremely unsatisfactory and continued to be so. From the top of the steps Oberstleutnant Gillman explained to the men in the cellar that their attitude was mistaken as well as unpatriotic. Being shot by a firing squad was not even painful because the immediate shock of the impact of high-velocity bullets anaesthetised the body against pain, and they would be dead before they had time to feel any, whereas the injuries they would be likely to sustain in an attack by his own troops, who were utterly in-experienced in mercy killing, would be excruciating. But the men would not come out of the cellar. They had already begun to feel that they had made a mistake in merely disarming the two soldiers who had been sent in; they should have been kept as hostages.

Who was to flush these fellows out? The scratched-together battalion was not equipped, as any normal infantry battalion would be, with machine-guns, anti-tank weapons, mortars or even grenades. Nor had the twenty men of the William Joyce Company, employed for so long on ceremonial duties in Berlin, either the equipment or the experience to storm a cellar. Standartenführer Hawkins was reluctant to risk them in this action, and the semi-independent command structure of the SS made it difficult for General Allenby to insist. Meanwhile the film unit had set up in the farmyard.

An experienced tactician might have flooded the cellar with water, or better still poured petrol down the steps and set fire to it, which would have ignited the smokeless fuel already there and made a rare inferno. But General Allenby had never seen combat and Oberstleutnant Gillman was from the Legal Department. They were working to a deadline which was synchronised to a press release at noon, and were already behind the clock.

Also their pride was involved. A battalion of the Wehrmacht, no matter how inexperienced in action, *ought* to be able to take on thirty-three semi-naked civilians in a cellar, half of them past fifty, and armed with only two rifles which they must be unaccustomed to using. It was a disadvantage that the soldiers could not come down the cellar steps more than one at a time, but from an arc around the top they could safely direct fire into the cellar and any bullets which hit the edges of the stone around the door would be deflected at odd angles and be bound to inflict casualties in so small a space. That should be enough to soften the cellar people up, and an assault would follow.

The preliminary rifle fire lasted twelve minutes, and one could hear that many of the bullets found a body. The actual assault was over in four. The first two soldiers slipped on the blood in the doorway and were shot by their comrades: they were the only military casualties. Some of the men in the cellar not yet dead tried to surrender, but there was no time for that any longer, and they were finished off by the soldiers of the assault party, hyped up with fear and incensed by the death of their comrades. Then the Tilley lamp was relighted and General Allenby came down to look. 'What a shambles!' he said, and it was.

The dead men in the cellar were carried to the trench and thrown in: in the general muddle and vexation nobody thought to count the bodies. The wooden posts were pulled out and thrown on top of the bodies, and the trench filled with earth. Bulldozers knocked down the barn, covering the trench and the execution ground with masonry and rubble.

Meanwhile soldiers of the scratch battalion made bonfires of the villagers' furniture and household objects. Farm vehicles and machinery were broken up, private cars set on fire. Nothing was to be taken from the village; there was to be no looting; the soldiers would be searched before they left the site. Pets were killed in various ways, though a few dogs and cats managed to escape. Ponies were shot. Nothing was done about the farm animals, most of which did not belong to the villagers anyway: the Public Health Department of Berkshire County Council would be informed after the press conference and instructed to arrange for immediate care and eventual disposal.

The bulldozers moved into the village and began to knock down the buildings. The council houses in which the old villagers had lived went down easily enough, but some of the older stone houses resisted destruction for a while, and most of the Norman church could not be demolished at all. The bulldozers did what they could: the rest would have to be cleared up later with more specialised equipment.

This was to be the final stage of Operation Strong Example: the site of the village would be grassed over and its name erased from the map. It had sounded well in the Cabinet Room, looked well on the confidential report submitted to the Council in Berlin. People may give such orders without having the imagination to visualise them being put into effect. They lack a sense of the ridiculous as well as a sense of pain.

The Rolls Royce and Austin Twelves of the MI5 contingent had gone already. The Deputy Prime Minister departed, the command vehicle departed, the detachment of SS from the William Joyce Company departed, most of the scratch battalion departed, leaving only a token force to oversee the demolition. When as much demolition as was feasible had been completed, the remaining soldiers departed, the bulldozers and the JCB departed, the road blocks were taken down and the police departed.

It was long gone noon, gone four o'clock, gone six. Thursday, 24th September 1992. The day had come and gone; it was dusk and then dark in what was left of the village.

In the cellar the darkness and stench were intense; they had closed the door when they took the last body out. Something moved behind the pile of smokeless fuel, something which had been covered completely by it, had breathed through it and had listened through it, listened first to the sounds of the destruction and then to the soldiers leaving, then to silence, hour after hour of silence.

Little Billy Wilsher emerged from the pile of smokeless fuel. The floor was sticky. He sat quietly in the dark and continued to listen. Nothing. But with the door closed he could not be sure of that nothing. No help for it, he would have to open the door. Cautiously he did so. Nothing. Six steps up to ground level, to be taken slowly, and keep your head low. Done. Nothing. He could see now; his eyes were well adjusted. There was rubble all over the farmyard. If he could see well enough to walk without tripping over or stubbing his toes, his bare feet would be an advantage because he would make no noise.

Manor Farm had gone, its barn gone. He walked down Main Street by the light of the gibbous moon, moving from one patch of shadow to another. Wrecked houses all around and the smell of bonfires. He could see the church up ahead, but there was something wrong with the tower. He heard a noise – grunting . . . snuffling – something ahead, just round the corner in Peacock Lane. Suicide to run, to throw himself to the ground, to move at all. He had broken into houses in his time to take whatever the occupants had carelessly left about, had heard them wake upstairs, and knew the drill; he must behave as if he were not there, did not exist, and they would go back to bed. Billy Wilsher, a shadow within a shadow, behaved as if he were not there. It worked. Two pigs came round the corner and trotted on up the street, ignoring him.

Where there were pigs there was food. Fridges and freezers had been dragged out of the wreckage of houses and, since they would not burn, broken up with axes. It stood to reason that not all the contents would have been thrown onto the bonfires – people were not that thorough – and it would not have gone bad in the course of one September day.

On his right were the remnants of what had been the Gills' house. The Gills had been rich people, did themselves well. He picked his way through the rubble in the Gills' front garden and found the wreckage of both fridge and freezer by what had once been the kitchen door. Foil dishes had spilled out of the freezer, and the soldiers had left them there for the contents to rot. Billy Wilsher picked one up, sniffed at it and held it close to his face. There was writing on the top. He squinted at it by the light of the moon.

The inscription in Mrs Gill's best Gothic calligraphy, studied at evening classes, meant nothing to him:

Fondue de Poulet à la Crème
23 Sept '92

but the stuff might be worth a try. He took off the top, dipped in his fingers and began to eat.

Consequences

The move from the Operational Base required careful preparation. When they went, they would have to go quickly and silently and by night so as to avoid the notice of the couple in the cottage, and they would need to have covered a fair distance before dawn. Cakehole made out a Provisional Movement Order in the proper form. They would leave on Sunday, 20th September, Estimated Time of Departure 0300 hours. The moon would be entering its last quarter, and would give them some light but not too much, and there was still the possibility of good weather for the journey, both by land and sea. They chose Sunday because the couple, whether they were police spies or not, liked to lie in of a Sunday. Also there would be fewer people around.

They gave themselves no Estimated Time of Arrival; the journey to the coast would take as long as it took. They would travel by bicycle, eat only picnic food in picnic places, drink from their water-bottles which would be refilled from the wash-taps of Public Lavatories, and sleep in the open. They would carry food for the first two days with them and thereafter it would be bought only from small village shops and by Juliet.

Travel by bicycle – but they only had three cycles for five people. Carry food with them, and at least a change of clothing – but they only had two rucksacks, which would have to contain bolt-cutters and a crowbar as well as the guns and grenades. Sleep in the open – but they had no tents, sleeping-bags or waterproof ground-sheets. All these deficiencies must be made up.

Forget tents: they were not Boy Scouts. Even if they could steal a

277

tent, it would be extra weight, a bugger to carry. Cakehole despised tents. If it rained, it rained: that would be the time to look for shelter. The solution was bedding-rolls, blankets reinforced with plastic in which extra clothing could be rolled, to be strapped on the carriers of bicycles or slung across backs or both. There were blankets in the Base and sheets of thick plastic could be found in any garden shed and most conveniently in the sheds of the village allotments, deserted after dark in September and inadequately locked, often not locked at all. Cakehole went out at night and returned with plastic sheeting, which Carrie and Juliet cut and sewed to blankets.

The stealing of another two bicycles was a more delicate matter, and could not be done until just before they left since, with the cottage occupied, the cycles could not be brought into the Base but would have to be hidden in the woods. It was galling that Cakehole and Juliet did each own a bicycle, left behind at Cakehole's cottage, but it would be folly to take those; attention would be aroused. No, the cycles must be stolen, and from nowhere nearer than Henley.

In order to steal the cycles at a distance they must first steal a car locally, and return it before the theft was noticed. On the Friday night, Cakehole left the Base by the emergency exit, taking Sinclair and Parry-Jones with him. They wore dark clothing and had blackened their faces. They moved swiftly, quiet as foxes, and were soon at the village. There was a choice of vehicles in the street, and none in that village was fitted with an alarm. But they were looking for a particular car – yes, there it was, Don Bushell's old DKW, parked outside his bungalow at the top of the road which ran downhill all the way to Assenden.

Don's car was not special; it was the hill they needed. Cakehole would not risk starting the car outside a house in which people might wake. They had brought a wire coathanger with which they unlocked the door. Then Cakehole sat in the driver's seat, holding the open door so that it did not bang and released the hand-brake, the two volunteers got behind and pushed, and they were off. They stopped in a lay-by halfway down the hill, well away from all habitation, and started the car by hot-wiring the ignition. There would be a problem if the DKW were low in petrol; they would have to find another which might not be so easy to move silently. There was no problem. The tank was half full.

They drove to Henley, parked the car outside the Congregational Church Hall, stole two cycles without difficulty, and drove back to their own patch of woodland. They hid the cycles and returned Don's car to the spot just outside his house from which they had borrowed it. Well before dawn they were back in the Base.

They had given much thought to the problem of disguise. Photographs of Sinclair and Parry-Jones, Attlee and Cape continued to appear in the newspapers and on posters. The two volunteers, presenting themselves as part of a group of cyclists on holiday, must look different but not villainous. Sinclair was not difficult. The lock of dark hair falling over the forehead had gone already. His hair was cut short – what the French called *en brosse* – and he had grown a beard and full moustache, which he kept trimmed with nail scissors. No longer the romantic poet, he had become a student in a Chekov play. But Arwen, ah Arwen! Arwen's hair was fair and fine. His beard would not grow. He could manage no more than bum-fluff.

The solution came early to Carrie, but it was some time before she could communicate her thoughts since it was still impossible to talk to Arwen privately. Finally she passed him a note, watching his face while he read it.

First there was a controlled reaction, nothing either way; she could see him thinking. Then he looked across at her, grinned and nodded. Carrie said, 'I thought the best thing with Arwen . . . the best way of disguising him, I mean . . . would be to go the other way from Ian. No beard. Long hair, not short – as long as he can grow it in the time; he could wear a headscarf. Shave his arms and legs . . . and chest . . .' It would hardly be necessary to shave Arwen's chest: there were so few hairs on it, only a few curling golden strands between the nipples. Carrie could not have loved a hairy man.

Arwen said, 'Couple of melons down the front.'

Bless him for taking it so well, but he must not make too much of a joke of it or he would end up looking like a pantomime dame. Carrie said, 'I could stuff a bra; there's cotton wool in the First Aid box. Make-up – not too much. Alter a couple of shirts – turn them into blouses.'

279

'Skirt?'

'There's that dressing-gown of Ian's.'

Ian loved that dressing-gown. It was of navy-blue towelling, bought at the Men's Casuals Shop during one of their visits to Windsor, and it had to be admitted that he looked handsome in it, like someone in an advertisement. Well, they would all have to make some sacrifices, and anyway he wouldn't be able to take it with him.

So it was agreed, and with acclaim. She and Juliet set to work, and made an attractive skirt out of the dressing-gown, with buttons all down the side. They had no curlers, no blow-dryer, and only the scissors from the First Aid box, but they washed and styled Arwen's hair, turning it by daily attention from short-back-and-sides to what might look like a boyish cut on a young woman. They altered shirts into blouses and discovered that a cotton polo-neck of Arwen's needed no adapting at all; just the breasts made all the difference. They experimented with what make-up they had, which was not much. Of course Arwen's legs and arms were far too muscular and his shoulders too wide, and his dear feet would not fit into any woman's shoe, but that was no problem. He would wear gym-shoes like Carrie herself and Jules; that was what cyclists wore. And nobody would be able to look at him closely because, except when they were lying up overnight or eating a picnic lunch in some field or copse well away from the road, he would always be on the move.

Arwen said, 'What happens when I need to use the Ladies?'

'You won't use the Ladies. You'll go behind a hedge.'

They left at the estimated time on the estimated day. They took out what they could through the emergency exit but the three bicycles had to be taken out through the outside privy, each separately lifted up through the trap-door, then out through the privy door, and left in the garden while the same operation was repeated for the next, all this without waking the couple in the cottage. It was the most dangerous part of the operation. Cakehole was in a muck-sweat by the time they were done.

By daybreak they were well clear of Nettlebed and on the road to Checkendon. They had decided to keep north of Reading, then aim for Salisbury Plain, then travel westwards to the coast, using minor roads as much as possible and avoiding all towns. They would move as a group of four with one outrider, usually Juliet, to give warning of any road block. If they were stopped by a cruising police car and asked for identification, Cakehole and the volunteers would have to kill the policemen before they had a chance to use their radio, and the car would be left at the side of the road; it was bound to be undisturbed for at least a while, since no passing motorist would wish to tangle with the police.

But there was no reason for the police to be suspicious of a party of cyclists on holiday – two young women, a teenage girl, an old man and a young, in their holiday clobber with their rucksacks, their bedding-rolls, their water-bottles and plastic carrier bags slung over the handlebars. They were a world away from the four desperate American terrorists for whom the police and security services were searching.

The press release from the Cabinet Office on 24th September went out a little late, at one o'clock instead of twelve, but it was there in all the evening papers in London and every major British city, a large box on the front page, headed:

THE PRICE OF SILENCE

and below it the story, bald and official, informing the British public that the inhabitants of Lidlicote, a village in Berkshire, who had given aid and comfort to enemies of the state, had suffered a condign punishment for their treachery by order-in-council of the government in Westminster. The men had been shot in a disciplined and humane manner by a firing squad of their own compatriots and the women and children been taken to detention centres where they would remain for the duration of the Present Emergency. The buildings of the village had been destroyed, the site would be grassed over, and the name of the village removed from the Ordnance Survey. Meanwhile the public was forbidden to approach the area. The people of Lidlicote were now known to have had important information regarding the presence of American terrorists in Britain, yet they had failed to inform the authorities. They had chosen to remain silent and this was the cause of their punishment. Members of the public were reminded that silence amounting to the support of terrorism was itself a form of terrorism, and would continue to be punished as such.

That evening the Prime Minister appeared on radio and television, speaking from 10, Downing Street. He was sad but stern. The men of Lidlicote had suffered the extreme penalty. He had consulted with Church leaders, and prayers would be said this coming Sunday in every church and chapel in the land, asking God to forgive them their trespass and have mercy on their souls. Their punishment had been condign, but though it was a condign punishment it was not a new punishment. To give aid and comfort to an enemy of the state was treason, and the punishment for treason was and had always been death. There was a cancer in their midst, which must be found and removed; silence was the only way it could hide itself and spread. Photographs of the terrorists had been and continued to be published. There was no excuse for ignorance; the men must be somewhere. It was the duty of every citizen to watch and search. The police and security authorities were doing their best, and had made some progress, but without public co-operation they were tied hand and foot. It was with the utmost sorrow that he must emphasise that anyone in possession of information about the terrorists who should withhold it was as much a criminal as the unfortunate people of Lidlicote. Any suspicion, however slight, must be reported: it was better to be safe than sorry. He prayed to Almighty God that further punishment would not be necessary, but it could not be ruled out. He wished the viewers and listeners good night and asked God to bless them all.

The final image of the Prime Minister on the TV was very still, only his head moving slowly across the screen as if gazing individually at every one of the viewers. Then he was faded out and there followed fifteen minutes of film of ancient monuments and unspoiled countryside (what the BBC called 'heritage footage') backed by the music of Elgar, Handel and Eric Coates. Then came the News, when the whole message was repeated and reinforced with the comments of persons of distinction, mostly judges and bishops. The television audience for the Prime Minister was thirty-three million, with a further seven million of the old, the poor and the blind who still listened to the radio.

Next day the same box appeared on the front pages of the morning papers, but there was an addition. This was variously presented by the different papers, from the *Daily Mirror*:

'I WAS THERE!'
MP SAW IT ALL

to *The Times*:

EYEWITNESS ACCOUNT OF THE EXECUTION AT LIDLICOTE
By Sir Gervase Acland MP

How had this come about? Surprisingly easily. It was dynamite, and the editorial staff of all the newspapers knew it, the printers knew it, the men who parcelled up and loaded the newspapers onto lorries and the night mails at the railway termini knew it, even the newsboys and street vendors knew it when they saw the headlines and read the story. But it was printed in good faith since it had come – although late at night – by fax from the Ministry of Information under the same reference code as the original press release.

When, later that morning, too late to stop the distribution of the papers, the shit hit the fan, Mr Stephen Grenfell, a permanent official at the Ministry, was discovered to have disappeared. Sir Gervase Acland MP was not at his home either, but made his way that afternoon to his place of work, the House of Commons.

On Friday 25th September, Cakehole's group were lying up in the Quantock Forest within easy reach of the Somerset coast. There was no point in getting there early. The weekend, when the pleasure craft would be in use and the harbour would be hopping, was the worst time to try to steal a boat. They decided that, as drifting and apparently aimless holiday-makers, they could safely reconnoitre the harbours at Watchet and Minehead over the weekend, but that they would maintain a shifting base in the forest until Monday. So they sent Juliet to buy supplies at the village shop in Crowcombe.

There were newspapers in the shop, and Juliet bought *The Times*. She always bought a newspaper for Sinclair because he liked to know what was going on. She did not look at the paper, but folded it and put it in the carrier bag with the bread and cold meat, apples, cheese, milk and salads. She slung the bag over the handlebars of her cycle and began to push it up the hill.

The hill out of Crowcombe is steep, one in four, a good half-mile: there is no pleasure in it for a cyclist, going up or down. Carrie was waiting among the gorse and heather just outside the forest area and together they rejoined the others. Juliet gave the paper to Ian. He opened it and his face changed. Juliet knew at once that she had made a mistake. She should have had a quick look at the paper herself before bringing it back. Then she would have known that there was something in it to upset him, and thrown it away.

'Have you read this?'

'No.'

Sinclair continued to read, Juliet to watch him reading. The others felt the tension, stopped what they were doing, and watched also. Sinclair heard the silence, felt the tension. He lowered the newspaper, turned on his heel and walked away further into the forest, calling 'Arwen!' over his shoulder. Parry-Jones followed. Cakehole, Carrie and Juliet watched them go.

Out of sight of the others, Sinclair gave Parry-Jones the newspaper, and watched him as he read the front page. Parry-Jones said, 'Christ! Oh, Christ!' several times as he read, 'Oh, Jesus Christ!'

Sinclair said, 'We were wrong: we did it wrong. We were never intended to survive. This is what happens if you survive.'

The Times had printed a photograph of Sir Gervase Acland MP. Parry-Jones said, 'It's the mouse.'

'Right. He takes the risks. We run away.'

'We didn't know, Ian. Couldn't have. They must be mad. Sick. Where is this Lidlicote place? We've never been anywhere near it.'

They supposed that Cape or Attlee or both might have been given refuge there. But Cape and Attlee had not been responsible for killing the Reichsprotektor. That was what had caused the execution. A whole village. And it might happen again. In Battersea to Dorothy's neighbours and patients. In the Chiltern village they had just left. Don Bushell shot for the use of his DKW. Mrs Brooking. Sally Miles at the post office packed off to detention. The Framley twins. The upwardly mobile vicar. The people with addictive disorders in the Convalescent Home.

Sinclair said, 'We could give ourselves up.'

'If you like.'

But Cakehole would not hear of it. 'Solves nothing,' he said. The Auxunits had been warned of this sort of thing, which was to be expected under a German Occupation. 'Give yourselves up? Rubbish. Only encourages them: that's why they do it. There's a lot of effort been put into keeping you two out of trouble, not just from me and Juliet. And Carrie, of course. If that mouse of yours had wanted them to have you, they'd have had you; he could have shopped you any time. Instead he's put his own head on the line, so don't you let it go to waste.'

He was right. It was a dirty business, stomach-churning, but logically Cakehole was right. When they reached Ireland, they could go public, take the responsibility, make it clear that nobody in Lidlicote or any other village – nobody but Cakehole: they would not mention the mice – had known anything about their real identities or their mission. They would not mention Megan and Hastings in Wales either, or Dorothy and Jack; they would not tell lies but be economical with the truth. They wondered about the landlady in the hotel on the cliffs. It seemed unlikely that she would keep her mouth shut.

They ate little of the food Juliet had brought from the shop, and grew increasingly silent. They went to bed as usual when it grew dark; they would rise at dawn. This was Cakehole's rule: he would not allow a light.

Except for the night spent on Salisbury Plain, which had been unpleasant, with heavy dew and no cover but a dry-stone wall, they had found woodland every night, and had constructed shelters of leafy branches. Carrie and Arwen slept in a shelter of their own at a distance from the others, and Sinclair with Cakehole and Juliet; both groups were protected by trip-lines. On this Friday night, Sinclair said, 'I'll sleep alone, if you don't mind. I shan't be far away,' and walked off with his bedding-roll in the opposite direction to Carrie and Arwen.

Juliet, alarmed that he might be going to do a Sydney Carton, looked at her grandfather, and Cakehole said, 'Ian! No nonsense, eh?'

'Don't worry. I'll still be here in the morning. I'm too restless to sleep in company. Don't want to keep you and Jules awake.'

Juliet watched Sinclair go. Several hours later she set off in the same direction to find him. Her grandfather would hear her go and know where she was going and why, but he would not oppose her or even speak of it unless she spoke first. They had respect for each other.

She knew where the trip-line had been set, and avoided it. She found Sinclair within thirty metres; he had not bothered to make a shelter. She knelt at a little distance from him. If he was asleep and woke suddenly, there would be danger until he recognised her. She said, 'Ian?' quietly.

He was not asleep. 'Go away, Jules.'

'You're unhappy. I've come to be with you.'

No point in pretending not to know what was happening. Ian said, 'Juliet, don't be silly. You're much too young for this. You know I'm fond of you –' he could not say 'love you', although he did love her, and they both knew it – 'but it won't do.'

He had forgotten that Juliet was never silly, just as she was never dishonest, known throughout the village for common sense as well as for clear-speaking. She said, 'I'm only nine years younger than you. When you're thirty-five, I'll be twenty-six: that's no difference. Katie Martin, four doors up, was pregnant at fifteen, breast-feeding at sixteen, had a couple more kids and a husband by the time she was twenty-one. I have got breasts, even if they're not very big yet, and I started having periods when I was twelve. I'm going to get in the bedding-roll with you now.'

She got into the bedding-roll and snuggled against him. There was enough room; she and Carrie had made all the bedding-rolls on the generous side. He put his arms round her, saying 'It's all very well for you, but I'm supposed to be responsible,' and they lay close together, her head on his chest. After a while she put one arm up, and touched his cheek. It was wet. She climbed up his body until her face was on a level with his, and licked away the tears. Then they kissed.

Juliet knew what a naked man looked like from classical statues and biology textbooks and television documentaries about the

Trobriand Islanders and such, but she had never actually felt one against her own body and tumescence came as something of a surprise. Perhaps in the daylight, even with someone as gentle and careful as Ian, she might have been alarmed, even a little repulsed, but they were close together in the darkness, as she had for so long wanted them to be, and any alarm, she was sure, would have been quite washed away by the strength of the emotion his own touch aroused in her, which led to moisture and participation far beyond what she had ever experienced during teenage masturbation. And what they had told her at school was rubbish, what some of the older girls had said, rubbish, Mrs Dawes' Education for Womanhood classes rubbish. There was no blood, there was no pain beyond a little soreness, just a deep physical satisfaction and a kind of triumph.

Friday 25th September. Sheets of a newspaper blowing along a village street. Terraced cottages of slate and granite with small windows, dark inside and out against the weather. A sudden squall of wind whipping round Moel y Feidiog has plucked the newspaper from the top of a shopping basket. Since it is only a tabloid and comes to pieces easily, the sheets have separated almost at once.

Sudden rain follows the wind, a downpour of heavy drops with some sleet. The woman who bought the paper runs back inside the village shop to complain and buy another. Rain beats the sheets of newspaper to the ground, and the wind lifts them again, but with more difficulty now that they have become heavy with rain and dirt. Sailing before the wind is no longer an option; they can hardly leave the ground. Like dying butterflies they flop forward once, twice, and then give up. The squall passes. The rain stops.

A vagrant wearing a woolly hat, an old blue donkey jacket and corduroy trousers which have become trichologically challenged at the knees, stoops to pick up the pages. He looks about him for an owner, but there is nobody near. The newspaper is damp and dirty and torn; nobody would want it now. He takes what he has salvaged to the shelter of a doorway, and begins to put the paper together again.

There is a box on the right-hand side of the front page, covering two columns. The headline and text within it are both in bold type:

THE PRICE OF SILENCE

It is some kind of official announcement; he will read it later. On the left-hand side, across three columns, the type is also bold. The whole front page of the *Daily Mirror* seems to be shouting at its readers:

'I WAS THERE!'
MP SAW IT ALL

with a picture of some politician beneath the headline.

He begins to read.

Members of Parliament cannot be arrested inside the precincts of the building, but there are always policemen to challenge anyone who may wish to enter without the right to do so, and on the afternoon of Friday 25th September, they were particularly thick on the ground. Every taxi, every private car was stopped, every would-be entrant required to show indentification; even those with tickets to the Public Gallery were turned away.

Most MPs had arrived at the House well before lunch. They had gathered in little groups in the bars and tea room, groups which formed for a while, fell apart, and reformed in new groups. They drifted between each others' offices. None of them wanted to be too long in the company of the same people; it might be dangerous, though nobody knew why. The PM was to make a statement to the House at two-thirty on a matter of Internal Security – which must be this business at Lidlicote. Two-thirty on a Friday of all days: the times were out of joint. Many members felt that the statement should have been made to the House before the PM had gone public on TV and radio the night before, but the House of Commons, now that it had become merely the legislative assembly of a provincial government, had grown used to taking a back seat.

At two thirty-five a van belonging to the Acme Roller Towel Company, which supplied fresh towels to the wash-rooms of both Houses, turned into New Palace Yard as it always did at this time on a Friday, and the identity documents of the driver and his assistant were checked by the police, who knew perfectly well who they were. The van drove on and stopped at a side door. The driver and his assistant opened the back of the van, and began to take out the fresh towels which they would substitute for soiled ones. Sir Gervase Acland MP rose from the box of towels on which he had been sitting, handed it to the driver, said 'Thank you, Henry,' and went on into the Palace of Westminster.

He made his way to the Chamber, and entered. Nobody stopped him; he had a right to be there. He stood at one end of the Chamber between the benches. The Prime Minister was speaking, as sad and as stern as he had been the night before but a little more prolix, yet the quality of attention was intense: Honourable Members were well accustomed to prolixity. Nevertheless on both sides of the House, at first on the back benches and those nearest the door, heads began to turn. The Prime Minister sensed the diminution of attention. He saw the heads opposite begin to turn. His own head turned.

Silence. Total silence. Not a cough, not a foot scuffed, not an order paper dropped, not a bum shifting on its seat, nothing.

The Prime Minister's throat was dry; he wished to continue, but the words had gone. He looked down at his notes on the despatch box, but could not make them out. He swallowed. Why did the man stand there like the Messenger at the end of some bloody play, why did he not break the silence, walk on in and take his usual seat? He would give Acland time to do that, and then he would continue. Let the buggers wait.

The Home Secretary was sitting at his side. Proper place to be: Internal Security was his department. Whatever Julian's private feelings might be, he would have to sit there and give support; that was what Cabinet responsibility was about. Except that he was no longer sitting, but standing, which he had no right to do since the PM was himself on his feet, making a statement on a matter of grave national importance, which by convention could not be interrupted. The Home Secretary was standing, he was moving towards Acland, he was taking Acland's hand. The Leader of the Opposition had also left his seat on the bench opposite, and was running towards Acland. He held him, embraced the fellow, and the Home Secretary embraced him, open and unashamed like three queens at a party, and together they began to lead Acland forwards.

Then the whole Chamber, which had been silent for so long,

came to noisy life. Members on both sides were shouting, cheering, waving order papers, running to greet Acland, trying to touch him, shouting, 'Thank you! Thank you!'; many were weeping. The Deputy Prime Minister got up and left the Chamber, head down and swearing. 'Sod the lot of you! Sod you all!' but he was weeping also.

What would come of all this could not be guessed and would have to be considered. Since nobody was taking any notice of him, the Prime Minister sat down.

The news of Lidlicote affected Cape and Attlee in opposite ways. Cape became very angry, Attlee very depressed; Cape violently energetic, Attlee hardly able to move at all.

Cape took his machine-gun and four grenades, and stuffed the pockets of his donkey jacket and the inside of his shirt with clips of ammunition. The Ingram Eleven is not large; it could be wrapped in newspaper to look like a parcel and carried in a plastic bag. He was glad that at last there was a use for the weapons; they had been dead weight for so long. He cycled to the nearest town, and stole a station wagon from the car park of the railway station; he wanted something solid and heavy in case of road blocks, but nothing as identifiable as a three-tonne truck with a name on the side. He drove south and east towards Gloucestershire. Attlee remained where he was, sitting with his back to the wall of a deserted barn.

Why was Cape going back to the abbey? There was no obvious reason: Cape was not in a rational state. Perhaps he thought that, after what had happened at Lidlicote, the monks might be in danger, and intended to protect them. Perhaps he was simply returning to the only place in this bloody country where he had felt happy and secure.

Five miles out of Hereford he realised that there was not enough petrol in the station wagon to finish the journey, and since he had no coupons he would have to steal another vehicle. He stole a milk tanker from outside a farm while the driver was socialising in the kitchen. It had the weight he wanted, though not much speed. The theft would be quickly reported; he would not be able to keep it long, but did not have far to go.

There was a road block on the main road to the abbey, a red and white wooden barrier on a swivel across the road and a police car by it. There were two cars waiting on Cape's side of the barrier and two on the other side, coming the other way.

A policeman was talking to the occupants of the first car on the opposite side of the road. Cape stopped the tanker behind the second car on his own side as if taking his place in the queue, rolled down the window on the driver's side of the cab, then took a grenade from his pocket, withdrew the pin and held down the lever. The car under examination received clearance, was allowed past the barrier, and continued on its way. The policeman turned to question the driver of the first car on Cape's side. Cape pulled out into the road, revved his engine, and drove straight at the barrier, smashing it to pieces. As he went by, he lobbed the grenade under the police car. He heard an explosion behind him and screams. That should hold them for a while.

There were two security guards on sentry duty outside the abbey. Cape stopped the milk tanker near the front door, and shot them from the cab. He wondered whether to drive the tanker straight at the door, smashing his own way in and making a way out for the monks, but was reluctant to damage the fabric of the abbey. Probably the guards would have keys. He found a large iron key attached to the belt of one of the guards, and dragged the man's body into the shelter of the porch, since he did not wish to come under fire from the windows. What next? The guards inside would have been alarmed by the gunfire. If he opened the door and went in, he would be shot as he entered unless he himself came in fast and shooting, and in that case he might injure any of the monks who happened to be in the hall. Hard decisions, and nothing planned.

What did he think he was about? Did he intend to rescue the monks, and if he did, where would he take them? Cape did not think so far ahead. If he opened the doors and eliminated the gaolers, the monks themselves would know where to go. His immediate object was to kill as many security guards as he could.

They made it easy for him. Eight guards armed with automatic rifles, in two groups of four with no officer, came round each side of the building, running and tumbling over each other, shit-scared and utterly inexperienced at this kind of thing. They were no match for a trained Free British volunteer armed with an Ingram and three grenades. Ten down – how many to go? It was unsettling for Cape that he had been unable to kill them cleanly; some of them were still blubbering and moaning and calling for help. Perhaps he should finish them off, but they had dropped their weapons, they were no danger, and he could not bring himself to do so.

The front door opened from the inside. The abbot and Father Theodemar came out to meet him. Father Theodemar said, 'Pack it in, Bernard. This isn't the way.'

'They won't let you give me sanctuary this time.'

The abbot said, 'No, I don't think they will. You'd better come inside while we do what we can for the people you shot. There's an ambulance on its way.' The herbalist and a couple of assistants with bandages and a First Aid box were waiting by the door and came scurrying out at the abbot's signal. 'Please give me the machine-gun. I've promised the officer in charge that you'll allow yourself to be disarmed and he's promised not to interfere. You'll remain in my charge until the police arrive from Gloucester.'

So Cape gave up the Ingram and went indoors with the abbot and Father Theodemar and as he entered the Great Hall he was shot through the chest with a dum-dum bullet by a marksman from an upper landing. 'You promised. You promised,' the abbot said, and the officer in charge of the security guards replied, 'Ends and means, father. The man's a killer,' and again a light went out in the mind of the patient, David Piper, who, although he was incapable of speech and there was no one about to hear, spoke one sentence clearly: 'Into thy hands, oh Lord, I commend my spirit.'

Father Theodemar said, 'Let me.' He knelt by the body and made the sign of the cross with the fingers of his right hand on the dead man's brow. Then he tried to put his arms under the body to lift it, but he lacked the strength, and two monks came forward to help him. 'Into my arms,' he said. 'I brought him here.' The two monks lifted Cape's body into Father Theodemar's arms, which they supported from beneath with their own arms, and somehow, with very little grace, the three of them managed to carry the dead man to the Infirmary.

He was horrible and hairy. The monks washed the body, shaved the beard and cut the hair. They had no shroud so they dressed Cape's body in a monk's habit, and put it in the chapel before the altar, with candles at head and feet. Then they sang '*Laudate, Domine*'.

None of them had any experience of boats. They knew – or thought they knew – that one could hot-wire the ignition, just as with a car, and they assumed that any sea-going boat would have a compass; one would point the boat's nose in the direction one wished to go, maintaining that direction by a commonsensical use of the wheel, and the engine would do the rest. Probably there would be charts in the wheelhouse, though they might not be able to read them.

They had no idea how long the journey would take, regarded a boat as just another vehicle with an internal combustion engine, and grossly overestimated the speed at which it would travel. They thought they knew about tides. Tides came in and went out. An incoming tide would slow the boat, an outgoing tide help it to go faster. The concept of a tide which would pull them south when they wished to go west was beyond their grasp.

It would be important to have their own supply of fuel. Boats ran on diesel, which they would steal from a petrol station, and bring with them in a plastic can: they would also have to steal the can. Bad weather might be a problem, but they would face that if it happened; they would not begin their journey in high winds or fog, and the coast of Ireland was not that far away. As for the eventual landfall, they would not attempt it in the dark: they would land wherever they found a calm bit of coast with no rocks.

They were innocent, they were ignorant, they were all of them landspeople. A recce, to be of any use, requires a degree of knowledge, and they had none. Carrie and Cakehole cycled to Watchet to take a look at the harbour. They had expected the marine equivalent of a car park, with stone piers and rows of suitable vessels tied up side by side; they would have to find one with nobody on board, lying between others equally deserted.

The reality was disconcerting. The harbour at Watchet is shaped like the claw of a pair of pincers which is not quite closed. Cakehole and Carrie stood on the East Pier looking down into a basin of mud.

Resting on the mud, as if they were stuck in it, were seven boats of a suitable size, well separated from each other, each attached at one end to an iron chain which also rested on mud. Near the boats were buoys and they seemed to be stuck in the mud also. The only way of reaching any of these boats would be by descending one of the rusty iron ladders attached to the side of the stone pier and walking across mud of unknown depth. And then what?

At the end of the pier, where it curved to make the left side of the not-quite-closed claw, there was a miniature lighthouse, too small for a crew but large enough for a light, with a stone seat around it, on which sat two old men. They wore waterproof capes of transparent plastic and plastic covers over their flat tweed caps and they were eating chips out of newspaper. Carrie approached them.

'I'm sorry, I'm very ignorant, but do those boats ever float?'

'Do when the tide's in.'

'And when is that exactly?'

The left hand of one man, the right of the other, reached simultaneously into the newspaper, each lifted a chip simultaneously, masticated simultaneously. The chips were long and may have once been firm, but they had been well dowsed in vinegar, and they bent at the ends as they were lifted. They had that soggy quality which foreigners despise and the English find so succulent. Carrie felt a rush of love for her country. *This is my own, my native land.* Would there be chippies in Ireland?

'High tide nine forty-five.'

'And then they float?'

'Then they floats.'

'It doesn't seem very long.'

'Twice a day.'

'Six hours. More or less.' Fingers in; chips up. Chips in; jaws chomp. A pause in the conversation. Old men with false teeth do not masticate chips and talk at the same time.

'Three hours before, three hours after. More or less.'

'Twelve hours out of twenty-four. More or less. Can't ask for better 'n that.'

She must move away or she would reach out and take one; her longing for chips was so great. If the boats floated, the buoys must float also, but they would still be in the middle of the harbour basin. What about those iron chains? They could not be expected to float. Presumably they came up with the boats. It all seemed rather unlikely, but the boat people must know their own business. Oh God! the enticement of the vinegar! 'How do people get to the boats?'

'What people?'

'The people who own them.'

'Dinghy.'

They were going, going, the last of the chips were going; they had gone. One of the two men crumpled the newspaper and handed it to the other, who threw it off the jetty and into the mud. Barbarians! 'Thank you,' Carrie said.

Three hours before, three hours after. The boats would be back in the mud at a quarter to one in the morning – more or less – and remain there until a quarter to seven, by which time it would be light. They would have to steal a dinghy as well as diesel and a can. What would they do with the dinghy afterwards? One of the old men reached inside his plastic cape and withdrew a second parcel of chips from inside his jacket. Carrie rejoined Cakehole. 'Well, we're not going from here,' he said. 'Look at the mouth of the harbour, like some bloody animal ready to bite, and there's all rocks outside. We'd better move on further down the coast.'

It was the same all along the coast: there was a singular absence of marinas. The harbour at Minehead looked like their best bet, well away from the centre of town, a curving stone wall like a button hook at one end of the long muddy beach, and no buildings nearby, just a lot of parking spaces and the lifeboat station. But Minehead was a tourist town with caravans, a holiday camp and amusement arcades; it had a night-life. The latest practical time to steal a boat and get it out of the harbour would be half-past eleven, and there might still be people about.

Nevertheless it would have to be Minehead. Although they had left all their gear, even including the weapons, hidden in the Quantock Forest, and left their bicycles further down the beach, they were still a party of five, burdened with two fifteen-litre cans of diesel and a large plastic bag which contained the implements they would need to carry out the theft – a bolt-cutter, crowbar, torch and a length of washing-line. In any smaller place, if they were seen at all, they would attract suspicion. In Minehead they might just pass as holiday-makers.

Also the harbour there had another great advantage. When they had visited it on the Sunday, they had noticed a boat, a real sea-going vessel, moored to ring-bolts set in the harbour wall beside a narrow flight of stone steps. The mooring seemed to be rather elaborate and even inconvenient – the nose of the boat faced the wall with two lines on either side at the front and an anchor chain behind – but it ought to be easier to steal than something in the middle of the harbour basin. Fastened to the iron railing on top of the wall was a blackboard on which was chalked:

LEOCADIA
Deep Sea Fishing
M20 PER HOUR

Perhaps the boat was only for hire at weekends this late in the season; perhaps they would not find it on the Monday night. That was why they had brought the washing-line. It was too chancy to try to steal a dinghy and then a boat. If the *Leocadia* had gone, Sinclair would have to swim out, carrying one end of the line, to one of the boats moored to a buoy, cut the mooring, and Arwen, Cakehole, Carrie and Juliet, standing in line on the narrow steps hidden from public view, would pull the boat against the tide into the wall where it could be secured to the ring-bolt until they were all aboard.

They had decided to use the same principle as that employed for the theft of Don Bushell's DKW. They would not risk starting the engine in harbour, since anyone who noticed them would have time to alert the Coastguard. Instead they would drift silently with the tide and start the engine when they were already some way from the shore. They did not know that a drifting boat has no steerage and is at the whim of wind and tide and that it is not easy to start the engine when your boat is already entangled with another boat or being smashed into the harbour wall.

Leocadia was at her mooring and available for theft. No tourist was enjoying a stroll before bedtime, no householder walking the family dog along the harbour wall. Cakehole went first down the narrow stone steps, carrying one of the cans of fuel. Arwen, still in his polo-neck with padded bra and the buttoned skirt of navy-blue towelling, followed him, then Juliet, then Sinclair with the second can. Carrie remained at the top of the steps, keeping watch.

There was a public toilet near the end of the jetty by the lifeboat station: Carrie and Juliet had both visited the Ladies for a safety pee. Someone came out of the Gents' side, and hovered. Carrie must not be seen to be watching him. She turned her head and looked across the harbour, as if admiring the moonlight on the water and the distant prospect of the amusement arcade. Silence. Was he creeping up on her cautiously in rubber-soled shoes? Had he simply zipped up his fly and gone away? She risked a peek. He had moved away from the area outside the Gents, where he could be easily seen, and was now standing in the shadow of the harbour wall. He was all dark – dark hair, dark sweater over dark trousers, just the white blur of his face turned towards her.

Was she about to be propositioned? If so, she could handle it, though she would have to walk back to him in order to keep him away from the action at the bottom of the steps, and the others would wonder where and why she had gone. There was also the possibility that he might have some connection with *Leocadia*. She crouched down as if re-tying the laces of her gym-shoe and spoke softly to Ian below her. 'Someone interested. A man. Do you want me to talk to him?'

'No. Come on down. I'll look after it.'

'It might just be sexual. I could tell him to get lost.'

'If it's just sexual he'll get lost anyway as soon as he sees me.'

Sinclair came up the steps, lazy and easy as a cowboy in a Hollywood musical, put an arm round Carrie's shoulders, and stood there, enjoying the moment. He glanced at the hovering person at the end of the wall, who did not get lost but continued to hover. Sinclair, still in character, squeezed Carrie's shoulders and patted her bum, indicating that she should go on down the steps, and she did so. Then he strolled back along the harbour wall, still lazy and easy, neither challenging nor evasive, just a young man on holiday with somewhere to go and something to do. He nodded to the hovering person as he passed, and said, 'Evening.' There was no way any casual loiterer could out-run a trained Free British volunteer dedicated to pursuit, but it would be normal caution to cut off his retreat. The hovering person did not reply. Sinclair turned.

There was a couplet of verse running through his mind. *No retreat, no retreat! They must conquer or die who have no retreat.* He must be quick; he must be kind. No unnecessary suffering. The volunteers were not barbarians; they would do what had to be done, but take no joy in it.

A boy stepped out of the shadow of the wall. He wore a blue heavy-gauge fisherman's jersey, probably knitted by his mother, black jeans and black plimsolls. He looked to be about Juliet's age, not much older. A lock of dark hair fell Byronically over his brow just as Sinclair's used to do, and there was a pimple at the side of his mouth: Sinclair's own back was still pocked with the marks of teenage acne. The boy said, 'I been watching you.'

'I know you have.'

'What you doing?'

'Nothing for you to worry about.'

It must be done immediately and without noise. The tide would not wait. The others would already be aboard, the hatch-cover forced, the door to the wheelhouse opened. The boy had seen too much already, and would see more if he were allowed to live. He could not prevent them from getting away, but even at night, even with the engine running, the Coastguard would catch them if he gave the alarm. Sinclair said, 'What's your name?'

'Werner.'

'You're German?'

'My grandad was German. I'm named after him.'

So much killing, all down to himself and Arwen. The Reichsprotektor – well, that was the mission: that had to be done. Peter. Bobby the policeman. Some man murdered in a train, the mouse had said. The people of the village, taken out and shot before being tumbled into a trench. He remembered – would never be able to forget – Acland's description . . . men vomiting before execution, the wounded battered to death in a cellar, the two children running in the dark, the professor tied to a post and shouting, 'What's going on?'

It must be done immediately, and he could not do it.

'Turn round.' The boy turned. 'Walk to the top of the steps.' What did he think was going to happen to him? He must be scared: would he try to run? Perhaps if he tried to run, the thing could be done. The boy did not try to run. He stood at the top of steps and said, 'My mum and dad . . .'

'Expecting you home?'

'Right.'

'Can't be helped. Go down the steps.'

The boy walked down the steps, Sinclair following. Only Cakehole was waiting; the others must be lying low in the cabin. Sinclair said, 'This is Werner. He's coming with us,' and then to the boy, 'I suppose you don't know anything about boats?'

'A bit.'

It was that bit which, against all the odds, got them to Ireland.

Lieutenant Attlee remained where Cape had left him, sitting with his back to the wall of the barn. Time passed. He did not eat, drink or shit. When he wished to piss, he unzipped and pissed in front of where he sat. Mostly he slept – if it could be described as sleep; his mind had rejected what he had read in the newspaper and nothing came in to take its place.

Friday turned to Saturday and Saturday to Sunday. On Monday morning Attlee opened his eyes. His mind was no longer empty: a conviction had formed there.

He saw now that he had been in error. He should not have allowed Cape to take control, not have agreed to evade capture, not have sought survival. The British government-in-exile did nothing without a purpose. There had been a purpose in sending the volunteers and there must be a purpose in betraying them. What had happened at Lidlicote was a consequence of the volunteers' refusal to be betrayed. They should have had faith; they should have fulfilled the purpose by allowing themselves to be taken; their efforts to escape were tantamount to disobeying an order. There would be a purpose behind the purpose, of course, which he had not yet been able to fathom, but his immediate duty as an officer on the ground was to comply with the first purpose, and the second would follow.

There was water to drink. He drank. There was very little food, since Cape had brought none back from the village, but what there was Attlee ate. He cleaned himself up as well as the facilities of the place would allow, which was not very well, then he packed his weapons and the plastic explosive into a rucksack and then he walked. He walked over hilly country, rough turf and boulders. He came to a pool into which he threw the Ingram, the grenades and the explosive, and left his empty rucksack by the side. He came to a road and followed signposts to what seemed to be the nearest town of any size. A village would not do; his requirements would not be met.

There was a shop in the High Street, B Madog Williams & Nephew, Gentlemen's Outfitters. He entered the shop. He still had plenty of money; he had not left that by the pool. 'I want a gentleman's outfit,' he said.

The shop-keeper was cautious. Over the past weeks Attlee's hair had been roughly clipped and occasionally dowsed in water, but his beard was uncontrolled and his body odour rank. However, he did not seem to be drunk. 'For yourself, was it?'

'For myself.' He pulled out a roll of currency secured with an elastic band, and separated four fifty-mark notes. 'I have money.'

'When you say "an outfit", the implication . . . how shall I put it? Head to toe? You don't intend to retain what you stand up in?'

'No. I want the lot. Do you sell shoes?'

'We're not a shoe-shop as such. We do stock a small selection of up-market footwear, however, for country wear. Brogues mainly.'

'Brogues will do very well if you have my size.' They had his size: Attlee bought a pair of brogues. He bought underwear, socks and a couple of linen handkerchiefs. He bought a double-breasted suit with belt incorporated in the trousers, a white shirt with a collar, cuff-links of imitation opal and a silk tie which caught his fancy: it was the Llanidloes Bowling Club tie. When everything had been packaged and paid for he said, 'Do you happen to know where the public baths are in this town?'

'For swimming?'

'For bathing. Soap and water. Large towels.'

There were no public baths nearer than Chester.

Attlee said, 'Ah!' and stood in thought. 'Do you live above the shop?'

'There is a flat above the shop.'

'How much would you charge for a bath with use of razor and cologne?'

So it was arranged. Attlee took all the packages upstairs and changed into his new outfit after he had bathed and shaved. There could be no doubt; he looked a treat and every inch a gentleman: the brogues in particular added a touch of class. Then he asked the way to the police station.

Everyone at the police station, everyone in the locality, had read the piece in the paper by that MP the Friday before. On the previous evening they had listened to the Prime Minister's Address to the Nation, and what he had said seemed harsh, but he had explained the reason for this punishment and how it was a harsh necessity and that sort of thing. He had not described what had actually happened to the people of the village; instead he had used words like 'extreme penalty' and 'condign punishment'. Now they knew what had been done, the details of it, and that made a difference.

It had to be thought about, but somehow could not be. There was a numbness in people's minds; it would take time to sink in. This had not been done by the Germans, but by their own government in their name. It seemed so strange that British lads – there would have been Welsh-born among them – could do such a thing, even under orders.

Attlee arrived at the police station as the day shift was going off duty. He announced himself at the desk. There was a silence. They asked him to confirm his identity, and he went over to the poster of the five volunteers stuck up on the wall, and stood beside it. A protective routine took over; the process was automatic. Nothing was said, no opinions uttered, which could be held against anyone later. It seemed to the desk sergeant and his colleagues that proper procedures ought to be followed; the report must go upwards through channels. Documentation was completed, and Attlee was confined in a cell. There was no occasion for hurry, since he was no threat to anyone and nobody could come from London to collect him until the morning.

301

There was talk in the town. Mr Williams talked to his family and neighbours, and the off-duty policemen talked, mainly to other policemen, since policemen have so few friends outside the force. The two reporters on the local paper picked up the news and spread it; it was their job to be out and about. There was talk in the pubs and the bar of the Red Dragon Hotel and even people from the villages, who had come in to town for a noggin, heard and spread the news. By next morning it had become widely known in the town and surrounding villages that one of the American soldiers had given himself up to the police.

Of course there was no need for anyone to come from London. It would have been perfectly easy for the local constabulary to have sent the prisoner for interview in a police van with adequate escort; it would have been easy to have incarcerated him in a local goal. But for the investigating authorities this was an occasion, the longed-for success, the proof that the strong example of Lidlicote had paid off, a proof made all the more necessary by the unedifying scene at the House of Commons the Friday before, about which the public had not been told.

Since the surrender had been made to the police, the Head of Special Branch decided that he himself would collect the terrorist; he would take a photographer and make a little ceremony of the handing over. But MI5 had its own spy at the yard, just as Special Branch had in MI5. Mr Phibbs made two telephone calls, the first to the Home Office, the second to his opposite number, and it was decided that, in the interest of inter-departmental harmony, they should both go.

In the little town, people began to gather near the police station from eight in the morning. They could not be called a mob at that stage, not even a crowd, just a group of interested observers. They hung around in the local cafés and in the street, and kept an eye on the police station; any who had to wander away for a while would be replaced. They were there all morning, and more of them as the morning wore on.

MI5 and Special Branch arrived at half-past two in an armoured car with an armoured van for the prisoner, a motor-cycle escort and an entourage of photographers and public relations personnel. By then the press of local people was thick, but not threatening; they would have heard what was to happen, and come for the show, which was only to be expected. They readily made room for the official vehicles, and then regrouped around them. During the regrouping, the motor-cycles fell over. Luckily there were willing hands to catch them, no harm was done, but some of the local people suggested that the motor-bikes would be less of a public hazard if they were propped against a wall a little distance away.

Meanwhile Mr Phibbs and the Head of Special Branch had entered the local police station, where they remained for twenty minutes. The ceremony of handing over would take place just outside the front door. The public relations people cleared a space for the photographers. In this they received enthusiastic co-operation from the townspeople. Although it was not noticed at the time, during this process the tyres of all the police vehicles managed to get themselves slashed, as did the tyres of the motor-cycles propped against the wall of the Red Dragon Hotel.

The front door opened and Mr Phibbs and the Head of Special Branch came out, followed by Attlee between two uniformed police constables and behind them the desk sergeant and the chief constable of the local force who was to do the handing over. Attlee had been handcuffed but still looked quite the gentleman. Since the ceremony had to be photographed several times and from several angles, he was passed from hand to hand like a doll, but he kept his head high and his dignity survived it. Flashlights popped. The crowd, which might have been expected to applaud, was strangely quiet.

The ceremony was over and had been recorded, and it was time to take Attlee to the armoured van, but the crowd in front of the police station did not part to make a corridor. Instead its constituents seemed to press more tightly together, and within this pressure the photographers and PR people were gravely squeezed. The photographers' cameras were crushed into their bodies, rubbing against chest or stomach, before being wrenched away by unknown hands to disappear underfoot: their owners dared not stoop to recover them because they feared being unable to surface again. The motor-cycle escort found themselves pressed back, against vehicles, walls, crushed and squeezed along until they reached a gap, when they were ejected from the press of people, popping out like corks from a bottle into back alleys or the delivery bays of shops. The chief constable said, 'Come along now! Make way there, please!' but the crowd did not make way.

Mr Phibbs was not having any of this; he felt like Moses confronted by a Red Sea which had become intransigent. Together he and the Head of Special Branch linked arms, put down their heads and pushed forward; the crowd would have to give way for them, and it did, closing up again behind them. It was then discovered that, even when reached, the police vehicles could not be used since all the tyres were flat, and the two heads of the Security Services could not get back again; they had been separated from their prisoner. Politely the nearest members of the crowd opened the doors of the armoured car, assisted the two men to get in, pushed the PR people in after them and shut the doors again.

The chief constable said to the desk sergeant and the two constables, 'We'd better take him back inside while we get this mess cleared up,' but the local police inside the station had already locked all the doors and windows, so as to protect government property from the mob, and could not hear the chief constable shouting to be let in.

The desk sergeant said, 'Under the circumstances, sir, and bearing in mind the safety of all concerned and the importance of avoiding the arousal of disorder or other public malfeasance, do you agree that it might be better to take his handcuffs off?' The chief constable said, 'You'll do no such thing,' and the desk sergeant replied, 'Thank you, sir; I was sure you'd see it my way,' and then to the two uniformed constables, 'You heard the chief constable instruct me to remove the handcuffs?' and they said they did, so he complied with the order of his superior officer.

Lieutenant Attlee rubbed his wrists where the handcuffs had chafed them. He looked over the crowd, from face to face, a leader of men appraising his troops. He had not anticipated any of this, but that was of no consequence. The new Attlee did not anticipate events, but accepted them and followed his star.

A man in the crowd, a man of presence – he was an auctioneer in the cattle market, a back-row forward of the local rugby team – said, 'Where do you want to go?'

'London.'

'Some of us better go with you. See you right.'

'If you don't mind walking.'

'There'll be no objection.'

So Attlee set off, walking to London. Some of the people of the locality, those who felt strongly and could be spared, took food and a few necessaries and went with him, while others remained outside the police station for the rest of the day to make sure that the chief constable and their other visitors were comfortable.

The news spread quickly. In every village, every town on the way, the streets were lined with people applauding, and always some would join the march. Those employed in the public service – firemen, police, nurses, railway staff, bus conductors – wore their uniforms.

They marched on, Attlee always a little ahead, their numbers growing all the time. They marched through the afternoon and into the dark, then stopped at a cathedral city for the night. They were five hundred by then, but they found people to give them shelter. Seven hundred left the city next morning.

That was on Wednesday 30th September, six days after the massacre at Lidlicote. Seven hundred marchers is not so many, and during the morning it began to rain so that their number was not much increased. Attlee himself strode on as if indifferent to the rain, but his followers were not indifferent; fewer people were in the streets to see the march go by, far fewer joined, and some dropped out. They were a rabble, wet and increasingly uncertain, and could easily have been dispersed by the police, but they were not dispersed because, also on that Wednesday, the government fell on a vote of no confidence moved by one of its own back-benchers. There would have to be a General Election as soon as possible. Meanwhile the caretaker government of Liberals was not sure what to do about Attlee and his followers. It would rather depend on the attitude in Berlin.

For the time being it seemed prudent to do nothing and say

305

nothing. D-notices made sure that Attlee's surrender was not reported by the news media; what had happened in the little town was not reported; the march was not reported. Yet people knew. And, as first one day and then another passed, and the sun came out again, and the police did nothing more than to ask the marchers to keep moving please and not obstruct the traffic, seven hundred became a thousand, a thousand fifteen hundred, with Morris Dancers in costume and a Silver Band, until almost five thousand people, in increasingly carnival mood, were on their way to London.

Then news came from Ireland. Sinclair and Parry-Jones, Cakehole and Carrie, gave a press conference: they could safely do so: the German Empire had no extradition treaty with Ireland. Attlee, it was now clear, had committed no capital crime whatever. He had known nothing about the murder of the Reichsprotektor, had not been with Cape when the guards at the abbey were shot or with Alloway when Pargeter was killed on the train. Attlee might be technically a spy, but was in other ways squeaky clean.

And news came more covertly from Berlin. The Council of State had no objection to a change of government in Britain; it could work with Liberals just as conveniently as with Conservatives. The political complexion of a provincial government was of no great account to the Council of State since provincial governments had no real power anyway. What did matter, in view of the fuss which had been caused internationally by the affair at Lidlicote, was that the world should know that the whole unfortunate business had been a purely British error, and a change of government in Britain would give some credence to this.

It was decided to deal with the march by treating it as a celebratory occasion, with fireworks and roasted oxen at a tent city in Hyde Park. 'Tell you what,' said Tony the Choccie Bar Terrier, now a junior minister at the Home Office, to Sir Gervase Acland, 'I'll walk the last two miles with them myself, if it keeps fine. We'll want you to make a speech, of course.'

So speeches were made, and rockets whooshed up into the night sky, and there was gravy on everyone's chin, and next morning the marchers dispersed happily and Lieutenant Attlee was popped into preventive detention until he should be formally charged. About the formulation of those charges there would be no great hurry.

At the General Election shortly afterwards, the Conservatives were reduced to a rump of thirty-seven members, smaller than the Labour Party which then became the official Opposition to the Liberals. More importantly, the war ended. Although Lidlicote had been a purely British matter, there could be little doubt that von Neustadt had received encouragement unofficially from military sources in Berlin, and what with that and Desert Storm, the influence of the military in the Council of State was much diminished. The civilians were heartily sick of the war, which was a cause of unpopularity and expense without any compensatory successes. Since, as all sides knew very well, there was a similar feeling in Tokyo and Washington, making peace required no more than a formula which would save face all round.

It was found. All three empires withdrew their forces from the Gulf; Iraq withdrew from Kuwait. Peace within the Middle East would henceforth be the responsibility of a newly created organisation, the Pan Arab League, which would also ensure that all nations had equal access to oil and would fix its price.

The government of the USNA withdrew recognition from all the European governments-in-exile which had maintained their embassies in Washington. The move was unpopular with the Washington wives, but there is a price to be paid for peace. The governments-in-exile retained their own funds and premises, and became semi-charitable organisations, sponsoring cultural events and caring for members in distress.

Someone had to carry the can for Lidlicote; heads had to be seen to roll. The civilians in Berlin and the civilians in Westminster agreed that it had been a military operation, and luckily there had been that shambles in the cellar, which nobody in government had ordered or anticipated and in which the military had lost control and gone too far. General Allenby and Oberstleutnant Gillman were both court-martialled; Allenby was shot and Gillman sentenced to life imprisonment. Standartenführer Hawkins and the twenty men of the firing squad were dishonourably discharged into civilian life, where they had considerable difficulty in finding employment.

307

Acting Reichsprotektor von Neustadt was moved to a dead-end diplomatic job in the Soviet Union, and died of gangrene brought on by frostbite during the Black Winter of 1998.

Sinclair and Parry-Jones, Cakehole, Carrie and Juliet had been interned in Ireland, and were released, and Parry-Jones and Carrie were soon married. He took her back to Idaho where she settled happily into the lifestyle of a faculty wife. Cakehole and Juliet could not return to the village in the Chilterns – the British government would have to do *something* about a confessed murderer – and in any case Juliet was by now already pregnant, though determined to finish her education. So they accompanied Sinclair to the USNA and settled in Madison, Wisconsin, where Juliet was able to enrol as a student at the university and Sinclair became the happiest of house-husbands, combining care of their child with a little quality journalism and the freelance coaching of students on football scholarships in Basic English and Philosophy. Attlee was re-patriated, settled into the family's legal practice and married his cousin, Louise, by whom he had two children, neither of whom could be considered officer material but they did well in Manitoba. The life-support system of the patient, David Piper, was removed at the request of his parents, and he died shortly afterwards without any obvious signs of distress.

Was it all so tidy? No, nothing is tidy. Cakehole, for the first time in his life, found himself with nothing to do, entirely surplus to anyone's requirements. He pined and died within a year of his arrival in Wisconsin, was cremated and his ashes scattered at Chippewa Falls by his grieving grand-daughter. Her children, with Sinclair's assistance, have constructed an Operational Base in the garden, but it does not measure up to the original.

The village of Lidlicote has been rebuilt, every house and garden exactly as it was. Nobody lives in the houses; the families have been rehoused elsewhere at public expense. Instead Lidlicote has been declared a national shrine. Once a year there is an Easter service of celebration in the church and a Midnight Mass is said at Christmas; these services are attended by pilgrims from every Christian country, but the church is not otherwise used for any religious purpose. A rose garden has been created just outside the village, and it is usual for visiting celebrities to plant a rose; in spite of regular spraying the roses are seldom free from black-spot and mildew because of the singular purity of the air.

Tourists flock to Lidlicote from all over the world at every season of the year. They are given the full tour with nothing shirked. Authentic posts have been erected at the back of the Manor Farm barn and a trench dug with a mound of earth behind it; both trench and mound are kept free of weeds. There is a museum with a Roll of Honour and photographs of all the men who were shot, and tourists are able to have their own photographs taken by a professional photographer in the company of Billy Wilsher, the only survivor, who sells the tickets at the door. A cinema is part of the museum complex in which students with a genuine professional interest may view the film of the massacre made at the time by the Central Office of Information.

All tours end at the tourist shop, which is crammed with memorabilia. There are container-grown Lidlicote roses to take home, postcards, books and brochures, coloured slides, vases, mugs, pottery figures of Nell the Faithful Dog, Berkshire honey, soaps and country comestibles. Most of all there are T-shirts, racks and racks of them for children and adults, each with 'LIDLICOTE LIVES' on front and back. They are the most popular item.

Viewed objectively, the massacre at Lidlicote was, for all but the parties immediately concerned, the best thing that could have happened.

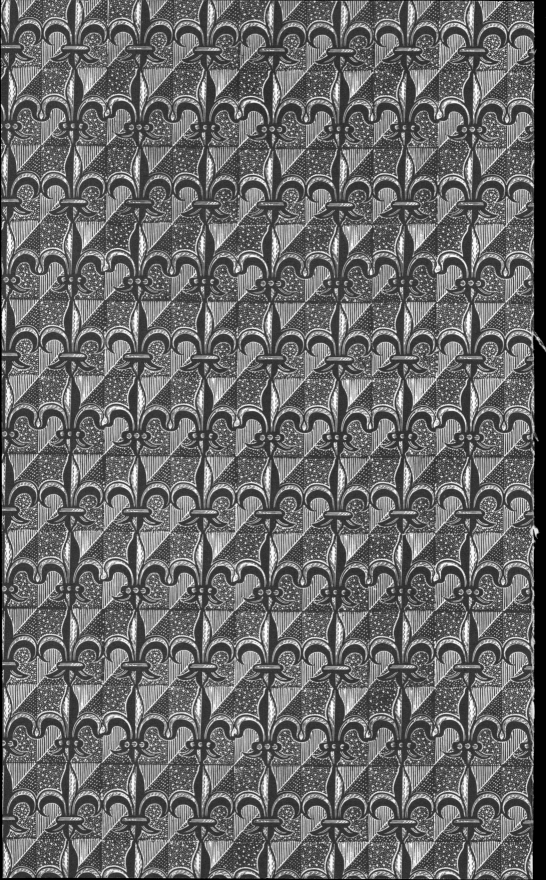